The Astonish

Saint of Cabora

BILINGUAL PRESS/EDITORIAL BILINGÜE

General Editor
   Gary D. Keller

Managing Editor
   Karen S. Van Hooft

Associate Editors
   Karen M. Akins
   Barbara H. Firoozye

Assistant Editor
   Linda St. George Thurston

Editorial Consultant
   Ingrid Muller

Editorial Board
   Juan Goytisolo
   Francisco Jiménez
   Eduardo Rivera
   Mario Vargas Llosa

Address:
Bilingual Press
Hispanic Research Center
Arizona State University
P.O. Box 872702
Tempe, Arizona 85287-2702
(602) 965-3867

The Astonishing Story of the

Saint of Cabora

Brianda Domecq

translated from the Spanish by
Kay S. García

Bilingual Press/Editorial Bilingüe
Tempe, Arizona

863
DOM

© 1998 by Brianda Domecq

ISBN 0-927534-78-9

Library of Congress Cataloging-in-Publication-Data

Domecq, Brianda.
　　[Insólita historia de la Santa de Cabora. English]
　　The astonishing story of the Saint of Cabora / Brianda Domecq ; translated from the Spanish by Kay S. García.
　　　　p.　　cm.
　　ISBN 0-927534-78-9 (alk. paper)
　　1. Urrea, Teresa—Fiction.　I. García, Kay S., 1951-　　.
II. Title.
PQ7298.14.O35I513　1998
863—dc21　　　　　　　　　　　　　　　　　　98-2821
　　　　　　　　　　　　　　　　　　　　　　　　　CIP

PRINTED IN THE UNITED STATES OF AMERICA

Cover design by Kerry Curtis
Interior design/typesetting by John Wincek, Aerocraft Charter Art Svc.
Back cover photo by Miguel Ehrenberg

Table of Contents

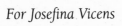

For Josefina Vicens

Introit

The agnostic is an individual who doesn't believe in the certainty of knowledge but can play with possibilities and weave hypotheses that might be enchanting, or terrible.

—JORGE LUIS BORGES

The angel meekly approached the Lord and whispered into his ear: "There's someone asking for you at the gate. A woman requests your permission to enter."

"A woman? What's her name?"

"Saint Teresa, Lord."

"Saint Teresa? . . . Oh, the one from Ávila!"

"No, Lord; the one from Cabora."

"Cabora? Where's that?"

"I don't know, Lord; I can't find any record of it. There are plenty of capes: Cape Barren Island, Cape Coral, Cape Fear, Cape of Good Hope, Cape Porpoise, Cape Tormentine, Cape Yakataga, Cape Charles, Elizabeth, Vincent . . . but no Cabora. There's a dam called Cabonga, a place called Cabool in America, another called Caboolture in Australia, and a Caborca in Mexico, but she swears that's not the one. C-A-B-O-R-A is the name of the damn place. I found a whole slew of Cabots, a few Cabras, some Cabreras, and then there's Cabrobó, Cabulo, Cabure, Cabruta, and even Caca near Stalingrad. . . ."

"What other information did she give you?"

"None. She said she wanted to see you, that you would know who she was if I told you she was Saint Teresa of Cabora."

"Doesn't ring a bell. Let's see, bring me the list of saints; maybe one slipped by without my noticing. There are so many of them now!"

The angel returned in a short while with a lengthy scroll and slowly began to read.

"Let's see: Saint Rita, Saint Roberta, Saint Rose . . ."

"The Ts! The Ts!"

"Saint Tabatha, Saint Tacha, Saint Tamara, Saint Tamarinda, Saint Teresa of Jesus—that's the one from Ávila—here's one! Saint Teresa of the Baby Jesus and the Most Divine Countenance, amen."

"Let me see. Yes, canonized in 1925. What's the year down there?"

"It's only 1906, Lord."

"Then that's not the one. Are you sure she calls herself a saint? She's probably one of those false saints that pop up all over the place every time there's an uprising. Do you remember what happened with Jesus? There were so many self-appointed messiahs running around that we could hardly tell which one he was!"

"Well, *she* says . . ."

"Forget it! Tell her that she's not registered. Either she's got the wrong name or the wrong year or the wrong heaven. And just ignore her if she cries. Women always cry when they don't get what they want; they cry or pray or produce a false hymen from somewhere to prove that they're virgins and therefore martyrs. Nonsense. If she makes a fuss, ask for her genealogy. Women can never trace their genealogy back more than two generations. Tell her we don't admit saints without genealogies. . . ."

Daughter of Amapola, daughter of Marcelina. Marcelina bore Tula, Tula bore Juana. Juana bore Anastasia, who bore Camilda. Camilda of Rosalío bore Nicolasa, Nicolasa bore Tolomena, and Tolomena bore Rocío. Rocío bore Dolores, who bore Silvia María. Silvia María bore Epifania, who bore Agustina, and Agustina bore María Rebeca, who bore the harlot Cayetana, who bore the one called Teresa of Cabora. . .

I

"Cabora . . . ," she thought as she climbed into bed, "the place must exist somewhere." She set the alarm for five and turned out the light. Everything was ready. On the table, her plane ticket, hotel reservation, and car rental receipt lay like concrete evidence that she would make a strange journey to an unknown place. On the floor was the briefcase full of documents, notes, and photographs that she had gathered over so many years of research. Next to it stood her suitcase with a few clothes, just the essentials. She closed her eyes, realized she wasn't going to sleep, and turned the light on again. In her stomach the queasy feeling of nerves and excitement stretched out the night hours before her.

"Cabora . . . ," she thought again. It was the last thing she had to do, the last piece in a complicated and chaotic puzzle she had slowly put together with gatherings from archives and libraries, rumors, facts, legends and false leads, discoveries and disillusionment. It had been like a spiritual pilgrimage for which, at times, she had felt herself chosen. Cabora was the last step; after that there would be no more. "And if Cabora doesn't exist . . . ?" she queried her tired mind, only to receive the answer she had given herself over and over again: "If you don't go, you'll never know."

And then there was the dream, relentless, beckoning, threatening. It had all started with that inexplicable dream that had invaded her solitary nights like a sign that she had to decipher. In October 1973 she had dreamt, three nights in a row, that she stood in the middle of an arid landscape, an interminable, flat desert. In the distance, the horizon undulated with the fierce heat of the day, cut only by an occasional jutting stone, a dead tree, the

3

soft slope of a dune. The sun blinded her and burned her skin. She stood alone facing the endless expanse of desert, an overwhelming sensation of extreme fatigue coursing through her body as if she had been walking for days, searching for a place called Cabora. That was all she knew: she had to find Cabora. Suddenly, she would spy in the distance a human figure, a tall, thin man dressed all in black. He beckoned to her and then turned and walked rapidly in the opposite direction. Afraid of being left alone, she ran after him, calling, but as she seemed to draw near, she would stumble on a rock and fall, not to the ground but out of the dream, awakening drenched in sweat and remembering that in the silence of the dream she had heard a strange cry.

Sitting in bed, she lit a cigarette. That had been a long time ago, and the dream had not repeated itself until recently, again three times in a row. It had been this occurrence that had made her decide to go to Sonora looking for Cabora; it was a signal. Perhaps there she would finally understand why she had so obsessively pursued this woman's story for so many years; perhaps there she would finally be able to lay this madness to rest or write the whole saga from beginning to end.

After the first series of dreams, she had rushed to the library to look up "Cabora," unsuccessfully, for there was no such place either in the atlas or the encyclopedias, nor was there any record that it had ever existed. Believing it to be a figment of her imagination, she was about to give up when the librarian placed a book in her hand. It was Heriberto Frías's novel *Tomóchic,* published in 1906, and it included a chapter on the once "famous" saint from Cabora. And there, as if by magic, was the name "Cabora." She took the volume to the nearest table and avidly began reading. When she finally raised her eyes from the book, it was dark outside and someone at the far end of the room was turning out the lights.

All the way home the printed words whirled about in her head, creating a multitude of feverish images: "A woman whose very memory would sustain the sullen obstinacy of a strong race," "a deluded woman . . . vibrant, sweet, and tenacious, who carried in her eyes a disturbing flame, sometimes stimulating and fierce like a shot of whiskey and gunpowder, sometimes benign and placid and soporific like the smoke from opium." Her eyes, "eloquent and resplendent—whose rays surrounded her face with a halo that incited miraculous enthusiasm in the poor pilgrims who came to her from distant hills—had inspired the mountain people of Sonora, Sinaloa, and Chihuahua to rebellions that could only be controlled by smothering them in flames and blood. . . ." Who was she? How had she achieved such influence at the turn of the century only to be forgotten a short time later? An amorphous and fascinating figure arose from the impassioned descriptions in the book: "Was she perhaps a fine instrument, a crystal controlled in the shadows by hidden hands so that, inspired by her facets and sparkling edges, strong, rough men . . . would, from their impregnable mountain strongholds, perpetrate a horrendous war of Mexicans against Mexicans, in the sacred name of God?" How was it possible to reconcile such sublime descriptions with phrases such as "that poor hysterical girl," "a victim of passive epilepsy," and "that deluded, highstrung creature"?

From that moment on she felt possessed by a cantankerous curiosity that gnawed at her peace of mind. She began to haunt libraries, to lend an ear to anecdotes and incredible tales, and to follow the winding trails of forgotten stories. Over the years, her search became obsessive; the more she uncovered, the more convinced she was that something still lay hidden. She so wanted to penetrate to the very soul of the forgotten woman and so identified with her that she ended up losing almost all notion of her own reality and was living only to retrieve the other's existence.

The documents, clues, references, facts and lies, the myth and reality that had been written or shouted or whispered or sung or recited all accumulated on her desk in a disorderly heap: testimonies found in dusty files inside dark, silent archives; photographs located in neglected drawers; tapped-out telegrams that had traveled back and forth in some forgotten time and now

lay silent; articles in yellowing newspapers; essays in discontin-
ued journals; interviews with living people who recounted
memories of the memories of others—she searched in the most
remote corners, but everything only led back to the dream of
Cabora and the terrible possibility that Cabora was no more than
a dream.

The alarm rang at exactly 5 A.M. Sometime in the early morning hours she had fallen asleep. Tired, fraught with nervousness
and a strange excitement, she dressed, checked the apartment
once more, picked up her suitcases, and descended to the street
where the taxi, ordered the evening before, awaited her.

It was a cold, cloudy November dawn in Mexico City. A tenuous gray light was beginning to invade the neighborhood. The
taxi took an unfamiliar route "to save time" and began to ramble
through dismal, narrow sidestreets full of potholes. Famished
dogs huddled against the walls, seeking a bit of warmth; a child
headed for school with tattered pants; discolored, crumbling
walls sported remnants of random, violent graffiti. Everything
seemed to increase her anxiety, to underline the sense of futility
of human life, its anonymity, its insignificance. Who, after all, was
remembered? Who stood out? Who would not be fodder for
obscurity? Jesus Christ and Porfirio Díaz, and they had both been
converted into myths. The rest, herself included, were insignificant, lost in the common dust of the past. And Teresa? Also gone,
meaningless, erased as if she had never existed.

The streets seemed eerie in the first light of dawn. Faded
walls displayed the remnants of political campaigns: Abelardo
Jiménez for deputy; Soconucio Pérez, senator . . . unknowns who
shone briefly and then were forgotten. This is how Lauro Aguirre's
"revolution" ended, she thought. And what had happened to
him? He also was swallowed up by the vicious circle of oblivion.
Teresa died just a few months before her friend Lauro joined the
Flores Magón brothers to sign the Mexican Liberal Party's pro-
gram in St. Louis, Missouri. A while later he was arrested for the
third time. The man hadn't given up; he was just as stubborn as

Porfirio Díaz, or more so. Had Lauro lived the Revolution when it finally began? Did he believe that his dream had come true or had he become disillusioned?

Her rambling thoughts came to an abrupt halt as the taxi pulled up at the airport. She felt a shiver of anticipation run through her body: the journey was about to begin.

 II

On the day of her second death, Teresa would remember the long, dusty journey that took her from the ranch of Santa Ana near Ocorini, Sinaloa, to the settlement of Aquihuiquichi in Sonora. It was the beginning, those first days when she was scarcely becoming aware of herself and her dream of living some day in Cabora began to take shape. She was seven years old, with waist-long, silky red hair, fair skin, and enormous amber eyes that never blinked.

"Your mother's shame!" her Aunt Tula said every time the girl stared at her with a piercing gaze that seemed to penetrate everything it touched. "Stop staring and go play with your cousins!" Her cousins were all legitimately dark-skinned, with black, submissive eyes like Cayetana's when Tula yelled at her, accusing her of things that Teresa would only understand much later.

"Slut! Even worse, you're a stupid slut! I took you in and fed you and this is what I get! With a bastard daughter so light-skinned that anyone can see you're the boss's whore! You've shamed our whole family!"

As the shouting continued, Cayetana would shrink into a corner of the hut, a shadow amidst shadows, and sheltering her daughter with her slender arms as if the child were a wounded animal, she would wait for the storm to pass. Sometimes the older sister's shouts were interrupted by the more vociferous bellows of Uncle Manuel, who came home drunk every day and had to be put to bed before he destroyed the furniture.

As soon as she could, Cayetana would slink away from the whirlwind of insults, pulling Teresita after her. They would cross the clearing that served as a corral, walk quickly down the path through the dense thicket, come out on the wide banks of the wash where groups of women were scrubbing clothes in deep pools, and then continue on until they were alone in the shade of a group of mesquite trees far from the settlement. There Teresa played, picking up branches or pursuing beetles while her mother lost herself in dreams and secret desires hopelessly aroused since the day Cosimiro had approached her.

At that time Cayetana, barely fourteen, had her innocence intact, a pair of fresh round breasts, and the innate desire to go on playing all her life. Even though she had occasionally observed the violence with which the rooster humped the hen or the bull mounted the cow, nothing linked these observations to the disturbing changes that had been occurring in her own body for some time. Tula, who showed her how to cover her private parts so as not to stain the furniture when it was that time of the month, didn't see any reason to explain further. Thus, on the day of her "disgrace"— as her sister called it now—Cayetana was still immersed in blissful ignorance about masculine appetites and their possible consequences. That afternoon she had remained alone at the wash, rinsing her nephews' clothes. The sun was already sinking on the horizon and the evening's chill was beginning to reach her bones when she felt herself being observed. She turned and saw Cosimiro, the boss's right-hand man, staring fixedly at her newborn breasts and tight little waist. Cayetana hid her face in a sudden flush of embarrassment that she didn't understand and immediately untied her long black hair so as to cover her shoulders and back. Cosimiro kept staring for a while. Then he told her that he would come for her in a couple of hours because the boss needed her.

"Wash yourself," he said, "and dress properly, though little good it'll do you."

Cayetana thought that there was some job for her in the main house; whenever there was a party many of the women in the settlement went to help in the kitchen. Instead of finishing her washing, she doused herself with the cold water of the pool and put on a white cotton dress that had already dried. Then she tied the rest of the clothes into a bundle, hid it in the underbrush, and sat down to wait.

It wasn't long before Cosimiro came out of the shadows and signaled for her to follow. Cayetana was surprised, first by the secrecy and then because there were no lights on in the house, but with customary docility she followed the servant to a large door at the end of a hall. Cosimiro pulled it open, gave Cayetana a light shove, and shut the door behind her. The girl was overcome by fright to find herself in the boss's bedroom, and even more so when he began speaking to her in a low voice and touching her in all those places that Tula had told her should never be touched. She scarcely had time to realize that his fervent caresses were awakening in her something akin to the urgent desire to pee, when she felt the man's thrust and began to moan. If she didn't lose consciousness it was only because her consciousness was being transformed into a whirlwind of sensations and feelings that burst into an irrepressible craving. When the boss finally fell asleep, she was left only with that hunger that would not be satiated that night or any other. Hours later Cosimiro came to take her back to the settlement. She arrived at the hut at dawn with her hair uncombed and her dress half undone; she didn't even hear her sister's shouts or begin to imagine that the craving inside her would have any consequences. She couldn't think about anything but Cosimiro's next visit.

But the young boss prided himself on never using the same woman twice, especially when they were virgins, because that way, he said, he didn't corrupt them. It had been a lot of work to achieve the prerogatives of top man on the ranch, and he wasn't going to jeopardize them for some horny Indian girl who wanted him to fulfill his duties as a stud. Although bereft of a father—but not of ambition—since he was twelve years old, Lady Luck had bestowed upon him a rich, childless uncle who adopted him with no more to do than the approval of his mother, Apolinaria Ortiz, who was happy to entrust her brother-in-law with the education and care of the boy. Tomás, who was not even consulted, had to exchange maternal warmth for the benefits of money, which were not meager. Don Miguel Urrea, besides being the owner of several very productive mines and the Santa Ana hacienda in Sinaloa, also had acquired by marriage haciendas at Santa Rita de Aquihuiquichi, San Antonio de Cabora, San Ramón del Cocoraqui, and the ranch at Vizcárraga, which made him the second most important landowner in the state of Sonora. All that fertile terrain undoubtedly helped to compensate for the barrenness of Doña Justina Almada y Zayas, but it left unsatisfied the paternal macho in him and unresolved the fundamental problem of an heir, which Don Miguel sought to remedy with a putative son who unfortunately would turn out to be more of a Don Juan than a Don Miguel.

Doña Justina, although disapproving of her brother-in-law's dissolute life, which led to his premature death, refrained from dampening her husband's hopes for the adopted son. Prudent and cunning, she preferred to let blood speak for itself before she took a stand. At first the boy proved worthy of the benefits he received. He grew strong, though not very tall, with blond hair and green eyes that made him the favorite of the women in his family. He became an expert horseman, dressed like a gentleman, and acted like a feudal lord when his uncle was not around. The role of boss's son fit him so well that tales of his despotic and prepotent attitude soon reached the ears of Doña Justina. She waited for an opportunity. The day she caught him with riding whip in hand, giving peremptory commands to the servants, she decided it was time to confront her husband with the imminent usurpation of his authority and the need to get his headstrong nephew under control.

"I'm afraid you've spoiled Tomás," she said to him; "if you aren't careful, he'll go sour on you. You may not want to admit it, but he inherited your brother's insolence and the irresponsibility of your sister-in-law, who didn't even blink when she handed over her son. You'd better get control of the situation before it's too late."

Don Miguel had to admit that Tomás had a certain presumptuous air that wasn't appropriate for his age, but he thought that could be remedied by a good education and a stint away from the permissive atmosphere of the hacienda. There was nothing that a couple of years in Europe wouldn't whittle down to size. But Tomás, besides being conceited, vain, and spoiled, also turned out to be extraordinarily stubborn: he was already too involved in his favorite pastimes—pretty Indian girls, unbroken horses, and the idle life of a young gentleman—to allow himself to be sent to a cold, inhospitable country across the sea. To the weak protests of his tired old uncle, the young man responded with subtle circumlocutions that abounded with an irrefutable logic. He managed to convince Don Miguel—despite the protests of Doña Justina, who called her husband "deluded"—to name him administrator of the Santa Ana ranch so that, face to face with reality and the daily problems of running a hacienda, he could become a respectable man. Consequently, Tomás moved from Alamos to Ocorini and installed himself as owner and lord of Santa Ana with the triumphant air of one who deserved all that and more.

Although it's true that there he became a man, he wasn't necessarily a respectable one, and it definitely wasn't thanks to the management of the ranch but rather to every fresh-as-a-hot-tortilla Indian girl who was willing, and many who were not. The rumors of his debauchery quickly reached Don Miguel, who called the young upstart back home and clearly drew the line.

"Either you get married, become respectable, and stop carousing with the Indian girls and scattering about illegitimate children, or you leave my ranch and make your own way in the world."

For once Tomás didn't doubt that his uncle meant business, and he felt a sudden desire to be married and respectable. The obvious choice was his second cousin Loreto, who for a long time had been making futile advances to him. Loreto had undeniable advantages from the perspective of the young gentleman. Enough years had passed for her to be considered an old maid, so rather than make demands and create a fuss, she would be deeply grateful and would ask few questions and look the other way when her husband felt the need for a little "fresh air." Of course, Loreto was no raving beauty, with her hooked nose; small, brown eyes; dull, bristly hair; wide hips, narrow shoulders, and indistinct waistline; and a character so sour and sanctimonious that it would have made even the Holy Father despair, but she also had positive attributes—all in the form of property that Tomás would inherit from his uncle if he married her—that made her more than attractive, even downright desirable. The engagement was forthcoming, and thus Tomás assured his position as owner and lord of an elegant home in Alamos called "La Capilla" and as the undisputed heir of the prosperous ranches of Sonora.

The arrangements were formal and precise. The young man got married with no illusions but with much pomp and circumstance. Once the ceremony was over he installed Loreto in La Capilla, stayed with her long enough to get her pregnant, and went back to running around on the Santa Ana ranch, only now with more discretion, employing the services of Cosimiro to parade daily through his bedroom those dark, submissive women with indistinct names like María, Lupe, Panchita, Hermenegilda, Rosaura, Chabela, and finally Cayetana, whose madness he ignited by whispering in her ear—as he did to all the others—that her hair was like a flowing brook, her breasts like smooth, rounded hills, her brown skin like the earth after a rainstorm, and her eyes like deep, refreshing wells. Then he opened her secret mouth, undiscovered and insatiable, only to condemn her to endless yearning because Cosimiro never returned for her and the craving became embedded in her gut like a tumorous frustration that kept her from sleeping or eating and that seemed to grow day after day until weeks later it turned into a whirlwind of nausea and vomiting that convinced her that she was about to die.

On the seventh day of uncontrollable vomiting Cayetana began to suspect that it could have something to do with the secret hunger in her womb, and seized with panic, she ran to see Huila. Whimpering, crying, and throwing herself on her knees, she begged the healer to take that thing from her body. She swore that she was possessed and that the devil had entered her. Huila looked at her dispassionately.

"No devil entered you, little one, just the desire for a man and his seed. Prepare yourself to give birth like a woman because you are no longer a child. You see, I've been waiting for you since the night that you mooncalfed with the boss and you conceived, because I know things unknown to others and hear what others can't hear. Into my ears flow the murmurs of gossip and the silence of thoughts and every move that is made in Santa Ana. Thus it was that I heard you rutting with the boss that night. I knew that desire had made you a slave and that his seed had impregnated you. I've been waiting for you for some time. What a strange voice you carry in your womb! But don't be afraid; I'm going to help you."

Cayetana understood little of what she heard and less of what was happening inside her. She was like a wild animal, prisoner of an impulse that dominated her and of a body that betrayed her, harboring mysterious voices heard by the healer and a menacing presence that grew within her. Nevertheless, she instinctively surrendered to the care of the old crone who, due to an age-old limp, hobbled and lunged about the hut like an enormous vulture more likely to devour her than to cure her. She drank the tea that Huila offered "to relieve the panic," she pocketed the herbs and spices that she was supposed to take with each meal so that the baby girl would grow strong and healthy, and allowed the old healer to spread lard on her belly and breasts to avoid stretch marks. Then she returned to Tula's hut and fell asleep. When Tula saw her little sister moping around and dozing in corners, she began to suspect that something was amiss.

"What's wrong with you? What bug bit you? Has your character gone sour so soon? Why don't you go wash clothes? Why did you forget to stir the beans? You're getting lazy. Do you think I'm going to let you live here as a freeloader? Go on! Who do you think you are, you thankless wretch? If I let you stay here it's so you'll help with the chores. Go on, get out of here!"

Cayetana would force herself to get up and leave the hut, dragging her rebellious body and hiding the nausea until she arrived at the river, where she would throw up and then fall asleep again. But Tula became suspicious and began watching her every step, spying on her when she slept, keeping an eye on her as she stirred the beans, peeking at her to see if there was some sign as she entered or left the hut, until one day the scrawny, frag- ile-boned child-woman could no longer hide the bulk that was growing inside her and she began to cry. Tula grabbed her by the hair and buffeted her from side to side until she extracted from her the name of the culprit. Then she threw her to the ground and spit on her.

"Whore! Stupid slut! At least you could have gone with one of ours; at least you could have done that so you could go live with him. But no, you let the boss mess you up and now I have to support both you and the son of a bitch you've got inside." Cayetana lowered her eyes, hunched her shoulders, and tried to hide as best she could the sinful swelling.

"It's a daughter, not a son, of a bitch," she murmured to herself.

On October 15, which fell that year on a hot, cloudy day with no redeeming grace whatsoever, Huila heard the first sounds of the impending birth: there was a slight crackling of bones, a creaking of tendons, a sudden cry of tensing muscles. She gath- ered her equipment and headed for Tula's hut. When she arrived, Cayetana was alone, rolled up in a ball in the corner, moaning like a sick cow. Huila cleaned the center of the room, spread a straw mat on the earthen floor, picked up the frightened bundle of bones, and deposited her on the mat, holding her down so she couldn't run out and give birth in the middle of a field. Firmly, she made Cayetana crouch and then, hunching down behind her, she circled the swollen belly with her arms, lifted the young mother up from the floor, and brought her down with a jolt against her old woman's knees. Cayetana, feeling as if her innards were about to spew out, emitted a terrified cry. Huila calmed her by murmuring ancient formulas in the Yaqui language to dispel the evil spirits, and lullabies to welcome the newborn.

Slowly Cayetana stopped moaning and surrendered in determined silence to the movement of Huila's arms as they raised and lowered her with great force, opening her to the inevitable desire of her body—up, down, wham!; up, down, wham!—until the trembling of her bones, the tearing of skin and muscle, the stretching and twisting of tendons became flesh in her hands, a cry in her ears, a new life that had survived the violence of birth.

When she saw her, Tula felt the first spasm of a searing envy that would last for the rest of her days. Huila had left and Cayetana was cuddling a beautiful baby girl with very fair skin, reddish hair, and eyes like two morning stars, already open to the world. Tula was just about to let loose another string of insults when she had the strange sensation that the child was staring at her defiantly and she felt a violent shiver that ended in a series of hiccups.

Teresa would remember very little of her childhood: her aunt's scolding, her cousins' rejection, a certain joyful solitude that she discovered in the shade of the thicket where she hid; the warmth of Cayetana's body when she cuddled up close to her in the early morning hours, and the arrival at nightfall of her uncle Manuel, who started yelling before he crossed the threshold: thorns that left little scars in her memory. Such as when her cousins called her a "nit" because she was so pale or maliciously asked about her father and then began to laugh. Or when her drunken uncle shouted: "Tell the boss's whore to bring me more booze!" and it was always Cayetana who ran to do his bidding. Words that lacked meaning but that remained like knots in the intemporal fabric of her childhood. She didn't know if the memories that she had of the hut in which they lived, of the animals in the corral, of the acrid, moldy smell of beans, of the patient patting of tortillas, of the sun, the wind, the plants, the cold and the heat belonged to that distant time or to the other time, after the journey, when everything seemed to go away forever just to come around to being strangely all the same again.

But the journey . . . That was different. That she would remember very clearly on the day of her second death: the journey . . .

Until then she hadn't been more than a extension of her surroundings, an undifferentiated piece in the family puzzle, scarcely separated from her mother's body. The days followed each other indistinctly in an ever-flowing present, lacking a character of their own, repetitive and continuous, fixed in a daily routine marked by the strident notes of her aunt and the drunken baritone of her uncle. Without the concrete perception of her own existence that is derived from an act of separation, Teresa felt like part of the furniture, of the food, of the dawns and the evenings, part of all that was constantly merging. But the change came, the pattern was broken, the routine was disrupted, and Teresa suffered an abrupt interiorization of reality. That night it wasn't the shouts that woke her, it was the silence.

She found her aunt and uncle outside in the clearing, strangely together, strangely speaking in soft voices, and even more strangely, sharing the conversation with Cayetana. When her mother gestured to her to approach and Tula didn't yell at her to go back to bed, she felt suddenly alone, isolated by the abrupt change in reality. She saw herself standing there, indecisive and confused, trying for the first time to choose between responding to her mother's call or compensating for her aunt's indifference by retreating voluntarily.

In the following days the fabric of time continued to unravel and Teresa found the clothing of her existence uncomfortable, as if the sleeves were too short, the waist too long, the hem uneven, until she finally became very concretely aware of her own corporeal existence, individualized by the necessity or the hindrance she became in that new situation: "Get out of the way," "Bring me that," "Don't bother me," "Put that over there," "Careful where you step," "Pass that to me."

As the hut was emptied, the everyday utensils disappeared into boxes and baskets, the marks of daily life were wiped out, pigs and chickens were tied to the wagon, and the familiar space became an unknown vacuum, Teresa felt increasingly differentiated, isolated, alone, and pensive. For the first time she pronounced her name out loud to be sure that she existed: "Teresa, Teresa, Teresa," as if she were fanning the air with a pair of new wings. She thought that she would take off flying if she continued to repeat it very, very quickly, and she was astonished. There was a marvelous sensation of absolute freedom in her that she would not feel again until many years later when she jumped on the back of a horse for the first time and galloped off across the countryside. At the end of those disconcerting days reality took on a new name: moving.

One morning moving became a palpable event and time was split into a concrete past that remained behind, empty, and an uncertain and changeable future that stretched ahead. At that moment Teresa learned that she, space, and time existed separately, although years later she would have to unlearn that lesson.

Suddenly everything was movement. It seemed that the whole settlement was whisked up into the air and thrust forward, everything except the mesquite huts that remained there like points in the past: silent, vacant, insignificant. Twenty-five carts, seventy-five men on horseback, two hundred head of cattle, dogs, pigs, chickens, a hellish cacophony of shouts, orders, crowing, neighs, moos, and children's voices: "We're going to Sonora, right, Mama?" The world was moving, reality was shifting. They—she, Cayetana, her aunt Tula, her uncle Manuel, and the four cousins— were riding in a wagon pulled by two oxen; her aunt and uncle in front with the two smallest cousins; she and Cayetana in back with the other two, poorly accommodated on top of the bundles, along with three laying hens and a piglet. She was full of a sense of adventure and even the cousins, intoxicated with the change, stopped harassing her. Uncle Manuel didn't get drunk once during the five-day trip, and he didn't use that mysterious phrase "the boss's whore." Even Cayetana seemed to free herself from her stubborn habit of sighing like a bitch in heat. Everything was new: reality took shape and made itself present; the desert wasn't the one that had always been there, even if it appeared to be; familiar things suddenly had a name like organ cactus, mesquite, or tumbleweed. The movement was filled with questions, and it seemed as if she heard for the first time the dark cries of the grackles, the neighs of the horses, the murmur of the wind, the river's song, and the guitars of the ranchhands around the campfire under a sky that displayed an amazing array of stars. And, with all that novelty, with all that "why didn't I ask before?" or "why didn't they tell me?" she suddenly saw him and her mouth fell open in newfound astonishment.

He was at the head of the caravan, mounted—upright and strong—on an imposing chestnut stallion. Even though he was no tall man, to Teresa, from the perspective of her seven years, he seemed like a divine being on the most beautiful animal she had ever seen. He was blond and his light skin shone under the rim of his hat. He had a mustache and wore a black *charro* suit full of silver trimmings that surrounded him with magic sparkles. His confidence and authority over that group of human beings lent him the aura of a benevolent god caring for his flock. From the first moment she caught a glimpse of him in the distance she understood that he was different. She observed him closely, as his horse pranced back and forth along the length of the procession, giving orders, making the horse's agile feet dance, observing everything. Several times he passed near the wagon and Teresa thought she smelled the sweat of the man and the horse combined in the afternoon heat. She was filled with a new sense of marvel, of amazement, and she wished with all her soul that the man would stop and look at her, that he would realize that she existed. Abruptly, during one of his runs, the chestnut stallion stopped. The horseman looked first at Cayetana and then at her; he smiled. He had clear green eyes like spring water and Teresa thought that she had never known anyone so magnificent. She laughed with pure pleasure, and to her surprise the god on the horse laughed in return. Teresa laughed again, but this time to herself, when she observed that Uncle Manuel, Aunt Tula, and even Cayetana lowered their eyes and scarcely murmured: "Good afternoon, boss."

"Very good," he said. "Everything all right?"

They responded affirmatively without raising their heads. Teresa couldn't take her eyes off him; he glanced at her once more, turned his mount, and rode away, full of his own importance and lordliness. Teresa followed him with her eyes until he disappeared among the wagons in the distance. Impulsively she lunged toward Cayetana and hugged her.

"He's my father, isn't he?" she said, with her voice full of pride. Cayetana blushed. "Oh, Cayetana! Oh, Cayetana! He's so wonderful!" she exclaimed and hugged her again.

From then on she learned to look at Don Tomás not as a boss, not as a stranger, but as someone who in some mysterious way belonged to her.

What Teresa didn't know then was that this move, this kind of pilgrimage of the whole settlement from Sinaloa to Sonora, had not resulted from a free and sovereign choice but from threats that were more or less concrete, from rumors that were more or less true, and from a very definite order for the arrest of the boss. The truth was that Don Tomás was fleeing, because if he appreciated anything more than young virgins, binges, and bets in the bar, it was his freedom, so he decided to preserve it by moving from the comfortable life in Santa Ana to the ranches in Sonora he had inherited when Uncle Miguel died. And the truth was that all this had come about because Tomás had made the mistake of abandoning his carousing in favor of politics and aligning himself publicly with the enemies of Porfirio Díaz.

Backed by a group of ranchers and landowners, Tomás organized the opposition and was elected their leader at the beginning of 1880. Enthralled with his own passionate rhetoric, he did not perceive the trap that was closing in around him. He publicly

accused the engineer Mariano Martínez de Castro of having risen
to the governorship not by popular vote but by Díaz's machinations. He made fun of the presidency of Manuel González, saying
that it was nothing more than a clumsy sham that allowed the
man from Oaxaca to maintain his hidden power and manipulate
the state governors. His close followers applauded him with
increasing enthusiasm.

Little by little his existence had become more complicated.
Rumors began to circulate that the nocturnal meetings at the
Santa Ana ranch had to do more with dishonest motives than politics, that the ranch owner was covering up rustling activities, that
he was trafficking in contraband, that he was prostituting indigenous women, and that he was inciting Yaqui and Mayo Indians to
rebellion. It was even insinuated that a corpse discovered outside
Ocorini could be traced back to him.

What was really decisive was that the governor told him in
no uncertain terms to take his distinguished self to another state
or suffer the consequences, a threat that was followed two days
later by an order for his arrest.

Tomás understood that not only his freedom but also his
health and fortune depended upon his willingness to comply
with the governor's request. For the first time in the four years
since his uncle Miguel's death he remembered the ninety-six
thousand acres of land in Sonora that he had inherited, and it
seemed less onerous to make that abandoned property prosper by
enduring hard work, a few mortal dangers, and the general dis-
ruption of his carefree life than to face the consequences of
staying in Sinaloa. Without a second thought, he packed his
belongings, herded together his ranchhands, ordered the wagons
and the mules to be loaded, and taking everything that was mov-
able, he fled toward Sonora.

For Teresa that first pilgrimage ended in Aquihuiquichi,
where some huts were still standing in spite of years of neglect
and attacks by Indian bands. There the ranchhands and their
families were to settle. For a long while Teresa stood outside her

new home, playing deaf to her aunt's shouts, watching the man-god gallop off into the distance. She didn't want to move until his figure had been completely lost on the horizon and the dust raised by the horse's hooves had settled. She heard someone say that the boss was going to Cabora, and at that very moment she decided that some day she would follow him. Then she entered the dark hut, looked indifferently at her enraged aunt, and began to put away the bundles. She had decided that Tula ought to be afraid of her because she was the boss's daughter. For the first time she felt free, even of Cayetana, whose dark skin contrasted so visibly with her own. With no remorse or nostalgia, she stopped belonging to her mother. Cayetana was expecting another baby and didn't even notice the change.

III

The flight was delayed. There was no departure time. A thick blanket of pollution and fog covered the airport. In spite of the early hour, the wide passageway was already busy with people. An unbearable confusion and noise mixed in her head with cut-off phrases from the piles of documents she had read and reread throughout the years. She went to the cafeteria and ordered a cup of coffee, thinking that surely she would have breakfast on the plane. She chose a table in a remote corner and sat with her back to the crowd, but the tangled, meaningless voices continued to weave in and out of her consciousness, bewildering her. At the next table a fat man with a pounding voice spoke about someone named Aguirre.

Don Lauro Aguirre has intentionally circulated the rumor that the Mexican government intends to assassinate Doña Teresa Urrea. Another mystery, another missing person. Had he died in the Revolution? Had he gone home to grow old anonymously? In a book written before 1910 about the massacre at Tomóchic, he had recorded the history of Teresita, *who escaped death when an individual attacked her with a knife.* Nevertheless it was a work that nobody had read; if it hadn't been for an old edition discovered in an archive, she herself would never have seen it. All those unexpected finds were due to Teresa, she thought, to the uncanny way in which she had led her, almost by the hand, to discover so many old papers, so much contradictory and forgotten information. Secret connections amid chaos, a mysterious, significant pattern: Díaz was born on Teresa's saint's day; Madero was born fifteen days later, but on the same geographic parallel. Was there something in those dates that determined the historic spotlight for the men and obscurity for Teresita? *Teresita Urrea, alias the Saint of Cabora, is in Arizona performing her miraculous cures, or should we say, making fanatics of ignorant people.* The quirks of fate.

She took a sip of coffee. How difficult it was to put her thoughts in order, to find the thread in so much scattered material, to know why she was doing all this. . . . Once again the question: Why? What did Teresa have to do with her life? She had been possessed, losing herself for fifteen years, only to become a receptacle for someone else's life. What a strange obsession! Similar to the obsession of Don Porfirio, who for ten years carried on a secret war to silence the young girl's voice. *In regard to the conspiracy plotted by the seditious Aguirre and his accomplice, the so-called saint, I have the honor of informing you that, by order of the President of the Republic, the following conducive measures are hereby decreed.* Conducive to what? To eliminating Teresa or simply to taking . . . *the necessary steps leading to the extradition of Lauro Aguirre, Tomás Urrea, Benigno Arvizu, and Teresa Urrea. . . .*

She took another sip of coffee; it was cold. On the monitor, the flight was still "delayed." Blocking out the sounds of the cafeteria, she turned her thoughts back to Díaz and the numerous cryptographs, telegrams in code, secret reports and dispatches from spies that he had received, all referring to the Saint of Cabora. A complex and vast network of espionage had kept him informed of every restless stirring in the country, even in that remote Sonoran ranch called Cabora. *After extensive investigations we man-*

aged to find Tomás Urrea's baptismal certificate, which states that on September 14, 1841, he was baptized in the Villa of Sinaloa. . . . . Díaz had been paranoid in spite of his absolute power. The proliferation of "saints," the Tomóchic rebellion, the attack by the Mayo Indians, skirmishes at the border, raids on customs offices, Lauro Aguirre's journalistic bombardment, all in the name of Teresa Urrea. *Enclosed you will find newspaper clippings from El Progresista, edited by Lauro Aguirre in El Paso, Texas, so you can assess the constant insults to the Mexican government and the exaggerated praise of Miss Teresa Urrea.* It seemed like a personal war between them, between the dictator and the saint, evil and good, a kind of mythic battle in which tyranny had triumphed.

Nobody would forget Don Porfirio. No matter what happened, he was firmly installed in history and his ghost still hung over the present like a cyclical threat. Far from forgotten, he had been said to unite "in his person the sum of all virtues and perhaps even more; he had taught the wolf to live peacefully with the lamb as if there were not the slightest antipathy between them." She could almost hear him speaking to the Nation: *It's true that there are some abuses to correct, reforms to initiate, and an enormous task ahead of us in order for the people to be able to brag of having walked down the path of progress and become a modern nation. It would be a true miracle if that weren't so, and miracles are not frequent in our days.* . . . . Miracles weren't frequent in those days? What about Teresa's miracles? The profusion of "saints" in the north, the appearances of the Wandering Jew in Chihuahua, the hope of making rain with a machine? Miracles weren't frequent *now!* Or maybe they weren't recognized. It would be a miracle if a national flight left on time. The monitor still registered "delayed." Miracles were never frequent, but there was Don Porfirio, mythic, eternal, invincible, still receiving the echoes of honors as *the First Patriot, one of the most honest and sincere men of all the countries of Latin America; with his infinite patience, his almost prophetic power to anticipate actions and remain one step ahead, his self-control, and his unequaled authority over his constituents. The*

miracle had been Díaz; the miracle had been Madero. . . .
Everlasting, with their permanent place in history.

She ordered another cup of coffee and lit a cigarette. The
cafeteria was full. At the next table a man read a newspaper; the
headline proclaimed: "Mexico Will Never Be a Hotbed of
Revolution." Díaz had said something similar in one of his
speeches: "There are no revolutionaries in the country today for
the simple reason that there are no motives for revolution. The
governmental line of peace and justice, law and order, more
administration and less politics has produced abundant fruits of
prosperity and happiness. There is work for everybody; public
employees earn more than ever; families of the middle and upper
classes are better housed, better fed, and better dressed than ever
before. Those who speak lightly and thoughtlessly about present
or future revolutions in this nation do not realize the tremendous
forces that are continuously working to avoid such a contingency.
I assure you that it would take a perverse miracle"—again, a miracle—"to disturb the peace that this country has enjoyed under
my leadership."

Suddenly she felt weak, her mind fuzzy as if it were losing
track of time, merging past and present in the hubbub of the
restaurant. *Rebels are crossing the mountains, heading toward
Cabora.* Airports were places of transition; they made her feel
anxious. *I will lead a detachment to Cabora with whatever orders you
send.* In between the tables, through the ample corridors, anonymous beings were rushing from here to there, from there to here,
all with the same expression, the same senseless hurrying, from
here to there, from there to here, from here to nowhere. Where
was *she* going? To Cabora. *On the fourteenth about thirty-five
armed men passed through Mayacoba, saying they were going to
Cabora.* And if Cabora were nowhere? She didn't want to think
about it anymore. Porfirio Díaz consolidated his control when he
was named "The Necessary One." *Captain Emilio Enríquez was
killed this morning by the rebels on their way to Cabora: please send
orders.* When Díaz publicly received the archbishop's blessing it

was celebrated with a round of thunderous applause, which he acknowledged with a brief "Thank you very much." That was reality. *Tomás Urrea, Teresa's father, has a case pending in Sinaloa for robbery and rustling.* Or was there more than one reality? *In regard to the extradition of the Urreas, we should not attempt that now because we have pending the case of an American, who after committing a crime in the United States, came to Mexico and became a citizen and my government has denied his extradition.*

Words, documents, telegrams, secret messages . . . voices blending together, reporting the news, repeating the lies, praising, criticizing . . . all inside her head, pushing her toward Cabora where *a sick woman professes to be inspired by God. After suffering a cataleptic fit, she is delirious. Superstitious people have declared her a "saint," claiming that she cures the blind, the crippled, and lepers with dirt and saliva. A multitude of people are flocking to her in search of health, believing firmly in the alleged miracles.* . . . Aeroméxico announces the departure of Flight . . . *that the delirium* . . . 901, to Navojoa, Ciudad Obregón, and Guaymas; passengers . . . *has planted in the head of this poor woman* . . . please board at Gate B.

▨ IV

As she lay dying for the second time, Teresa would remember with particular intensity Don Tomás's love for Cabora, perhaps the only sincere and disinterested love of his life.

He was not a man to whom loving came easily, especially at the age of forty and with no previous experience of any relationship that surpassed his testicles or his ambition. Actually, he hadn't loved anybody and if asked, he would have confessed his total indifference in regard to that emotion. He scarcely knew his father, a jovial man who rarely appeared at home during daylight hours and who had the bad judgment to be standing in the trajectory of a stray bullet during a brawl in his favorite bar. For his mother, Apolinaria, he reserved mixed emotions that, considered altogether, canceled themselves out. On the one hand, he was grateful to her for turning him over to his uncle Miguel for his education and upbringing since this had such tangible benefits to his material well-being; on the other hand, he despised her for the same reason, sensing that giving up her only son without a fuss was definitive proof of maternal indifference. With Don Miguel he had to expend so much effort plotting how to get what he wanted that he never had time to develop any real affection for him, and he distrusted his aunt Justina as much as she distrusted him. Loreto was almost a stranger with whom he rarely spoke but who offered him a convenient excuse to avoid other emotional commitments. The days he spent with her were just for the purpose of making another son or baptizing the newborn. His relationship with his children demanded obedience and respect on their part, authority and tolerance on his, but no demonstration of affection. The Indian girls who bore him so many illegitimate offspring left his mind as soon as they left his bed. Therefore, he was not prepared for what happened to him when he arrived at Cabora.

Spurring on his chestnut stallion, he approached the outskirts of the ranch, followed by four of his most trusted ranchhands. What he saw was a disaster; the place was completely in ruins. Apart from the neglect it had suffered since his uncle Miguel's death, there had been attacks by bands of Yaquis who, infuriated by new expropriations of their lands, had reduced the buildings to rubble, dispersed the cowhands, left a trail of dead cattle, and set fire to everything else. There was nothing left. Don Tomás faced a panorama of destruction and death. Staked to the only wall left standing was the skeleton of a child, carefully picked clean by the vultures and whitened by the burning rays of the sun. Tomás took it down and, with the help of his ranchhands, buried it without ceremony. While the others went to check the well and to see if there was anything redeemable on the other side of the wash, Tomás went up a nearby hill to get a better view of the desolate panorama. He stopped his horse and looked around. It was then that he saw her for the first time: her tanned earth, her hair of meadow grass combed by the wind, her smooth, firm hills, her velvet belly stretching out toward the horizon, her infinite air of freedom. He perceived the unmistakable aroma of native soil and its soft, sweet dust, its fertile, virgin flavor nestled deep into his gut; the name of Cabora curled up on his tongue, and he was overcome by an emotion so powerful that it left him breathless. Tears came to his eyes and he was filled with a ferocious tenderness that sparked his creative passion. Suddenly he knew she was his: Cabora defeated, destroyed, looted; Cabora on her knees, her pride burned, her fences torn up; Cabora deserted, solitary; Cabora miserable but blessed, needy, yearning, his to do with as he wished. She came into his heart like an unquenchable desire and into his head like hope; she aroused for the first time his dormant homing instinct, and he fell to his knees and began to caress her earth, her dust, her destruction. Inside himself he was already creating his new world.

Perhaps there he found what he had been looking for in the arms of so many Indian girls, in the procreation of so many fatherless children. Perhaps there he found the meaning of his manhood as he never had found it in Loreto's passive resignation. Perhaps there he finally understood the frustrated illusions from which his father had fled and the quiet self-sacrifice of Apolinaria. For the first time in his life, he surrendered to something outside of himself. He molded his entire ambition to the needs of Cabora, shaping her, recreating her in his own image. On top of the rubble, on those ruins still wounded by the memory of violence, Tomás conceived his life's work. He converted the fury of the recent destruction into a chaotic, crazed passion. In each crevice of the dry land, in each hole, on each carbonized rock he poured his desire and caresses, his macho tenderness. To the chaos of the looting he added his own chaos: he ordered his ranchhands to bring adobe, flagstones, yellow bricks, red bricks, glazed bricks, flat red tiles and curved red tiles for the roof, thick tiles and thin tiles, gutter tiles and tiles for the eaves; he ordered them to cut beams and planks, oak boards for the floor, mahogany for the doors; he sent for paving stones, stone slabs, and hewn stone; he brought lime and mortar, sand and pebbles for the concrete; he ordered tiles with geometric patterns, tiles with bright-colored birds, tiles with stylized flowers or in solid colors, six-sided tiles, square tiles, delicate, elongated tiles to go around the lower edge of the walls, floor tiles for the entranceway; he had iron forged for the windows and grilles and balconies and doors; he ordered a three-tiered stone fountain for the patio. He made great piles of everything, sorted by textures and colors, shapes and thicknesses, lined up like troops on his own battleground, a contest of materials and consistencies under the command of Don Tomás, compiler of dreams and fantasies, architect of hope. The war had begun.

From the disorder there gradually emerged smooth, logical walls, tall and thick against the merciless climate, imbued with pride that seemed to emanate from his hands and from his orders. Walls for the six bedrooms, for the long hallway, for the library— lofty and wide, to be covered with bookshelves—white walls for the kitchen, square walls for the chapel, long walls for the spacious living room, open walls with windows, with arches extending to the patio and to the hallway. Then came the task of creating ceilings: domed ceilings, solid, cool, poised on giant beams and corpulent columns, on arched curves; a tiled vault for the chapel, a white marble altar, chimneys for the kitchen, long tables for kneading bread and making tortillas, roofs covered with curved red tiles, with rainspouts and eaves. The center patio was left open like a shameless invitation to the sky, with an enormous laurel tree to provide year-round shade, the fountain in the middle surrounded by flowerpots of hewn stone, displaying red and white roses, yellow brooms, orange cress, and geraniums of every color. The floors were laid with care, tile by tile: huge brown squares bordered by rows of lemon-colored rectangles. The heavy doors were set in their frames with iron hinges; for the master bathroom Tomás designed a huge tile tub decorated with paintings of birds and flowers. He had the exterior walls painted white to reflect the heat of the sun, and he made openings to assure that the desert air would flow through the arches and cool off in the shade of the high ceilings.

Finally, he put up miles of fences that wed the land and the house to the owner, the beloved to the master. Cabora began to fill with the slow, steady steps of cattle, the rhythmic canter of horses, the whistling of faithful cowhands; the owner's illusions were expressed in the walls and ceilings and floors and arches and patio of that great white house, product of his hands and his passion. Tomás had taken possession of the spirit of the land, and the land in turn had granted him the miracle of sustaining his dream. The man rejoiced in his achievement, finding in it a higher meaning for his existence, a concrete expression of his creativity.

It wasn't until after he had filled the house with furniture—soft beds, easy chairs covered with fine leather, walnut tables, carved chairs, bookshelves with glass doors, thick curtains, handwoven rugs, and everything that he might possibly need—that he was hit by the first wave of anxiety. He was checking for the hundredth time the workmanship in his library, feeling so satisfied that he was congratulating himself out loud, when suddenly he heard it and felt its power: the silence, a thick, heavy stillness that encompassed everything, snuggled into the corners, slept in the bed, covered the furniture, inhabited the kitchen, prayed in the chapel, and converted the air that entered from the patio into a cruel, foreboding caress. Don Tomás realized immediately how absurd it was to build that immense marvel, so beloved and carefully created, without having someone with whom to share it. Sitting down in the leather chair he began to think, or rather, he heard himself think, surrounded by a deepening silence that was becoming more and more distressing. What good was it to have created a work of art if nobody was there to appreciate it? To whom could he pour out the joy that contemplating Cabora produced in him? He needed someone there to whom he could say: "Look how I've arranged the arches so that they open onto the patio and serve as frames for the greenery; notice the equilibrium of the beams; what do you think of the harmonious integration of the library, the coolness of the living room, the coziness of the bedroom?" All this he needed to express out loud and receive a response; without it the house, in spite of its beauty, was incomplete, an empty work of art. It didn't exist as long as it existed only for him.

He served himself a glass of brandy and paced several times around the room. Through the window he heard the cowhands' voices and the neighing of the horses and he was besieged by a second wave of anxiety: he imagined bands of Yaquis with their cries of death and destruction, falling upon Cabora to reduce it once more to ashes. He remembered the boy's skeleton and the trail of dead cattle; he recalled the pile of rubble that he had found that first day; he imagined the flames that would consume his labor of love, and he felt himself die. Mounting a defense of the ranch would be almost impossible: half of the workers were Yaquis and the other half were Mayos. With the first sign of danger they would disperse, or worse yet, they would join the enemy. The other option—to make a pact with the tribe—would seem like a cowardly act as if it were just to protect his own hide, and who else was there to protect in this forlorn place? As he sipped his second brandy, he thought—for the first time in a long while— of Loreto and his children, not with the usual irritation but with a certain need that he disguised as compassion: poor Loreto, it was easy to see that he hadn't been exactly fair; he would even admit that he had been a bit abusive, always thinking primarily of himself. And the children? There were three of them now . . . no, four boys who by this time certainly needed the presence of a father, whom they had never known.

By his third brandy, the alcohol was enhancing the novelty of his thoughts with a delicious warmth; it sweetened the tepid remorse and deepened the desire to share all he had built with someone who could appreciate it on a daily basis, which exclud- ed the one-night women, the cowhands, and certain friends from the cantina. Don Tomás felt himself reconciling with life, the life of a respectable man, a responsible family man, a father and hus- band who was, if not loving, at least present. He thought of his sons and he imagined that at Cabora they would also become men and they wouldn't be stuck in church all the time or attending teas with their mother. He could teach them to ride, to speak the rough language of the ranch, to deal with cowhands, and to survive the difficult life in the country. Loreto would have her chapel—as long as she didn't bring in a permanent priest—so she could pray all she wanted, and her kitchen where she could shout orders until becoming hoarse. During the winter nights they would light the fire and she would keep him company while he sipped his usual brandy. When they had guests, Loreto would tend to their needs and feel proud to be the owner and mistress of such a beautiful home. The rest of the children would be born on the ranch; there would be commotion and laughter. . . .

By the fourth drink, Don Tomás was convinced: he'd send for Loreto and the children. Once he had the family there, anything he did to assure their safety was justifiable, even if it meant making a deal with the devil himself. Once the decision was made, his anguish was over and the future lay ahead of him full of joy and security. He wrote a brief note to Loreto, informing her that he had installed in Cabora all the commodities that she might desire, and since he was sure that she wanted to be reunited with him forever, he expected her and the children as soon as possible. Without giving it any more thought, he sent for Cosimiro and gave him orders to deliver the letter and return with the family to Cabora.

The next day, accompanied by Aniseto Wichamea, a fugitive Yaqui who had sought refuge from federal troops among the ranch hands of Cabora, he set out for the eight villages of the Yaqui valley. There were ten days of riding horseback, and when that wasn't possible, of advancing on foot, skirting the thickets that were too dense, avoiding the thick fields of prickly cacti that would hurt the horses' hooves, camping near a stream when they were lucky, and if they weren't, wherever they found themselves at nightfall. They traveled from west to east, passing through each town, speaking in each place to the governor, waiting patiently while he consulted with the townspeople, watching how they

deliberated and spit, how they listened and spit, how they sometimes just spit until the ground was full of prudent and wise
spittle. When they had obtained the consent of the eight governors, they returned to the meeting place, Vicam, which means
Arrow's Point. There all the governors and representatives—men
and women—of the eight villages got together and set up the
Council. Three days of deliberations and spitting followed. The
elders argued that "the boss" couldn't hide enough warriors, and
Don Tomás drew on the ground for them a map of his land and
all the places where the fugitives could "disappear" among the
regular workers. They said that the *yoris* could not be trusted and
that the boss surely would betray them, and Don Tomás spit on
one side and the other and looked fiercely into their eyes before
he swore on the lives of his wife and children that he would not
be the one to turn them in to the *yoris,* but they should watch
their own people who sometimes betrayed them for a cow or for
a position in the state militia. By the third day they were negoti-
ating quantities: how much milk, how many head of cattle, how
much cream, how much cheese. It couldn't be rushed; one had to
offer little and then let them bargain until they were satisfied that
they had made a good deal. The bargaining lasted deep into the
night, and then the governors retired to make a decision. Tomás
decided that things were going well and sent Aniseto to Cabora
for a head of cattle to give to them as soon as the deal was closed.
The governors debated until dawn and then ordered their women
to bring mezcal and *bacanora* and to prepare the enormous flour
tortillas, as big as tablecloths, tasting of the arms and thighs on
which they had been flattened until they were as transparent as
the skin of a newborn baby. They killed the steer that Aniseto
brought and hung it over the coals; they prepared a place for the
celebration, surrounding the group of participants with sticks and
branches of mesquite until all of them were encircled. An agreement had been reached: they would respect Cabora.

Aniseto asked to stay in his village since the soldiers had
stopped looking for him. The boss gave him the mare he was rid-

ing in appreciation for his help. Don Tomás headed home. He felt satisfied; he had spent two weeks away from the ranch and the pact had cost him several milkings a month, a head of cattle every so often for the *huacabaquis* that were held for weddings and funerals, and the formal commitment to hide fugitive Indians among the peaceful workers, but he had the assurance that Cabora would not be attacked again. He spurred on his horse, impatient to welcome his family, which was surely waiting for him at home.

But in Cabora he found the same silence that had reigned before his departure and, as the only response to his order, a brief note from Loreto: "I can't go. My health is delicate. Yours, Loreto." He couldn't believe his eyes. Delicate? She had the strength of a bear and gave birth to babies as if she were shelling peas. No, it wasn't a question of delicate health, but rather of disobedience. Blind with rage, he sent for Cosimiro and demanded to know the truth.

But the truth—which Cosimiro couldn't know, although he probably had his suspicions—was that Loreto was very nicely established in Alamos and hadn't the slightest desire to join her husband. If there were a greater sacrifice than putting up with Don Tomás's permanent presence in La Capilla, it would be to move with her family to a ranch in the middle of a desert in order to take care of him. Thus the written order, far from filling her with loving gratitude, infuriated her. First she consulted Doña Justina—who sided with her completely—and then her confessor, Father López y Sábana, from whom she received the blessing of God himself and permission to defy her husband's authority. How could he presume that she would leave Alamos, the center of Sonora's social, cultural, and religious life, to bury herself alive with the cattle and cowhands? Not a chance. She had her children and her friends, the cream of Alamos's society, including Doña Justina, now a widow and recognized benefactress of the city. Furthermore, Loreto belonged to the Catholic Mothers who ran the orphanage and to the Society of the Sacred Heart of Mary; she participated with Father López y Sábana in organizing the May devotions and the Friday Communion. Nevertheless, all that was beside the point: since it was an indisputable marital obligation, she was willing to sacrifice her life—as she swore with total humility during her Friday confession—and to go to bury herself on the ranch if necessary. No, it wasn't for herself that she refused to comply with her husband's order, it was for her children, poor things. Where did Don Tomás plan to educate them? Among the atheist ranchhands who didn't even know how to speak proper Spanish, much less attend sacred mass like decent people? As a mother, she couldn't accept that, and even though as a Christian she recognized her conjugal obligation, her children came first and she wasn't willing to take them out of the best school in Alamos and drag them to the country to be raised in ignorance and without the proper religious instruction. And furthermore, what about her offsprings' health in that barbaric environment? She couldn't even consider it. She was very sorry, but for the good of her children she had to contravene her husband's orders.

Of course, Cosimiro knew nothing of all this, but it was enough to see Loreto's face livid with rage as she read the letter, to catch certain phrases of the tantrum she threw behind closed doors in the company of Doña Justina, and to hear her pronounce that decisive, self-justifying no! in order for him to understand that this woman was not going to be moved by anything, any way.

Don Tomás, as soon as he had Cosimiro before him, understood that more elaboration would mean more humiliation and that he ran the risk of making a fool of himself in front of his right-hand man if he insisted on knowing the details. He realized that if his mind hadn't been blurred with brandy-colored dreams, he would have known from the beginning that Loreto would not come, and he could have avoided the outrage.

"Don't feel bad, Cosimiro; it's really better this way. What would we do anyway with a sanctimonious hypocrite who goes to bed with the Lord's Prayer and gets up with a Hail Mary? That's all we need here! Thank God I've been spared such an annoying mistake. At least I've fulfilled my duty to her and she will not be able to reproach me for anything. Run and get me a young girl to my liking, clean and brown-skinned, and bring her to me as soon as it's dark."

That night he poured all his love for Cabora into the poor little creature, who felt as if she were dying under the passionate onslaught and didn't understand a word of what the crazed man was murmuring: "I will mold your long lines like the night, I will penetrate your spaces and reach the womb of your secret pride, hidden in the foundations of your dream; I will cover with caresses your aching forms, I will allow myself to be drawn into your dark silences, in me you will find your structures chiseled beneath the force of my desire. . . ." When the young girl left, Don Tomás swore that, henceforth, Loreto would never set foot in Cabora.

V

From the air, the profile of Mexico City sank beneath the unmovable gray smog and disappeared from sight. She leaned her head against the seat. At last she was on her way, her stomach tied into a tight ball of nerves, excitement, and hunger. She closed her eyes. The plane's vibration sedated her and her mind was occupied again by word-images, sound-images, as if they were memories or dreams of memories, or memories of memories, or memories of dreams, as if her mind were a register of meaningless phrases she had read, snatches from here and there. . . . *These were the last days of 1889 . . .* everything was muddled . . . *and in the capital of the Republic preparations were being made for the biggest and most sumptuous dance of the New Year. . . .* Before 1888 the New Year wasn't celebrated in Mexico: that had been one of Díaz's innovations. . . . *In Cabora, in spite of the cold, more than two thousand souls congregated in the company of the new Saint Teresa to receive the Baby Jesus . . . and in Mexico City . . . the best families of the capital greeted the year 1890 with whistles, confetti, streamers, balloons, music, merriment, fireworks, laughter* . . . and an infernal drunken spree that left a hangover until after Epiphany. . . . *The miraculous apparition of young Teresa Urrea on the ranch of Cabora is a confirmed fact.* . . . Was Teresa an apparition? *Internal peace reigned at the end of 1889. . . . Miss Urrea, with complete knowledge and malice, planned and led uprisings against the legitimate government.* . . .

The saint visits God whenever she wishes, speaks informally with Saint Peter, and corresponds with the Holy Ghost . . . and with me, she thought fuzzily; if not, why would I be going to Cabora?

In his New Year's speech, President Díaz assured the people that the restlessness and revolutionary spirit of his opposition had not been repressed, merely put to rest. . . . *Teresa Urrea sells secrets to remove calluses, puts curses on Catholic priests, and eats dirt with tomato sauce.*

All signs indicate she is possessed. . . . Possessed? It was *she* that was possessed; that would be an explanation, wouldn't it? *Teresita Urrea was a Mexican Joan of Arc who received divine inspiration and was declared a saint by the people, who loved her.* . . . *What's the best cure for sainthood? Ah! With ice water, antispasmodics, and sometimes a husband, the roster of Catholic saints would have been reduced to a minimum.* . . . *General Marcos Carrillo has ordered that operations against the Indian rebels resume in the Bacatete Mountains.* . . . Could Cabora be near the Bacatete Mountains? Did Cabora exist? *Teresa joined the spiritist movement and didn't recognize any authority other than her own.* . . .

. . . *of all the crimes Díaz committed there were none more monstrous than those against Tomóchic and Temosáchic, where more victims were sacrificed than in Río Blanco.* . . .

Don Tomás Urrea took advantage of the crowds gathering around his daughter by selling meat, eggs, chickens, tacos, milk, and even the water that the poor fools drank. . . . The words seemed to churn about in her head, strung together by the monotonous droning of the plane. . . . *in the ranch of Santa Ana, near Ocorini, Sinaloa, there is still a small cemetery where a white cross marks the spot of Teresa's birth.* . . . *Once the curtains fell on the rebellions of Chihuahua and*

Guerrero, it was believed that nobody would dare provoke a new uprising against a ruler who, like Don Porfirio, had the necessary elements to squelch it. . . .

Young Teresa was of imposing beauty, with long black hair and clear, luminous eyes. . . . There is an old saying that one shouldn't believe in saints who stay for lunch . . . lunch: when would they serve lunch? She hadn't eaten since . . . since 1888, the Mayo Indians have respected the peace . . . peace, Porfirian peace, peace of the sepulchers . . . the rebel Indians were totally defeated and taken prisoner along with their families and supporters . . . there is no doubt that the fanaticism of Teresa Urrea was responsible for the deaths at Tomóchic. . . .

In 1890, near the Cocoraqui Wash in Cabora, a young girl named Teresa Urrea began to have visions. Her father encouraged the girl's spirituality, believing that he would thus gain a place in heaven. . . . The Saint of Cabora has ruined her father, Don Tomás Urrea, who is from a good family and does not believe in the miracles performed by his daughter. . . . Did Teresa really perform miracles or did popular hearsay invent more than what was there? Would she ever know? The whole northern region of the country was infested with spiritist circles whose motives were more political than religious. . . . His almost prophetic power to judge the acts and character of men has given General Díaz control and authority and made him the most respectable ruler that Mexico has ever had. . . . How incredible! Where had that tidbit come from when it was generally known that during the Veracruz rebellion, Díaz himself had given the order to squelch it from the start, strike while the iron is hot and take the necessary measures. . . .

The young lady had strange powers of suggestion; she could heal a patient by just looking at him. . . . Only faith is capable of moving mountains; people without faith are like pieces of straw blown about in the wind. . . . The Mexican government estimates that due to the sinister influence of Lauro Aguirre and Teresa Urrea more than one thousand people have been killed in the past few years. . . . The past few years . . . , she had lived, breathed, and dreamed about

Teresa; now she was going to her encounter. *After an epileptic attack that lasted three days, this young woman "came back to life" endowed with a strange power in her hands and voice . . . refined and beautiful, she preached only peace, meditation, and patience as a means to achieve justice. . . .*

President Díaz is a man of simple tastes who finds his greatest pleasure in methodical work, God bless him. . . . The young fanatic is usurping the sacramental rights of the true religion and blessing people in the name of a power supposedly conferred upon her by God. . . . "Peace reigns in Mexico," declared Porfirio Díaz before the Congress. . . . The Tomochitecs, inspired by Teresa's preaching, resolved not to recognize any authority other than that of God and not to obey any rule other than divine law. . . .

Teresa Urrea was not the leader or the inspiration of the insurrections in northern Mexico. . . . Wasn't it more rewarding to receive the sacraments from the hands of a lovely young virgin than from those of an exploitative, ambitious, and treacherous priesthood? In times of revolution, it is not sobriety, audacity, bravery, or wisdom that triumphs: it is magic. . . . She was in a trance for three months and eighteen days. . . .

On the main altar in the Church of Tomóchic, the image of Teresita was surrounded with candles and flowers . . . thousands of pilgrims arrive at Cabora . . . the so-called saint is the illegitimate daughter of Don Tomás Urrea, a man with a criminal record, wanted by the law for rustling and other crimes in the State of Sinaloa. . . .

Lauro Aguirre converted the saint into a symbol and banner of his struggle against Díaz . . . Teresa's preaching incited the Indians to rebellion . . . fanatics claim Teresa to be the future mother of Moctezuma . . . reliable sources have informed us that Teresa Urrea is an ordinary young woman, with no special power; it seems that she is living in sin with a rebel named Aguirre. . . . Soon the young Teresa became quite wise: she denounced abuse and corruption; she called for justice for the disinherited and liberty for mankind. . . .

The North American press has published several inaccuracies about Teresa Urrea, portraying her as a martyr, unjustly persecuted, deprived of her property, and sentenced to death by Don Porfirio's government. . . . Cabora has become a pestilent place, full of cripples, amputees, lepers, blind persons, and all kinds of undesirables. . . . In other words, law and order have replaced struggle, disorder, political restlessness, and the insincerity of previous administrations. . . .

On the ranch of Cabora there are new miracles every day. . . . According to the latest reports, the new saint doesn't have a shadow. . . . President Díaz declares: "In Mexico, there is no censorship of the press. But the government acts severely towards any publication that is anarchistic, subversive, or revolutionary. . . ."

Teresa Urrea performs miracles at a distance. Yesterday, without moving from her room, she saved a baby girl whose father had left her on the railroad tracks because he wanted a boy. . . . Two nations unite in the persecution of the false saint. . . . News of miracles spreads as tens of thousands descend on Cabora to celebrate the saint's birthday. . . . A youth named Mariano fell in love with her, and one day she was surprised kissing him on the beach; one malicious follower chanted: "Long live Teresa, pretty and quaint, long live the fools who think she's a saint" . . . the young mystic had innate intelligence; she taught herself to read and write. . . .

Bands of Indians were followed to the ranches where they took refuge and were summarily rounded up. . . . As the years passed, Teresa was forgotten by her followers and she became a slovenly old woman who for a long time was known as "The Witch of Nogales" . . . this beautiful young woman died at the age of thirty-three, having exhausted her spirit in the service of others.

The church denounces the fact that Teresa Urrea drinks blood in order to have power over her followers . . . the public condemns the hypocrisy of the so-called saint and the villainy of her father who exploits the ignorance of the people for his own benefit. . . . Mr. Melbourne will produce three rainstorms in Sonora for the price of twenty-five hundred dollars each, so as to end the drought that has produced the fanaticism around the Saint of Cabora. . . . Government maintains constant vigilance of the Cabora ranch due to great concentrations of people. . . .

One cannot understand the fuss made over a woman who is illiterate, ignorant, and dirty, and whose sole purpose is to achieve power for her lover, Lauro Aguirre, by leading rebellions against the legitimate government of Mexico. . . . Teresa of Cabora is considered by everybody to be a threat to public tranquility . . . does she read minds or practice witchcraft? . . . a woman full of pride and vanity, she condemns to death anyone who doesn't believe blindly in her. . . . Good news for the bald! Teresa Urrea makes hair grow by blowing across the scalp of the interested party. . . . It is recommended that an all-out war be declared against the saint. . . . After three weeks, Mr. Melbourne produced four drops of rain and wanted to collect his money. . . . Two hundred Mayo Indians, shouting, "Long live the Saint of Cabora," attacked the town of Navojoa. . . . Navojoa . . . she felt someone touch her shoulder. She opened her eyes. It took her a moment to remember where she was as the tangle of words in her head slowly unraveled.

"Please, put your seat in the upright position. We are about to land in Navojoa." She shook off her numbness and looked out the window: they were approaching the runway. Navojoa, Cabora, Teresa . . .

VI

On the day of her second death, Teresa would remember that she herself was all that changed with the move to Aquihuiquichi. Everything else was as if the world had gone in a complete circle. They set themselves up in a hut just like the previous one, with the same walls of mesquite branches, a similar reed roof, identical dirt floors, and equivalent common rooms: the main room and the family room. The former, open on one side to allow the smoke to float out and the chickens to come in, continued to function as a kitchen, dining room, bedroom for poor relatives, and pantry. There they ate on the same wooden table, sitting in the same three homemade chairs, and in the same hierarchical order: first Uncle

Manuel with the older boys, then the younger boys, and finally the women, including Teresita. Just as in Santa Ana, she and Cayetana slept on a straw mat on the floor, both of them huddled against the wall to avoid being stepped on during the night; there was the same big clay urn for fresh water that perspired its monotonous drop into the same small dish for the chickens, and the same pot of beans that boiled daily, permeating everything with a moldy smell. In the corner, a counter served the double purpose of shelf for kitchen utensils and cover for the nocturnal shelter of the chickens; from the roof hung the same huge basket with dishes and pans, washrags, and a rusty knife, and at the entrance there were the same old flat stone for grinding corn every other day and the griddle for cooking tortillas. Against the wall was a stack of firewood gathered from the surrounding area. The other room, an exact replica of the one in Santa Ana, was where her aunt and uncle and cousins slept. It had four walls and a door that was closed at night but open during the day. It also served as a storage room for everything they had brought from Santa Ana, from clothes to tools and old furniture in need of repairs. There, Uncle Manuel passed out every night on a cot made of sticks supported by two forked props and covered with a straw mat, while on the floor Aunt Tula and the younger children shared one straw mat and the older children shared another. Everything the same, interchangeable, homogenous.

Everything the same, even time—the hours of the day that during the trip had become so long and full of novelties, each one with its own identity, each day individualized by different, concrete events, by new landscapes and unexpected sensations— coiled back upon itself and reinitiated that obsessive repetition of tasks whose results were always ephemeral: wash clothes, refill the pot with water, poke at the fire and stir the beans, grind the corn to make tortillas, sprinkle water and sweep the floor to clean up the chicken shit, look for mesquite branches for the fire, roll up the straw mats in the morning and spread them out again at night, sweep the corral and feed the animals, rescue the eggs before the pig ate them, wash the dishes in the creek, wash herself from time to time, go to bed and get up and go to bed again: an endless daily routine that made time stand still, each day a copy of the previous one.

Everything the same. From early in the morning she heard the same shouts of her aunt and at night she suffered through the same drunken bouts with Uncle Manuel. Cayetana continued being a humble shadow except that each day she was heavier with child, this time by someone from the settlement whom she would not marry either, in spite of the same threats and renewed insults from her sister. Outside, the same sun scorched the hard earth in an identical corral, where she felt the same heat in the summer and where a similar frost fell in the winter; there, the same roosting hens continued laying or not laying their identical eggs according to their emotional state, and the same pig that Teresa had fed in Santa Ana continued to get fat under her faithful care. From the mesquite thicket, the indistinguishable grackles cawed their black dominion from one branch to another as the sun set; the remembered sounds of the other settlement floated in the air: the wind howled in an identical manner or stopped blowing to leave everything in a familiar stupor. Nothing had changed: each object seemed to have sought an analogous place to manifest itself with the same sad disposition and the same futility of all that was eternally repeated in a way homonymous with the time before the move.

Everything the same, except Teresa, who became restless and even rebellious and surly at times, as if that sameness made her annoyed and impatient. She did her chores unwillingly or left them for later; she slipped away in the morning and came back well past midday. She seemed to have entered another world, her head full of dreams, her eyes brimming with the vision of the blond man, gestating an illusion of the future.

In October she turned eight without anybody noticing. A few days later Cayetana gave birth to a baby boy and Teresa had to concede him her place on the straw mat. She began to sleep alone. Some time earlier she had stopped seeking her mother's warmth or expecting any kind of consolation from her. Soon she abandoned her childish dresses in favor of Cayetana's and Tula's hand-me-down cotton blouses and skirts. She learned to braid her hair and care for herself. In one year she grew faster than a mesquite tree and became taller than her cousins. Her hair hung down to her waist, her eyes were increasingly intense and luminous, her arms and legs grew long, and she had hands that were strangely large and coarse compared to the rest of her body.

A year later the first school was established in the settlement, and the children, including Tula's sons, began to attend. Teresa didn't want to go: she preferred what she learned from life on the mountain, from the birds and the fox. She roamed around in a world of her own, oblivious to Tula calling her "wild" and her cousins' jokes about her illegitimacy.

Nevertheless, as the boys ganged together in school, they became more and more aggressive and offensive, repeating and elaborating upon taunts and insults, until a solid ball of rage swelled up inside of her, along with an ardent desire for vengeance. She allowed that desire to fester, and she waited.

The wait ended one afternoon when she was caught off guard by her oldest cousin, Manuel, who approached her from behind, grabbed her skirt, and began to dance around her, forcing her to turn with the garment. The other cousins and their friends began to laugh. Teresa flailed her arms, trying to swat him, and this excited her tormenter even more.

Abruptly, she stood still as a statue, her body completely erect, her muscles tense, and her eyes fixed straight ahead. The surprise movement forced her cousin to face her, and in that instant she glared at him as she imagined Don Tomás would do with a subordinate.

"Let me go or else I'll . . ."

She couldn't finish her sentence or take her eyes off her opponent: it was as if Manuel had been turned to stone; he couldn't move a muscle, pronounce a word, or even blink. Only his eyes

revealed the enormity of his terror caused by the sudden immobility. The others looked on, horrified. When she realized what
was happening, Teresa was frightened also, and she closed her
eyes: in that instant her cousin collapsed like an empty gunny-
sack. There was a moment of absolute silence, and then everyone
took off in opposite directions, abandoning the defeated cousin.
Teresa, shaking from head to toe, opened her eyes and understood that something terrible had happened. Manuel, still
overcome by an inexplicable weakness, got up very slowly,
glanced at her fearfully, and ran off hopping and stumbling as if
he were badly wounded.

If any of the witnesses had told on her, nobody believed it,
because Teresa was never scolded. Her cousins stopped harassing
her and kept as far away as possible, but she was scared. She
remembered Tula remarking more than once on the strangeness
of her eyes, and she started noticing that nobody, not even
Cayetana, could hold her gaze. She began to feel afraid of herself.
She sought her own reflection in a pool of water, but saw only two
amber eyes that looked up at her with anguish. The fear of repeating the incident kept her more distant than ever from the family.

Her apathy wore down Tula's patience; finally her aunt gave
up and opted to leave her the only chore that she seemed to do
willingly: collecting firewood. Early in the morning Teresa would
wrap herself in an old shawl to protect herself from the sun and
head off to the hills to look for dry branches and fallen logs. She
carried a small bag with two bean tacos that she ate around midday. Many times she returned with her hands, arms, and bare feet
scratched by the mesquite thorns and by the "cat's claw" that
grew in the thickets, but she liked the task of collecting good
wood, breaking the branches into the same lengths, and tying
them into a bundle that she slung across her back with the shawl.
It was a solitary job, quiet and peaceful, that allowed her to
dream. Some day . . .

Illusion and waiting became an infinite plain on which she
wandered every morning, looking for firewood and searching for

a way out of her menial life. Each day she roamed a little farther, and she often returned home long after dusk. One of those afternoons, nightfall surprised her when she was still far from the settlement. To orient herself, she sought the light of the cowhands' campfire. Many times she had heard the noise of their gatherings from a distance, but she had never approached because they were just for men. That night she was guided by the flickering glow, and when she drew near she was astonished to hear their singing and laughter. With hoarse voices, some already thick with alcohol, the cowhands were singing, accompanied by a guitar. Between songs there were jokes, laughter, and quiet conversations in which Cabora was often mentioned. Teresa crouched down at the edge of the festive circle. The music and gaiety were a new experience that filled her with delight, and the realization that these men had contact with the world of her dreams filled her with hope and the hunger to hear more. When she arrived home that night, the family was already asleep. Only Cayetana opened her eyes to make sure she had returned and then closed them again without a word.

From then on Teresa arranged things so she could attend the nocturnal gatherings. She hovered in the shadows, listening, learning, absorbing every detail of that masculine life that knew the secrets of Cabora. She memorized the songs and learned that the ranch house was big and white and beautiful. She found out about the daily chores of the cowhands, the fences they repaired, the lost calves, the death of cattle, and the gossip about the boss. She found out that her father's name was Tomás Urrea, the cook was Josefina, and the trusted servant, Cosimiro; Doña Huila, the healer, lived in the back part of the big house now and was very respected by the boss; two young girls who did the cleaning had become pregnant and it was rumored that Don Tomás was responsible; he had other children with women in the settlement, and she even heard some of their names, like Buenaventura Ramírez, Antonio Salazar, and José de la Luz Estévez. She found out that one day a bronco threw her father three times and after the third time he shot the horse. She discovered he had a family in Alamos, and she was glad that they didn't want to live on the ranch.

Little by little she became part of the group of men, making herself indispensable. As soon as something was needed, she brought it: the alcohol from Doña Mati's house, wood for the bonfire from the bundle that she had collected, some tacos from Miss Rosarito's, the guitar from Don Epifanio's. She was careful not to get in the way and to allow her presence to be felt only as something useful. When she was sure she wouldn't be sent home, she dared to sing the songs that she had already learned. She had a well-rounded voice, harmonious, a little hoarse, and full. The one who played the guitar was called Anastasio. He was a young ranchhand with a clean-shaven face and high cheekbones; his hands were tanned by the sun and his fingers were long. Teresa was fascinated by the way he plucked music from the instrument; she began to memorize the finger movements for each chord, and when she was alone she practiced with any stick she could find, listening to the sounds in her imagination.

One night Anastasio did not come. Don Epifanio had brought the guitar as usual, but nobody else knew how to play it. Someone tried to sing without accompaniment, but it wasn't the same. The instrument was set aside, covered in silence. Teresa, incredulous at her own daring, picked up the instrument and started to pluck out the notes she had heard so often.

By the time Anastasio returned, Teresa was playing and singing like one of the men.

"You don't play so bad. Where did you learn?" he asked her. Teresa shrugged.

"Watching you," she said.

From then on, Anastasio was committed to teaching her his art and sharing the playing with her. For Teresa, those classes were the happiest moments she had ever known, and she learned quickly. She had heard that Don Tomás liked music and at night she dreamed that some day the cowhands would say to him, "Hey, boss, did you know that your daughter strums a mean guitar?"

The same motivation she had for learning to play the guitar induced her to learn to read: she heard there was a library in Cabora and that her father was an avid reader. She consulted Anastasio.

"The one who knows a lot is Doña Rosaura," he told her.

Doña Rosaura was a very old lady with a big belly, a curved back, and snow-white hair. She lived alone and she smelled of wet earth. She had never married and had no children; she was the oldest person in the settlement, and some considered her wise because she had read so much. She had spent her life in Aquihuiquichi, except for the four years between Don Miguel Urrea's death and the arrival of Don Tomás when she moved to Guaymas to work in the home of a wealthy family. There she had the pleasure of taking care of someone else's children and reading at night by the light of the kerosene lamp the newspapers and magazines that the family threw out. When she returned to Aquihuiquichi, she brought all the journalistic material that she could carry. Since then she spent hours in her hut reading over and over again the news from years past as if it were current, mumbling to herself comments about obsolete events and offering her opinion to whoever would listen about issues that were ignored in their time and by now had been completely forgotten. But she was going blind, so when Teresita came to her asking for lessons, Doña Rosaura was happy to have found someone who could continue rereading her tattered newspapers for her.

. Teresa put so much effort into learning that soon she was able to slowly read the fading words of the paper. Although she didn't understand much of what she read, she was learning new words and the way in which they should be strung together to make sense. Thus she read that in early 1876 Cajeme had exacted a toll on the boats that ran between Guaymas and the municipality of Médano, and that affront had made Governor Pesqueira turn blue with rage; toward the end of 1879 Generals Ramírez and Márquez de León had led an uprising in Sinaloa with the intention of overthrowing Governor Cañedo, a henchman for Don Porfirio and

reputed assassin of the journalist José Cayetano Valdés, who
founded the opposition newspaper *La Tarántula;* on May 5, 1878
the Tuxtepec revolution's supreme promise not to reelect the
President of the Republic or the state governors was proclaimed
an article in the constitution; the government of General Porfirio
Díaz lacked funds for the army's payroll and this had made Lerdo
de Tejada bold enough to demand, from his exile in the United
States, the return to "legality"; the Wandering Jew was making one
of his routine visits to the north of Mexico, convinced he had
found his lost people because he saw a wooden wagon pulled by
oxen as in Pharaonic times and women carrying jugs on their
heads like Rebecca; for lack of rain the grain crops were in danger
in the district of Ures, Sonora; Don Porfirio was taking advantage
of the existing corruption in order to consolidate his dictatorship;
the government of General Díaz, concerned about the improvement of the country's equine stock, had imported sixty-five
hundred colts, thanks to which the young gentlemen of the country would ride in style while the peasants died of hunger; in order
to do away with raids and assaults on the border and to avoid the
incursion of American troops into Mexico, the government had
ostentatiously deployed federal troops along the Río Grande; the
U.S. government finally had established formal relations with the
government of Mexico under General Díaz's command; in the year
1877, forty million pesos worth of exports and forty-nine million
pesos worth of imports were registered; Mexico continued to
export mainly precious metals and import consumer products;
Porfirio Díaz had named twenty-two ministers for six ministries in
only four years; the government of Porfirio Díaz had let in foreign
capital to solve all its problems and had made an example of all
Mexicans who didn't recognize the infallibility of the system by
punishing them severely; contracts were signed with three foreign
companies for the construction of railroads in the country; a boy
under hypnosis had seen his sister who had died years earlier; the
heavy rains in the north of Sonora were delaying the work on the
railroad between Guaymas and Hermosillo; even though reelec-

tion had been abolished by the "regenerative" revolution led by President Díaz, there had been established in its place a system of "transference" by means of which the incumbents turned over their command to their brothers, relatives, and intimate friends with the condition that they would receive it again in 1884; General Porfirio Díaz was taking advantage of any opportunity to back the candidacy of General Manuel González; General Porfirio Díaz denied having supported anyone's candidacy for the next elections; no sooner had General Díaz taken over the helm of the Republic, when the official exploitation of the pernicious vice of gambling was authorized, and public opinion was demanding corporal punishment for the one responsible for such an outrage against morals and ethics. . . .

"Who is Porfirio Díaz?" Teresa finally asked.

"He's somebody who goes in and out of power as if it were his home. They say he was a carpenter, he was a general, he had people killed in Veracruz, he has come to save the nation, he's going to be president again, he's not good for anything, he's irreplaceable. You see how people talk about so many things that here on the ranch we never learn about: that so-and-so rebelled, that this other fellow was removed from office, that one struck a blow and another one received it. Some people say he can barely read or write, others that he is a genius, but it isn't important. He will never bother with the likes of us here on a ranch in the middle of the desert."

"How can he be president if he doesn't know how to read or write?"

Doña Rosaura opened her eyes, looked at Teresa and shrugged.

"He must know something," she said. "Keep reading."

Teresa went back to reading. When she looked up again, Doña Rosaura was asleep.

During the long months of her tutelage she insisted on hearing many times about Porfirio Díaz, convinced that if a simple carpenter could become president of the country, anything was possible. When she had mastered reading to Doña Rosaura's satisfaction, she began teaching herself to write. Using her index finger, she copied all the printed letters in the dry dirt of the desert. It was more difficult than learning to read and the symbols rarely turned out even, but with practice she learned to write one name almost perfectly, her true name: Teresa Urrea. From then on she left her signature here and there in the dry, barren world of the Sonoran desert, under the mesquites, next to the organ cactus, in the sand by the wash, scratched on a stone, over and over again, affirming her determination with that act of writing, until suddenly something happened that was to change her life completely.

▣ VII

At the dusty airport of Navojoa only she and two other passengers left the plane. The main building was deserted and the heat was suffocating; of the four car rental agencies, only one was open and it wasn't the one she had contacted. She approached the employee, who didn't stop yawning and shooing flies while he talked to her. When she showed him her receipt, he murmured a heartfelt "Oh, boy!" and swatted a fly on the counter.

"Nobody from that agency has been around here for more than two months. I think they're closed." And he yawned again.

She had to wait an hour until a beaten-up, bottle-green Renault arrived from "downtown." After signing the contract and taking the keys, she requested a map of the city. The young man looked at her as if she were crazy.

"Of Navojoa? Nobody needs a map of Navojoa!"

She told him the name of the hotel she was looking for.

"Oh, that's easy. When you leave here, head north on the highway and in five minutes there's a turn-off; you can't miss it. When you enter the city, at the second . . . no, the third light you turn right. . . ."

She thanked him, and as she leaned over to pick up her baggage she noticed that the briefcase wasn't there. She panicked; nobody had come near her in all that time. The only explanation was that she had been so drowsy she had left it on the plane. All the documents! Fifteen years of work! She felt overwhelmed; she couldn't believe it. It wasn't possible! But the briefcase wasn't there. She felt the irrational desire to turn back time, to repeat her arrival, to not forget something that was so much a part of her existence. She had to make an effort to control herself and not cry. *The voice of the public condemns the behavior of Teresa Urrea and Don Tomás Urrea and accuses them of being the principal instigators of the disturbance and the setback suffered by the Eleventh Regiment.* . . . She walked over to the Aeroméxico counter. It was closed. The schedule board announced the next day's 10 A.M. flight; somebody with a dark sense of humor had written the facetious question: "delayed?" There was nothing she could do. *There's no doubt that the fanaticism that I have been battling for two years was the motive for this surprise attack and that the only culprit is the "saint" from Cabora.* . . . She found a scrap of paper in her purse and wrote down her name and address and a description of the lost object. *Nowhere in Mexico is there a woman whose name is as well known as that of Teresa of Cabora.* . . . She left the note under an ashtray so the wind wouldn't blow it away, and walked out of the airport feeling completely empty. *This is to inform you that there is an order from our superiors to the effect that the rebels be severely punished as soon as possible.* . . . She headed toward Navojoa.

Thanks to the agent's precise directions, she got lost. *The young Mexican woman to whom the peasants attribute divine powers is now among the Yaqui Indians.* . . . She drove around on back streets that all looked the same, until she came to a gas station. *Even though they say that the Indians are irreconcilable in their hatred for the white people, they revere and obey this young woman as if she were their queen.* . . . She got gas and asked for directions again. The hotel was just a few blocks back that way, she was told. She finally arrived, drenched in sweat, desperate because of the loss of the briefcase, and frightened to find herself in a strange town for reasons that seemed increasingly absurd and confusing to her.

The building definitely needed a good coat of paint. There was nobody at the doorway to receive the car; she had to park it herself. At the reception desk, she asked about the dining room hours. The young receptionist looked reluctantly up at the clock above her head. It was 3:21 P.M.

"They close at three. But there's a diner one block from here. If you're lucky you'll get there before everything's gone. When they run out of food, they close too. Since today is Thursday, we don't open for dinner. On other nights it's from seven to nine."

She couldn't tell any more if the void she felt in her stomach was from hunger, rage, or just despair. She asked the young woman if she had heard of the ranch called "Cabora."

"I'm not from here," she answered and kept writing.

Picking up her purse and her unpretentious suitcase, she went up to her room, which was small and barren, but clean. There was no air conditioning, just an enormous ceiling fan that turned so slowly it produced more noise than a breeze. Navojoa was suffering from an unseasonable heat wave and the atmosphere was asphyxiating. She put her things on the chair and threw herself down on the bed. She felt defeated by the disappearance of the documents. Now nothing made sense. Fragmented memories of the records filled her head again in a bewildering jumble of facts and quotes. *That young woman whom you invoked for her virtues and her love of truth will avenge you. . . . The lesson learned by the rebels has been severe. . . . And the poor people will follow her and will die with her because poor people are always ready to sacrifice themselves. . . . The meetings in Teresa Urrea's house are frequent and Lauro Aguirre continues to form bands to attack Mexico. . . . For the sake of the redemption of humanity . . . it will be difficult for them to rise again. . . .*

She closed her eyes; the answer was there, silently waiting for her: she was crazy, totally mad. *Teresa Urrea belongs in body to psychopathy and in spirit to the disciples of Allan Kardec. . . . To think* that she had been "chosen," that her footsteps were guided by the will of a woman who had lived a hundred years ago, that the information reached her by divine order . . . divine? . . . *with these weapons, the so-called saint would not have gone beyond being a hopeless neurasthenic if it hadn't been for the fanaticism of the masses . . .* so she could fulfill an unknown mission! Insane! *The moral and intellectual qualities of the young woman were in direct contrast to the vices and ignorance of the social environment in which she had been raised. . . .* If not, where was her supposed saint when she forgot the briefcase? What "mission" was she going to accomplish with empty hands? *The priests, the government, and the personal enemies of Mr. Urrea took advantage of the first opportunity to persecute him and deprive him of his legitimate inheritance. . . .*

Tears began to roll down her face in silence. *I observed, huddled in a dilapidated building, hundreds of sick people, cripples, lepers, blind people, and amputees that were dedicated to making the most ridiculous demonstrations of fanaticism to the saint. . . .* Breaking into sobs, she felt torn up inside without understanding whether she was crying for herself, for the loss, for so many wasted years, for the directionless future, or for a past that didn't mean anything. She just cried. *It is necessary to suffocate this movement at its inception because its fanatical nature makes it dangerous. . . .* She cried uncontrollably until she wore out her desperation and anguish . . . *Extraordinary cure: Mr. Vidal García, who had been blind and deaf for four years, recovered his speech in two days under the care of the saint and can now see sufficiently well to get around town without help . . .* and she finally fell asleep. *Yesterday there circulated a false report that Teresa Urrea, the Saint of Cabora, had been executed in the plaza of Cibuta in Sonora. This report was sent by the Mexican government in order to calm down the Yaqui Indians who are arriving in Nogales by the thousands to see their patron saint and receive her blessing. . . .*

She was woken by two flies that were taking advantage of the fan's placidity to get drunk on her sweat. It was 4:30 P.M. She had slept profoundly, without dreams or words or voices or unsettling phrases. She felt encouraged. *Teresa, rather than support her patients' religious ideas, combatted them, saying that to God religions didn't mean anything, they were just empty words, exterior practices that didn't penetrate the soul.* . . . Tomorrow she would call the airline office; they would surely find the briefcase.

After taking a shower . . . *what God wanted was the feeling of love that is only found in the disinterested practice of good* . . . she decided to tour the city. At the reception desk she asked how to get to the main plaza.

"Oh, that's easy. . . . Let's see, as you leave here you turn . . ."

She got lost again. All the streets had the same appearance. The avenues were too wide for the few vehicles that circulated, as if at some time Navojoa had expected a surge in population that never occurred, that happened somewhere else. Indistinguishable streets of faded colors, burnt by the sun and gritty with dust, a totally antiesthetic, misguided, third-world attempt at modernity. Nothing that made her think of Teresa. *The cases of zealotry inspired by Miss Urrea have had fatal consequences and have caused much blood to be spilled.* . . . What was Navojoa like back in 1892 when, *at 4 A.M. on May 15, General Otero received the first news of the movement of the Indians toward the city; a few hours later he was informed that* . . . a horde of two hundred Indians descended on the town, shouting, "Long live the Saint of Cabora!" . . . *the Indians had taken over the plaza, looted all the stores* . . . and left behind a trail of cadavers? *At dawn, the Mayo Indians, who had been peaceful until then, assaulted the towns of Navojoa and San Ignacio, looted Mr. Morales's store, killed the mayor and wounded two townspeople.* . . . What was Navojoa like when Don Tomás's enemies snooped around, looking for a way to ruin him? *In spite of the surprise attack, the neighborhood was able to resist and defend itself; after three hours of battle they made the assailants retreat, leaving behind fourteen dead.* . . . What was the city like when child-saints appeared throughout the state . . . *any Indian captured was hung without the slightest investigation; suffice it to say that they ran out of nooses in the town because they hanged so many Indians* . . . or at the time of Tomóchic, *General Otero had been notified in advance of the attack* on Navojoa and not only refused to make preparations but also sent away the detachment of federal troops in order to implicate the saint and take revenge on his enemy, Mr. Tomás Urrea . . . or the day that seven-year-old Teresa passed by here on her way to Aquihuiquichi? *The fact that they confiscated eighteen rifles in Cabora does not prove the owner's complicity with the rebels since all the ranches have weapons to defend themselves against the attacks of the Yaqui rebels. . . .* Definitely not the way she saw it now. *During the attack on Navojoa, the emissaries of the enemies of Don Tomás—not the Indians—were shouting, "Long live the Saint of Cabora!". . . .* She asked herself again what she was doing in such a godforsaken town that mistakenly called itself a city.

For the third time she drove down the same unmarked avenue . . . *well-informed sources have assured us that on the boulevard of this city . . .* flanked on both sides by houses painted washed-out pink, washed-out blue . . . *at night a ghost has been appearing that scares everyone who passes by . . .* washed-out yellow, ocher . . . *it shrinks, it stretches up, it flies, it sneaks into houses. . . .* At the corner she turned left on a kind of boulevard with an island in the middle . . . *it causes terror and disturbs minds. . . .* Judging by the dry sticks stuck in the dirt of the dividing strip every few yards . . . *the people blame the apparition for the lack of rain . . .* it was obvious that at one time the municipality had had the illusion that it could create a tree-lined avenue . . . *the recent train derailment, and everything bad that happens in the region.* Suddenly she turned onto what had to be the central plaza.

On one side was a big church with just one tower; it wasn't even a cathedral. In the center of the plaza stood an enormous laurel tree where crows, sparrows, doves, and other birds were raising a ruckus, quarreling over the branches for the night. She parked the car and contemplated the church. The façade was too modern to have been constructed in Teresita's times. *The appearance of a saint is a serious, lofty, and transcendental occurrence that is of even greater interest if one considers the fact that this saint came down to earth to produce a revolution in medical science. . . .*

Nevertheless, there was nowhere else to start. By that time the city hall would already be closed; it was doubtful that the town had a library. Perhaps in some corner of that unimpressive religious construction there was a historical record. As soon as she entered the building, she felt the change.

The nave of the church was spacious and cool, with tall, smooth walls painted white; the area was covered by a nondescript dome. Two women wrapped in shawls were reciting the rosary. *Mr. President, it seems that misfortune is hounding me. . . .* The last rays of the setting sun entered through a cut-glass window, dispersing lights of variegated colors on the rustic wooden pews. *I was in charge of the forces that were defeated by the Tomochitecs and of the troops that withdrew from Navojoa before the recent attack by the Mayo Indians. . . .* The altar was in shadow. *Therefore, it is my duty to inform you that almost two years ago I advised the governor of this state to take severe measures against the farce of the so-called saint. . . .* Only the murmur of the Hail Marys ruffled the silence.

She stood in the middle of the center aisle, feeling the calm spread through her. She liked the thick air of tradition and magic in churches. *Our General Díaz orders that the saint be kept away from the troops, since they are ignorant and could be influenced by her spell. . . .* There everybody minded their own business, nobody bothered anybody. She always felt a little overwhelmed by the slow, monotonous prayers, the rites of the mass, the smell of incense. *Young Teresa Urrea is admired and respected by all that know her; she only offers health and well-being to the poor, consolation to those who are sad, and love to all of her cherished ones. . . .* Churches were magic, isolated spaces, capsules of time held still, cloisters of oblivion, libraries of lost hopes, archives of sin. *Due to the seriousness of the matter, I believe we should not make any mistakes this time.*

A dizzy spell reminded her that she hadn't eaten. *Everybody has enemies, Mr. President, and I fear that mine are distorting what has happened here. . . .* She was just about to go when the door to the vestry made a loud noise as it opened and a short, slender person with features she couldn't quite distinguish in the shadows appeared as if out of nowhere. *The ghost has not deigned to speak to any of the mortals that have seen it. . . .* The figure approached her with determined steps . . . *they only know that it moans and cries, wears white, and is twenty-four hands tall, and thus they believe without a doubt that it is the Wandering Jew.* It was a woman of indecipherable age, black eyes, and white hair pulled back in a bun.

"May I help you?" The sound of the woman's voice reminded her of the purpose of her visit. She hesitated.

"I was looking for . . . I mean, I wanted to know when the church was built."

"I think it was around 1920, after the great flood. They reconstructed the whole city, thinking then that it would be a center of commerce, possibly the most important one in the region because it's so close to Alamos. But when the gold ran out and the silver could only be extracted in small quantities, everything went north, to Ciudad Obregón and Hermosillo. I suppose they were going after dollars. And Navojoa remained as you see it, an unfulfilled promise. I don't live here, I live near Tesia. I only came to do a favor for the priest, who requested it months ago and today, for some strange reason, I remembered. I'm getting so forgetful! But tell me—you never know, I may be able to help you—were you looking for something in particular?"

"Have you heard of Teresa Urrea, the Saint of Cabora?"

"But of course! Why, I'm almost a relative of hers, since the fellow who married her daughter was courting me first. That was so many years ago. . . . " The woman got lost in her recollections.

"And . . . ?" she insisted. Once again she felt the tingling in her body, the excitement. Her fatigue had disappeared.

"Ah, I was saying . . . What was I saying? Oh, yes. Well, that louse dumped me and went and married Laura Van Order, Teresita's daughter, and I, well, I stayed single. I think it would have turned out the same, anyhow. He died many years ago and they never had children, so today I would be just as alone. Such is life."

"And the saint?"

"I don't know anything about her, just that her daughter stole my husband. I don't think you'll find anyone to tell you much around here; you hardly hear about her anymore. Maybe in Hermosillo. They have a Center for Historical Studies there, if I'm not mistaken."

"And the ranch of Cabora?"

"That probably doesn't exist anymore, all that area became communal farmland after the Revolution. The haciendas were destroyed when the troops passed through. They didn't leave anything. Excuse me, miss. I need to go. I have to get back to my town and it's already dark."

"Sure . . . thanks," she mumbled.

Nothing. It had all ended in nothing. *Teresa died in Clifton, in poverty, after having lost her beauty and her powers: the sanctified young woman from Sonora had been forgotten.* . . . She looked again at the empty nave, now deep in shadows, full of silence. Suddenly she felt someone touch her shoulder.

"Excuse me, I just remembered . . . didn't I tell you that I'm losing my memory? But not completely. I recall that some relatives of the guy I almost married still live around here, in the town of Chiripas. They ought to know about your saint. The family's last name is Soledad; you can't miss them. They have the only grocery store in town. If you take the highway . . ."

She returned to the hotel in a state of total distraction. She didn't even see the streets or the houses; she didn't notice if she had passed another car on the way or if the city was really as abandoned as it seemed. The excitement was growing inside her again, the astonishment, the sense of magic: the fortuitous encounter, the unexpected information, a solid lead. How had she found that woman? Once again reality was producing strange coincidences, as if everything were planned.

That night she hardly slept. She spent hours tossing about in the heat of a feverish exaltation, a state of limbo between slumber and vigilance, full of confusing voices . . . *dreaming isn't exactly the word, says Mr. Myers of the Psychical Research Laboratory in London*

. . . scattered phrases . . . *the spirit of the dead does not abandon the earth brusquely and totally, rather, for some time it preserves bonds with loved ones* . . . words . . . *the rivers and streams have overflowed their banks* . . . images . . . *the dead think about earthly matters, about loves they left behind, the grave matters that they did not reveal, and the profound injustices they suffered* . . . *and the torrential rains have destroyed the fences around the fields* . . . in that chaos . . . *the thoughts of the dead person can reach such intensity and energy that they have hypnotic effects on the living* . . . that she was almost used to . . . *provided that the dead can find a favorable person whose will and strength of thought are weaker than hers* . . . *and they swept away some cows, pigs, and horses* . . . *these communications usually take place during the sleep of the living person when her state is similar to that of death.* . . .

VIII

On the day of her second death, as she perceived the gradual transformation of her flesh that seemed to be detaching itself from her bones, she would remember how many times she had cursed that flesh of a woman. From the time she had seen Don Tomás, so splendid on his chestnut stallion, she wanted to be a man, but not just any man. She would never have aspired to being Uncle Manuel or one of her cousins; nor did she want to be one of the cowhands, not even Anastasio, for whom she had a great deal of respect and admiration. No. She wanted to be Don Tomás, to have his power and authority, to command the respect he commanded and to produce the fear he produced. All of her games and fantasies during those years in Aquihuiquichi had developed around the same theme: she was Don Tomás; the image she had of herself was the image of him, only without a mustache. Learning to play the guitar and sing was learning to be a little like Don Tomás; being haughty and contrary with her aunt and cousins was treating them the way he would treat them; fulminating Manuelito with that glare had resulted from imagining how Don Tomás would look at someone he wanted to annihilate. She saw herself becoming more and more like her father. That's how she felt until her body betrayed her and her breasts began to grow.

At first she only perceived a certain painful sensitivity around her nipples, but when she reached the age of twelve the irritation turned into two obvious swellings on her chest and she understood that the problem wasn't going to go away unless she did something about it. She searched among her mother's old rags to find one of adequate length to make a binding for herself, and she tied it around her chest so tightly that those early lumps could not be detected. She didn't harbor the slightest doubt that the baneful growth of those little bulges would have irreversible consequences if left unchecked. If the cowhands saw her transformed into a woman, they wouldn't allow her to be with them anymore. She contemplated the results of the binding, and was satisfied. She thought the problem was solved until she was visited by her first moon.

Some time before she had seen the rags that Tula and Cayetana burned in secret, far from the house; she had perceived the smell of rancid blood that they sometimes released into the air, but she thought that was a special disease of the two sisters. Faced with the reality of her own blood, she thought she had been contaminated by the nefarious illness, and she tried to cure herself by going to the waterhole at night to wash herself repeatedly with cold water. Her affliction, far from disappearing, intensified with the cold baths; finally she had to look for some rags so the blood wouldn't run down her leg. She wanted to die. She was more frightened than when she had paralyzed Manuel. She secretly blamed her mother for having given her the disease, and she hid it as best she could. It was the longest week of her life, but finally her body's zeal to bleed to death began to wane. She waited a few more days to make sure that it wasn't coming back and then returned to her daily routine. One month later it happened again and she had to do the same thing. The third time she couldn't find any rags and she resorted to a handful of dry grass. This not only caused an incredible itching and kept her wriggling like a snake in a hot tin pan, but it also did not absorb the blood very well and she accidentally left a stain on one of the chairs in the hut. Aunt Tula, who was warier than a hoot owl, understood the significance of the stain, scolded her for having hidden such a portentous event, and took her to see Doña Rosaura, who, being the eldest in the settlement, was in charge of educating young girls in the ways of womanhood. All the way there Tula grumbled about her bad luck, convinced that she would soon see Teresa in the same state as her slut of a mother. She left her there, in front of the old lady, who had taught her to read. Between her shame and the prickling of the grass, Teresa couldn't stand still, twisting and turning this way and that.

"Stop jiggling. Don't make such a fuss," the old lady said to her as she watched her hop from one foot to the other, trying to keep the grass from going where it shouldn't. "What's happening to you is both a blessing and a curse. A blessing because you are finally a woman and God has made your blood run so that you can give your husband children; a curse because from now on men are going to smell you, and when they do they are going to go after you, wanting to stick their thing in you, and they aren't going to leave you alone. That's why you'll have to be careful, to keep your legs together so they don't surprise you, to hide yourself so they don't smell you, and never go out alone so they don't tempt you with their thing. Very soon you need to choose a man that you like for your husband and marry him. Then you can have children and the others will leave you alone. If you don't do that, Teresita, and you let yourself be surprised by just anybody, God will punish you, making you a whore, and from then on you will be condemned to bring children into the world without a father, and you will go around like a bitch in heat and nobody will want you for a wife. Do you understand?"

She understood perfectly. She understood that there were only two alternatives: Aunt Tula's way or Cayetana's way, and she was terrified. She pressed her legs together as tightly as possible in spite of the grass as she listened to Doña Rosaura's advice and thought about how simple and clean everything had been before she became a woman and wished she could go back to being a child. Then the old lady told her she could go and she shouldn't use grass anymore because her little baby bag might get infected and she could die or at least never have children.

Teresa left, determined to use all the grass she could find to do away with the cursed baby bag once and for all, but the possibility of dying made her reconsider. She was stuck with those disgusting rags. She ran to hide in the hills, feeling unbearably impotent due to her uncontrollable body, which she hated more than anything else, more than her cousins and more than her aunt Tula. She was convinced that, sullied as she was, Don Tomás would never accept her and all of her dreams and fantasies were in vain. When she was able to calm down a little, she solemnly swore three things: first, that she would always keep her legs together; second, she would hide in the hills every time she bled so no man would ever smell her; and third, she would never, never get married or have children. Only when she recalled those vows on the day of her second death did she realize that she hadn't fulfilled any of them.

Fortunately, that unpleasantness only happened during a few days each month, and the rest of the time she went back to being herself. Her breasts, to tell the truth, never put up much of a struggle against the binding, and she soon stopped paying attention to them. Once her time had passed, she went back to singing with the cowhands, and since they didn't seem to notice anything and continued treating her as always, little by little she lost her fear and strengthened her conviction that with a strong enough desire sooner or later she would overcome so many feminine encumbrances and become a man. To achieve this, she redirected toward herself the powers that she had discovered when she hurled the look that froze Manuelito, turning them inward, berating her body every time it insisted on fulfilling its feminine functions. All to no avail. She changed tactics and decided to ignore the fetishisms of the moon as if they didn't exist and to continue becoming in all other aspects the man she wanted to be, but Tula intervened, and this time with a determination and severity that gave her no choice. For starters, she forbade her to go out into the countryside by herself and she gave that task to Cayetana, who "didn't run any risk, seeing as she was carrying another bundle." Since Cayetana was gone for most of the day, Teresa had to take care of her little brother, "because don't you or your slut of a mother think that's the aunt's responsibility." She also had to wash clothes, "so you get used to being a woman, and we'll see if you turn out like your mother."

It didn't do Teresa any good to walk around all day long like a soul in mourning, gloomy and crestfallen. Tula ignored her except to scold her, and Cayetana seemed to have lost all interest in her. The weeks degenerated into monotonous eternities. She hated going to the wash, she hated listening to the other women while she scrubbed clothes, and worst of all she feared she would be doing the same things for the rest of her life. But even washing was better than taking care of her scrawny, sickly little brother, who cried all day. After all her illusions, was she going to become just one more woman in the settlement? She preferred to die. To make matters worse, her maximum pleasure had been forbidden: she no longer could go to see the cowhands at night. She would never sing again; laughter and gabbing were over for her, and worse still, she no longer heard any news from Cabora. For the first time in her life Teresa suffered imposed solitude, not that freely chosen solitude that she had enjoyed for so long, but a bitter emptiness in the center of her being that never went away. She became quiet and taciturn; she scarcely ate and lost so much weight that she didn't even need the binding any more to dissimulate her shrunken breasts.

As the days passed she became more and more soul sick. She felt her own desert growing inside her, thorns and all. She walked hunched over as if she had suddenly become old, and she was convinced that her life from then on would be nothing more than prolonged agony. Her illusions, dreams, and fantasies were shattered, leaving her with little pieces in the rosary of petty chores that filled her day, pieces that dissolved in the soapsuds, drowned in her brother's incessant crying, and swirled off into the air like the dust when she was sweeping. Cabora ceased to exist, and Don Tomás was more distant than all of the saints to whom Tula commended her so she wouldn't become a slut.

Finally she rebelled: it was better to get lost in the desert and die than to continue in that endless travail. One day she got up at dawn, gathered the dirty clothes in order to hide her true intention, and left before the family awoke. Instead of heading toward the wash, she walked through the half-asleep settlement, listening to the cowhands in their huts preparing to go to Cabora and envying that freedom that was denied her. As she passed Anastasio's hut, she saw him mounted and ready to go. She was gripped by a deep, furious nostalgia; angrily she remembered the nights of music and joy and felt an unpostponable need to speak with her friend, to confess her incurable sadness, to share with him her desperate situation. Rapidly she approached the man on horseback, but as soon as he turned to look at her she felt herself blush from head to toe. She understood that she couldn't tell him anything, it would be admitting the inadmissible: that she was a woman and everything that she hated was her lot in life. She was just about to run away when the cowhand called out to her.

"Hey, Teresita! Why such a stranger?"

Since she didn't know what to answer, she approached and petted his mare.

"She's pretty," she said, to avoid the question.

"Just like a guitar: half female, half male. If you tame her, she becomes a part of you just like the instrument when you know how to play it. A horse is like that. When you're on one, you forget where your own body ends and the animal begins."

"Do you think I could learn to ride?" she asked without thinking.

Anastasio looked surprised.

"I don't know," he said; "you know women don't ride anything except donkeys, and that's only when they have to go somewhere. I don't know."

"They don't ride because they don't want to; they don't play the guitar either, and they don't know how to read or write. But I *do* want to, I want to learn to ride." Teresa didn't know where she had come up with such a daring idea, but once she said it, it seemed like the most important wish of her life. Immediately she remembered Don Tomás on his chestnut stallion and a tiny spark of hope flared up once more. If she could ride, if she ever had a horse, she could go to Cabora and then . . .

"I need to learn to ride," she insisted; "I know I can do it."

Anastasio was pensive, looking into the distance.

"I'll meet you at the entrance to the settlement before sunset. I'll teach you to ride Mi Nena." And without waiting for an answer, he galloped away.

At no time during that day, or afterwards, did Teresa think that in order to ride Anastasio's mare she would have to spread her legs and break her vow. This was totally different, it didn't have anything to do with that other matter, with sickness; it had to do with Don Tomás on a horse, it had to do with being a man, it had to do with becoming a god. She went to the stream and washed the clothes as quickly as possible; after she had tied them in a bundle and hid them, she returned to the hut to wait. When the afternoon began to wane, she announced that she had to go and wash clothes and she ran to the entrance to Aquihuiquichi; Anastasio didn't take long to appear. The mare was all sweaty. For an instant the cowhand looked at her with surprise as if he didn't remember his promise, and Teresa was afraid he would go back on his word.

"I'm all ready," she said. Anastasio got down and unsaddled the horse.

"First you ride bareback so you feel her and the mare gets to know you," and he picked Teresa up and put her on Mi Nena. She wrapped her skirt around her legs. Afterward she wouldn't remember feeling fear, just the dampness of the mare's sweat, which made her think, "We are melding together and becoming one, she and I."

"Now think of the guitar. Caress her neck as you would the strings of the guitar, speak to her as you would speak to the instrument, with your hands, with your legs that hold it. That's it. Always think that you and she are going to make music together."

She didn't need any more coaching. As soon as she touched the sweaty neck of the mare with her fingers, she perceived the harmony between the animal's blood and her own. She spoke to her in a hushed voice and told her she wanted to fly, squeezing her legs together slightly, and in an instant they were one, racing across the countryside. She let herself go, converted into a mare; she had inside herself all that power, the veins, the muscles, the sweat, and the velocity of the beast. She held on to the mane and flew, beyond any dream, beyond the earth, feeling the extraordinary lightness of the willful harmony between the two of them. Her braid came undone and the wind joined them, like a third rider, in a crazy race across places she had never been before. Afterward she wouldn't remember how long they had run, how much distance they had covered: it was like entering another dimension, as she imagined death would be. Suddenly she was back facing Anastasio and he was looking at her with amazement.

They both smiled with a secret complicity. Teresa got down from Mi Nena and hugged her, covering her face with sweat. Then she hugged Anastasio, too, kissed him on the cheek, and ran away, impelled by an irrepressible joy. At last she knew where freedom could be found: she had ridden it. All dreams were possible.

IX

She got up at dawn with the fragments of the lost documents tormenting her. She was ferociously hungry. She called downstairs;

the dining room wasn't open yet, but they promised to bring her some coffee and a roll. The order took more than half an hour, and when it arrived the coffee was tepid and the roll was stale. She ate half of it. Her stomach was churning with nerves. Today, she told herself, today something has to happen. *A ranch called "Cabora," situated between the rivers Yaqui and Mayo, has become the center of attraction for an increasing pilgrimage. . . .*

Outside the air was cool. The sun was just peeking out over the horizon; an abrasive blue sky promised another day of heat. She found the way out of town easily and headed down a narrow highway toward Chiripas. *The peace that has reigned in the whole state has been slightly interrupted by the small bands of Yaqui Indians who gather in the most remote areas of the mountains, not to continue a war that they themselves judge to be impossible, but to live in idleness and from the fruits of looting. . . .* After driving about fifteen miles she reached the turnoff and veered to the right on a wide street of compacted dirt. One hundred yards ahead she saw the faded sign that boasted "Soledad Groceries," painted in black letters on the white wall. She felt a slight tremor that indicated that the internal turmoil was beginning. *Teresa Urrea is a charming young woman whom I saw at the time of one of her cataleptic fits; she speaks at length and with a rare ability; she says she is sent by God, and she expresses a certain acrimony toward the clergy in general; this makes one think that Heaven will soon be sending us another Messiah. . . .* The door of the store was open; on the wall to the right were announcements of mail and long-distance telephone services. Inside everything was in shadows. She entered, waited a while for her eyes to get used to the dark, and then addressed a woman who was sitting behind the counter.

Mrs. Soledad was about seventy years old. She received her with a friendly smile. She had porcelain skin and a thick gray braid that hung down her back. Something about the woman's manner made her lose her timidity, and without further ado she announced her interest in getting information about Teresa Urrea. Immediately she noticed the change: the woman hesitated; a glimmer of distrust flickered in her eyes. She asked her to wait a moment and then disappeared through a curtain in the back. *Because of the healthy effects that the presence of the apparition might have on misguided souls, we believe that it would be beneficial for her to come to the capital so that she can enliven certain performances with a sideshow of miracles: it would be a great business. . . .*

The woman reappeared accompanied by a younger woman of approximately the same height but more slender, with black hair severely swept back and knotted at the nape of her neck. There was a wary expression on her face. *I am secretly following the steps of Aguirre, Urrea, and Teresa's principal sectarians in order to demonstrate their complicity in the unfortunate events of the other day. . . .*

"This is my daughter, Gracia. The lady," she explained, "is asking about our Teresita."

"Why?" queried the younger woman, scrutinizing her carefully. "We don't like busybodies."

She didn't know what to answer. The expression "our Teresita" was whirling about in her head. *It is incredible that at the close of the nineteenth century a virgin has appeared who is not the one from Lourdes. . . .*

"I just want to know . . ."

"Know? Know what? There's nothing to know here," Gracia interrupted brusquely. "That's what they all say. They come, they rummage around, they invade our lives and Teresa's life, and then they spread pure lies. We don't need more people asking questions. You don't have anything to do here. You better leave."

She felt the veiled threat but it was too late to retreat. Besides, what right did this woman have to challenge her? Following a hunch, she dared to murmur timidly:

"She has brought me here."

There was a spark of interest behind the hard look.

"Teresa?"

"Yes."

She began to speak hastily, without taking her eyes off the rigid young woman who was trying to close the door without even knowing her. She spoke with the hope of penetrating her armor, of piquing her curiosity, of opening a crack through which she could enter into the secrets that the other woman guarded so zealously. She told her of her first accidental encounter with Teresa's name in a book, the years of research, the unexpected discoveries, the secret messages, the obsession, and finally the dream that had brought her to Navojoa, the extraordinary encounter with the unknown woman in the church, and the hope she had invested in this visit to Chiripas. When she finished, she was disturbed, confused, and trembling inside. She kept looking at Gracia until she perceived or imagined an ambiguous sparkle in the eyes of the other woman, who without saying another word pushed the curtain aside and gestured to her to enter. She passed through the door, followed by Mrs. Soledad, who in contrast to her daughter seemed to rejoice at the unexpected visit.

"Oh, miss! If you knew what things they have said about our Teresita! That's why my Gracia doesn't want me to tell anything anymore, but . . ."

She stopped short, as if the other woman had cut her off.

The room was clean and decorated with severe simplicity, in solid colors: brown and beige, with ocher walls. She was surprised by the absence of objects on the tables or in the corners. She turned to Gracia; with a nod of her head, the young woman indicated that she should look at the opposite wall. There was an enormous photograph of Teresita, with huge, luminous, profound eyes, contemplating her as if from a distance. *The young Urrea is a woman without notable physical attributes, with common features and a hysterical nature. . . .* Through the years she had found many photographs of Teresa and what they all had in common was that they seemed to be of different women, except for the look in her eyes. That was the only thing that didn't change. But this was a photo she had never seen before, of a Teresa transformed into a woman of the world: beautiful, suave, mature, wise. She felt as if she recognized the expression, perhaps it reminded her of something she had seen in herself: the look that decried having searched for years without finding an answer. Teresa was wearing an elegant dress, very stylish for the period. Her thick hair arranged softly around her face formed a chestnut halo rich in highlights; her eyes, slightly turned away from the camera, seemed to be looking at something tangential to reality. There was no mark on her skin, no wrinkle: it was the fresh face of a young adult just entering her prime. Her mouth played with the idea of a smile, but didn't smile; it was a soft mouth, full of sadness. In her hair she wore an enormous white feather, as was the custom back then; her neck, wrapped in the ivory lace of her blouse and framed by the stand-up collar of a black cape, was slender and firm. She was beautiful, with an almost ethereal beauty, full of nostalgia but, at the same time, hard. She gave the impression of being alive, as if the photograph were just another kind of waiting.

"There she is," she murmured, overwhelmed, and blushing from the sound of her own voice. She turned quickly toward the younger woman. Gracia was observing her without saying anything. Mrs. Soledad intervened with a smile.

"Yes. That was the last photograph they took of her. When I look at it, I think that she is somehow here. Oh, Gracia, I have a hunch that the lady is telling us the truth. When she looked at the photograph, Teresa became more luminous. Come, sit here by me," said Doña Ausencia—which was her first name—as she made herself comfortable on the sofa.

Hesitant, she looked at Gracia as if to ask permission, and the young woman responded with an enigmatic smile; her eyes shone with strange intensity and for an instant seemed surprisingly similar to Teresa's eyes. She settled down on the sofa while Gracia occupied a chair facing her. *Zealotry is on the rise due to the inventions and hypocrisy of the so-called Saint of Cabora and with the thievery of Don Tomás Urrea, who exploits the people's ignorance for his own benefit.* . . . Once she began to talk, Doña Ausencia didn't seem to want to stop. The hours began to string themselves together with anecdotes, facts, memories, inventions, and myths.

Gracia observed in silence, only intervening from time to time to correct a detail or to ask her mother to tell about something in particular.

From an ancient trunk or chest they extracted some old clothes: a worn, moss green vest; a yellowish white glove with little pearl buttons at the wrist; a lace blouse stained by humidity. *Supposing that the Indians' gatherings could only be for the purpose of conspiracy, the leaders of the expeditions proceeded to apprehend all the so-called saints and their most avid followers. . . .* She was surprised by the diminutive size of the clothing. Everything she knew about Teresa had made her think that she had been taller and stockier, but she had been wrong: she had been tiny and delicate; only her hands were disproportionately large, like the hands of a man, attached to a feminine body.

At her mother's request, Gracia took out a small lapel button with Teresa's photograph. It was probably taken in Nogales, perhaps to be distributed among her followers. *Tomás and Teresa Urrea, fearing the persecution of the Mexican government, have traveled to Tucson to request American citizenship and thus be safe from any threat of extradition. . . .*

"Gracia never goes out without it," said Doña Ausencia, referring to the tiny portrait; "it's like her guardian angel. We all have a lot of faith in our saint. Did you know that she promised to be reincar—"

"Mother! You swore never again!"

"Oh, dear, you're right! I always forget; I start talking and things come out without my noticing, but not anymore. Let's see, where was I?"

A photographic composition made years after Teresa's death showed her with her two daughters, Laura on the left and Magdalena on the right. Her hair hung about her shoulders, a cascade of locks that fell outside the range of the camera, thick and heavy. She had never seen her children at that age; nevertheless, the work of the photographer created the illusion. Rescued from oblivion. *She was only thirty-three years old when she died, and it was said that she had exhausted her spirit in the service of her people.* . . . Doña Ausencia continued speaking, ". . . and, you see, Auntie, as we always called Mariana, had many photographs and even interviews that they had done of Teresita . . . *in the United States our enemies' great interest* . . . because she took care of her until the day of her death, and then she came here with the daughters . . . *is to make people believe that there exists in Mexico a nucleus of revolution, using Miss Teresa Urrea's nonsensical declarations as proof* . . . but she wanted to be buried with the photograph of Teresa as the queen of the Yaquis, so that one went into the coffin with Auntie, and others were carried away by the flood, with newspaper clippings and many other things. But we heard about everything from Auntie—we called her that because she was such a close friend of my mother's—like the story about Aunt Jesusa. You see, Aunt Jesusa didn't believe in Teresita's miracles; she was Mariana's cousin and she lived on another ranch, far from Cabora; so one night she says to Marianita that all those stories about Teresa aren't true and she insults her and says bad things about her, and Teresa wasn't there to defend herself. Well, the next day Mariana finds Jesusa with her mouth all swollen up, and she asks her what happened, and her cousin doesn't answer. But when Auntie arrives back home, Teresa laughs and asks: 'See what I did to your cousin for being such a blabbermouth?' And that's how she was, Auntie used to say, sweet as a dove, but she didn't like people to go around bad-mouthing her or not believing in her miracles. *Many arrived to see and consult with this marvelous young lady; the present war that the Yaquis are waging against the Mexican government is attributed to her influence.* Don't you want another cup of coffee?"

"No thank you, Doña Ausencia, don't bother."

"Well, you see, another time when they were in the United States, I think it was in Los Angeles, I don't remember well, but Teresa and Auntie were there, and Teresa says to her: 'In a little while a man will come looking for me and he is coming to kill me,' and Auntie gets frightened and tells her she's not going to answer the door, but Teresa tells her to go ahead and open it and not be afraid because that man isn't going to kill her, he's coming with that intention but she's not going to die by the hand of man. *Certainly the American government will refuse extradition, arguing that the crimes were political in nature, and thus the hopes of our government will be dashed; I suggest that a more effective means of achieving our goal be sought.* Then there's a knock on the door and it was a man asking for the saint and he enters and says: 'Are you the saint?' and Teresa tells him no, that she's not a saint, although they call her that . . . *this marvelous young woman, sweet and kind, never accepted being called a saint . . .* but she is Teresa Urrea and she knows that he is there to kill her, but he will repent and from now on he will be a good man, and then Mariana sees the man drop the knife he has in his hand and throw himself on his knees in front of Teresita, asking for her pardon. They say he was sent by the government of Porfirio Díaz, who wanted to kill her; that's how evil he was."

While she listened, she turned to look again at the photograph on the wall; she could have sworn that Teresa was observing her out of the corner of her eye and smiling.

". . . until her last day, it's true, Auntie took care of her, and then she raised the daughters that she brought back here when they were just little tykes, since Teresa was only thirty-three years old when she died, and she brought them back here to live after the Revolution, and my kids were young, too, and she came to help me with them, Auntie did. Until they were big and Laura married my cousin; and they were living here awhile and then they went north of the border. They never had kids. She died about fifteen years ago, and then my cousin died. They say Magdalena is still alive, up there in Arizona, that she's really sick, and she changed her last name so they wouldn't be bothering her about her mother. She never got married. We lost track of her a while ago.

"Oh! they say so many things that you don't know what to believe anymore. It seems like everyone makes things up as they please . . . *the presence of the so-called saint and her father in the hacienda at Cabora is considered by everybody to be a threat to public tranquility* . . . but here everything was told to us by Auntie. You see, one day Mariana arrived at Cabora with her husband, Fortunato. She was accompanying her very old mother, who had a crippled hand, I think she had stuck a needle in it and the hand stayed that way, all curled up. Well, they hardly had arrived when Teresita called for them because she knew they were coming. And Mariana was surprised because Teresa hadn't seen them, but she and her mother approached the little house where Teresa did her cures, and when she saw her it was like she almost recognized her, and Teresa extended her hands and invited them in and said, 'How good it is that you have arrived, sisters! I was waiting for you.' And then she cured the old lady's hand, like so, she took the withered hand and turned it upward and spat in it as if that were the most natural thing in the world, she rubbed it and there it was! Like new!"

The hours floated awhile in the atmosphere and then suddenly disappeared. Many of the stories she had read before, others were new; some perhaps were inventions of time itself. Gracia sat on the edge of her chair, stiff, like a huge bird about to grab its prey. Doña Ausencia's voice twisted and turned, repeated itself, looped back, and began anew, as in a reiterative dream that never ends. The atmosphere of the room became unreal, outside of time, belonging to another dimension. Once in a while she looked at the photograph. She perceived her own excitement as a kind of bridge between Gracia's resistance and the unconditional surrender of her mother. Teresa's presence was more and more palpable, as if her arrival were imminent, as if in some invisible way she were already there. The midday heat was increasingly heavy. *Teresita Urrea, a pleasant young lady from Sonora, through her social position, intelligence, and medical knowledge achieved the respect and admiration of the people of the region.* . . . Tireless women weaving magical stories, stringing together memories in colorful patterns, embroidering the fabric of dreams that belonged to them. *She suffered an attack that lasted several days, and when they had given her up for dead, she came to; the common people consider it a case of resurrection.* . . . Who was Gracia? Where had she come from? *Maintain strict vigilance of activities in Cabora and keep me informed.* . . . Why did she, too, seem so obsessed with Teresa, so possessive? . . . *converted into a political banner against the dictatorship* . . . Priestess of a private religion. Gracia didn't take her eyes off her. What was she looking for? *Nobody could resist her look without bending to her will.* . . . She began to ask herself if this verbal circling around the same theme was leading somewhere. *A young woman from Sonora suffers a cataleptic attack and remains in a deep sleep.* . . . *The public opinion in the whole region condemns the farce in Cabora.* . . . Only the photograph seemed to be telling the truth: there were no more words, just oblivion, the tireless repetition of what someone else had said, memories of memories, reconstructed truths invented in retrospect. *Teresa never came back to Mexico.* . . . Nevertheless, she felt hypnotized. She didn't want to leave, there had to be something more there besides that photograph and those poor, worn-out clothes. *Teresa Urrea, the so-called saint, has been responsible for more deaths than the last great epidemic of yellow fever.* . . . The air bristled, filling up with secret silences, with things unsaid. She began to feel exhausted, her head was spinning, it was difficult for her to concentrate on the words. *Definitely, I am a victim of tyranny in my country from which I was exiled for no reason.* . . . *Everybody was executed, and thus ended this strange episode of our history and the kind of collective insanity provoked by the hysterics of an abnormal woman called the Saint of Cabora.* . . . *Peace reigns in Mexico.* . . .

Suddenly she realized the two women were looking at her. She hadn't heard what they said. She apologized. They asked her if she wanted to drink something, a little tequila perhaps, or to have lunch with them. She wanted to make an excuse; she felt very tired and needed to sleep. But Doña Ausencia, insisting, got up and set another place at the table. Then she returned with a bottle of tequila and three shot glasses.

"Let's drink a toast to Teresita," said Gracia, who tossed back the whole shot at once and set the glass on the table, making a noise that sounded like a period at the end of a sentence, and without waiting for the others to finish she rose and went to the kitchen.

She sipped her tequila slowly, remembering her fast of almost two days. Doña Ausencia set her glass aside and leaned toward her. *Obviously her followers were fanatics, but their fanaticism was revolutionary. . . .* "There is a family secret," she whispered. "Teresa promised to return one day and she did so, briefly, when Gracia's little sister was born. As soon as she opened her eyes we knew it was Teresita: they shone like morning stars, even in the dark. Poor thing! She died three days later."

She would have liked to ask what purpose could there be for such a fleeting reincarnation, but Gracia appeared in the doorway of the kitchen and with a stern voice announced that the food was ready. *This surge of messianism was caused by a young woman named Teresa. . . .* The three sat at the table in silence.

The lunch was simple, homemade, and nutritious. She ate with real appetite. The images of the morning danced chaotically in her head. She had asked about Cabora—it existed!—and Gracia's cousin knew how to get there. Doña Ausencia immediately sent a neighbor to get him. She was drinking a cup of coffee when the curtain was drawn to the side and a young man appeared. She glanced at his face, their eyes met, and she suddenly felt a profound shiver run through her body.

 X

On the day of her second death, one of her sweetest memories would be of Anastasio: their mutual friendship seemed to her, at a distance, more fulfilling and satisfying than the few days of love she had experienced in her life. Many times she had asked herself if perhaps she would have been happier living with him, having children, adjusting to life in the settlement. Even though

Anastasio was married, some men had more than one woman and nobody thought anything of it. There was Don Palomino, for example: he had taken in the widow of his brother-in-law and the three of them—he, his wife and her sister—lived quite peacefully. But back in those days Teresa didn't know everything that she would learn later; she couldn't even imagine the complications of love, the subtle motives that it hid, how ephemeral it was once passion was satisfied, and the thousands of ways that it could wound. She just had the feeling that her destiny was elsewhere, and all of her being was dedicated to reaching it. Anastasio was her friend; her feelings for him were frank, open, with nothing hidden. There were no limitations or requirements, just a sharing of mutual interests. Once she overcame the obstacles that Tula put up against their friendship, the terrible urgency to lose herself disappeared and she was happy again; the future opened up full of renewed illusions. She understood that true desperation came not from losing one's liberty but from losing hope, veering away from one's destiny, because that produced an internal silence that turned into emptiness.

She found excuses to slip away as frequently as possible and went back to the activities that were to take her, one day, to Cabora. What she liked the most was to gallop across the open countryside, get away from everything, and dream. Some afternoons when Anastasio returned from Cabora, he lent her Mi Nena when the mare wasn't too tired, but that brief period of time before nightfall allowed her to ride around only a short while, without the possibility of venturing further. Don Epi, on the other hand, had a gray mare that seemed older than her owner and was no longer of any use for roundups. She was called Goldie because at one time she had looked somewhat like a palomino; she didn't run anymore, at most she trotted a few paces and then went back to a walk. Don Epi allowed Teresa to take her out for a while in the morning and then again in the afternoon "so she doesn't get so stiff," he said. One day Teresa took this opportunity to guide the slow steps of the animal toward Cabora.

She had already gleaned quite a bit about the ranch from the cowhands' conversations but she wanted to see it herself. At the same time, the idea of something so daring produced in her an amorphous and ferocious fear that was related to the terror of losing her illusions again. Each day she went a little further, but a vague foreboding always made her turn back before reaching the outer limits of the ranch. So she went back and forth, without making up her mind, feeling her urgency and fear growing at the same time. It was like stretching toward something that she really didn't want to reach except in her fantasy, where everything could resolve itself to her liking. Thus she imagined that some day she would go the whole distance and arrive. . . . What was she going to do the day she arrived at Cabora? As soon as she asked herself that, she would turn Goldie around and slowly return to the settlement.

But, as does happen, that "some day" arrived. Cayetana fell ill and Teresa had to be sent for firewood. Tula grumbled, skewered her with all kinds of warnings, and ordered her to return as soon as possible. Teresa ran to Don Epi's house and took out Goldie. She was determined: it was still quite early and she would have time to arrive at Cabora, return, gather firewood, and be back at the hut before nightfall. She was full of palpitations and fears, but this time she refused to think about what she would do once she got there: she would just go see and come back. The sluggish pace of the old mare prolonged the journey to exasperation. With each plodding step her fears grew. What if she ran into Anastasio? Or worse yet, Don Tomás himself? What if they kicked her off the ranch, saying that wasn't her place, that she should go back to the settlement with the Indians? A direct rejection would dash all her dreams, but still she kept going. Seeing the cowboys rounding up the cattle in the distance, she turned toward a low hill to the right of the road so as not to be seen. As she emerged from behind the hill, she stopped abruptly in her tracks: two hundred yards away stood the Big House.

She contemplated the white, stately construction that dominated the landscape with its enormous arches at the entrance, red roofs, and walls like those of a fortress. It was an edifice more massive and elegant than she could ever have dreamed; she stood very still, incredulous, incapable of looking away. Goldie, believing it was time to go home, pulled at the reins from one side to the other. Teresa ignored her. Something was crumbling inside her. What she had imagined so many times was, in reality, much more imposing. The Big House loomed like an impregnable citadel, an inaccessible castle, a closed world. This had nothing to do with settlements and huts, earthen floors, and old wooden furniture; it was overpowering and majestic, a dwelling where only gods and angels could abide, their feet not touching the ground as they passed through the long hallways, their eyes never contemplating the faces of mere mortals. She felt small, poor, dirty, a bumpkin with bare feet, a braid, and humble clothes. Her dream crumbled; she wasn't Don Tomás, she didn't belong to Cabora, a world that was so distant she hadn't been able to approach it even in her imagination. Tears came to her eyes and she wept with disillusionment and rage.

She regretted having gone there, like someone who wakes from a dream to confront the nightmare of reality and regrets not having continued sleeping. How could she have imagined, with what crazy thoughts had she aspired . . . ? She bit her lip and turned her eyes away from what was wounding them and undermining her confidence. She was just about to turn Goldie around and head back the way she had come when she noticed a hill behind the Big House. It was remarkable enough to pique her curiosity. It didn't look like any of the other hills. Around there, the bluffs were all smooth, soft, rounded. This one, in contrast, seemed like a pile of giant rocks in delicate equilibrium, a miracle of divine architecture, always about to collapse and at the same time immovable. The boulders were pink, and here and there they formed profound hollows, natural arches, enormous caves, and dark passageways. The hill rose above the rest and on the top it had an opening, a small cave like a smiling mouth or a vigilant eye that watched over the land.

Moved by a strange impulse, she guided Goldie toward that gigantic hill, making a big circle around the house so she wouldn't be seen. The vexed mare resisted, but Teresa was determined. She rode her to the foot of the hill, dismounted, and tied her to a mesquite tree where she would have some shade. It was almost noon and the sun beat furiously on the immobile landscape. She found a narrow path between the lowest rocks and she started to climb. Every little while she ran into insurmountable stone barriers that she had to circumvent to find the path again. Several times she stopped to rest in the shade of some monumental boulder. Her goal was to reach the top and gaze at the countryside from a distance, perhaps see inside the patio of the hacienda; she wanted to reach the eye of the bluff, the sacred mouth she had seen from below. She climbed for more than an hour and finally came out on the narrow, flat space outside the cave. It was much smaller than it looked from afar and she had to crawl in; it wasn't very deep, either, but it offered shade and, because of the altitude, it was cooled by a gentle breeze.

She sat down and looked toward Cabora, which in the distance had regained human proportions. It was still white, very, very white and beautiful, but set against the incommensurable expanse of the plain, surrounded by so many hills and bluffs and fields and pastures, measured against the extraordinary distance of the horizon, it didn't look at all imposing; it even looked a little lost and solitary. Far away the cattle grazed peacefully; the ranchhands, gathered in the shade of a small grove of trees, were eating or resting. Down below, the dry bed of the Cocoraqui Wash showed signs of its subterranean water with rows of tall *huamúchiles;* inside the hacienda nothing moved. The patio, with its leafy laurel tree, seemed to doze in the midday heat. A little smoke wafting from the chimney marked the kitchen where lunch was probably being prepared. Teresa smiled: in order to put in perspective what seemed so unattainable from down below, she only had to reach the appropriate height one way or another. Once again her dreams became possible. Don Tomás was no bigger than the minute cowboys that she saw and the mansion could belong to dwarfs: it was all relative. Suddenly she felt that her destiny was in her hands; it was just a question of time. She looked around: the cave's floor was covered with a fine, pink dust, the product of the slow crumbling of the rock. She scooped up a little in the palm of her hand, and looking toward Cabora, she pronounced half in her Indian language, half in Spanish, words that seemed appropriate for the occasion.

"By the blood of my people . . . " She placed a little dust on her tongue. It had no flavor. She added some more phrases about destiny, the future, purity, and strength, and after each one she ate another bit of dust. Finally she concluded, "Cabora will be mine."

She was filled with such euphoria that she ran down the hill, jumped on the dozing horse, and returned as quickly as possible to Aquihuiquichi. In her excitement she forgot the firewood and had to put up with the routine scolding, but nothing, absolutely nothing could undermine the decision she had made up there on the hill. From then on, every act, every thought would be directed toward fulfilling her vow.

Teresa distanced herself more and more from the customs of the settlement. There was no possibility of getting clothes that would make her look more like a "young lady" or even a pair of crude sandals to wear, but that didn't worry her. She devoted herself obsessively to her personal hygiene, bathing twice a day whenever possible and washing her clothes so often that they became more faded than a blanket left in the sun. She stopped braiding her hair, piling it instead on top of her head and tying it with colorful ribbons. She avoided the humble chores of the other women, just doing what was absolutely necessary in order to remain in Tula's house. When it was her turn to wash clothes, she waited until nobody was at the creek before surreptitiously completing her chore. She took advantage of every opportunity to return to Cabora until she became accustomed to seeing the mansion without feeling fear. Secretly she continued writing her name in the dust, the name she didn't have yet, until the letters turned out almost perfectly: Teresa Urrea, she wrote tirelessly, as if repetition were capable of creating reality. One day she dared to ask Cayetana if she could use her father's last name. Her mother, who was breastfeeding the newborn baby, looked at her as if from the other side of an abyss of oblivion.

"No. Only if he recognizes you and gives you permission. Be content with Chávez; don't bother him."

She went back to waiting. She observed the modest way of walking that the women of the settlement had, as if they were asking forgiveness from the earth, and forced herself to walk upright with her head held high, a firm stride, and her feet pointing straight ahead to the future. She practiced every gesture, every attitude that would distinguish her and advance her one more step toward her destiny, until she could make it her own.

For the same reason, she watched for any chance to be seen by the inhabitants of the Big House, even if just from a distance. She didn't speak to them, but neither did she look away if she was observed. She had hopes that trivial reports of her existence would begin to reach Don Tomás's ears, so that perhaps some day he would come to see for himself.

Teresa was fourteen years old when Cayetana left, but she was so engrossed in her dream world that for several days she didn't even notice her mother's strange absence. Finally she asked Aunt Tula about her.

"I thought you were never going to ask. Your mother left and she took your two little brothers with her. Not even thanks, not even goodbye, not even 'Please, take care of Teresita for me.' She felt the itch and she went after that Tolentino and left me with the daughter with who-knows-what fuzz in her head, who goes around like a zombie all the time. It's better, it's better that she left, and you're next if you don't start chipping in with the housework. . . ."

Tula kept chattering, but Teresa didn't listen any more. She saw the image of her mother disappearing into the distance, trotting as usual after a man, with a child by the hand and another on her back, a little bundle of clothes, nothing more. A shadow.

What her mother saw in Tolentino Teresa didn't understand; she didn't understand what she had seen in any of them with the exception of Don Tomás. Suddenly she felt that she was hovering over a void, a there-is-nothing-here, a silent farewell. That night she curled up on the straw mat that her mother had occupied for so many years and cried. She wept without knowing why, with tears leaving her body the way her mother had left her life; it was a weeping that didn't ask for anything, that didn't miss anything. Her mother, Cayetana: a shadow without threads. She couldn't even remember her face; it was as if she had never really existed. She wouldn't see her again until a few days before her second death, and by then Cayetana would consist of so much forgetfulness that they wouldn't even say a word to each other.

XI

Doña Ausencia brought a cup of coffee for her nephew and made the introductions. Gracia had changed when he entered: she became possessive, hovering around him, touching him here and there as if brushing some lint off his shirt. Her eyes shone in a special way, and she seemed to want to isolate him from any contact with the others. Doña Ausencia explained that Javier was more like a son than a nephew.

"He always lived with us until he went to Piedras Negras a couple of years ago to work in the mine. Just imagine! In those black, horrible tunnels! How many times did you almost get killed, Javier?" The young man silently raised the five fingers of his hand. "That's why . . . you know what nickname they gave him? Death! That's what they called you, right? Because only death cannot die. But I think you were saved by something else: because Teresa was protecting you. Every day we commended you to her and she has never failed us."

Doña Ausencia kept talking; from time to time Gracia inserted some comment in her inflexible tone. Javier didn't say anything; he

didn't even seem to be listening. He sipped his coffee without lift-
ing his gaze from the cup. She contemplated him at her leisure.
He was tall, very slender, with black hair and mustache, his skin
slightly olive-toned. When he came in, she noticed that his eyes
were also black but with a series of strange lights, like oil wells on
fire. He was attractive, strangely sensual, but there was something
dark about him, something threatening. She remembered the
chill and realized that when she saw him against the curtain he
had looked just like a shadow, not a person. Observing him now,
sitting there so serenely, she felt a little ridiculous and suddenly
very tired. Doña Ausencia had refilled her glass with tequila; she
sipped it, trying to find new energy. Gracia, with veiled sarcasm,
repeated what she had told them in the morning about her obsessive search for Teresita. In that hostile, distrustful mouth, the
story sounded absurd, incredible, the product of a sick mind. *The
North American press takes every opportunity to insult us; they call
Teresa "a martyr persecuted by the government of Porfirio Díaz. . . ."*
She raised her eyes and met the coal-black eyes of Javier, who had
said something to her.

"Pardon?"

"When do you want to go to Cabora?" he repeated. He had a
slightly hoarse voice but it was smooth and suggestive as if the
words were wrapped in a veil of insinuations. *Cabora is a hacienda with 107 inhabitants; far from any center of civilization, it has to be
self-sufficient. . . .* She trembled inside again, without knowing
why; the young man intimidated her. What's more, that whole
unreal atmosphere was beginning to cause her uncontrollable
anxiety. "It takes an hour and a half from here; the road isn't good
and we'd have to take it slowly. We don't have a car, so we'd have
to go in yours."

"Yes, yes, no problem. We could go tomorrow. I would come
pick you up." She listened to her own clumsy voice. Perhaps the
tequila had gone to her head. She felt embarrassed. *The common
people are easily impressed, and when this fiery young woman speaks
to them of sin . . .* She blushed. Suddenly, she was engulfed by the

need to get out of there, to be alone, to put her thoughts in order. Sleep, yes, that's what she needed, to sleep all night without interruptions. "It's late. You have been too kind and I'm afraid I've imposed on you. Really, I ought to go; I don't want to be caught in the dark. Thank you . . . ," she spoke hastily as she stood up. "No, please, don't get up; I'll just say goodbye here," but Gracia was already at her side, taking her arm.

"You can't leave without saying goodbye to Teresita," she said, pushing her toward the photograph and leaving her there alone. She felt absurd. She no longer found anything luminous or smiling in that image; she saw a vain woman, disillusioned with life, bitter and morose, who looked at her with an enigmatic semismile. *This woman produced extraordinary phenomena of psychological pathology, both individual and collective; she manipulated people's consciousness at her whim to satisfy her intense pride. . . .* She closed her eyes and felt dizzy. Gracia took her arm once more and guided her to the curtained door. Doña Ausencia gave her a kiss on the cheek.

"How good it is that you came! We almost never have visitors. Tomorrow, after Cabora, you'll stay for lunch, okay?" She took both her hands and leaned toward her.

"You know what?" she said in a low voice. "You have big hands like Teresita's." Gracia, at her side, laughed scornfully. *Saint Teresa was such an outstanding person that her mere presence in a room relieved one's soul, and when she extended her hands toward the crowd she radiated a celestial light. . . .* She thanked them and her own voice came to her from far away; the dizziness was increasing. She turned to go and stumbled into Javier, who was waiting in the doorway to accompany her to the car. He grabbed her elbow.

"Do you feel sick?"

"No, I'm fine. I think it was the tequila. I'm not used to it."

"If you wish . . ."

"No, I should go. I'll be back tomorrow."

Javier accompanied her. As soon as she got outside, the fresh air cleared her mind and she felt silly. *Marvelous cures are performed by the blessed child. . . .* The sky reflected a thousand shades of red and salmon; a tenuous breeze was blowing. In the street some children were playing kick-the-can. *Long live Teresa, pretty and quaint; long live the fools who think she's a saint! . . .* The town was tranquil, almost asleep, and the air was cooling off. She breathed deeply, with relief.

"We'll see you early tomorrow, so we can have the whole day," said Javier. *I don't believe in saints who stay for lunch. . . .* She answered affirmatively and started the car.

All the way back she couldn't understand why she had felt so frightened. She reviewed the events of the day and didn't find anything strange, except her own reaction. On the contrary, she remembered the strong emotion she experienced before Teresa's photograph, the ease with which the hours slipped away during Doña Ausencia's pleasant conversation, and Javier's friendliness. She could even comprehend Gracia's hostility and her reluctance to open up in front of a stranger. She decided that it had been the tequila. When she arrived at the hotel she still felt full from lunch so she went upstairs to bed immediately. "Tomorrow is going to be an important day," she thought and smiled to herself. *Cabora has become a kind of Mecca; thousands of people have converged upon this isolated ranch, seeking physical and moral relief; they are all attended to. . . .*

She suffers through another restless, feverish night, thrashing around in bed, sweating, drifting in and out of dreams. She dreams of Cabora again. This time she's inside the Big House, in a huge room full of people, shouts, confusion. Gabriela and Huila are there, and so are Don Tomás, Lauro Aguirre, and even Gracia, Javier, and Doña Ausencia. They are all running around and shouting at the same time: they are looking for Teresita. She observes from a corner, without moving. She has lost track of Javier in the chaos, and she wants to find him; she has something important to tell him, but doesn't remember what. She dreams that by finding him she will remember. Suddenly she sees him on the other side of the room. As she crosses over to him, the confused voices sound accusatory, shouting that she is crazy, deluded, deceived; she doesn't pay attention, she just wants to reach Javier. When she arrives at where she thought she saw him, she realizes that it is not Javier, it's actually a stranger, who is watching her; she looks around and locates Javier again. She moves toward him and bumps into Doña Ausencia, who tells her, "Take care of your hands. Teresa needs them"; she pushes forward. Gracia abruptly blocks her path, threatening her. "You aren't the chosen one," she shouts at her, "you can't be the chosen one," and disappears. Then she suddenly finds herself face to face with Javier. He looks at her, extends his hand and takes her by the hair, pulling her near and murmuring, "Oh, Teresita, how I want you, come, Teresa Urrea, you're going to be mine"; she begins to shout that she isn't Teresa, to let her go, that he's made a mistake. She tries to get away; she falls. . . . She wakes up bathed in sweat.

▩ XII

She didn't have much time to think about Cayetana's disappearance; other worries immediately surged to the forefront. At first it didn't seem like anything serious: there were rumors in the settlement about Don Tomás's new affair, but the whims and entanglements of the boss had been daily fodder for many years. Nonetheless, when a few weeks passed and they kept gossiping about the same thing, Teresa began to pay attention. They were talking about a young woman, this time not indigenous, but the daughter of a nearby rancher. Someone said it was shameful, another said it was embarrassing, and a third that it was enviable: Don Tomás was more than thirty years older than his new conquest. It was said that it seemed to be serious: the "suitor" had been frequenting the house of his "beloved" for almost a year and a half now, buttering up his future "father-in-law." They made jocular bets about Mrs. Urrea's reaction, since the women from the so-called good families tended to be much more squeamish and

possessive than those from the settlement. Different versions
came and went: that it was settled; that he repented; that they
rejected him. Until finally the definitive news was announced: the
young woman would be set up in Cabora as the "lady of the
house," but not legitimately. The news upset Teresa, who found
out through Anastasio about when the other woman would arrive
and decided to go and observe the arrival from a distance.

Gabriela Cantúa was scarcely a year older than Teresita.
Besides the freshness of her youth, an air of complete innocence
highlighted her natural beauty. The ranch of her father, Don
Ramón, shared a boundary with Cabora. And even though it had
good pasture land, it lacked water and never would have provided old Cantúa with a comfortable life if it hadn't been for Don
Tomás, who permitted him to water his cattle in the northern
pool of the Cocoraqui Wash. That's how they initiated their
friendship, which continued to grow because the two of them
shared a well-entrenched solitude. Cantúa had been a widower
since the birth of his only daughter, and Don Tomás, who was
already pushing fifty and had slowly given up his affinity for
young Indian girls, only saw his family on his trips to Alamos,
which were less and less frequent. They began to get together
every week on Don Ramón's ranch to play chess, drink a little,
chat awhile. Cantúa was delighted: his friendship with Don
Tomás not only provided him with access to the watering hole
and pleasant company, it also lent him the prestige of rubbing
elbows with a member of Alamos's high society, an added benefit
that, he thought, could be useful in the future when he wanted to
marry off his daughter.

Gabriela had grown up in the care of domestic servants, from
whom she assimilated timidity and modesty, and of a maiden
aunt brought from Guaymas, whom Cantúa instructed to educate
her like a "young lady"; with this arrangement the father considered his responsibility fulfilled and he turned his attention
elsewhere. The aunt, who made up for a lack of intelligence with
an excess of sanctimony, interpreted the father's orders by means

of the Sacred Scriptures. From then on she set out to supplant all of the girl's real needs with surrogate rituals. If Gabriela cried for lack of a mother, the self-righteous old maid had her pray rosaries to the Virgin Mary; insomnia, fever, colds, and itching were all cured with exaggerated doses of the Lord's Prayer. When she was hungry, she was supposed to entertain her stomach by reviewing the twelve Stations of the Cross; she learned to read by memorizing passages from the New Testament, and her games always included the Baby Jesus as a playmate. She practiced drawing angels by copying religious images, learned to weave little altar cloths for the chapel, and to embroider in cross-stitch a replica of the cape of the Virgin of Guadalupe. The divine family had always been *her* family, and she spoke with God and his Holy Mother with more ease than she demonstrated with her own father. The celestial representatives always had time to listen, never interrupted, and gave unambiguous answers that never varied one iota from what was already dictated in the sacred texts.

Thus Gabriela grew up with a strange mixture of absolute abandonment on the part of her real family and complete permissiveness on the part of the divine family. She passed through puberty erroneously convinced that she knew everything she needed to confront life's problems, had the best company for her solitude, and possessed all the answers; but when she entered the torturous tide of adolescence, her world became a turmoil. With menstruation her peaceful character went out of kilter and she began to suffer mood swings that took her from irrepressible euphoria to profound depression, from religious exaltation to total apathy, from docility to rebellion, and from an amorous surrender to God to a desparate longing for love. She alternated laughter with tears, verbosity with silence, and joy with desolation in such a bizarre sequence that she ended up feeling completely confused. One day, finding herself in an open field and bathed by a resplendent sun, she could not contain her jubilation, for at that moment she knew she was intensely alive; she shouted to the sky an inebriated "Thank you, Jesus!" and at that same instant, just as suddenly and absolutely, she understood the irrevocability of her own mortality. Drowning in sobs, she ran to take refuge with her celestial father. Weeping, she confessed her terror and prayed that he change her destiny; the answer, rather than sweet and tranquilizing, was inexorable: "Ashes to ashes, dust to dust."

Her mystical world crumbled around her. That was the cruelest of rejections; she was invaded by an unbearable loneliness and couldn't think of anything but recuperating her lost love. She imposed on herself an almost monastic regimen, but it was of no use. Her prayers no longer produced answers. She had discovered the insurmountable silence of her spiritual progenitors. From then on she opted for the only possible solution: her flesh-and-blood father.

Cantúa found himself suddenly overwhelmed by the unexpected attentions of his daughter, who spared no effort to wait on him, accompany him, and caress him as much as possible within the norms of the relationship. After the initial surprise, the ministrations began to please him; he received them as a natural manifestation of gratitude for everything that he had provided for the young lady. The change in his daughter coincided with the period of Don Tomás's frequent visits, and the neighbor also reaped the benefits of Gabriela's subtle and pleasing attention. Gabriela and the soothing shots of cognac became indispensable elements in the smooth sliding away of the hours of those shared afternoons.

Little by little Don Tomás began to notice something that was totally unknown to him: that warm presence of the daughter, the little kisses that Gabriela deposited on the paternal bald spot, the "Daddy, what would you like?" in a very tender and sweet tone, the complacency and satisfaction in Cantúa's face, the minute gestures interpreted immediately as an invitation to refill his glass, but especially the regal air that all that gave the father, converting him into an absolute monarch of the special kingdom created by his daughter. Don Tomás had never experienced anything similar. He reached the point of feeling nauseous while contemplating the gratified face of his friend under the care and pampering of the apparently angelical young woman. He felt that his life was incomplete. For him, women had served only three purposes: the servants, completely anonymous, attended to his daily needs; the Indian girls, who had first names, satisfied his male impulses; and Loreto, to whom he had given a last name, corresponded to his ambitions as a hacendado. None of them had ever made him feel like a king. His children were mere lackeys (the illegitimate ones) and sissies (the ones Loreto was raising in Alamos). All good for nothing. What he needed was a daughter!

"What damn luck you have, Cantúa!" he exclaimed one afternoon, when Gabriela had gone to prepare coffee. "What a daughter! And I have never managed to make one! Just boys who, when they aren't ignoring you, are rebelling. Sons of bitches, all of them. And Loreto just had another one. Damn woman, she only produces cursed colts, no fine fillies."

Cantúa smiled with deep satisfaction. When Gabriela returned he hugged her, something he rarely did, and from then on he never missed an opportunity to sing her praises to his friend, thanks to which Don Tomás got a bee in his britches that would not let him sleep, eat, or drink in peace, until he began the siege. Gabriela, although surprised, did not reject him. The unexpected advances conferred upon her a feeling of importance and individuality that she had never experienced in her relationship with her father or with the divine family. Don Ramón, who felt that he had acquired a new stature in the eyes of his neighbor, didn't even realize what was happening until Don Tomás laid his cards on the table.

"Cantúa, I'm taking your daughter home with me."

Don Ramón couldn't believe his ears, and even less so when he found out that they had already come to an agreement.

Gabriela hadn't put up the slightest resistance, even when she was informed that there would be no formal marriage. Her naïveté allowed her to confuse his need with the love she had never received and her own need with the love she had never felt, and she immediately created for herself the insatiable desire to be as necessary to this new family as she once believed she was to the celestial family. She was prepared to surrender without questions or requirements. A week later, Don Tomás took her to Cabora.

Teresa, mounted on Goldie, witnessed the arrival from a distance. She felt a twinge of jealousy when Don Tomás held Gabriela by the waist as he lowered her from the wagon. She observed her father: next to the young lady he didn't seem as tall as she remembered him on the horse, but he made up for his lack of height by shouting orders, gesticulating, and assuming lordly poses. He didn't leave the slightest doubt about who was in charge. Gabriela, on the other hand, looked timid, insecure, frightened; she had remained quietly to one side as the servants unloaded her things, and she even hesitated when Don Tomás invited her to enter the house. She was wearing a white dress that brushed the ground, with long sleeves trimmed in lace and a frilly collar that covered her neck. She was pretty, with translucent skin, big, black eyes, and dark hair that fell in spirals around the nape of her neck, but there was something terribly delicate in her manner, almost fragile, as if she were afraid to step on the earth for fear of harming it. Teresa laughed to herself.

"Let's go, Goldie," she murmured, pulling the rein, "there's nothing to worry about here."

From the first night they spent in Cabora, they both realized their mistake. Don Tomás, upon deflowering one more timid young woman, realized that far from having found a daughter, he had taken on the burden of another wife, and Gabriela, who discovered with astonishment the secret delight of her body, finally understood the profound meaning of sin. The next day Don Tomás went back to his routine duties on the ranch, conferring a certain tranquil but dispassionate gratitude on Gabriela during his free moments, as if her presence, while not being annoying, did not add much to his life.

Gabriela, on the other hand, was filled with remorse, recriminations, and doubts that she immediately confided to the divine family during long, solitary hours of confession. She spent the day praying in the chapel with the hope of exonerating her sinful desires to cavort with her man again that night. All of her energy, which wasn't much, was consumed with trying to reconcile this new contradiction. A fierce feeling of guilt that had been almost unknown to her produced a visceral fear of rejection, by God as well as by her husband. The only remedy was to wear herself out in the constant service of both: she became the personification of abnegation, self-denial, and sweetness; she aspired to absolute servility and the immediate fulfillment of the slightest desire—real or imagined—of either of her owners. Nobody ever rejected her, but she never knew, not even after the death of Don Tomás, if that was because they loved her, they forgave her, or they didn't even notice her existence.

The news of Gabriela's installation in Cabora did not take long to spread throughout Alamos, where there existed an abundance of good souls willing to whisper in the ever attentive ear of the legitimate wife. After spending four hours shut up in her bedroom throwing a tantrum because of the affront to her pride, crying all night long in sorrow and outraged vanity, cursing in every way possible her fate as a betrayed woman, ruminating for a while on the possibilities of making a scene, and having lengthy consultations with Father López y Sábana in the secrecy of the confessional, Loreto decided that it was her obligation as a good Christian to abandon the comforts of her home and rush to her husband's side so as to return him to the straight and narrow path of virtue and ensure the continuance of her marital rights. In order to avoid adding more fuel to the fiery gossip, she opted to make the trip alone.

Cosimiro, who was inspecting the fences, saw her coming from afar and ran to notify the boss that a problem was approaching.

"Your wife is coming!" he shouted, bursting into Don Tomás's office.

"Gabriela?" he asked, surprised.

"No. The other one."

"That's all I need!"

Don Tomás leapt to his feet, ordered his chestnut stallion saddled, and galloped out to meet the wagon before it arrived at the
outer limits of Cabora. He took the reins from Loreto's hands and
glared at her.

"What are you doing here?"

"Oh, you have to ask? I'm not willing to be the laughing stock
of the whole town. I want that woman out of here. If it's necessary for me to come live with you in order to achieve that, I'm
ready to make the sacrifice." Don Tomás was quiet for a moment,
sizing up the situation without losing sight of the machete-sharp
glare in Loreto's eyes. Then he took a deep breath, smiled, and
spoke with a firm voice, but without anger.

"No, Loreto, you do not belong on the ranch. Once I invited
you to share my life here and you refused; now, you're not even
invited. In Alamos you have your house, your children, your
well-deserved social position; there you give the orders and you
can do as you like. But here I give the orders and what I do is
none of your business. Don't come back and don't pay attention
to hearsay. You will always be my legitimate wife and you will
always have whatever you need to live your life with dignity. Be
satisfied with that."

And ignoring her tears of rage, he grabbed the horse firmly,
turned the wagon, gave the reins back to Loreto, and set everything in motion with a crack of his whip. His wife returned the
way she came without saying a single word or looking back. Don
Tomás remained there, watching her straight spine that shook
from time to time as if from some interior tremor, and something
in its hardness gave him a bad feeling. He thought about calling
her back, but then he remembered the image of the sweet and
innocent Gabriela, who was waiting for him at the ranch. With
ambiguous omens churning around in his head, he slowly
returned to Cabora. There, two good slugs of cognac cured him
of his misgivings, and he dismissed the problem at once.

Teresa didn't learn of Loreto's one-time visit until years later
when it was necessary to think seriously about the problem that

her father had foreseen. At that moment she was too busy redoubling her efforts to catch her father's attention. She allowed herself to be seen galloping over the countryside as fast as Mi Nena could go or trotting on the reluctant Goldie in the direction of the strange hill, her head held high, a haughty look in her eye, as if she had always belonged on the ranch. Nevertheless, all of these premeditated activities didn't seem to produce more than the renewed ire of Aunt Tula, while Don Tomás didn't even show any signs of being alive.

The situation in the hut took a serious turn for the worse with Teresita's increasing absence. Tula, realizing that her niece was ignoring her, became as ornery as a mule and every day she dealt her a heavier hand. It became a duel between two obstinacies: one shouting and the other resisting passively. Finally, total war broke out:

"Either you go wash the clothes and get back here before this saliva dries," howled Tula, depositing a huge wad of spittle on the floor, "or you don't ever come back here."

Teresa realized that it was not an empty threat. She grabbed the clothes, looked defiantly at her aunt, and spit on top of the other woman's saliva.

"I'll be back before it dries," she said, and left. After hiding the bundle of dirty clothes behind the house, she dedicated the rest of the day to her own affairs. When the sun was about to set, she picked up the clothes, went to the waterhole, and washed them. It was already dark when she returned to the hut.

Tula was beside herself. Her shouts resounded against the shaky walls, degenerated into insults, and finally ended in orders for Teresa to leave the next day. The young woman waited until the storm had calmed a bit and then, in that tranquil voice that drove her aunt mad, she said:

"The clothes are washed."

"I told you to wash them before that spittle . . ." and she couldn't pronounce the last word; her eyes were riveted on Teresa's saliva, which was still damp and shiny as if she had just deposited it there. She stared incredulously; she looked at her niece, but the young woman hadn't moved from the doorway. It wasn't possible for her to have spit again. And then Teresa saw, for the second time in her life, the look of terror that the proof of something supernatural provokes in mediocre beings.

"You aren't normal. You're possessed. Go away from here; don't get near me. Don't ever get near this family again."

Without further warning, they threw her straw mat and few clothes out of the hut. She accommodated herself under a small lean-to that had previously sheltered the pig while they were fattening him. Nobody spoke to her, which wasn't a problem, but they also refused to provide her with food. Instead, they left her a small sack of dry beans, another one of maize, and some utensils so she could cook. That was too humiliating; she preferred not to eat: nobody was going to see her making tortillas! She lasted two days. On the third day she went to Doña Rosaura's house, thinking that perhaps the old woman would take her in while she made up her mind about how to take the definitive step toward Cabora.

She stood at the fence and called for a long time so as not to commit the impertinence of entering without being invited. There was no answer. She approached the door and knocked and again there was silence. She thought that maybe the old lady was asleep. The smell of cooking beans wafted out the window, and hunger goaded her to knock harder. With the force of her blows the door opened a crack; once more she perceived the heavy silence, then she saw the quiet bulk on the bed.

She tiptoed in, approached the cot, and looked at Rosaura's face. She touched her skin: it felt waxy, as if it had just begun to get cold. She was dead. Suddenly Teresa heard a sound, something between a sigh and a sob that seemed to come from the other side of the room. Frightened, she peered into the shadows but didn't see anything. The sound came from the corner; she looked more closely and the noise ceased; there was absolutely nothing there. She searched in vain around the rest of the room.

In a little while she heard it again. This time she wasn't scared; rather, she felt sad. She remembered what Anastasio had told her: when death takes someone by surprise, the shadow is left behind, and until it dissipates it can be heard weeping and sighing near the body of its origin. She went over to the corner again.

"If you lie down with her, you will feel better," she said in a soft voice. "Maybe there's still time to catch up with her."

The soft sobs were quieted once more. She waited, but she didn't hear the sound again. She looked at Doña Rosaura's body; in the tenuous light it seemed as if she could just make out the thin outline of her shadow. She smiled, thinking that death was much simpler than life.

Without Doña Rosaura, she had to make a decision. She couldn't go back to the animal existence in the hut; she had already discarded the possibility of asking Anastasio for help because of what it would imply; there was nothing left except Cabora: the time had come.

She looked for the paper and pencil that Doña Rosaura always kept tucked away, and after apologizing to the dead woman in case she was showing any lack of respect, she served herself a heaping plate of hot beans. The nourishment gave her courage, and a little while later she had produced what she thought was a convincing letter written with great care in her best handwriting. It consisted of just a few lines, beginning with "Dear Don Tomás: Your daughter is writing to ask you to receive her," and ending with her signature: "Teresa Urrea."

She folded the paper, left the pencil in its place, put out the fire under the beans, deposited a kiss on Doña Rosaura's cold forehead, and ran as fast as she could to Anastasio's house. He was the safest messenger because of their friendship and because he didn't know how to read. As soon as she handed him the letter, she realized that this was her only opportunity. If her father rejected her, she would have no alternative but to wander off into the desert, like Cayetana. Nonetheless, instead of fear, she felt extremely calm: the wait was over. Finally she would know the answer.

▦ XIII

By morning she had forgotten the dream but she awoke full of anguish; the memory of the briefcase came to her as if she had lost it countless years ago, as if the documents were fragments of memories of another life that senselessly invaded the present. As if time crumbled into pieces and stopped flowing. She didn't even know what day it was. . . . No! She did know: it was *the* day. Finally: Cabora. *Cabora is a most miserable spectacle with lepers, cripples, blind and lame people, all huddled together in subhuman conditions.* . . . She had rushed to get dressed and set out for Chiripas, and now, with Javier and Gracia in the car, she was on her way.

According to Javier they had to go north on the Navojoa highway to a place called Fundición. There they had to turn right on a dirt road that led toward the mountains. *The dispersed fugitives from a riot in Chihuahua crossed the mountains and headed for Cabora.* . . . She was driving, feeling the security of the steering wheel in her hands like a solid contact with reality. *Cabora is a ranch with no more authority than its owner, the father of the so-called saint.* . . . Javier was at her side, Gracia in the back seat. Due to the bumpy road she had to drive at a snail's pace, and even so the holes and stones made the car rock back and forth, constantly bringing together her shoulder and Javier's. All that remained of her memory of the dream was a vague uneasiness each time she felt the contact.

When she saw him again in the morning, she decided that it hadn't all been the tequila. He had a strange animal sensuality that was distressing to her. His movements were almost feline, his physical stillness and his silence insinuated veiled threats as if he were a beast of prey ready to leap. Then there was the gloom: a darkness seemed to emanate from his body as if he had absorbed the coal or the obscure shadows of the mine. To top it off, he was dressed in black. In contrast, his hands were too long, slender, and white for a country man, almost feminine. Seeing them made her feel nauseous, as if their whiteness were a symptom of a contagious disease. *They say that psychic illnesses are also contagious, and there's no doubt that the father of the hysterical young woman is beginning to suffer from the same disease. . . .* But, once in the car, she had decided that it was all her own prejudice. The young man was friendly, attentive, respectful, and he spoke very little.

Gracia, on the other hand, had replaced her surliness of the previous day with comments made in a sarcastic and mocking tone, as if she wanted to feign complete indifference to anything that had to do with Teresita. She seemed to want to bother her, addressing her words exclusively to her cousin, whom she insisted on calling by his strange nickname. Gracia had said something scornful about Teresita's saliva, but she, with her eyes fixed on the road, scarcely had listened.

". . . and they say that Auntie sold her bath water, can you believe that, Death? As if people were so foolish."

"So there was money made from the powers of your saint?" she asked, simulating innocence. There was a sudden silence, loaded with tension. Then, Gracia spoke but she had lost the mocking tone.

"Teresa never charged for anything. Ask Death, here. Those are the lies that the busybodies make up. Right, Death? Isn't it true that Auntie said that if she had charged, Teresita would have lost her powers? Well, that's if she really had them," she added, changing her tone again, "I mean, if one can believe in her supposed universal hearing and the miraculous cures with saliva."

Gracia's hostility, which had made her anxious at first, was becoming exasperating. Fortunately, after the turnoff the other woman stopped talking, and she could concentrate on the landscape and think of Cabora. *The caravan of those who were coming to visit Teresa, stretched as far as one could see. . . .* Her excitement grew, like a tingly effervescence, as though the movement of the car and the country air itself were intoxicating.

Now they are traveling in silence: she can only hear the squeak of the suspension as the car hits potholes and bumps, and the monotonous rumbling of the motor. The windows are down; the air begins to heat up and she feels the sting as it beats dryly against her cheeks. *Since the month of April symptoms of an imminent insurrection began to be felt in the Yaqui Valley. José María Cajeme preached to his people the need to regain their independence, awakening the pride of that bellicose race. . . .* The coastal plains spread out on both sides of the narrow road; in front and to the right the aggressive and imposing peaks of the Sierra del Bacatete—the sacred mountain of the Yaquis . . . *the center of the world, where God's declaration took place: that the rainbow would be his sign and never again would a flood destroy humanity . . .* their last refuge from the federal troops before the massacre—form a wall of silence and anonymity. The contrast between the plain and the mountain strikes the eye abruptly and aggressively; the massive hulk seems to emerge from the center of the earth without warning, tearing through the intricate cloth of the prairie like a cruel, virulent god. *The Yaquis are commanded to surrender their weapons even though two hundred poorly armed Yaquis do not represent a threat when they are guarded by two battalions and a regiment of federal forces. . . .*

A turn in the road and almost imperceptibly they begin to climb. *Investigate case of so-called saint. Advise me of any evidence of conspiracy. P.D. . . .* On both sides tall, platinum yellow grass waves in the breeze. Grass whitewashed by the sun, trimmed by the wind, soft grass, gently combed. Javier tells her that this is communal property.

"Before they were great haciendas; the cattle grazed here, the fields were cultivated. The land is fertile, it produced well, but only for a few. Now it doesn't produce for anybody: it's abandoned."

"That's how Lauro Aguirre's revolution ended," she murmured to herself. *Considering that the violation of property rights by the so-called government of Porfirio Díaz has led to the confiscation of land from the legitimate owners as has happened with that belonging to the Yaquis and Mayos . . . and considering that land should belong to everybody just like the sun and the air. . . .*

Suddenly she brakes. A quail and her family cross the road. The motor stalls. The birds don't seem to notice the presence of the humans. "It's as though we didn't exist," she thinks. Minute by minute she feels reality slipping away, her little apartment seems more and more distant; the library, the archives, the lost documents recede farther and farther from her. The images of her daily life are fading from her mind. *My dear General Bandala: Before you undertake your duties in Sonora, you ought to know that the Cabora ranch is a focus of insurrection where Yaquis and Mayos gather for the purpose of conspiring against the government. . . .* There is something in those interminable expanses, an enormity, that eclipses the human dimension so manifest in Mexico City. She feels overwhelmed by the beauty of the landscape, so arid, yet so full of life. She doesn't want to go any further. She wants to listen to the sounds of the countryside. A roadrunner appears and disappears. In the distance, vultures sit on a cactus, enormous black fruits that conclude the cycle of life. *The Tomóchic rebellion had its inception in Cabora. . . .* She starts the car again; in her ears there remains the whisper of the wind sifting through the wild grasses. *As you can see, Mr. President, the "Teresistas" are doing their best to discredit your venerable government. . . .*

The road continues to ascend gradually. The bushes, the mesquite, the twisted vegetation of the desert begin to close ranks, becoming increasingly tall and dense. The automobile bumps and rattles as it passes over the dry beds of unruly washes that fill with water during the rainy season. *The multitude gathered outside Teresita's house and at dawn they sang "happy birthday" to her over and over until she came out and began to attend to them one by one. . . .* On the right three horizontal hills appear, flat, ancient, worn by time, smooth as horses' backs: they look like tables for a picnic of the gods. *Mr. Governor: You must understand that it is not possible to do away with the bandits because they take refuge in the haciendas, mixing with the "law-abiding" workers; the landowners, in order to protect them and maintain their work force, wipe out their tracks by driving cattle over the roads. . . .* There are plenty of mesquite trees, tumbleweed, prickly pears; the grass is more sparse; here and there a lone organ cactus stands tall like a sentinel of the desert. Ahead and still far away, the craggy peaks of the big mountain. "Over there must be Alamos," she thinks, "where at one time Loreto, the silent enemy, lived." *Some say that her eyes roll back and her face becomes as luminous as the moon; they say that she is so kind that she is capable of forgiving her staunchest enemies. . . .*

She has almost forgotten her companions. Her eyes rejoice in the delicate hues of the countryside; she expands inside, trying to absorb the landscape. It's another world; it's . . . yes, it's Teresa's world. *From Cabora the news of the saint spread throughout the country and then throughout the world. . . .* Across these expanses she probably rode her chestnut horse, making it gallop wildly until both of them, beast and amazon, were exhausted. She feels the emotion, she imagines the muscular animal transporting her as if they were flying toward the aggressive spirituality of the mountains; through her pores she soaks in the indomitable will of the prairie, the crude, strong vegetation, the sun that envelopes that world in an incomparable luminosity reflected by the white dust of the ground, the almost white grass, the limpid, limitless sky. *When she came to, she thought she was inspired by divine voices and that she possessed extraordinary faculties; from then on, she exercised her power of suggestion to cure people, and she devoted her time to performing miracles. . . .*

They arrive at a fork in the road; there are two signs. To the right one travels to Quiriego; on the left, the faded letters say "Cabora." She cannot believe what she reads. As if she had waited her whole life to see that dilapidated sign, she is overcome by an emotion that chokes her. At that instant, Javier puts his hand on her shoulder and gestures toward the left; she trembles. She turns the car slowly and heads for Cabora. *Watch Cabora; keep me informed. P.D.*

 # XIV

As she was experiencing death for the second time, she would remember another death and subsequent burial; that of Doña

Rosaura. After she had given the letter to Anastasio, Teresa went to spread the news, which was received with the customary solemnity and the corresponding joy: there would be ceremonies and festivities for two days! Doña Rosaura, being the oldest in the settlement, was very highly respected. Teresa joined the retinue of women who were going to prepare the deceased for her party. Since Doña Rosaura hadn't married, they couldn't bury her in her bridal gown as was the custom, but had to honor her as a child saint. They chose a simple, blue cotton dress that made her look almost like a little girl lying there on the mat of reeds and sticks that was used to carry the deceased to their grave. They tied her hands over her chest with a ribbon that was also blue, tenderly placed a small pillow of the same color under her head, and improvised an altar on the table with two candles and an image of the Virgin of Guadalupe. From the communal house they brought the usual objects for the ceremony: the eight candles that should burn around the beloved dead person during the rituals, the drum and flute that would accompany the songs and dances, and a sprig of mature wheat that they placed in her hands as a symbol of her long life.

When the cowhands returned from Cabora, they began the procession that would wind silently and solemnly through the whole settlement in two long lines, up to the house of the deceased, where the women were busy making coffee and tortillas. First they stretched the little balls of dough with their hands, then on their forearm, and finally on their thighs until they reached the required size and an almost transparent thinness. Once cooked on the flat griddle, the tortillas were folded in four and kept hot inside a huge basket, next to which sat an enormous pot of boiling coffee. When the procession arrived, carrying the small wooden cross to mark the grave, night had already spread its darkness over the marchers.

A cousin of the deceased and six companions initiated the ceremony by placing two lances made of mesquite branches in the form of an X at the foot of the mat. Immediately the women knelt around the deceased while the men began to file past, one by one, saying farewell with the sign of the cross. Teresa, who was close to the head of the mat, noticed that Doña Rosaura was already beginning to stink. Nobody else seemed to realize it. Outside they lit the twelve bonfires that were to burn for the two nights and one day that the ceremony would last, while the guests—some holding candles in their hands to illuminate the way for the spirit and others lighting firecrackers at irregular intervals to push the soul toward heaven—ate, drank coffee, sang psalms in their Mayo language, danced to the melancholic rhythm of the flute and drum, or were busy swinging reed rods to stave off the demons who might try to enter the defenseless body of Doña Rosaura, stiff with that incommensurable patience of death and stinking more and more with each passing hour as the sun rose and set again.

At dawn of the second day, Don Ramiro began to play a funeral march. It was time for the burial: Doña Rosaura's soul was well on its way to heaven, and they had successfully combated all the demons that wanted to possess her body. One by one the attendants filed past the foot of the mat for the last time, to give thanks to the deceased for the occasion to celebrate such a worthy death.

At nine in the morning four men and four women raised the decomposing body, placed it next to the grave, and untied the hands, which immediately flung out wide to both sides as if Doña Rosaura were still alive and wished to offer everyone a heartfelt hug. When she was deposited in the tomb, her mouth joggled open and her head slipped to one side; nobody bothered to close or straighten anything but they did place the little pillow under her head, apparently more concerned about her comfort than about her physical appearance. Then all seemed to be in a hurry to finish their task. The first shovelful of dirt fell directly on her face, entering her mouth and her ear, and that was the signal for them to use their hands and feet to help fill the grave as soon as possible, as if the deceased suddenly embarrassed them. They had no sooner finished than they turned and disappeared in the direction of their homes.

Teresa remained a while at the grave, contemplating the small cross on the pile of dirt. Rather than sad, she felt empty, as though everything she had experienced until then—joy, disillusionment, fantasy, disappointment—had been buried there with the dead woman. Abruptly she realized that she ought to prepare to leave and she was certain, without knowing why, that her father would send for her soon. Slowly, using her index finger, she wrote in the loose earth: "Here lies Doña Rosaura, Teresa Urrea's teacher." Then she went to the waterhole, washed her skirt and blouse, and bathed herself with utmost care, scraping the calluses on her feet with a stone, and scrubbing behind her ears with dry grass to be sure she was clean. When her clothes had dried, she changed, tied her hair with a ribbon, and went to the outskirts of Aquihuiquichi, where she sat down to wait. When the foreman of Cabora arrived, she climbed up on the back of his horse, held on to his waist, and without looking back abandoned Aquihuiquichi forever.

It was a triumphant journey, the culmination of a will that she had exercised over her circumstances for many years, proof that it was possible to forge the future according to her own desires. Since she believed she was made in the image of Don Tomás, she had no fear or doubts about her new life. She felt she had every right to be his daughter: the rest was merely a long awaited change in residence. Fantasy and reality were merging. Teresa, having just turned sixteen, held in her hands the reins of her life.

For Don Tomás it hadn't been so simple. When he read the brief letter, the determination and confidence of the young girl, who dared to use his last name without his having bestowed it upon her, caused him such a pleasant surprise that he laughed and thought, "She's like me." Without pondering any further, he ordered Miguel to go get her. As soon as the foreman left, the order he had given so lightly began to gnaw at him. He felt weighted down with bad omens, premonitions, doubts, and fears about the imminent encounter. He was afraid he had taken on the

burden of a white Indian, ill bred, ignorant, and dirty, who would
be an embarrassment in Cabora, so he did what he always did
whenever he didn't know what to do: he set out precipitously for
Alamos and left the problem for others to solve. He gave a strict
order to Huila:

"Disinfect her," he said and took off on his chestnut stallion.

Huila was waiting for her at the doorway. She was a tall, thin
woman of undefinable age, but well past her prime. She always
wore black, which gave her the appearance of an enormous vulture. Her face was a whirl of wrinkles scarcely punctuated by two
small, lively eyes and a big nose. When she held still she could
stand erect and firm, but as soon as she walked she did so with a
strange hobble due to an old lesion in her left leg. Thus she
looked like an enormous rat trudging clumsily around the ranch.

"Welcome, Miss Teresa," she said as Miguel helped her down
from the horse. It was the first time anyone had called her "miss."
"We were expecting you."

The "we" included Gabriela, whose shyness had kept her
waiting in the living room. But, as soon as she saw Teresa, she
burst out laughing.

"You must be my new daughter," she said, taking her hand
and guiding her into the house. "Huila! Why didn't you tell me
that we were the same age?"

Teresa, who was unfamiliar with the pleasure of laughing at
simple things, felt suddenly intimidated. Her contemporary could
have been from another planet, with her fine clothes and elegant
hairdo. She turned to Huila and asked about Don Tomás. At once
the old woman took command and, ignoring the adamant
protests of Teresa, who swore she had bathed herself thoroughly,
she set about following the peremptory orders of the boss.

For two hours Teresa was subjected to a process of transformation that went from delight to torture. Huila was worse than
an English nanny. She submerged her in a tub of hot water,
kneaded her as if she were preparing bread for the oven, scoured
her three times with a scrub brush, soaped her, rinsed her off, and

disinfected her until she tingled from head to toe. That was the delight; the rest was torture.

Once she was dry, Huila proceeded to insert her in an endless array of strange clothing that Teresa was sure would render her completely immobile: silk stockings, a corset, slips bordered with fringes, and finally a floor-length white dress with a thousand buttons up the back. All those garments restricted her, squeezed her, hardly let her breathe; she remembered with a certain nostalgia the cool freedom of the native skirts, but she didn't protest. Above all, she wanted to learn, to know what it meant to be a "young lady"; underneath her discomfort there was a gnawing curiosity to see her new image, but Huila said no, not until they finished.

After dressing her, Huila seated her in a chair and began to arrange her hair. The scissors appeared and she had bangs, the curling iron and she had ringlets; the ribbons and hairpins and that whole universe of waves and coils were fastened on the top of her head. She thought that they had finished, but the worst was yet to come. Huila took out a pair of dress shoes with heels and, in spite of Teresa's violent protests, she forced them on her. Now she didn't have a centimeter of freedom; she was immobilized. Her toes, accustomed to spreading out comfortably on the ground, were cramped and shoved on top of each other inside the two white prisons. That was martyrdom. From discomfort it progressed to burning, from there to outright pain, and finally she couldn't feel anything.

"I think they died," she said, looking mournfully at Huila.

"What did?"

"My toes."

"Silly girl, you just have to walk around a little. You'll get used to it."

Teresa stood up shakily and tried to take a few steps; her ankles, surprised by their new angle, buckled in brazen disobedience to the will that demanded firmness of them. Huila had to hold on to her so she wouldn't fall down. She felt ridiculous and humiliated; tears pressed against her eyes. It was turning out to be so complicated, whereas in her fantasy it had all seemed so simple.

At that moment Gabriela entered and, seeing her swaying back and forth, started to laugh and gave her a hug.

"You're new at this!" she said to her tenderly. "You look beautiful, but you have to learn how to walk. Look, put down the point and your heel at the same time, like so, taking little steps," and holding tightly to her hand, she instructed her in the proper management of feminine footwear. Teresa felt as if she were walking along the edge of a precipice.

On the day of her second death she would remember that first pair of shoes. It was the only thing that she never got used to. From then on, any excuse to take off her shoes was welcome, and she did so during almost all the important moments of that life and of her other life also. She took them off to ride horseback and to play the guitar, under the table during dinner, and for the more difficult cures; she took them off during the long train trip when she was exiled, and she was always barefoot during Lauro Aguirre's subversive meetings as she painted the rebels' faces black; she almost never used them in Solomonville in spite of the cold, and she took them off to run after Guadalupe Rodríguez on the train track and on the day she received her first kiss from John Van Order and immediately after the beauty contest in New York; barefoot she had given birth to her two daughters; barefoot she set out to save Don Simón the night of the flood in Clifton, and barefoot she awaited her second death so they would bury her like that, according to her instructions. But that first day in Cabora she had to put up with those glorified miniature coffins on her feet until it was time to sleep.

Gabriela patiently led her to her room, where she had a full-length mirror. Teresa didn't recognize herself. She was someone else. She was Miss Urrea from head to foot. All the humiliations and discomfort disappeared before the reality of her transformation. She didn't even worry about the fact that the dress emphasized the breasts she had desperately tried to hide for so long, or that it pulled in the waist she hadn't even noticed until that moment. She couldn't stop looking at herself; it was as if she were looking at somebody else and wishing to be like her; she was prettier than anyone she had ever seen. She liked herself so much that she was overjoyed; she hugged Gabriela, she hugged Huila, she hugged herself and, forgetting that she didn't even know how to walk with the new shoes, she danced around the room, thinking how surprised Don Tomás would be that night.

As for Don Tomás, he traveled the whole road from Alamos to Cabora struggling with doubt and fear. First he hoped that Teresa suddenly had refused to come to Cabora, but he discarded that idea. Then he thought that perhaps she would have already fallen asleep by the time he arrived so at least he could postpone the dreaded encounter until the next day. He implored the unknown powers of heaven that Miguel hadn't carried out the order he had given so thoughtlessly, but when he got there and heard the happy laughter of three women in the dining room, he readied himself to face the inevitable.

They had just dined on empanadas and *atole,* and they were chatting cheerfully around the table. Gabriela had taken on the task of explaining to Teresa the routine and customs of Cabora, preparing her for the authoritarianism of her father, who exercised an absolute dominion over everything that happened on the ranch. She explained to her that he was a good man as long as nobody crossed him; he was generous in his own way; he drank but he almost never got drunk, and when he did so he shut himself up in the library; he wasn't very affectionate and he didn't like to be pampered, but he did want his every need fulfilled, and immediately. She told her something about her own relationship with him, something that hinted at her immense solitude and spiritual affliction. She insinuated that Don Tomás was emotionally inaccessible, he spoke very little except when there were visitors, and he was rather serious and introverted, dedicating his life to the ranch above all else, including his family. She informed her of his institutional relationship with Loreto and the seven children; she told her that Don Tomás rarely became enraged, but when he did he became violent and he was someone to fear; he didn't believe in God or the saints, he cursed the clergy, and he only spoke of politics with his friend Don Lauro because they were both 100 percent anti-Porfirians. She had just added that he was a real womanizer and then, realizing what she had said, she looked apprehensively at Teresa. Both she and Huila laughed. At that moment Don Tomás appeared in the doorway.

Gabriela stood up at once and took his arm. Teresa and Huila stood up also. Teresa noticed the timid way the young wife greeted him, lowering her gaze as if she were afraid of being rejected, and she chose to look him straight in the eye. He returned her look, and Teresa was surprised to perceive in his green eyes a profound yearning for affection. Instinctively she approached and kissed him on the cheek. Immediately he began to shout orders so as to cover up a sudden wave of tenderness.

"Josefina! Bring the cognac! Gabriela, the guitar! Huila, don't just stand there like a scarecrow, go get some glasses. This we have to celebrate. You don't find such a beautiful daughter just any day. So your name is Teresita. Let's see, let me look at you, turn around. Not bad, not bad at all. Sit over there; no, better sit by me so I can ask you questions. So I have a daughter. Gabriela, you can tell your father that I don't envy him any more!" Gabriela blushed and lowered her eyes, but Don Tomás didn't even notice. He kept shouting, exclaiming, ordering, until finally he sat down at the head of the table, at last in control of himself.

That night they partied as they would many times throughout the first months. It was an idyllic period, complete happiness. Life had bestowed upon the inhabitants of Cabora the fulfillment of all their dreams: Don Tomás had a daughter, Gabriela a companion, and Teresa was finally Miss Urrea. There was merrymaking at the ranch day after day. Don Tomás didn't tire of inviting friends and neighbors so they could meet his daughter; Gabriela was so involved in organizing parties that she forgot about her fears, her solitude, and even her sins; Teresa became the queen of the castle.

Cabora overflowed with songs and joy. Don Tomás and
Teresa engaged in long conversations until the wee hours of the
morning, during which they gradually got to know each other.
She confessed that ever since she was seven years old she had
wanted to come and live with him; he admitted that he had
always missed having a daughter. She soon realized that his
authoritarianism was mainly defensive; he noticed that her gaze
was like that of a man, direct and penetrating; they both discovered that they shared an intelligence that differentiated them from
the rest and isolated them in entertaining discussions about life,
religion, and the country's politics. Teresa learned a lot during
that early stage. Don Tomás wanted to teach her everything he
knew: he was delighted to have somebody with whom he could
share his opinions. Little by little he was discovering more of himself in her than he had ever found in his other children.

Teresa was enthralled, wanting to learn every detail of his life,
to understand every thought. Thus she found out that, according
to her father, religion served to oppress the poor, the clergy lived
off the misery and fear of others, Porfirio Díaz was consolidating
an ironclad dictatorship, all the governors had sold out, the high
military officials were taking land from the Indians and creating
enormous haciendas, the country was selling out to the foreign-
ers, Don Tomás harbored Yaqui rebels in order to ensure peace in
Cabora, which he loved above all things, Don Lauro Aguirre spent
his life preaching revolutions, Doña Loreto rubbed elbows with
the high society in Alamos and was a close friend of the bishop,
deep down Doña Justina Almada was stingy and ambitious even
though she put on airs of a great lady, and Gabriela would always
be a child but he liked her that way. But most importantly, Teresa
learned to have her own way in spite of Don Tomás's orders, without his getting angry, sometimes without his even noticing.

Thus she was able to impose her will and ride bareback instead
of with that strange, useless saddle that "young ladies" used; she
managed to get everybody accustomed to seeing her barefoot
when she couldn't stand the shoes anymore; she convinced her

progenitor to let her call him "Don Tomás" because she felt strange calling him "father"; she began to address him in a familiar tone that none of his sons had ever employed, and she entered the library whenever she wanted to, even without an invitation. Although she realized that the enormous mustache, the shouts, and all that arrogance were covering up his fear of tenderness, it didn't occur to her then that he had a weak character. During those first months, Teresa saw in her father the strong man who was to protect her for life. Far from making her dependent, it made her feel more free as she herself imitated the leadership qualities that she thought she perceived in him.

Happiness spread throughout Cabora. That year there was no extreme heat and no drought; the cows gave birth to twin calves and had so much milk that it had to be distributed among the ranchhands. The workers' children became chubby and smiling; the women sang songs as they washed clothes; the harvests doubled, the grass grew thicker; the *huamúchiles* were laden with bittersweet fruit; the parrots kept up an unending and joyful chatter; water ran in the Cocoraqui Wash for three months in a row. Teresa completely forgot her previous life and set about administrating the new abundance at her pleasure. She grew in wisdom and in vanity under the constant attention of her father, in beauty and pride under Gabriela's care, in self-assurance and arrogance as she saw her most trivial desire fulfilled. She accepted without question the admiration and praise of all. She felt she had fulfilled her destiny.

XV

"We're almost there," Gracia's voice reaches her as if from afar, hoarse and muted. Once more, the capsule of silence closes about them. The road is getting bumpier and she has to concentrate on driving. It seems as if time has stopped and everything exists only in dreams. *People who find themselves in her presence say they feel a special awe. . . .* A buzzard flies over the road and lights on top of the twisted branches of a dry tree. She doesn't think, she's all expectation. Heat makes the air seem scarce. Suddenly there is a small rise and then they are out on a wide plateau bordering the foothills of the mountain range.

"We're there," announces Javier, and she shakes herself out of her reverie and looks around. There is nothing. Cabora no longer exists. It's a faded sign by the road, a space doomed to oblivion; it's absence itself. She stops the car. *I ordered the arrest of the Urreas, father and daughter, whom I have sent to Guaymas, either to be kept there or to be imprisoned somewhere else. . . .* She feels like crying. *For now it wouldn't be prudent to allow them to return to Cabora under any pretext; it would be like authorizing the fanatics to continue carrying out their farces. . . .* It's all been in vain.

"There's nothing here," she says in a husky voice.

"Don't you feel it? Don't you feel it?" Gracia asks mockingly.

"What?"

"Her presence. Isn't that what you expected? Didn't you want to find Teresita here? Don't you feel her presence? Or were you deceiving yourself?" *The false saint continues to preach her false doctrines to a few gullible people. . . .* Javier looks at her in silence.

"I don't feel a thing," she responds. The derisive expression on Gracia's face bothers her; she doesn't understand Gracia's violent rejection of her. Why can't she perceive her profound disillusionment?

All is lost: lost documents, lost Cabora, lost identity. Nothing makes sense. She wants to breathe, to think, and go back to something that was trying to emerge as she was driving along the road and then was cut short. She wishes she could be alone. Slowly she gets out of the car; her eyes wander across the desolate expanse of landscape. She leans on the car a minute. The others get out. There's not even the wisp of a breeze. The sun is high above them.

To the right are three huts; in front of them two little boys with bloated bellies are playing in the dirt. On the other side a small concrete construction sports a battered sign: "The Little Miracle Grocery Store." *In Cabora the miracle has been reborn right now in the nineteenth century; for the nonbelievers, the saint is capable of making hair grow on bald people!* . . . It's closed. "Teresa isn't here," she thinks, feeling like the penitent who discovers after a long wait that heaven doesn't exist. *Yesterday young Teresa Urrea arrived in Arizona from her own country, where she says she was persecuted by government agents.* . . . So much wasted time, on such an untenable dream! She has arrived at nowhere, which is all that is left of Teresita's world . . . *after the flood four Yaqui prophets joined a group of angels and walked along the border of their territory, preaching and singing.* . . . an extensive plateau; beyond that, the dry bed of the Cocoraqui; on the far bank, the enormous *huamúchiles,* their roots reaching deep down to the dampness, their tall branches sheltering the babble of small parrots, their knotted, grotesque trunks thickening in the shade . . . *they defined the dimensions of the Yaqui territory and established clear points of reference, starting at the mouth of the Cocoraqui Wash and marching to a point about sixty miles from what is now the ranch of Cabora; from there they headed toward Guaymas* . . . farther on, the peak of the hill called "Cerro de la Mina" on the right, the soft, round hills on the left, and in the middle, directly behind the trees, that strange formation that doesn't look like any other: a world without memory, a world that forgot Teresa Urrea long ago.

She looks at the bald hill that could be part of a moonscape. It has a reddish hue. *The saint performs all types of cures, using only red dirt and saliva as medicine.* . . . At its base are huge boulders, piled up haphazardly, creating enormous hollows. It's completely out of place. In the distance stands the steep mountain range that they had seen from the road and beyond that, Alamos, the ancient capital of the state of Occidente, where the rich paved the streets with gold ingots for their daughters' weddings; where Loreto established her court in the house called La Capilla and educated her sons in the Frenchified style of the period; where Teresita was condemned from the pulpit of the cathedral; where the families of high society sat in patios shaded by huge laurel trees in the summer, milking gossip and grazing on the destinies of others; where Don Tomás never felt comfortable; where Gabriela, afraid of scandal, refused to set foot; where Don Miguel Urrea had died, leaving his fortune to Doña Justina Almada, who invested it in charity and thus earned the title of benefactress of the city. *The city of Alamos has just suffered a grave loss with the death of the distinguished Doña Justina Almada, the widow of Miguel Urrea. . . .* What was left of all that? Nothing. *Owner of a substantial fortune, her main task was to take on charitable causes, and many families depended on her entirely because her generosity was inexhaustible. . . .* Now it was a colony of retired gringos who had reconstructed the old capital as a historical monument, a museum piece. Cabora had disappeared, Teresa was forgotten, and she herself was a useless accumulation of meaningless data.

What had she expected? Actually, she didn't have the slightest idea; she had never conceptualized it; she just knew that she expected something, not this, not this absence of traces, not in Cabora, the place where five thousand people had gathered on each of Teresita's birthdays; where day after day for two years the earth had been subjected to constant trampling by the needy, the curious, the ambitious, the impertinent, the doubters, indigenous dancers, tribal chiefs, dying old men, incurable drunks, crippled women, the lame, the lepers, the deaf, the blind, the fleabitten . . . *the rebels of Tomóchic surrendered their arms, knelt down, and sang praises to the so-called saint; when they discovered she wasn't there, they cried like children . . .* all looking for a miracle, a small one, a large one, or at least a little hope. Hadn't she come, also, hoping for a miracle? Hoping to see Cabora, to feel Teresa's mark on each rock, the magnetism of her presence in every inch of earth. There was nothing. *I am sorry to inform you that the tranquility of this state has been slightly disturbed, which is due exclusively to religious zealotry . . .* On the left, where Teresa's house was supposed to have been, just an open field; straight ahead, a slight hint of the Big House: a dirt path that seems to circumvent an old, half-buried wall. *Peace reigns in the country.* . . . She starts walking; Gracia and Javier follow her silently. Soon she stops by an insignificant piece of old wall that stands half a yard tall and about two yards long. At one place, the crumbling red bricks still form the crown of an arch, as if the house had been slowly sinking down into the earth, swallowing itself until it disappeared. In a few years there would be nothing left. Once again she perceives oblivion as something concrete and palpable, the only thing left in the end, after all. Human life seems like a sterile struggle against anonymity, its whole meaning summed up by the wall that is gradually disintegrating, returning to its origins, to dust and silence. That which once was, no longer is. *They say she is capable of dreaming the future, hearing voices from all over the world and traveling outside her body to wherever she wishes, but we have no proof of this because she looks like any other mortal.* . . . Teresa was dead, twice dead: first in body, then in history.

She turns her head slowly, her eyes full of tears, and encounters Javier contemplating her with an enigmatic smile. She is surprised to feel a sudden desire to lose herself in something tangible and human, to become oblivious to oblivion. *A man without faith is like a leaf in the wind.* She shakes her head and carefully passes her hand over the rough rocks of the crumbling wall.

"It makes me sad," she says. Crouching down, she picks up a smooth, round stone and throws it far away. She feels destitute. The abrupt return to reality has depressed her. *Young Teresa was never to return to her beloved Cabora; she would end her days far, far away.* . . . Gracia was right to be scornful: she was crazy; she was a poor, contemptible soul who had allowed herself to get carried away by an empty obsession. Coming here was insane. If she could just fall asleep and wake up again in her own apartment in Mexico City, alone, without problems. . . . *I am willing to grant all kinds of guarantees to those who repent of their rebellion and wish to return to peace; but those who insist on perpetuating the armed struggle will be treated without consideration and as enemies of public tranquility.* . . . She would look for a job. She would abandon this obsession.

"I think the sun is getting to me." Javier takes her by the arm. As they turn to go, a boy approaches, vacillating between wariness and daring.

"Do you want to hear about Teresita? I'll take you there, to Doña Josefa's; she tells the story and you give me some pesos, yes?"

◈ XVI

But the merrymaking had to end one day. Little by little Cabora returned to its routine. Don Tomás left early each morning to take care of the ranch; Gabriela spent hours praying in the chapel or organizing meals in the kitchen; Huila went back to her duties as healer, and Teresa was stuck with something called "idleness": she didn't have anything to do. The hours stretched out interminably in straight lines of boredom that disappeared later without leaving a trace, as if life were just one big yawn. That was completely unexpected. In the settlement there was always something to do, and if she didn't do it, it was because she didn't want to. If instead of washing clothes she went for a walk across the countryside, dreaming of Cabora, that wasn't idleness, it was building her future. If instead of watching the pot of beans she joined the cowhands, that wasn't idleness either, it was learning to play the guitar, sing, and be a man. Free time in the settlement always had a meaning, it was marching toward a goal. But the goal had been reached; the dream, fulfilled; illusion had become reality, and as always, reality didn't measure up.

All day long she paced back and forth in the house, waiting for Don Tomás to return. After so much festivity and flattery, the limitations and prohibitions commenced. Her movements were restricted to the house and the surrounding area; she was forbidden to speak with the cowhands, the foreman, the stable boy, and of course the laborers, unless Don Tomás was present and there was an imperative reason to do so; she could not walk alone outside the house, or ride alone, and even when accompanied, she could not go more than a quarter of a mile away from the ranch or approach the area where the men were working. In other words: a young lady either stayed inside or was accompanied by the appropriate person, who in her case was obviously her father since her "mother" was subject to the same rules. In regard to his rules, Don Tomás was categorical, and there was no argument worth considering; if Teresa tried to change his mind, he threatened her with possible Indian attacks and with stories of kidnappings and violent murders of women. Teresa didn't dare to refute him by reminding him of her origins because her "ladyhood" was still too recent. Therefore, she was reduced to roaming around the Big House. She began to ask herself what her role could be in that monotonous routine; the only answer she found was "being Don Tomás's daughter." But what did "being a daughter" mean? If you were the cook, like Josefina, you busied yourself all day with the meals; if you were the chamber maid, like Camilda, you were in charge of keeping everything clean; as a wife, Gabriela had to organize the housework, order the meals for the day, see that Camilda didn't forget to dust any of the furniture, and do the darning or embroidering on various useful items. But with the title of "daughter" she didn't seem to have any specific function beyond being attentive to her father. Finally, out of desperation, she decided to be Gabriela's helper, and she asked the young housewife to teach her how to darn and embroider.

It was useless, not because she refused to learn, but because she had the hands of a cowboy. Even though the rest of her was delicate and feminine, her hands belonged to another body: they were big, wide, and clumsy. They were good for collecting firewood in the hills, taming a horse, or playing the guitar, but with needle and thread they could not achieve anything. Gabriela doubled up with laughter at the sight of those rough hands whose strength bent the needles, tore the delicate cloth, and left the thread in a hopeless tangle. In the kitchen the same thing happened. As soon as she raised a finger to help, a dish fell as if by magic. If she picked up a knife, she knocked over the glass of water that was beside it. Her apron got hooked on the table and before she could unfasten it, it was torn. Josefina, fearing more serious disasters, respectfully kicked her out of her domain. Once again Teresa was left with nothing to do.

That was the signal for which Huila had been waiting. The old woman began to spy on her. As soon as she saw her yawning, she sat down beside her and commenced speaking of mysterious knowledge from beyond the grave, unusual stories told in the interstices of a dream, coded messages in the scribbles of desert beetles, flights of sinister birds that sketched in the sky secrets that only she could see. Teresa listened without understanding much, more eager to be entertained than to learn; they seemed to be the meaningless ramblings of a old age. Huila spoke to her of signs and portents, of predestined lives, of babies born with their eyes open, surrounded by a special luminosity; she explained that there were senses that the majority of people didn't have and that allowed one to smell life or death, listen to the voices carried by the wind, and see the future as clearly as the present. She seemed to be talking to herself, without addressing anyone in particular, weaving her strange stories into an enigmatic and intangible cloth, just to pass the time. Teresa allowed herself to be lulled by the old woman's strange voice, full of susurrations and hisses as if it came from somewhere deep in her body, a cave full of whispers that strung together those fantasies and united them all into one. Many times she didn't listen to the words, allowing herself to be caught up in them as if they weren't fragments of sound but interwoven colors in a somnolent, comforting blanket.

"What is Huila talking so much about?" Gabriela asked her one afternoon, and Teresa was surprised that she couldn't answer her: in truth, she didn't know what the old woman was talking about. She shrugged her shoulders. "She just rambles on about anything, I suppose," she said, thinking that perhaps it would be a good idea to listen more carefully.

That's how things were until boredom took over completely. When Don Tomás announced that he was leaving for Alamos for

his routine visit and would be absent all week, Teresa felt the
bottom drop out of her days: she wouldn't even have her father's
company in the evenings to distract her. By eleven o'clock in the
morning she had finished her brief routine of practicing the guitar and the hours stretched out ahead, loaded with drowsiness
and tedium. She was sitting on the patio, absentmindedly
watching the intricate swirlings of a fly, when Huila approached.

"Child, come with me."

Without questioning, Teresa got up and followed the old
woman. They walked toward the settlement of Cabora, where the
families of the most trusted ranchhands lived. It was the first time
she had approached a settlement since she had left Aquihuiquichi.
She was surprised to see everything clean, simple, and in order,
in contrast to her memories of clutter and filth. Outside of the
huts hung plants and flowers; the entrances were swept clean, the
branches and firewood carefully stacked beside the doors, the
pigs and chickens shut up in little corrals. Teresa was gripped by
a wave of nostalgia and tenderness instead of the old rejection
that she had felt in Tula's house. She recalled certain freedoms
that she had lost, a time in which her life had a goal that gave
meaning to everything else.

It was the first of many days that she would accompany Huila
on her visits to new mothers, people sick with consumption or
goiter, and children with diarrhea. As the healer administered
medicine and advice, relief and compassion to each patient,
Teresa observed how she managed hope and despair, life and
death, the slow recuperation of health or the gradual acceptance
of death. One day she began to perceive a strange odor during the
ministrations. It had nothing to do with beans, earth, or sweat. It
was something else, and as soon as she smelled it she felt queasy
and became quite upset. The smell was independent from the disease: it seemed the same at a birth or a departure from life, in a
serious illness or a case of hiccups. It was an acrid scent, pristine,
like a swamp that decomposes and gestates life, a mixture of fresh
clay and acidic beans. She couldn't define it, but it produced in

her an almost uncontrollable desire to do something with her hands, anything, tie knots, knead the earth, caress, squeeze, sink them into some thick, dark substance. When she told this to Huila, the old woman looked at her and then continued walking.

"I thought I was wrong about you, that you would never smell it," she said.

"But what is it?" she insisted. Huila stopped.

"It's the spume of life," she replied.

After that Teresa forgot about boredom forever. She wanted to learn Huila's secrets: she asked her to teach her how to heal.

She started by memorizing the herbs and formulas, what diseases they alleviated, how to prepare and administer them. In the little room in the back of the Big House, Huila began to explain things to her.

"Three little sticks of *goma de Sonora,* boiled in water, a pinch of anise seed, cinnamon bark, and a little mint, all aged with spirits and stored in a well-covered clay pot. It's good for dysentery and delirium. . . .

Teresa carefully repeated all of the instructions three times in order to remember them: *molanisco* root beaten to a pulp and steeped in cold water on nights of a full moon, to be drunk while the patient is in the shade: it stops diarrhea, induces sleep, diminishes hiccups, and prevents compulsive blinking. Powder from a dried *balburia* root mixed with tallow, applied to the temples, cures a headache. Fresh mesquite leaves pulverized and soaked in water and urine from a newborn boy, for migraine. For stubborn pains, *huisache* bark made into a pulp and soaked three days in urine from an adult male, to be plastered on the forehead.

For typhoid fever, a tea made from the leaves of the immortelle plant. For scarlet fever, the yellow root of the *mochi* plant after it's been moistened with dew: it's given to the fasting patient for three days, three times a day; on the fourth day you abandon the brew and give the patient a thick drink made from corn flour, with three raw eggs. Hallucinations are cured with tea made from the stems and leaves of the *lía* plant; rattlesnake bites on the ankle, with milkweed. If the bite is on the thigh or the arm, all you can do is pray unless you have on hand the following concoction: the bile from the spleen of a dead rattler, mixed with alcohol and allowed to sit for twenty days; this is applied to the bite, taking care that the patient avoids drinking liquids during the treatment to slow down the blood running through the body and dispersing the venom.

For mange and some wounds, the juice of the century plant; for cuts and bruises, *hierba del manzo* with rosemary, *hierba colorada,* and *alucema* seed; to prevent whooping cough, a bracelet made of a calf's tendon, to be worn on the child's wrist; for frights, a tea made of the *torito* plant; for smallpox, a tea of made of dyewood or of the excrement of a *pinacate* beetle; for a cough, a brew of *torote* bark; for flatulence, mesquite bark boiled well in water and drunk at dawn; for mule kicks, the resurrection plant: this is placed in water, and when it begins to grow, the patient drinks the water; if the plant doesn't unfold, the patient is going to die.

Chest and back pains are treated by rubbing with lime mixed with urine; for fainting spells, a brazilwood stick with mesquite leaves; for rabies, a rubdown with saliva over the whole body and complete fasting; for an abortion, a tea made of corkwood, taking care that the mother doesn't die during the subsequent vomiting; for ground-in filth, a good bath; for gunshots, grass and dirt inserted into the wound to stop the bleeding. . . .

Teresa immersed herself in these lessons, memorizing Huila's words. All that had previously seemed mere adornment or bothersome in nature was being transformed into life-giving substances. Plants, weeds, cacti, bark, insects, animals and their excretions, all melted into one vital substance, a miraculous paste. What usually killed, under certain circumstances and with particular treatments, brought back life; the dregs became indispensable in critical cases, dirt cured, and hunger scared off sure death. Teresa felt that the world was becoming a purposeful whole, a cycle in which life and death were no more than the confluence of certain elemental juices in a constant flux with no beginning or end.

As she began to comprehend that previously unknown universe, the rounds with Huila took on new meaning. She stopped seeing sick and healthy people; she even stopped seeing humans and began to perceive, in each case, an intricate play of interdependent elements: a queasy stomach wedded to the delicate veins of the immortelle plant; a tenacious insomnia calmed by linden-blossom tea; a bleeding artery combined with tepid earth; a fatal cough entwined with the dry tendon of a calf. All that heretofore had seemed separate, different, distanced now flowed together, joining urine with forehead, beetle with wound, bark with eye, in an endless ebb and flow of pure life.

"Or pure death," said Huila. "You have to have good sense to distinguish between them. There's no use treating a patient who already has the shine of death in his eyes; but if that shine is from a fever, it can be cured. The important thing is not to be deceived, so you can free the patient from his illusions."

She explained that those with a light fever were more prone to think they were dying, while the true moribund always harbored the hope of a rapid cure.

"You have to help the moribund patient to die well so he goes peacefully and takes all of his belongings with him: his shadow, his anguish, his guilt; it all has to be in place when death arrives so that it doesn't stay behind, roaming around, bothering his family. And on the other hand, you have to take away the curable patient's conviction that he is dying, which—who knows why— gets into his head and sticks there."

Then she spoke to her about life, death, and reality.

"As my teacher Apolinio said: reality is a constant transformation where nothing changes; everything is part of the same thing. The problem isn't life and death, but the fact that as we speak we separate them. You have to learn to recognize things without naming them in order to perceive their unity. As soon as we give them names, we're left with just little orphaned pieces, so isolated that they don't mean anything. Look, if we call this 'plant,' that 'cow,' and the other 'manure,' and what's underneath it 'earth,' we're going to spend the rest of our lives trying to put them back together again so they mean something, and then we make it even more complicated by saying that the cow eats the plant and shits manure that becomes earth. Understand?"

Teresa was listening. It all had something to do with Don Tomás's long explanations of cause and effect, but it was like trying to see it in reverse. For Huila everything was very simple. It was a question of distancing yourself a little from what we call "reality" and looking at it in another way; for Don Tomás it was very complicated: one had to go deeper and deeper into "reality" in order to discover its ultimate explanations.

"The problem, child, is words: language doesn't bring us nearer to reality, it hides it. Just look: we take 'corn' and 'grinding stone' and 'hand' and 'water' and 'limestone' and we mix them all up. Do we have corngrindingstonehandwaterlimestone? No. We have 'tortilla,' another little orphaned piece detached from its origin. Then we join tortilla-mouth-stomach-intestine and what do we have? Excrement! And we've lost the thread again. Apolinio taught me all this, poor soul; he's probably become carrionbone-dustlaughtershadow."

Understanding that didn't mean repeating it with words but, rather, seeing it: it was the secret of healing, the secret of life and death. She learned to look behind the names of things, to look for the threads that joined them with the rest of life, and to discover hidden meanings in order to turn around the intellect, evade reason, free herself from language, and see that indivisible flowing that, according to her teacher, was the true reality.

As her new senses sharpened, she could distinguish the ailments from the moment she came in contact with the patient. Hepatitis didn't smell anything like hysteria; the hands of an insomniac would sweat; those of a drunk were dry. Scarlet fever produced arrhythmic palpitations and typhoid a kind of cardiac arrest; pregnancy smelled like earth in the abdomen, whereas a kidney infection produced an unmistakable odor of urine on the breath. Huila also explained to her that there were incurable diseases: prolonged solitude, for example, became a vice; forgetfulness left enduring marks; fear of life or of death was one of the most pertinacious ailments, together with despair and bad character.

She learned as well what time of day to collect the ingredients for the remedies, from what part of the plant, and how mature the bush should be. Some could be found in the vicinity; others came from far away and had to be requested through an elaborate chain of people in the know. One had to tell so-and-so to tell Juan or Pedro or María, who would contact Diego or Lupe or Rafael to request the root or the little bone or the stem from way off in the settlement of Yoquibampo, or the Sierra del Bacatete, or beyond the Río Fuerte. She learned which remedies could be prepared in advance and saved, and which had to be mixed at the last moment. She learned to distinguish the urine of an adolescent from that of an adult, or a woman's from a man's, to avoid inappropriate mixtures, and how to stimulate her saliva for full-body rubs. But above all, she learned the secret of avoiding contagion by evil spirits.

"Pity," said Huila, "only aggravates the illness and makes it extremely contagious. You can't heal when you feel pity because it's a locked-in sentiment, merely a twisted reflection of the fear that you feel for yourself. Beware of pity! There's nothing that opens the door to disease more quickly than the fear of suffering or the fear of dying."

Teresa became Huila's helper. She accompanied her on every visit, whether it was to the settlement or to a nearby village. It was her job to calm the hysteria of women in labor, quiet the tremors of feverish children, alleviate the pain of broken bones. She used her hands, eyes, and voice and gradually discovered strange healing powers in a caress, an appropriate word, or in looking straight into the patients' eyes and absorbing their anguish. The practice exhausted her. Huila said that she tried too hard, that she still had much to learn.

One afternoon in early September they were preparing remedies when a ranchhand came running. Tencha was dying in
childbirth; she had labored for days and the child wasn't appearing. They gathered what they needed, climbed onto the wagon,
and headed for the settlement. When they arrived, the mother
was in the throes of death; they could hear the cries from far
away; and when they entered the hut Teresa perceived, as with
Doña Rosaura, the unmistakable stench of impending death: it
was almost unbearable. She was seized by a sudden dizziness and
the room seemed to grow dark. Huila immediately entered into
battle; Teresa, controlling herself, sat at the head of that body
twisted in pain. She felt another dizzy spell and thought that she
was going to faint when she heard the shout.

"Help me!"

Suddenly she blacked out. When she came to, she was outside in the wagon in the shade of a mesquite, with Huila sitting at
her side, waiting. She felt profoundly ashamed and covered her
face so she wouldn't see her teacher. Huila lowered her hands and
stared at her. She had a strange look.

"What happened, child?"

"Oh, Huila! I don't know. I think I'm no good at this.
Suddenly everything went dark and I felt as if I were dying, I
couldn't breathe, and when you cried out to me to help you, I
fainted."

"I didn't cry out; it must have been her. I could feel her dying
in my hands; there was nothing I could do."

"Then, she died? And the baby?"

"You remember nothing?"

"How can you expect me to remember? I fainted. I couldn't
even watch what you were doing."

"I didn't do anything. You did it, child." Now Huila was looking at her with a mixture of amazement and sorrow. Teresa felt a
chill. "You didn't faint until it was all over. When death entered
that woman, you leapt upon her like a cat, took her face in your
hands, and shouted, 'Look at me!' and then Tencha, who had

already left us, opened her eyes and fixed them on you and her whole body became lax and still, all soft and pliant, as if she were simply going to sleep. Little by little what had been clenched shut began to open, and the baby, caught before by the spasm, was able to descend and be born, but so slowly that he seemed to come into the world through a strange, silent dance, and that silence, child, seemed to emanate from you. As soon as the baby cried, you collapsed, but by then the mother was resting. I left her with her baby and set about attending to you out here in the shade, where you could get some air. I've never seen anyone so pale. You gave me a good scare: I thought you were dying. There's something strange about you, child, something that not even I can explain."

Teresa was filled with fear. All this was linked to Manuel's paralysis, the saliva that didn't dry, the gaze that nobody could sustain, to all that was abnormal. She heard the echoes of Tula's deranged shouts, she felt again the terror when her cousin tumbled to the ground, and she realized that once more her existence was threatened by something that was beyond her control. She began to tremble, feeling trapped by dark forces that seemed to shape her destiny. She looked at Huila, but in the other's eyes there was only an opaque silence: the teacher was leaving her alone in the face of fear. In a rush, all the lessons learned about life and death came back to her, and suddenly she thought she understood: she had absorbed Tencha's death and now carried it inside herself. Now she was the one who was going to die.

▣ XVII

Doña Josefa lives on the other side of the Cocoraqui Wash, in a small hut with a low door, one window, a dirt floor, an aluminum vat full of dirty clothes, a cot made of sticks and a worn-out mat, an image of the Virgin of Guadalupe, and an unlit devotional candle. As they approach they see her hunched up on the cot like a pile of bones on the verge of collapsing. Her long, sparse, gray hair is twisted into a disheveled braid; her dirty fingernails are broken and uneven; her whole body dispels a disagreeable, rotting odor. The boy enters first, approaches the old woman, and shouts in her ear:

"Doña, these people here want you to tell them about Teresita!" And like a robot starting up, she raises her arms stiffly and turns her opaque eyes toward the source of the sound.

"Yes, yes, Teresita, well, you see, I didn't know her, but they shared many memories with me, and since there was only one house around here . . ." The old woman's voice is dull, scarcely audible. The boy pulls up two chairs for Gracia and her; Javier has remained outside. "Afterward you pay me," he whispers in her ear. "The ruins are over there, I'm not sure where, the Santinis had a card with a picture of the house on it, such pretty arches, and they say Teresa was blond, I saw the photo but I don't remember anymore, and that she was pretty, and they started to take the house apart, that's why there's nothing left, they carried it away. piece by piece, the wood, the stones, the bricks, the floor was so pretty, red adobe tile, they carried it away to Quiriego, to Ures, to Alamos, to the settlements of Jambiolobampo, Core, Vizcárraga, Aquihuiquichi, Agiabampo, Sonábari, way over yonder, that was a long time ago, they took it to Baboyahui, they came and went, piece by piece, at first they'd say because Teresita sat here, or here she prayed, or this stone was at the foot of her bed, or here's where she knelt down, that's how they took with them the good luck, the little miracle, the hope, the stone against the evil eye, the brick so the baby would be born right; later they took it without the memories, because the wood was still good for making a door, the brick for a kitchen, the stones for a wall, but I only saw, I told you, one picture of Teresita, and I remember what they told me, they say she was a child, that she was a saint, that she showed up here in Cabora and old Don Tomás, the father, was all upset, because I met Don Tomás, the son, but Don Tomás, the father, was all upset when Teresita came around, and they say there was a cripple there in the settlement, just let me remember now, I'm going to tell you straight. So they say that Don Tomás was all upset because his cattle were dying of thirst, and Teresita says to him, 'Papá, why are you sad?' and Don Tomás answers her: 'How else am I going to feel when my cattle are dying for lack of water?' and she says to him: 'Look, don't be sad. By tomorrow there'll be a spring and it will never dry up,' and the spring's called Tasilobampo and to this day it gives water, and they say that there are no stones around here, they say, and that's why they take the stones to where they live, over to the other side, by the mine, and today there's nothing left. I got to see the rooms of wood, the arches were still of carved stone, and one day they came carrying a crippled guy, four of them, and he was all scrawny, and, well, he came in good faith so Teresita would make a miracle for him, and he comes and says: 'Good day, miss,' and she says, 'Good day to you, little brother,' and then 'What's wrong with you?' and 'Oh, Teresa, if you could only see how sick I am!' he said. 'Really? Well, you're not sick at all,' and she looks at him close up and she's standing in the doorway, that's how they told it to me, and that door was taken away by someone from near Alamos, and Don Tomás, the son, who was my boss, did his best but he couldn't keep the cattle because the ranch was falling apart with all the stones they were carrying away, and then Teresita said to the cripple, 'Let's see, give me your hand; see, there's nothing wrong with you,' and Teresita grabbed him by the arms and he stood up quick as a flash and she took him to where she had an altar and from there the cripple left walking on his own two feet and afterward the people took the stones and carried them away, took more stones and carried them away. . . ."

She's not listening any more; a fly buzzes around the room with a monotonous hum; she thinks vaguely, as if from a distance, that tomorrow she will leave this place, go back to Mexico City: there's nothing here. It's all been insanity. The old woman doesn't stop; she weaves and unravels memories of memories of memories of others, for herself, for the silence; memories full of loose threads, with endless strands, lost roads, weaving the design of oblivion.

". . . but no, no matter how hard Don Tomás, the son, tried to rebuild everything, they kept taking away the stones, and then the troops came by and they said that the Revolution was coming, and the people came, that's why Don Tomás, the old one, left, because they wanted to arrest Teresita and the Tomochitecs came to meet her, but they didn't let them because they were going to take her away and, well, they were her followers and they suffered for it, and Don Porfirio himself, there in Mexico City, wanted to take her away to somewhere else, because she cured the Indians, just think about it, miss, the house was so pretty and they carried it away, for the town, for the Revolution, for their huts, for their own asses, and then, just be a little patient and I'm going to tell it just like they told me. . ."

That voice begins to reach her from far away, like the buzz of the fly, wrapped in fog, disjointed, a string of fragments out of place and full of images, a movie voice from a broken-down camera; the images recur, pile up on each other, muddled, incoherent.

"And one time they brought her a sick girl by force, and Teresa, seeing that they had forced her to come, said, 'You don't want me to heal you, right?' and the girl made a face, and then Teresa asked her, 'Do you like flowers?' and the girl said yes, and Teresita said, 'Well, you'll see what I'm going to do since you didn't come here in good faith: tomorrow, when you're in your house, your friends are going to crown you with flowers,' and that's what happened, for when she got back to Barebampo she died and all her friends brought her flowers, and the thing is that Teresita gave rubbings with saliva, and if she didn't rub she spit, and every day she went up to the bald hill, and there was a little cave up there and from there she got the earth that she rubbed with, and when they brought her the cripple who had only seen her in a photogra—"

Surprised by the sudden silence, she opens her eyes and sees that the old woman has fallen asleep. She turns her head; Gracia is looking out the window.

"Let's go," she says. "Doña Josefa, Doña Josefa . . ."

The boy runs in.

"Doña Josefa!" he shouts. "The ladies are leaving." The old woman raises her head. ". . . and I'm going to tell you straight, just like they told me, they said they carried away the house piece by piece, that Teresita was a seer, that . . ."

Thanking her, she places a bill in the old woman's hand and a smaller one in the boy's hand. Outside Javier is waiting, looking into the distance, toward the strange hill. Behind them, the old woman continues to unravel the tattered fabric of her memories.

They walk toward the shade of the enormous *huamúchiles*, and for a while they listen to the chattering of the parrots. Javier picks up a pod from the ground and opens it; inside the seeds are wrapped in a white, fleshy substance. He offers her one; it has a sour-sweet taste, refreshing; she has the sensation that she is repeating something only experienced in dreams. What had the old woman said about the hill? She almost didn't listen at the end, something about a cave, the earth that Teresa used for her cures. She looks toward the bizarre hill, once more impressed with its strangeness, with the boulders that form enormous arches, doors, profound cavities, precarious, massive sculptures. "I want to climb the hill," she exclaims suddenly and starts walking toward it. Gracia mumbles something about the midday desert sun, but she's made up her mind: she has to get to the cave.

Javier catches up with her.

"Do you really want to go all the way up?"

She looks at him; his eyes are challenging.

"Yes. Will you go with me?"

Javier laughs and, without answering, climbs up on the first rock with impressive agility and extends his hand to help her up. She grabs his hand, feeling extraordinarily light; with one hop she's next to him. From there they have to zigzag, circumventing the huge masses of rock that stand in their way. Javier goes first, waiting after each climb. Halfway up they encounter an enormous formation that looks like an arch or a gigantic doorway. They are both sweating; the veins on their temples pulsate with the heat and the effort of climbing. On one side, a lonely, twisted

tree struggles to survive, anchored in a deep crack. They take
shelter in the shade. She thinks of herself; her life is like that of
the tree: a frugal existence, clinging to a world that is foreign to
her and doesn't recognize her. She breathes deeply, trying to catch
her breath, but the air reaches her in hot gusts that burn her
throat. The heavy beating of her heart thumps in her ears. She
feels Javier's glance resting on her.

"Let's go!" she says.

✸XVIII

On the day of her second death she would remember how she had
tried to flee from the first one because it didn't belong to her. She
ran off to the Big House, wanting to distance herself from Huila,
hoping to get rid of the chill that was beginning to travel throughout her insides and return to life. She was filled with a viscous fear
that stuck like sap to her soul, and an impotent desperation before
the tremendous injustice: how, after scaring death away from
someone else, had it gotten into her? But there was no doubt: a
strange deafness was creeping into her bones, her tongue was
numbing, her breath reeked of death, and her body responded to
any cessation of motion by trembling and shaking with cold.

It was a week before her birthday when Teresa surprised her
father by begging him to throw her a big party. Then she devoted
herself entirely to organizing it, eager to deceive the dire intentions of death, with a boundless activity that left no opening for
it to squeeze through. Death was not possible when she was going
to celebrate for the first time her day of birth. She launched into
action, dismantling the hours, fragmenting the minutes, pulveriz-
ing the seconds with a hammering intensity that scarcely allowed
her time to breathe, much less to think. Upon seeing her sudden
display of energy, everybody confused hysteria with euphoria,
and soon the ranch overflowed with excitement, movement,
anticipation.

Camilda helped her make the invitations. They cut the paper, wrote in the names, decorated them, and had them distributed by cowboys on horseback. Under Josefina's guidance they planned the meal; various women from the settlement were called to collaborate on its preparation. Don Tomás made sure he had enough drink. Gabriela created new dresses for herself and Teresa with the fabric Don Tomás had brought from Alamos. Everyone helped sweep, mop, and dust the house more than once. They had invited Gabriela's father and two of his nephews; Don Lauro Aguirre and his wife would come from Ures; José María and Guadalupe Ortiz and their children, from the ranch San José del Yópori; the town mayor, Don José María Lozano, from Batacosa; Aureliano Guerrero, from the ranch El Sonábari. Don Miguel, the foreman, and his family were also invited. The Santinis, the Mendívils, the Alvarados, and many other families would come from nearby ranches. And Josefa Félix, known as Chepita, would come.

Teresa had met Chepita a little while after her arrival at Cabora at one of those parties in which she was introduced to society. She was the first and only friend of her adolescence. She lived with her family in Baroyeca, and even though she was five years older they got along immediately. All of Teresa's reserve was matched by Chepita's propensity to chatter. She was mischievous, imaginative, and a liar. Although distance kept them from seeing each other frequently, during Chepita's few visits Teresa had discovered the joy of sharing secrets and planning innocent mischief with a peer. Teresa anxiously awaited her arrival, and the moment Chepita stepped down from her wagon, the two separated from the rest and secluded themselves in Teresita's bedroom. After closing the door, Chepita gave her a long look.

"I have the impression there's something you want to tell me but don't dare," she said and waited.

Teresa was pensive for a moment; she was afraid to put it in words, but Chepita insisted. So she told her about her boredom and the empty days, about her attempts to embroider and cook, about Huila approaching her and the strange things she said, as if she weren't really addressing her; then she described the apprenticeship, the mysterious world of medicine and healing, how she had smelled "the spume of life," and the uneasiness it produced in her. Chepita was very attentive. Finally she told the story of the woman in labor; her voice shook a little and the trembling came back. When she had finished, she looked into her friend's eyes.

"I'm going to die, Chepita; I feel it. I'm stuck with that death inside me."

Her friend didn't move. For a long time she was quiet, not looking at Teresa. Then she shook her head.

"I don't believe you're going to die. I think you were just deeply frightened by what you did, that's all. But what you did isn't so strange. Look, when someone dies, their spirit has to leave, right? Well, when you jumped on top of that woman, it couldn't leave, you stopped it, see? So it's not that her death got out, but rather that her soul was trapped inside and she couldn't die."

"You think so? Just like that, so simple?"

"Of course! Don't worry any more. I know about these things because I've read books about spiritism. In them they tell about just that, about spirits that return after death to visit their loved ones, about voices and ghosts, souls in purgatory, oof!, about a whole world of things that most of us don't see. They even say that some people can separate themselves from their bodies and travel wherever they want without moving physically; later the soul returns, and it's as if those people had experienced everything that their souls saw." Chepita fell silent, gazing at her friend, and said abruptly, "I bet you could do that, Teresita."

"Why me? Why not you?"

"Because you're different; I've seen how your eyes shine in the dark; they light up the whole room. That light must come from your spirit, which wants to leave. Snuff out the lamp so you can see."

Teresa laughed. She turned off the lamp and waited. She didn't see anything, but Chepita insisted that when Teresa had her eyes open the room was lit up, and when she closed them, the light was gone.

"My aunt Tula said the same thing: she said I had the eyes of the devil; now you say that it's my spirit. But when I look at my reflection, I don't perceive anything; I look the same as anybody else."

"Let's see your ears. No, those eyes can't belong to the devil, because you'd have pointed ears and yours are normal. So forget about Tula. Now, try to leave your body. Close your eyes and concentrate; feel that you have a spirit inside you that can separate and then come back."

"Where do you want me to go?" she asked, laughing.

"Over there, to the corner of the room."

Teresa closed her eyes and tried to concentrate but she was overcome by laughter. Chepita insisted that she take it seriously. She tried again. She created an image of the corner and concentrated on it. Then she thought of walking over there, turning around, and looking at Chepita. The image was perfectly clear: she could see her friend staring at her from the bed when Chepita's voice made her open her eyes. She was in the same place.

"You left your body! I saw it, I saw your silhouette in the corner, looking at me, while you were sitting here next to me on the bed."

"You just imagined it."

"I swear, Teresa. . . ."

"I don't want to hear any more. Let's go to sleep."

The next day she had forgotten the incident because of the commotion of the party. The surprises started in the morning. Don Tomás woke her up early. He took her outside. There was the old chestnut stallion and next to him his offspring, all saddled up. It was the most beautiful colt on the ranch and Teresa had watched her father training it for a long time.

"His name is Spirit, and he's yours," he said. "But I want you to ride it like a young lady, not like an Indian." The animal was wearing a side-saddle. Teresa was so excited that she would have accepted riding on her head if necessary. She let her father help her up and show her how to place her feet, both on the same side ("so I don't open my legs," she thought, remembering Doña Rosaura's lesson). She felt awkward, like a heavy broach pinned to a flimsy lapel. When the animal took the first steps, she had to cling to him to avoid falling: that wasn't riding!

During the hours before the other visitors arrived, Teresa galloped around the ranch with Chepita. As soon as they were out of sight of the house, Teresa got down, unsaddled the colt, and rode bareback. Only then did she sense that the horse was hers.

When she came back, Gabriela handed her a beautiful white shawl. The surprise, however, wasn't the gift, but the realization that her young stepmother was pregnant: she had a definitely earthy odor. Gabriela hadn't mentioned it and Teresa, thinking that perhaps she didn't know, decided not to say anything until after the party, but she couldn't resist the temptation to look at her belly: she wasn't showing yet. Gabriela noticed the look and felt a sudden chill, there inside, where she kept her carefully guarded secret. When Teresa turned away, she crossed herself.

As the time for the party approached, Teresa and Chepita ran to get dressed. Once again Teresa allowed them to curl her hair and pile it on top of her head, cinch her waist, perfume and decorate her like the first day. She waited until the last moment to put on her fancy shoes.

At midday the guests began to arrive. The ranchhands hustled to attend to the animals and at the same time take care of the bonfire where they were roasting a whole steer and a pig. *Bacanora*, cognac, and all kinds of wine were flowing. The women drank a punch made of selected fruits. They all brought some little gift for Teresa: hand-embroidered handkerchiefs, rosaries, a little prayer book, a silk shawl, and other things she would never use.

Teresa was the center of attention and she felt intoxicated by so much commotion. Surreptitiously, she and her friend gulped down a few glasses of *bacanora*, which made them cough and laugh uncontrollably, but there were so many people and so much gaiety that nobody noticed.

At about five o'clock, after the meal, the young people gathered to sing; Teresa went for her guitar. They were just about to begin, when one of Gabriela's cousins, visibly drunk, got up brusquely.

"This is for sissies!" he said, stumbling toward the dinner table. "Let's see who can beat me at arm wrestling."

The young men accepted the challenge and left the girls alone with the guitar. Teresa, furious, had paled as if she had been slapped in the face. His attitude made her recall her cousins' mockery and scorn: she felt humiliated.

She tried to ignore the situation and continue playing, but the shouts and cheers of the boys drowned out the notes. One by one the girls, excited by the virile competition, abandoned Teresita's circle to watch the contest. Gabriela's cousin, a brawny youth accustomed to hard work in the country, was winning every bout.

Abruptly, Teresa put down her guitar and approached the table. The cousin had just triumphed over another opponent when she stood in front of him.

"Let's see if you can beat me," she said.

Everyone laughed, but Teresa sat down and placed her arm in position. She concentrated on her hand and looked her adversary in the eye. He was laughing.

"Come on. You can laugh later."

At that moment, some of the gentlemen who had been conversing in the library came back to the dining room. Among them, a muscular man named Ontilón was attracting attention by uttering vulgarities.

"Well, well, just look at this! Go on, boy, do the lady the favor, and then you and I will see whose balls weigh more! Excuse me, ladies, I didn't mean to offend you!"

The cousin was still smiling scornfully and, with a wink to his public, he prepared to do battle. He took Teresa's hand. No sooner had he done so than he felt the back of his hand touch the table.

"I wasn't ready," he protested with surprise; the smile disappeared. He placed his elbow on the table again. This time Teresa waited until she felt the push and then she defeated him again, apparently without the slightest effort.

"Anybody else?" she asked derisively, and now it was she who was smiling. The young man shook his head and got into position again. The result was the same. Mr. Ontilón's belly laughs resounded throughout the dining room. The cousin got up so precipitously that he knocked over his chair; he glared at Teresita and left the house. Mr. Ontilón was doubled over with laughter.

"Ah, what a girl! And she looks so delicate. Let's see what you can do with me, young lady. This fucking arm has conquered the strongest in the state."

His vulgarity disgusted Teresa. She looked at him maliciously.

"I don't think that would be fair, Mr. Ontilón. I'd rather give you the opportunity to beat my friend Chepita. If you win, then you can take me on."

Chepita jumped when she heard Teresa's proposal, but Teresa took her by the arm and sat her down at the table. In her ear she whispered, "Concentrate on your hand and on mine," and she placed hers on her friend's slender shoulder. Chepita, with a nervous laugh, took the enormous palm of Ontilón; next to the behemoth's arm, hers seemed like a fragile twig. By then everybody had gathered around to observe the match. Ontilón asked if she was ready. Teresa said yes, her friend was ready.

"Well, go on then, young lady, start pushing."

Amazed, Chepita felt a strange force in her arm that was overcoming the man's resistance. She thought he was letting her win, but when she saw the back of his hand touch the wood, she realized she had beaten him. At that instant Teresa withdrew her hand from her shoulder and everyone broke into applause.

"Okay," she said, "now that we've finished with this foolishness, let's sing awhile." She turned around to go back to where she had left her guitar and encountered the black figure of Huila.

"Don't ever play with that power again," the old woman said in a voice so low that nobody else could hear, then she turned and left the room.

▨ XIX

The climb is getting more arduous; the boulders are increasingly formidable, with smooth, rounded surfaces that resist being climbed; they have to look for detours or narrow, twisting openings. She's gone on ahead. Abruptly she comes upon an immense formation that completely blocks the way. She turns back. Javier is already looking for another way up. He has taken off his shirt. She observes the curvature of his back and, noting the tension of each muscle, thinks once more of a feline. She breathes with difficulty, trying to control the pounding of her heart; the hot air doesn't seem to enter or leave her lungs. Javier disappears behind a rock and she hastens to follow him. When she gets there, he's already on top, almost out of her reach.

"How do I get up there?"

"Over there," he answers, pointing to a small crevice between two boulders that offers a foothold for climbing. "Give me your hand and put your foot in the crack."

She obeys. Javier grabs her wrist, gives her a tug, and she's up. The hardest part is over. In front of them is a path where they can walk without much difficulty. Exhausted, she lets him lead; inertia keeps her moving. She doesn't feel her feet anymore and has to concentrate to put one in front of the other. She just thinks of reaching the goal and resting.

Suddenly they are there, on a narrow, flat area that leads to the niche in the mountain, a small orifice, not very deep, that smiles on the side of the hill; a smooth, pink opening, like the tender mouth of a calf. They bend down and go inside, scarcely fitting in the little bit of shade; half lying down, they can rest. She observes that the floor of the little cave is covered with a fine dust,

the same color as the rock, as if the stone were gradually pulver-
izing over time. She takes a pinch in her hand and tastes it: it has
no flavor. She closes her eyes, hearing the breeze that circles the
hill, punctuated by her agitated breathing. Drops of sweat roll
down her cheeks. She opens her eyes and looks down and then
toward the horizon and suddenly she sees Cabora in every detail,
not as she had seen it before, destroyed, nonexistent, but as if she
were seeing it forever, through Teresita's memories. She recognizes the land stretching toward the horizon and knows that she
has contemplated it a thousand times, in dreams, in her imagination; she recognizes the road to the Big House, the extensive
plateau, the long, flat hills, the peak of the Hill of the Mine: everything is just as she has always known it would be. Overcome by
a wave of emotion, she turns her head and realizes that Javier is
no longer at her side. Leaving the cave, she looks around for him.
Finally she sees him far away, he's already going back down, his
slender, black silhouette reverberates in the desert sun. He turns
toward her, signaling to her with his hand, then he keeps walking. She is suddenly gripped by anxiety.

"Javier, wait!" she shouts, but realizes that her voice has no
sound. She runs down the hill, feeling her throat tightening;
waves of fear rush over her as she tries to remember something.
She runs, slips, gets up, and runs again, trying to catch up with
him, so he won't leave her alone up there; she runs after the black
figure that keeps moving away from her. Suddenly she stumbles
on a rock and falls, but this time . . .

XX

Huila's ominous figure installed itself in Teresa's mind and she
realized that the party hadn't changed anything. The next day
Chepita returned to Baroyeca, and the old routine started up
again. They all went about their business, and Teresa was left once
more prowling around the house and feeling as though death
were creeping after her. Her friend's advice, which had sounded so

solid, soon evaporated in the idle solitude, making room for growing anguish and the trembling that invaded her every time she
stood still. She herself began to resemble a ghost, walking noiselessly and continuously from the bedroom to the living room to
the library to the patio and finally, even against Don Tomás's prohibitions, to the stables to get Spirit and ride him at least around
the nearby area, looking for a little relief from the deadly shadow
that seemed to hover over her soul. She stopped eating and was
losing her ability to speak. When she looked in the mirror she
observed a strange pallor, as though her skin were transparent and
allowed the skull to show through. Nobody else seemed to notice,
but the distance between her and daily reality was becoming
greater each day. She suffered from insomnia and spent the nights
wandering through the house while the others slept; during the
day, accumulated exhaustion obligated her to lie down and growing anxiety made her get back up again. She found no comfort, as
though suddenly concrete things, the five senses, all were her enemies, ambushing her at the slightest sign of distraction in order to
remind her that she was moving toward death.

One afternoon as the sun went down she was returning from
a walk when she felt someone observing her. Turning her head,
she saw once more the sinister figure of Huila, who was obviously watching her from a distance. She looked almost like death
itself. Teresa was petrified, her eyes fixed on the eyes of that
specter, which suddenly turned and, hobbling away like an enormous vulture, disappeared behind the house, leaving her with a
chill in her bones.

When she entered the house she looked for Gabriela to have
a little company, but ever since Teresa had gazed at her belly, the
young stepmother had taken refuge in the chapel all day long; the
house was empty and silent.

That night in her dreams she saw Huila again, black, enormous, and just about to envelop her with the wings of her gown.
She was hopping around the bed like a bird of prey, squawking
disconnected phrases: "don't play," "that power," "leave your
body," "that power," "you took her death," "never again," "you're

strange," "power," "leave your body," "play," "you have a luminous look," "never," "strange powers, child," "powers of death," "by playing you die," "never," "you're possessed," "that power." She woke up, startled, and heard again the thick, palpable silence that surrounded the house. Not a cricket or an owl or even a wisp of a breeze. Silence. "And if I die, who will jump on top of me so my spirit doesn't leave me?" she thought, remembering Chepita's words, but even her own thoughts sounded hollow as if produced within a strange muteness, or as though they were materializing far from her, in another room, behind a closed door. She couldn't sleep anymore. She lay there with her eyes open to the thick shadows and her ears listening to the silence, which grew more and more solid. Only her soundless thoughts floated like wraiths around the room, obsessed with the proximity of death, someone else's death, a death that didn't belong to her but was making her increasingly insignificant and defenseless, less and less herself and more and more eternal stillness.

Suddenly she realized that if she stayed there in the dark she would never see the light of day again; the shadows of the room were inside her and the silence was covering her ears. The dawn she so anxiously awaited would not arrive if she didn't go out to meet it. She had to flee. Seized with panic, she leapt from her bed, abandoned the house, and ran to the stables; she hugged Spirit's neck, where she felt life beating. Mounting without even putting on the horse's reins, she entwined her numb fingers in his mane, clung with her knees to what seemed like her last hope, and galloped off without knowing where she was going. Her terror was contagious and Spirit, affected by it, became fearful even of the early morning shadows; he stopped without warning and twisted back and forth as if he had the devil himself on his back. She understood that even Spirit didn't know her: she was like blood running soundlessly, a muffled mind, an inaudible soul. . . . She was insonorous death, silent death, opaque death mounted on her own spirit and running so hard that she scarcely perceived the sensation of falling, not from the horse, but inward, toward the dead night of her inner self.

At that instant they felt swept away by death. Their bones filled with darkness and they dove inward through a long night, toward the center. But black isn't a substance or a sense, and they lost the boundaries of their bodies and of time; the infinite cosmos out there joined another cosmos that they had always carried within them and that was unfolding, pulled by the thread of an imperceptible breath. They perceived the absence of pain in that floating away, that disconnection full of nostalgia and compassion. They, or things, were projected along infinite, luminous trajectories: everything seemed to press outward, disintegrating the edges of life and opening consciousness to a limitless expansion, like rivers that overflow their banks, like air escaping into the void, like light that dissipates. Consciousness was, at once, infinite and centered, absolute freedom and restriction: it created itself just by being.

And consciousness was intent on reaching radiant oblivion. It spread out unchanneled, it was dispersed without ties or ruptures, in a motionless motion, fluid, whimsical, final: consciousness in flight.

They suddenly conceived their own absence and were filled with nostalgia for life, nostalgia for the body, like a warm cradle, thrown onto that inhospitable desert, surrounded by huge buzzards that, like black sins, like obscure doubts, were about to engulf the last remains of their existence. They saw Cabora in the middle of nowhere, the truncated dreams, the unfulfilled possibilities, with no future. They thought of the fragile breaking of a thousand dawns in their absence, and they conceived that absence as an infinite yearning for life, an enormous presence of oblivion. And afterwards, they saw the light. And then, nothing.

 I

At the very instant she fell, Huila knew it. She sent Miguel to look for her, to bring her back very carefully, and she warned him not to be so ignorant as to think that she was dead. Then she lit the candle. When the foreman returned with the body, chaos broke out in Cabora. Don Tomás unleashed a shouting spree of contradictory orders that Gabriela and Josefina, running in opposite directions, tried to carry out without being very convinced of their usefulness. Miguel placed Teresa's body on her bed, then backed up against the wall and stayed there, looking at her in a stupor. With all the confusion nobody, except Huila, heard him repeat several times, "She didn't weigh anything, light as a feather, she didn't weigh anything, as if she weren't there anymore, as if she weren't in her body." When Don Tomás saw the foreman standing there mumbling nonsense, he shouted another order.

"What the hell are you doing?! Get the doctor!"

The wait began. Don Tomás stomped back and forth from the study to Teresita's bedroom to the study again, over and over, weaving together fragments of a nightmare, barking orders that he immediately rescinded. He couldn't distract himself with anything, expecting from one moment to the next to return to the room and find his daughter sitting up and talking, or find her dead. The doctor arrived from Alamos twenty-four hours after the event. He tried all the homemade remedies that Josefina and Huila had already used: vinegar, ammonia, cold water in her face, thumps on her back, and nothing happened. There was no explanation. It was more than a fainting spell and less than death: an attack of hysteria, perhaps. They just had to wait. It certainly wouldn't last, but if it did . . . well, without food or water . . . who knows? Don Tomás's reaction to the doctor's insinuation was to let loose another barrage of shouts.

"Put covers over her! Don't suffocate her! Move back! Give her air! Don't leave her alone for one minute! I don't want you to touch her! Let me know if she gets cold!" and he went out, banging his fists against the walls and doors. In the library he was caught up in a labyrinth of guilt, his own and that of others: maybe Miguel hadn't been careful enough when he brought her, maybe he should have sent for her at the settlement seven years earlier, maybe she didn't pay any attention to him and rode her horse bareback, maybe the damn chestnut had suddenly gone wild, maybe Loreto had prayed to God for a tragedy to befall her unfaithful husband, maybe Gabriela had annoyed her that morning with her incessant Hail Marys, maybe he should have been more strict, maybe Huila had put a spell on her, maybe that worthless Cayetana shouldn't have left her . . . and back to the bedroom to see if she had awakened or died yet.

Gabriela took refuge in the chapel (selfish Gabriela, secretive Gabriela, Gabriela full of light, fertile, complete). She tried to think about Teresita, to pray sincerely for her recovery, but she couldn't concentrate; her mind kept wandering. She could already feel a slight flutter in her womb, the awareness of another life made her turn inward, and silently, with secret joy and secret guilt, she reveled in her hidden happiness. Instead of addressing God or the Virgin Mary, she spoke with her future child. From time to time she repented and said the Lord's Prayer for Teresita, but without conviction. How could she feel someone else's death when she was so full of life? "My baby," she said, because it was hers, there inside her, listening to her, and it responded with tiny, scarcely perceptible movements, in a way that all of her saints had never responded. She didn't want to share her secret with anybody, she wrapped it up in swaddling clothes of pride, she wove little camisoles of the future with yarn made of dreams, she played with the idea of hands and feet that would all fit into her two cupped palms. Gabriela was a greedy, finite goddess. She spoke the language of a cherished promise, to be heard solely by her hidden secret. It was the only thing in her life that had ever belonged totally to her. She avoided people's glances and took delight in herself, in her delicious egotism. She felt complete, integral in her solitude, special, different. Her life had meaning because of what was growing inside her. Her body had become a vessel full of mystery, a fertile land germinating miracles (auspicious Gabriela, narcissistic Gabriela, prolific Gabriela). That minute existence confirmed her own, her body belonged to it; she was strong, healthy, a magic chalice, a nourishing, protective cradle for her baby. She felt whole, overflowing, and deliciously guilty; she looked around her, fearful that someone would notice her joy (impassive Gabriela; Gabriela of ivory; Gabriela, mother of pearl).

Only Huila didn't seem to worry. She murmured to herself: "We must have patience, she'll come back, she'll come back," and she watched over her continuously, day and night; she came and went from her room to Teresita's. She took care of the child, she took care of the child's candle, as Apolinio had taught her. She knew: it was the candle of life and as long as it burned, Teresa wouldn't die; she had learned that from her teacher. He knew the secret of candles, he spoke with the spirits in charge of lighting them and putting them out, and he was entrusted with the art of making replicas for emergencies. In an old trunk, Apolinio had a collection of cut-off candles, a hodgepodge pile of bits of life from those who by pure chance had died before their time. "Oh, Huila!" he once told her, "Chance is the only thing that doesn't obey destiny. It leaps here and there, undoing the original plan, cutting off lives that still have many moons ahead of them by simply placing their owners in the path of a lost bullet, a bad slash with a knife, an unexpected fall." There in the trunk was chance's bounty, a heap of mistaken deaths. There was Froylán's death when he had just turned fifteen and the Cruz boy who died of fright a few days after being born and the child María who fell over the cliff. . . . So many that she didn't remember them all. Huila had cut a little piece from each candle, just a tiny bit so she wouldn't steal death from those who already had life stolen from them. With these bits she made a new candle, a candle of borrowed life for someone who shouldn't die yet. It was Teresita's candle. With its thin thread of light she had bound that fleeing soul, and as long as the flame didn't go out, the child's spirit couldn't depart from this world. So she went back and forth, taking care of Teresita, taking care of the candle.

Outside, in the settlement, the women whispered to each other.

"They say she's sleeping."

"Perhaps she'll die."

"Huila watches over her night and day."

"That old woman is always bad luck."

"She cured my little one."

"And Don Tomás?"

"He's going crazy. . . ."

"Huila doesn't do her rounds any more."

"She sent word to Lola to wait a while with her sick husband."

"Well, after so much waiting, the old man died."

"It's something serious; they say she doesn't breathe. Maybe she's possessed."

"And who do you think possessed her?"

"Don't be malicious, Nacha, I'm talking about witchcraft."

"Stop that chatter, here comes Don Miguel."

"How's Miss Teresa, Don Miguel?"

"The same. No better."

"I dreamed last night that they were burying her. . . ."

"I dreamed that I saw her flying. . . ."

"I dreamed she was leaving us. . . ."

"María?"

"Yes?"

"Huila asks if you could wait a little longer."

"I don't think so, Miguel; last night I felt it coming. I'd better go to Aquihuiquichi so Columba can take care of me. Tell Huila to forgive me; I tried, but this baby's coming and nothing's going to stop it."

"Then she says it's going to be a girl; you should name her Teresita and give her a nice burial and don't cry because the little boy'll be here soon."

"All right, Miguel."

"Poor María . . ."

"She's not the only one. Julia's little girl was born dead."

"Celestina miscarried last week when everything seemed to be going just fine."

"Hermelinda, too, and they can't stop the bleeding."

"Time is standing still."

"Celia cries all day because her womb doesn't move anymore."

"They say it's Teresa; she steals innocent lives so she won't die."

"What's going to happen?"

In Cabora, Don Tomás kept going round and round. The doctor had lost hope; she couldn't live much longer without food and, especially, without water. Huila hurriedly dampened Teresa's lips and all of her skin with rags: "If trees can absorb water through their bark, why not you?" she said in a low voice. Gabriela took it as a bad omen; she had heard the gossip from the settlement: not one baby had been born alive, not one fruitful womb was safe. Pregnant women, even those only a few months along, began to emigrate, hoping to escape Teresita's influence. Gabriela was tortured with fear; she felt that an evil spirit was pursuing her. She wanted to flee, to hide at her father's ranch, but what could she tell Don Tomás when she hadn't even revealed the pregnancy to him? How could she tell him that his dying daughter was bewitched and was stealing unborn lives? Just imagining his ire made her tremble from head to toe. And inside she was torn in two: on the one hand, she wished that Teresa would hurry up and die so she wouldn't have to nourish herself with more new lives; on the other, she was filled with guilt and remorse and fear of divine punishment for her unholy desires. She hid in the chapel so she wouldn't have to go near the enemy's room: she didn't want death to discover the life in her womb and feel envious. But once she was there she didn't know whether to pray for her baby or to do penance for her excessive selfishness. She did both and ended up mixing them up so much that she didn't even know what she was asking for anymore.

Josefina started repeating dishes for meals that nobody ate: soup and stew, stew and soup, day after day. Every time a pot broke, the milk spilled, or the food burned, she'd say, "This is for the child Teresita." Huila took care of the candle's flame so it wouldn't go out or burn too rapidly; she took care of the child, combing her hair, cleaning her face, touching her cold hands. "Don't go too far away," she'd say in her ear. Out in the settlements the rumors scurried about like frightened rabbits from hut to hut, from clearing to thicket, from waterhole to corral.

On the thirteenth day the mirror that Don Tomás put under Teresa's nose so carefully each morning didn't fog up. The doctor announced that there was no more pulse; a new silence reigned in her chest. Still they waited all that night for a miracle. The next morning the doctor could not find the slightest sign of life. He shook his head, embraced the father, and said, "I'm sorry."

Incredulous, Don Tomás looked at his daughter's body, so still under the white sheet; he touched her hands, her face, her feet. . . . She was stiff and cold. Without any hope in the face of the irrefutable scientific proof of her death, he sent word to the carpenter to make a simple wooden coffin; he had the women in the settlement notified so they could prepare the wake; he sent word to Gabriela to dress in black; he ordered Huila to stop muttering incoherences over a candle, over the little flame still burning—no, no, the child still had a little life left—and then he took refuge in the silence of the library and in his cognac.

Gabriela was shut up in her bedroom. The previous night, when she heard that Teresa was dying, she had suffered the first spasm; she prayed that it was only the effect of the fright, but the cramps in her womb continued until dawn. When she rose from her bed the next morning, a thin stream of blood ran down her inner thigh; she immediately lay down and covered herself up again to hide something she didn't want to decipher. During the whole day her body's eagerness to expel the life that was growing inside her continued and worsened as Gabriela cried and begged anybody, nobody in particular, the whole invisible and silent world of her saints, that her child not be taken from her, that they let it live and take Teresa if necessary but not her baby, her love, her secret little bundle.

When they notified her through the door that Teresa had passed away, she felt a pang of remorse and then that sharp stab, like a mortal wound, that pierced her abdomen. A warm liquid bathed her legs. She realized there was no hope: Teresa was gone, taking her baby with her. She sent word to Don Tomás that she was ill, that she couldn't come out, and then she curled up around her pain.

❀ II

In Cabora time has come to a standstill. No one works. Everyone walks quietly, wrapped in silence and sadness. At three in the afternoon the people from the settlement begin to arrive, the men with their hat in their hands, the women with a dark shawl over their head. They walk slowly, looking at the ground so as not to offend the dead. They form a long, silent line. One by one they enter, mournfully contemplate the dead girl, cross themselves, and go back out to join a group of people waiting patiently at the door of the Big House. They speak in hushed voices.

"Miss Teresa, she was so pretty. . . ."

"She was good. . . ."

"Remember how she cured Tencha?"

"Eyes like two morning stars . . ."

"The poor boss! They say she was his only daughter. . . ."

"She sang like a meadowlark. . . ."

"So lovely, Miss Teresa . . ."

"So good . . ."

"A saint . . ."

"She was so young, poor thing. . . ."

"An innocent soul . . ."

"Too bad! . . ."

Nobody mentions the rumors of a few days ago: it brings bad luck to criticize the dead. The act of dying wipes away all sins, even the suspicion of sins: the dead have nothing to do with life and its judgements.

Huila, half in shock, watches the preparations from her corner of the room. She asks for a miracle; she asks Apolinio, the only one she trusts. The child's skin is translucent, her stillness so definitive that it hurts. They have laid her on a wooden table covered with a white sheet; at each corner a tall candle is burning; her hands are tied together on her chest with a delicate, pink ribbon. Huila doesn't pray: she's arguing with Apolinio, she upbraids him for the ineffectiveness of his remedies—since the candle is still lit but Teresa is gone—and she asks for a miracle. But time stands still and Apolinio does not respond.

At seven o'clock the formal wake begins. The twenty women in charge of leading the prayers gather around the dead girl, all dressed in long, black skirts, black blouses, black shawls on their heads. The litanies begin, the Hail Marys, the Lord's Prayers, the entreaties to the protective spirits. Then the weeping, softly at first, scarcely audible laments that gradually increase in volume until they become howls and shrieks that smash against the silence. After a while the litanies start again; two voices break away from a Hail Mary and begin sobbing; two others slide down after them and then two more follow, until they are all wailing again. From her bedroom, Gabriela, curled up on her bed and hugging a sheet full of bloody remains, seconds the heart-wrenching cries with her own. Don Tomás has shut himself up in his library; he doesn't plan on leaving: saying goodbye to the dead is women's work; he doesn't want to have anything to do with rituals, he just wants it to be another day so he can gradually go back to his routine, fill up the void with daily tasks, remake his life. At his side the bottle of cognac is empty, but it hasn't even helped him to express his impotence with anger or with tears. In the kitchen, Josefina prepares the coffee for the women of the wake.

The chimes of the library clock begin to strike midnight. Josefina leaves the kitchen with a large tray of steaming cups and heads toward the room where the mourners are. As she enters, she is received by the heavy, gray sound of lamentations. She raises her eyes to contemplate Teresa's body, and at that instant she loses control of herself. Emitting a terrified shriek, she drops the tray, which falls crashing to the floor. Teresa is sitting straight up on the table, her eyes full of astonishment, contemplating the strange scene around her.

With the clanging of the tray, the frightened women leapt up like buzzards scattering at the sound of a shotgun and began to shout.

"Hail Mary, full of grace, she has risen! Our Father who art in heaven, Jesus, Mary, and Joseph! A miracle! She has come back to life! A miracle! A miracle!"

With his face pale and drawn, his eyes red, Don Tomás ran into the room and stood paralyzed in the doorway, looking at his daughter, who was looking back at him. For a moment he felt confused, believing that the delayed effects of the cognac were causing hallucinations. He rubbed his eyes and looked again: Teresa was still there, not saying a word, but indisputably alive. He hid his bewilderment behind the usual shouts and orders.

"Bring blankets! That doctor is an ass! Josefina! Make a beef broth . . . better make it from bull's meat! Doña Huila, get this pack of hysterical women out! Scram! There's no dead person here! Miguel, burn that coffin!"

"No, Don Tomás," Teresa interposed suddenly, in a hoarse voice that not even she would have recognized. "Leave the coffin there: it will be needed in three days," and she turned her eyes

toward Huila. Her words produced an abrupt silence and everyone looked at her, tearfully, incredulously, their mouths gaping
open, waiting for her to say something else. But Teresa had fallen
silent again. Hobbling, Huila approached her, tenderly untied the
ribbon that held her hands, and put it in her pocket. Teresa smiled
at her, extending her right hand and rubbing her twisted hip.

"You will no longer walk with shame," she whispered in
her ear.

Don Tomás started shouting again.

"Out! Get out of here! Everybody go! Teresita needs air.
Josefina! Where the hell's the bull's broth?"

With a flurry like the sound of a distant storm, the black figures retreated, leaving behind the swish-swash of their long skirts
and the secret murmurs that repeated, "Miracle, miracle." With
them went Huila, smiling, walking upright with even strides and
not even a hint of a hobble.

Josefina arrived with a broth that smelled like bulls' balls, but
Teresa made no move to taste it; she seemed to be in a trance, very
still, very distant except for her physical presence. Josefina started to pour the liquid into her mouth in patient spoonfuls. Don
Tomás noted that at least she swallowed. A little color was coming back into her cheeks. When she finished the broth, she
smiled, shut her eyes, and curled up on the table. Don Tomás
picked her up in his arms and placed her gently on her bed,
where she fell asleep as sweetly as a young child. He ordered
Josefina to keep watch all night and call him if there was any
change in his daughter. He returned to his refuge in the library
and sat thinking in the dark.

That was the beginning of the prolonged wait that was to last
three months and eighteen days. Teresa was alive, but she wasn't
present. She was like a ghost that had materialized, a concrete
absence walking silently through the house. The rumors started
circulating through the settlement again.

"They say she's the living death. . . ."

"She doesn't stay in her body. . . ."

"She goes away and then she's like that, like she's gone for a long time. . . ."

"She talks of strange things: spirits, kindness, justice, who knows what else. . . ."

"People say she hears voices that tell her to heal, to do good. . . ."

"And she's like that all the time, like 'gone.'"

That she was alive, there was no doubt. She walked and controlled her bodily movements herself, but that was all. She showed absolutely no interest in her own care. When she woke up in the morning someone had to bathe her, dress her, and comb her hair because if they didn't, she would go outside in her nightgown with her hair all tousled. She didn't eat unless someone spoon-fed her. It was necessary to take her to the bathroom like a child and undress her at bedtime so she wouldn't go to sleep with her clothes and boots on. She gave the impression that she was totally unaware of her own body and of everything that surrounded her. She almost never spoke, and when she did she mumbled things that seemed incoherent, in a voice completely different from the one she had used previously, as though it came from some dark abyss in her body, from a cave, some interior space that emitted sounds through her. When she was asked a simple question like, "How do you feel?" or, "What do you want to eat?" she would look at the speakers as if they were crazy and then respond with strange, disconnected phrases: "I am everywhere, kaboom!" she would say and throw her hands out as if she were dispersing something; or, "The voices follow me all day" or, "Truth is here," and she would point to her abdomen. Likewise, she didn't seem to look at the world around her; rather, she always seemed to be seeing a different fold of reality; hers was a tangential look that almost never rested directly on an object or person or, if it did, it gave the impression of going through them and stopping beyond the material substance.

Gabriela was in bed, twisted around her sudden emptiness, when she learned that Teresa had come back to life. The news caught her unprepared and she couldn't defend herself. She experienced it as punishment for her selfishness, a just dispossession of her first child, a divine sign of her fall, a loss of grace. She had no choice but to drink the bitter dregs of her contrition and search for some irreproachable way to do penance. On the third day she felt strong enough to go and look for Teresa and beg her forgiveness. As she left the room, she ran into Huila and asked her where she was going.

"To my room, to die," the old woman said, smiling.

"Huila! How can you say that? You look quite well."

"I've never felt better. The child performed a miracle for me so that I could arrive at death walking straight and proud." The old woman let out a raucous laugh and bade farewell to the surprised Gabriela, who watched her stroll away completely cured of her limp. Flustered by the revelation of a possible miracle, Gabriela retreated to her room again. If what she had just seen and heard was true, there was no doubt that the divine family had chosen Teresita over herself and that she was about to become spiritually orphaned if she didn't do something to make amends immediately.

The next morning they found Huila dead in her bed with a huge smile frozen forever on her face. When Gabriela was informed, she understood that only the miraculous child risen from the dead could forgive her sins and she hurried to confess.

Teresa was sitting on the edge of her bed, contemplating some astral spaces that seemed to inhabit her eyes, when Gabriela walked in, knelt down, and began a slow, anguished account of her real and supposed transgressions. Teresa didn't even turn her head, nor did she appear to listen to the litany of petty misdemeanors, perverse desires, hidden weaknesses, and insufferable vanities that the young woman was shredding piecemeal at her feet. After she had finished, Gabriela waited until the silence of the "risen one" became unbearable. When she looked up, the indifference she saw in the other's eyes frightened her and, feeling confused, she shouted:

"Teresa! Do you forgive me?"

Only then did Teresa turn toward her.

"They called me from far away; they're waiting for me outside," she said and, putting her hand on Gabriela's head to help herself up, she walked slowly toward the door. The young stepmother was dumbfounded; she had felt how, under the pressure of that hand, all of her guilt and remorse had dissipated, leaving her replete with sweetness and light. She followed Teresa. Outside the Big House a small group of people was waiting. She observed how Teresa approached them, spoke with each one, gently placing her large hands on the head of a little boy, on the shoulder or neck of a woman, on the temples of an old man, pronouncing words that Gabriela couldn't hear, and she saw how the sufferers started to smile, how they thanked her and went away peacefully as if they had received a great gift. "She's healing them as she healed Huila and me," she thought. "She's a saint working miracles with her hands."

III

Those were difficult times in Cabora. Don Tomás refused to call back the "sonofabitch of a doctor" who had declared Teresa dead. Nonetheless, he was the first to recognize that she wasn't the same person, and that had him in such a foul humor that he didn't want to see anybody. The only one he would let near him was his friend Lauro Aguirre, who arrived a few days after Teresa started attending to the ailing and the needy on the esplanade outside the Big House. Don Tomás asked his friend's opinion. Aguirre stood for a long time, watching the young woman through the window. Then he turned to the father.

"Everything has a perfectly scientific explanation, my dear Tomás, even if you, with your stubborn rationalism, refuse to accept it. Spontaneous somnambulism, preceded by a cataleptic attack of the mystic variety; possession by an astral body; possibly contact with other dimensions. She'll get over it with time. It's a simple phenomenon of magnetism and electricity that we still haven't mastered, but it's scientific, my friend, 100 percent scientific, I assure you."

"Hogwash, Aguirre," answered Tomás. "Miracles in our time! Hogwash!" But he felt a little better and decided to resign himself to waiting for Teresita to return to normal.

"It might be," said Aguirre, "but don't try to force her out of it. She could die of fright. And don't interfere with anything she wants to do. If she wants to heal because that's what the voices tell her, let her heal. Any opposition could be fatal. God knows what she hears: we're ignorant of the forces that reign in the afterlife that she says she visits. You have to be patient."

Don Tomás, however, found it impossible to be in his daughter's presence without feeling an overwhelming desire to slap her and send her to bed without supper until she came to her senses. So he avoided her and threw himself into the chores of the ranch with true desperation. When at home, he locked himself in the library. Gabriela was the one who set to work with real enthusiasm, finding in her ministrations, however menial, the most satisfying form of penance possible. She became the absolute guardian of her patient, determined to observe every gesture or any action that would confirm the other's sainthood. Her life would be dedicated to Teresa. She began to feel warm and loved within her new aura of humility: she was the one chosen to take care of the chosen one.

She soon realized that her task would not be easy. It was necessary to keep an eye on Teresa at all times so she didn't go out in her underwear, without taking a bath or with uncombed hair, or urinate in public places, or suddenly start talking nonsense when other people could hear. Sometimes Gabriela had to discipline herself and request divine enlightenment in order to avoid calling her charge a witch or a madwoman instead of a saint. Besides, Teresa was not grateful to her for anything, quite the opposite: she showed complete indifference, not even deigning to speak to her, but rather looking right through her as if she didn't exist. Nonetheless, Gabriela didn't let up one bit in her efforts to care for Teresa. Every morning she dressed her in white, braiding her hair carefully, washing her face, putting shoes on her feet, and watching her steps until leaving her before the needy, who formed an increasingly large group in front of the Big House. Then she waited, unflinchingly observing everything. Upon noticing that her charge was tired, she would guide her back inside, make her lie down for a while or spoon-feed her her favorite dishes, and ready her once more for her "public function."

Meanwhile the rumors were cropping up all around the settlement: Tencha told Lupe, who told Carmela, who told Epifanio, who told his wife, who told Hermenegildo . . . until everyone knew about the healing of Don Simón, the cripple who had been kicked in the head by a mule just three years ago and had been paralyzed on the left side ever since.

"What happened was," said Hermenegildo's wife to her neighbor Cuca, "that Lorenza told her husband: 'Go see Teresa, to see if she performs a miracle for you since it's been three years since I've lain with my husband.'"

"And that old fool Don Simón," said Cuca to Froylán, "went to see Teresa and—what do you know!—she was waiting at the door, like she knew he was coming."

"And then—can you believe this?—she made him take off his clothes so he only had his drawers on, right there with all of his shame flushing up his face," Froylán said laughingly to Eulogio.

"The poor guy," said Eulogio to Ignacia, "was red as a beet while Teresa rubbed him all over with saliva: on his face, his arm, his leg, until his skin was scarlet. When she finished, she told him he could go and took his crutch away."

" 'You're not going to need this ever again,' she said," Ignacia told her husband, Fortino, that night, "and Don Simón realized that he was standing straight with no support, and he smiled and his smile covered his whole face. He was so happy that he took off without his clothes, with just his drawers on."

"You should have seen him go," said Fortino, laughing, as he passed on the story to his close friend Román, "jumping around with his dick out and hollering to Lorenza: 'Here I come, baby, now I'm going to perform a miracle for you!'"

"Well, let's see if Teresa can perform the miracle of curing the boss of his foul mood," murmured Josefina when they told her. "He's so cross even his shadow can't stand him!"

But there was nobody who could relieve Don Tomás of the acidity that came gurgling up from his stomach, keeping him awake at night, burning his throat, ruining his taste for food every time he heard about another "miracle." That Don Simón was no longer a cripple; that Lula, who was dying of fever, got better with just a cup of tea; that a baby was born seeing out of only one eye and Teresa gave him sight by rubbing his other eye with her fingers; that a deaf fellow couldn't hear out of his right ear, and the saint spit in it and now he heard everything . . . Hogwash! Just plain hogwash! And Don Tomás would shut himself up in the library again, slamming the door behind him, while Teresa, under the strict vigilance of Gabriela, wandered through the house like a sleepwalker, on clouds. She walked so softly that nobody heard her, she seemed to float enveloped in silence; she hardly spoke, hardly looked at anything, all day long with a strange smile as if she heard music from somewhere else. Suddenly, in the middle of her room or while sitting at the dinner table, she would lose the gist of the conversation, turn her head aside, roll back her eyes, and get stiff and pale.

"She's in a trance again," Gabriela would say, and Don Tomás would reply: "I'm fed up with this crap! Why always at mealtime? Can't she do it when I'm not around?"

"He's coming. . . ." Teresa would murmur, or something similar.

"He's coming? He's coming? Who's coming? Tell me, who? We're not expecting anybody. Whoever said you can't believe in saints that stay for lunch was right! I'm going to my room and don't anybody bother me!" and Don Tomás, slamming down the silverware, would stomp out of the room.

And Gabriela would tell Josefina, and Josefina would tell Camilda, and Camilda would tell Abdulia, and Abdulia would spread the word that "ten minutes later the man arrived on horseback at breakneck speed, carrying the child with the broken leg, a bundle of screams, and Teresita took him and by just looking at him she put him to sleep, so peacefully, as if there were nothing wrong. Then she fixed the fracture, and the boy didn't wake up until Teresa told him to open his eyes. Then he smiled. . . ."

"I heard that the other day some fellow showed up just to thank her because Teresa had visited him at night to heal him. . . ."

"They say that Teresa goes around scaring people after dark. . . ."

"I heard she frightened death away from Elodio. . . ."

"They say that Lola wanted a boy and Teresita changed the baby's sex right there in her belly . . . ."

"They say that she cured Don Ramón's cough that wouldn't let him sleep at night . . . ."

"I heard she predicted Fortunata's death more than a month ago. . . ."

"They say she's a witch; she knows the future. . . ."

"I saw her pulverize a stone with her hands. . . ."

"I heard her speak with God in a strange tongue. . . ."

"Well, I heard that the other day she carried that big brute Maximino as if he didn't weigh a thing. . . ."

"They say she cures with the light that comes from her eyes. . . ."

"They say she heals with her voice. . . ."

"I heard she uses the powers of the devil. . . ."

"Hogwash!" Tomás repeated every time Gabriela tried to tell him about the most recent miracle.

But the rumors spread like floodwater surging across the plains, and people began to arrive, just a trickle at first, then more and more; they formed little groups, waiting for Teresa to cure them of paralysis, mange, diarrhea, cough, or mosquito bites; one woman wants a child and can't have one, another is going to have one and doesn't want it, so-and-so doesn't hear well, this boy was born blind, the old man just doesn't seem able to die and we don't know what to do with him, they stuck a knife in my son's belly, my niece hasn't eaten for three days. . . . And Teresa came and went like a sleepwalker, attending to the people, comforting, curing, or consoling, and sending people back where they came from, with the news of the miracles, the kindness, the justice of the child saint, the Sacred Child of Cabora, Teresita. And Gabriela observed everything so she could tell Josefina, who would tell Abdulia, who would tell Rosalío, who would tell Miguel, who would tell Lorenza, who would tell Celia, who would tell everybody. . . .

Don Lauro arrived again in February. He came from Hermosillo where he was in charge of establishing the boundary between that city and Ures.

"So the rich can have a little more," he said scornfully.

"Then why do you work for them?" Tomás asked, shrugging his shoulders.

"To keep up with things, to keep up-to-date. I've got 'ears' everywhere; you'll see, some day . . . By the way, how's your daughter?"

"Worse than ever. Now anything is a miracle. The other morning she starts talking about some dream of a cow having triplets, and she asks Miguel to be prepared, and that same day we have an orgy of cows giving birth that we couldn't keep up with. Now they say that was Teresita's doing, so there'd be plenty of milk and meat for the horde of beggars we have out there. The next day Miguel shows up, saying Teresa told him to open the dry well, and I tell him, 'Hogwash!,' but he opens it and—holy shit!—there's water, and now they're saying that the 'saint'—ha!—can extract water from the desert. It's so bad that if I get gray hair it will be another of Teresa's miracles! Frankly, Lauro, if this doesn't stop soon, I'm going to have to do something, even if she has another attack."

Lauro extracted a newspaper that he had in his pocket and handed it to his friend.

"You'll like this even less."

"What the hell is it?"

"A copy of a newspaper from the capital. Read the second page."

And there it was, eight columns wide: "Saint Teresa Urrea: The Miraculous Child from Cabora."

"What the devil is this?"

"Just read."

Teresa Urrea is originally from the state of Sinaloa and she presently resides with her father, Tomás Urrea, on his ranch in Sonora. She is not married and is scarcely more than sixteen, with almost no education.

"Sons of bitches! How dare they insinuate that Teresa is illiterate? Deluded, naïve, deceived, beside herself, perhaps, but illiterate? I'm going to . . ."

"Keep reading. . . ."

She was subjected to great suffering for a few days, which caused the extraordinary state in which she finds herself now. Today, Teresa Urrea alleviates all diseases, and some she cures completely, like leprosy, paralysis, and, in general, all kinds of nervous afflictions. She has knowledge equivalent to that of the best doctor: she knows where and what the disease is, what produced it, and all its symptoms.

One day, a young man arrived who was deafer than a doorknob, at the very instant that she was concluding a prayer, saying, "They have eyes and don't see. They have ears and don't hear," and the deaf man, for the first time in fourteen years, heard what was said.

"He probably had a wax plug the size of a horse's ass. Huila cured them by the thousands. That's what they call a miracle."

"The best is yet to come."

For her there is nothing hidden; she knows all the secrets of the heart, and to many she reveals the most private things of their lives. She hears at any distance and God made her understand all languages. The young Urrea also has a powerful force in her hands and in her whole body. With great ease she carries a sick man, using only one arm, and when she wants to use cinnamon for healing, she pulverizes it with her fingers, leaving it as fine as flour.

Teresa spits aromatic saliva, and a very pleasant aroma is left in her bath water, which the people soak up in their handkerchiefs to take the curative powers of the saint back to their families. She also says that her soul travels wherever it wants to, separating from her body.

This young woman is a treasure house of virtues. She preaches truth and abhors lies. She says that the most powerful of priests is the most evil and that God has declared all of their acts null. And if she wants to baptize or marry, she will do so because God has ordered her to. All this seems to have caused some horror among the clergy, and there are rumors that the bishop is going to excommunicate her. This does not worry the young woman, since she says she has higher orders that no bishop can rescind. She manifests a great interest in having everyone believe in her; on holidays more than five thousand visitors arrive in Cabora.

Don Tomás folded up the newspaper and put it on the table. He looked at Lauro.

"Do you know what will happen with this?" He didn't listen to his friend's answer; he had just decided to get his daughter out of her stupor no matter what it took and regardless of the cost; but before he could act, Teresa came back on her own.

 IV

On the day of her second death she would remember that long absence from which she returned after exactly three months and eighteen days. Without warning, she was there, aware of herself and of the anguish that reawakening caused her. It was like returning spilled water to a glass, an overflowing river to its banks, like enclosing fire in its own ash: it was dying twice over, reencountering the unequivocal prison of the body and of time. She woke up suddenly to the horror of oblivion, to the empty space without a speck or a scratch, to the hours, days, weeks, and months that had disappeared, to the opaque silence without a single resonance. Nothing: the void, a lacuna, a barren land without footprints. She realized she would have preferred to dissolve into death, into the blurring of forms and limits, into the absolute liberty of light, energy, mystery, but there was something that had held her, an invisible thread that didn't allow her to go and that brought her back to the restrictions of matter, hunger, sleep, to the ritual fragments of minutes and seconds: she was born again, and once more she had to confine the brilliance of a thousand stars in that simple human form.

It was three o'clock. Cabora was taking its traditional siesta. Everything was silent. She touched herself to see if she was alive, and her whole being awoke to not remembering. She made an effort to recover her memory but all she perceived, as though it came from an incommensurable distance, were the shreds of far-away days in Cabora, of Don Tomás's smiling face, of Gabriela's incessant prayers, of Huila's hissing voice: chaotic fragments that were rapidly traveling toward obscurity.

Between the present and what she remotely remembered there was an enormous blackness, a mirror with no reflections on its surface, a tear in the fabric of time, a lapse in the continuity of cause and effect: there were no reference points. Faced with this terrifying void, she lost control of herself and let loose a howl that split reality in two. Gabriela came running and threw her arms around her.

"Teresa! What's wrong?"

"I've lost myself! Where have I been? What's happened?"

"But you haven't budged from Cabora. The whole time . . ."

"How much time? How much time, Gabriela?"

More than three months, she told her: more than one hundred days, twenty-four hundred hours with all their minutes and their seconds.

"And all that time I've been asleep?"

"No, far from it! You've been all over, you haven't stopped . . . but, you really don't remember anything?"

She felt shipwrecked in a sea of immeasurable amnesia. One hundred days, lived daily, pass by like nothing, the myriad of motley and confusing instants is solidified in a few key memories that arrange them into a logical, manageable past. But, one hundred blank days! Not one entry! It was a vast span of time, longer than life itself! Under the threat of becoming a circular eternity, an inescapable labyrinth, each instant inexorably demanded its own registered reality. She had to reconstruct what she had left in the wake of her crossing so as not to go crazy. She lay down on the bed again and closed her eyes.

"Tell me about it," she said.

Gabriela felt a wave of emotion on hearing the long-awaited petition and opened wide the floodgates of her being. Rather than a river, what resulted was an inundation. She told her everything: her own recollections and those of others, what was seen and heard, the real and the imagined. Teresa took it all in, filling up the hole in time with an indiscriminate assortment of outlandish ideas, concrete facts, strange memories, verifiable occurrences, superstitions, credible events, and whimsical interpretations; everything was useful, provided it helped to muffle the colorless silence of that simulation of death.

She listened without protesting to the recounting of miraculous cures and of anathemas hurled against priests; of how she gave rubdowns with saliva mixed with earth from the hill and the newspapers made fun of her, saying she spit blood and cured hiccups; of how the people proclaimed her a saint and the priests said she was possessed by the devil; of how Don Tomás grumbled all day long and she foretold storms that appeared precisely when predicted; of how some people claimed she cured lepers, cripples, the blind, and the deaf and others said it was all falsified and made up; of how some believed that she had risen from the dead and others that she was hysterical; of how some said she was a mystic and others called her a lunatic. She told her about the cripples who had been healed, the miraculous childbirth of Doña Chucha, the deaf who could hear, the consumptive patients who got well. She said that sometimes she spoke of faraway voices and sometimes of sidereal silences, and all day long she seemed to be "gone," oblivious to her own needs, just thinking about the people waiting for her outside.

"I've seen it, Teresa: you perform miracles, you cure with your hands, with your saliva. . . ."

Teresa remained silent, receiving the muddled conglomeration of other people's memories. Finally, she sat upright on the bed.

"And what does Huila say about all this?"

When she found out that Huila was dead, Teresa felt that the net beneath her had unraveled. She listened with astonishment to the strange events that followed her "rebirth," as Gabriela called it: the tacit announcement of the old woman's death when she ordered the coffin to be kept, the healing of her limp with just one rubbing, the punctuality with which Huila fulfilled the prophecy, and the final smile that was fixed on her face forever.

"Huila said that Apolinio performed the miracle of returning you to us, but someone had to pay for it with a little bit of life, and that seemed to give her great joy. I had never seen her so happy: she walked all around the house, straight as an arrow, free of that ridiculous hobbling, and laughing wholeheartedly for no apparent reason, as if she knew something that the rest of us didn't. It frightened me, I didn't understand until I saw what had happened to you, that you had come back as a saint. . . ."

"Saint! That's absurd!" exclaimed Teresa, but she became quiet and pensive again. She remembered the days with Huila, what she had learned, Tencha's delivery, and that alien death that had latched on to her. Her teacher knew something that she hadn't told her, something about this unknown person that

Gabriela was describing, this new, incomprehensible "life." She lay down again.

"Keep talking."

When she had heard it all, she felt unrecognizable. It was as if she saw herself from a distance, standing upon a strange stage. She looked like herself, but enlarged, with something marvelous added that elevated her above all the rest. It did not displease her; it was just hard to believe. Once more she asked Gabriela to repeat the details of the cures, describing the people's faces, their gestures, their words. She wanted to know how she herself looked at the moment she laid her hands on a sick person, what expression she had, what phrases she used. Gabriela was delighted to repeat the stories of her kindness, her wisdom, the humility with which she accepted gratitude, the force of her presence, her generosity with the poor, her sense of justice, weaving such an imposing image that Teresa felt both admiration and fear.

"And Don Tomás, how has he taken it?" she asked.

"He says it's 'hogwash,'" and Gabriela laughed.

"Ah ha! So, tell it to me again."

And so she started the story again: "Exactly at midnight you came back from the dead. . . ."

Don Tomás returned at nightfall. Gabriela intercepted him before he could shut himself up in the library.

"She's come to," she said.

"Who? Teresa?"

Gabriela nodded.

"Does she laugh? Does she speak normally, without saying all those crazy things? Is she the same as before? My Teresa, the one who sang and rode and filled us all with joy?"

"Yes, but she's asleep now. You'll see her tomorrow. She's almost the same."

Tomás was so happy that he didn't notice the qualifier. He hugged his wife, swept her off her feet, and carried her to the bedroom. They made love until dawn, deciphering their bodies with caresses, measuring each other with kisses, until they lay exhaust-

ed. Immediately before falling asleep, Gabriela realized that in
their lovemaking she had surrendered her last trace of egotism.

"Tomás," she whispered, "I want to have your child."

Teresa got up before dawn; she yearned to observe without
being seen. She looked out the window and saw the multitude
that Gabriela had told her about. The encampment stretched out
on both sides of the ranch. Here and there small fires glimmered,
circled by silhouettes bent over the heat. Again she felt a mixture
of fear and astonishment. It was one thing to imagine all that and
another to confront the impenetrable reality of it. She sat down to
wait for morning. In the darkness she thought she heard Huila's
voice inside her head: "You have strange powers, child, strange
powers. . . . You tried to flee but you can't run from destiny,
because destiny is life. Apolinio sends his greetings," and then, a
kind of raucous laugh that fractured the silence into pieces. She
looked out again: the sun was coming up.

In the first light of dawn Cabora was unrecognizable. Rather
than clean, open space there were people everywhere, gathered
around steaming pots of beans, huddling under makeshift shelters. Indigenous worshipers executed their ritual dances in small
groups; lean-tos shielded entire families; there were booths set up
at the edge of the camp, selling trinkets, food, and objects of the
new cult of Teresita; far down the road, wagons and burros were
arriving, and men and women on foot; others were leaving.
Children were running around everywhere. So much commotion
was somewhat festive, somewhat of a circus, somewhat like a procession. From time to time the people would look toward the Big
House as if they were searching for something. She realized they
were waiting for her. That was the new reality created outside of
her consciousness. There was no escape. She felt a chill and heard
the raucous laugh once more.

At breakfast Don Tomás didn't stop talking, making plans,
organizing their life, scolding her tenderly for having fallen off her
horse, asking her to be more careful from then on, and repeating
how happy he was to see her well again.

"You realize, of course, the lunacy of what has been going on here?" he said, pointing outside. "I'm glad it's over! The beggars are turning Cabora into a pigsty. I already gave orders to Miguel to start dispersing them today."

"Yes, I know," responded Teresa and, breathing deeply, she continued, "I told him not to do it."

At first Don Tomás didn't understand; he thought he had heard wrong; he looked at his daughter, who returned his look without blinking. Then he felt the blood rush to his head, his ears turned red, his mouth filled with saliva, he couldn't speak and started to sputter incomprehensibly; finally, he banged his hand on the table, knocking over a glass of water.

"You did what? I give the orders here, I do, and no one else! How dare you contradict me in front of Miguel? Josefinaaa! Call the foreman; tell him to come here immediately!" And he fulminated his daughter with a fiery look. "That's all I need!" And turning his back on the table, he sat sputtering unintelligibly.

They waited in silence. Gabriela was trembling. Teresa didn't take her eyes off her father's back, as though she were taking his measure. Miguel came running, hat in hand. Tomás, gaining control of himself, turned to confront him.

"I gave you an order this morning. Did you carry it out?"

Miguel, disconcerted, looked at Teresa.

"Tell him the same thing you told me," she suggested.

"Well, you see, boss . . . how can I explain it? The truth is that the people are sneaking in everywhere and there's no way to stop them. Like ants. You should see what's happening to the grass. And yes, I can kick them out, but they come back, and no matter how many times I kick them out they just come back, or some go and others come and the more they walk back and forth on the grass, the worse it gets. So I told Miss Teresita that only she can get them to go, by telling them that there will be no more miracles. . . ."

"Don't talk to me about miracles! Hogwash!" He was pale, with the look of a cornered animal on his face; he turned toward

Teresa as if he were going to strike her. "Miguel's right! It's *your* fault and *you* should find a solution!"

"Of course, Don Tomás," she replied with the same tranquil voice, "but it's going to take time. Just as the word spread about my 'cures,' now it has to spread that I'm not doing them anymore so the people will stop coming. I'm going to need a few days. . . ."

"All right, a few days, no more, and don't come and tell me later that you believe in all this nonsense. Just ask Miguel about the cattle; they're saying that you reproduce at night what I sacrifice during the day. Just ask him how many animals they've eaten and how many head are left! That ignorant mob doesn't know how to count! A few days—and I don't want to hear anything more." He got up from the table and left the room, followed by Miguel. A few hours later he rode off toward Alamos without saying goodbye.

Teresa was left alone with the inescapable reality of the multitude that was waiting outside. Gabriela offered to accompany her. Together they walked to the esplanade in front of the house. As soon as they appeared, the hubbub of the crowd turned into a unisonous greeting.

"Good morning, Teresita!"

Teresa tried to grasp a fleeting memory that shone for an instant in the distance, but it escaped her. She looked curiously at the faces turned toward her and recognized what she had seen so many times when she accompanied Huila: an infinite hope that deepened with each individual gesture until it formed a substance that was almost tangible. She shed her fear. She knew how to cure: she had learned. She smiled and responded to the greeting; then she waited, but nothing happened. She looked at Gabriela.

"They're waiting for your blessing," she whispered.

"My blessing? What nonsense!" she said in a low voice. "Tell them to come forward."

"Miss Teresa says that the first one should come forward," shouted Gabriela. Nobody moved. They looked at her, perplexed; some had knelt down, others were waiting hat in hand, a few women were praying. Teresa felt irritated. Blessings were for the false ministers of hypocritical religions. She was just about to say that when she felt the strength of the looks, and she began to distinguish them, face by face, in all their intensity. She was flooded with a sudden shame, the same as when she thought she had fainted during Tencha's labor. At that moment a little boy, pushed forward by his mother, approached her.

"Aren't you going to give us your blessing today, miss?" he asked in a timid voice. Teresa extended her hand and drew him toward her.

"I want you to give it for me, little brother; surely you are cleaner in spirit."

A murmur of admiration ran through the crowd. The boy looked at her in amazement and then, adjusting his face to the seriousness of his task, he said:

"In the name of the child-saint Teresa, I welcome you, brothers," and he opened both arms as if he were offering to hug them. "May love be with you."

Miraculously, an orderly line began to form, and they began to come forward one by one. She attended to everything: diarrhea, colds, eye infections, menstrual cramps, a case of hiccups that had lasted a week; she gave out medicine for goiter and advice for curing insomnia; there were ear infections, festering wounds, wasp stings; for all of them she utilized Huila's prescriptions and that hushed, tranquil way she had of speaking to the patients. She caressed the children, hugged the young people, and took adults by both hands. All morning there wasn't anything beyond the ordinary ailments. But around five o'clock a young man who stuttered arrived.

He was about twenty-two years old and came accompanied by his mother, who explained to Teresa that her son couldn't manage to pronounce two words in a row and that shame had made him mute.

"Oh, Teresita! He needs to have a normal life, to get married and have children, but this way no woman could possibly want him; he isn't good for anything. Cure him for me; please, cure him for me."

Teresa doubted: she had never cured a stutterer. She felt a slight dizziness; the young man kept looking at her; she saw something in his eyes that she didn't understand. She extended her hand to touch his cheek and was instantly filled with anxiety; she began to tremble. Surreptitiously, Gabriela put a jar in her other hand; it was full of red earth. "This is what you use for these cases," she whispered in her ear.

She controlled her trembling, gently opened the youth's mouth, and sprinkled a little dust on his tongue. Then she took his head in her hands, covering his ears; she looked directly into his eyes. Under her gaze the youth closed his eyes. She began to speak to him so softly that nobody else could hear. She didn't even know what she was saying or where the strange, precise words came from. They seemed to come from a profound impulse, an urgency to wipe out the anguish that had spread to her and that had drawn deep lines in that young face. When she withdrew her hands and ordered him to speak, the young man said, without a single stammer:

"My name is Francisco Goicomea and I come from the community of Ures." The mother fell to her knees before her.

"Thank you, Teresita! This is a miracle. Oh, son, thank the young lady."

Teresa didn't listen to the words. Beside herself with joy, she shook from head to foot, possessed by an extreme exaltation; she was overflowing with tenderness toward the object of her healing and wanted to hug him. Gabriela had to hold her up so she wouldn't fall; for a moment she staggered like a drunkard and then collapsed.

The fainting spell only lasted a few minutes but the event exhausted her; she could hardly get up. Gabriela announced that she wouldn't see any more patients that day and the crowd dispersed. They all went back to their own business, lighting bonfires, reheating beans, speaking in low voices about the new miracle.

As soon as the euphoria passed, Teresa suffered a letdown that depressed her physically and emotionally. She allowed herself to be pampered by Gabriela, who surrounded her with maternal care, spooning a little soup into her mouth, breaking off small pieces of bread, tucking her into bed, and covering her with her favorite blanket. Teresa was too tired to protest. Finally, when she found herself alone, the silence bombarded her with memories.

Mixed with the images of the day were images of Huila telling her that more people were sick in spirit than in body; the ones who had a sick body were easy to cure; the ones with a sick spirit almost always needed a miracle; miracles happened in another reality that couldn't be expressed through words and to know a miracle one had to get behind the words. She concentrated on the image of the young man and saw, then, the circle—hard, red, angry. It was a circle of anger and she had broken it and absorbed it: that's why she became fatigued. It was a tenacious anger, vicious and self-destructive. But, what had happened? Had she spoken with the sick spirit of the youth in order to cure him? How had she managed that? She felt overwhelmed by a reality that transcended her but came from her: she had performed a miracle.

Immediately before falling asleep she thought of Don Tomás and felt a stab of compassion. He was going to be furious when he got back.

 V

The miracles became more and more frequent as Teresa overcame her fear and took a real liking to them. After the stutterer there were hysterical, feverish women who, after ten minutes of slumber under the influence of the "saint," woke up cured; kidney patients who passed massive stones after Teresa massaged the nape of their neck; the nearsighted and the blind whose eyes cleared up after Teresa blew on them; spastics and epileptics whose attacks ceased; deaf people who heard; others who left behind their insomnia, their tremors, their evil thoughts, their death wishes and fears. There were those who came to be cured of the evil eye, of shock, or of a spell put on them by some enemy or spirit. If she couldn't cure them, she told them, at the same time providing them with a good dose of resignation: the amputees went away giving thanks for their healthy limb, the moribund desiring to finally enter the other life, the barren blessing their orphaned nieces and nephews, the bachelors grateful for their freedom.

She acquired a new vision of the human body, different from what Huila had taught her, when she understood that pains in the extremities had to do with the head, those in the head with the heart, and those of the heart with the gut, and she discovered that by attacking the source the illness went away in the majority of cases. All this was strange and intoxicating to her. In each instance she understood exactly what she had to do without knowing why. It came to her not as a thought but as a feverish intuition that made her shake all over, feel anxious, and experience a strange, uncontrollable exaltation. But as soon as the cure was complete, that trance would dissolve in an almost indescribable euphoria that left her deliciously exhausted.

From doubt and unfamiliarity she progressed to astonishment and self-assurance: her anxiety melted into conviction and her fears into an irrevocable commitment. She began to crave the miraculous experience and hunger for the high it gave her. Nothing she had known was comparable to the vibrations of the mystery she experienced and shared. Anything routine began to bore her, and she was surprised to find herself actually wishing that the people who came would be struck with terrible diseases so she could perform a miracle again and feel the force that transcended her but that also elevated her above the rest.

She was no longer bothered by their worship and even accepted that the people called her "saint," although she preferred "child," as Huila had always addressed her. She never denied them her blessing again, and the simple rites of veneration they invented to please her filled her with tenderness. She comprehended that their ingenuous faith was part of the mystery, part of the whole that had been established between herself and the believers and that allowed the "miracle" to happen. Asking useless questions about the source, reason, or logic of the whole procedure would mean fragmenting it, destroying it, or as Huila had said, putting it into meaningless words in order to deny it.

Gabriela applauded the change she saw in her.

"What you are doing is so important, Teresa. You're not only healing bodies, but souls also. If it weren't for you, all of these people would be spiritual orphans. You provide them with hope and nourish their faith."

When Don Tomás returned two weeks later, Teresa was completely integrated into her own cult, and the multitude around Cabora, far from dispersing, had grown larger. She perceived his imminent arrival by the hint of violence, the scent of a storm on the breeze. A little while later she saw him crossing the plain at a full gallop. Pulling up his horse in front of the house, he dismounted and stomped in without looking around. She realized that a confrontation was brewing but continued attending to the sick people without allowing her calm surface to be disturbed.

The visit to Alamos, far from giving Don Tomás a chance to forget recent events in Cabora, had made the situation even worse. Everybody was informed; it was the daily grist. What they didn't know for sure, they invented, making it larger, exaggerating it, converting it into the greatest foolishness of the season, if not the decade. Don Tomás could read the mockery of society in the stifled smiles, the rejection in the reserved greetings, the malice in certain questions, and the disapproval in the conspicuous absences of some acquaintances. He felt naked and vulnerable; he realized that they attributed to him the responsibility for such brazen insanity and tried to defend himself by joking about it or telling that bunch of imbeciles to go to hell. But he was like an infuriated bull in a ring of rumors that he couldn't deny. Even though he tried to explain, Alamos refused to listen, it turned its back on him. That was unforgivable. Exhausted and humiliated, he lowered his head, and Loreto closed in for the kill.

She was beside herself. She confronted him with the ridicule she suffered, the offensive presence of Gabriela in Cabora, every one of the Indian girls of previous years, and all the illegitimate children. And, as if that weren't enough, she blamed him for the economic disaster that was hanging over their heads and over the innocent heads of their children, who, after practically not having a father at all, now had to put up with a foolish old man who was squandering their patrimony on a madwoman who supposedly healed people. And what for? For a horde of beggars, simpletons, spongers, and miserable, good-for-nothing idiots, gathered around an Indian woman who was usurping the legitimate rights of his children. A woman diabolically possessed! A messenger of Lucifer! An enemy of the church and of God himself! And all because *he* didn't have the balls to throw her out.

"How do you think Tomasito feels when they ask him in school if he's the brother of that lunatic, Teresa?" she shouted. "And Antonio, who came back from catechism crying because the nun made him recite three Lord's Prayers to save the soul of his errant father, who had dealings with the devil?"

Don Tomás could hardly believe his wife's crazed shouts. She had never raised her voice to him before, she had always been a model of abnegation. Now she was in a frenzy: she waved her hands, paced back and forth, and screamed as if she were going out of her mind. He felt like smacking her, but was afraid there would be repercussions throughout Alamos, to the greater detriment of his good name. To top it off, after scolding him, cursing him, and demanding immediate reparation for the damages, Loreto closed her bedroom door on him, denying him access to what was his by law. She kept yelling at him from inside. Not only was he to put an immediate end to the chaos in Cabora, but he also had to go personally to ask for a pardon and absolution from the bishop, who had denounced his heresy in public.

That was the last straw. If there was anything that Tomás had less patience with than rebellious women it was bishops and the clergy in general. At the top of his voice he told his whole family to go to hell, kicked the closed door of Loreto's bedroom, and fired all the servants; he threw chairs, hurled vulgarities and insults at the walls in a voice loud enough so that all the neighbors could hear, cursed the people of Alamos, the church, and his goddamn wife and the sissy sons she had given him, and when he got only silence as an answer he went to a nearby cantina and got drunk.

The next day he left for Cabora with a hangover the size of Chihuahua and Loreto's last words echoing in his ears.

"If you wanted a saint so much, you should have come to me: I've never reproached you for anything or complained about your whoring around on the ranch. Yes, I'm a saint for putting up with a husband like you. And if you don't believe me, just ask the bishop. But here's where I draw the line: either you put a complete stop to those heresies and diabolical practices, or you never set foot in this house again, do you hear me?"

Tomás heard her and continued to hear her even after he had put many miles between himself and the shouting. He heard her through the clouds of alcohol that exacerbated his senses and made his head feel as if it would explode; he heard her, and he heard all of Alamos laughing behind his back. He didn't stop hearing her until he had gone halfway back to Cabora. In spite of his hangover, he realized that his life, strategically ordered so as to offer him the best of two worlds—ranch and city, mistress and wife, freedom and high society—was crumbling around him, and for the least rational and logical reason possible: the struggle between two so-called saints; Saint Loreto and Saint Teresa, in whose sanctity he was the last to believe. Marx had mistakenly said that religion is the opium of the masses: it was actually the opprobrium of husbands. It was all Teresa's fault: she was the scorpion in the nest, in that rational and scientific nest that he had constructed for himself. And he had committed the error of placing her there, in the very center of Cabora. Between the humiliation and discredit suffered in Alamos and the irrationality installed in the ranch, they were destroying his sanity and his manhood.

He arrived home mortally wounded in his virility and in his rationalism. He was a cornered macho, a bull in a ring full of lances, and sharp *banderillas* brandished by a picador in skirts who obligated him to lower his head, a beast enraged by a scarlet cape of miracles that a taurine saint dangled in front of his eyes. When he discovered the increased throng at the ranch, he saw red and immediately sent for Miguel.

He began to stomp back and forth in the library, reaffirming his decision: the enemy was to yield or to leave, that was all. He was the master, the father, the maximum authority in Cabora—not even the powerful Díaz dared to intervene in his domain—and he was the good boss, the provider, the guardian of security, the generous protector. Nobody, much less the illegitimate daughter he had taken under his wing, had the right to challenge him. He would give the peremptory order and the enemy would fall, defeated by his fury.

Miguel arrived, pushing in front of him a poor wretch about fourteen years old, dressed in rags, dirty, and uncombed. He greeted the boss without letting go of the wisp of a girl, who looked around with wide, frightened eyes.

"I found her snooping around behind the house. She was trying to sneak in. Look at her, boss, just look at her. This is the kind of disgrace that is becoming the plague of Cabora. They're like roaches, everywhere! You see? There are more than a thousand of them out there!"

He had been waiting for the boss to return so he could vent his desperation. He let loose a string of accusations and complaints about the horde, how many times he had mended the fences that had suddenly gotten into the habit of breaking down to let the multitude pass, the posts that stubbornly insisted on maintaining a horizontal position. There was no way to keep things in their place with so many feet, so many animals, so many wagons, so many mules.

And the fences were just the beginning of the problems. There were the cows whose milk dried up as if by magic and the calves that got skinny instead of getting fat. There were the pastures whose grass became more and more raggedy with the endless stream of feet that trampled on it daily. There was a problem with the wells due to the increased demand, not only for drinking and watering the cattle but also for bathing, since Miss Teresa was bothered by filth, not to mention the fodder that they "borrowed" to feed horses, mules, and oxen, or the serious reduction of the herd. And then there were those like this one, he said, shaking the rag of a girl that he held in the grip of his hand; every day he caught somebody trying to breach the lines and sneak in through the kitchen to get to Teresita before anybody else.

The girl twisted and turned, trying to free herself from his grip.

"Hold still! And you know what this thing wants, boss? She's here so *your* daughter can do a 'miracle' for her," and he pointed at the girl's belly, "because some cowhand jumped her and knocked her up. And just like this one, boss, there are a thousand of them out there, screwing up your . . ."

In spite of his growing anger against Teresa, it seemed to Don Tomás that the foreman was bordering on disrespect and he ordered him to shut up.

"I'm completely informed of the situation and well on the way to finding a solution. Why do you think I sent for you? I understand they keep getting through the fences all around the ranch. You would need an army to guard the borderline between irrationality and pure reason. So, the evil must be torn out by the roots, its source must be dried up, and that's precisely what I'm going to do. Now, take that thing out of here and notify Teresa that I want to see her immediately."

Teresa saw him coming from afar, dragging the poor creature, who looked as if she were about to die of fright. She finished rub-

bing a consumptive patient with saliva and went to meet the foreman. But she wasn't looking at him, only at the girl. Nobody had
to tell her why the child had come; she had suspected it ever since
she saw her slip around the edges of the crowd and go behind the
house. What she couldn't have suspected was that when she saw
her close up, she would be reminded of Cayetana. It was like seeing her own mother at the age of fourteen, terrified by the foreign
body occupying hers, hunched over a rebellious belly that insisted on growing, her innocence wrenched from her by the
unwanted maternity. Like a whiplash she felt the cruelty of her
own conception.

"Possessed," Huila had said; "your mother felt possessed." She
stood looking at the little bundle of bones and fear, wrapped in a
brown skin, who said to her: "Get this evil thing out of me! I don't
want to die!" and it was as though she contemplated at the same
time—through her own eyes and Huila's—Saturnina Dórame, the
child-mother she had before her, and Cayetana Chávez, the moth-
er-child who had borne her. She confused past and present and
stopped distinguishing between Saturnina and Cayetana, who
seemed to moan: "I'm going to die; I need you to give me something to get rid of this little package that was left me by . . ." Had
she said "my father" or "your father"? Was it Saturnina's father or
her own father, Don Tomás? Was she going to save Saturnina from
being the mother of her brother and the sister of her son, or was
she saving Cayetana from the cruel process that robbed her of her
childish illusions and converted her into a shadow of herself?

She shook her head and looked again at Saturnina Dórame,
whose hopeful eyes were fixed on her, and then heard Miguel
repeating that her father had sent for her.

"Tell him I'll be there in a while; I'm really busy. . . . And,
Miguel, try to do something to feed all these people better. There's
no disease worse than hunger."

She began to prepare the thick, bitter brew of corkwood,
thinking that perhaps she was Huila, breaking the vicious circle
of her own birth, death, and rebirth at the beginning. She

watched Cayetana-Saturnina gulp down the venomous tea; fearing the death, not just of the product but also of the child-mother, she didn't leave her for a minute during the frightening process of spasms, contractions, uncontrollable vomiting, and dry heaves until almost twelve hours later, when she was sure that the poor creature had discarded her "bundle." She helped her bury it with the proper ceremony. Saturnina-Cayetana had recovered a little color and even a certain sweetness in her look when she finally kissed Teresa's hand and promised to be a good girl from then on and not accept any more indecent paternal advances. She watched the child slip away among the multitude as surreptitiously as she had come. Only then did Teresa remember that Don Tomás was waiting for her.

Still thinking of Saturnina, she walked toward the house. She didn't feel the least bit guilty for having alleviated so much suffering, even though it meant the termination of a possible life, but she asked herself why Huila hadn't done the same for Cayetana. The old woman had sacrificed her mother so Teresa could live. She felt strangely indebted for a life that could have been so easily wiped out. She thought again of poor Saturnina-Cayetana, no more than a little-piece-of-living-Indian-flesh, and of the violent irresponsibility, the unpardonable cruelty of both fathers, Saturnina's and her own. Suddenly she realized the irreversible damage done to her child-mother by that egocentric, insensitive man, and she was overwhelmed by guilt and repulsion for having taken up so joyfully with that violator of young girls. For the first time she felt a deep rage toward her father.

Don Tomás was waiting for her, surrounded by the silence of his books, his cigar smoke, and the vapors of the cognac that had slightly calmed the fury produced by Miguel's message.

"She said what?" Nobody had ever before refused to follow an order of his. "Bring her to me immediately, even if you have to carry her!"

"They aren't going to let me, boss."

"Who? Who's not going to let you, if I'm the boss here?"

"Well, no offense, but all those people don't see it that way; for them, Teresa gives the orders. . . ."

"Those people . . . those people eat, destroy, rob, and shit on *my* property! They've turned it into an outhouse."

"Maybe if you go personally, boss. I mean, with all due respect, she's your daughter and she has to obey you. As for me, well, frankly, with all this going back and forth, I'd be better off just looking for another job. Try to understand, a man feels put down when a woman doesn't pay any attention to him in public."

Tomás controlled himself as best he could. He told Miguel he was right and sent him away. But he didn't dare to go and call her himself. When he looked out the window and saw her there, surrounded by so many people, so sure of herself, so much in command of the situation, he realized that the esplanade, that part of Cabora, had stopped belonging to him: it was Teresa's inviolable territory. Besides, if she refused to come . . . He didn't want to imagine what would happen if she contradicted him in front of everyone. He preferred to wait. The first drink convinced him that he had made an intelligent decision: it was better to lure the enemy onto his own terrain. He congratulated himself for having drawn up such a good strategy for battle and celebrated it with another cognac, then sat down to wait. As glass after glass of the comforting liquid circulated through his veins, his arguments seemed more and more logical and convincing, and his enemy less and less formidable. So when Teresita finally arrived at about dawn and Don Tomás had drunk to the bottom of his rage as well as to the bottom of the bottle, he was sure of his victory.

When he saw her enter he didn't even recognize the enemy. He only saw his daughter and she looked tired, with a pale, tense face and an exhausted body. His defenses crumbled; he remembered all the nights of joyful singing and he yearned for their return. He was surprised by the air of docile gentleness that surrounded her, as if she were all goodwill and sweetness. He felt again that he liked his daughter, that he didn't want to lose her. Teresa, on the other hand, still had the scent of the cornered girl in her nostrils, the image of Saturnina in her head; she was alert and on guard.

"I'm here," she said.

 VI

Don Tomás started speaking slowly, measuring his words. He just wanted to remind her that he was her father and that thanks to his recognizing her and taking her into his home, she had the last name Urrea; otherwise she never would have left Aquihuiquichi. He wanted to remind her also that with that last name and while residing in his house, there were certain things that were not permissible, like bringing ridicule to the family or going against what was minimally acceptable to society. It was one thing to go barefoot around the ranch or to ride a horse bareback, and quite another to boast of so-called powers and get the whole state in a tizzy. This—Don Tomás was sure—she was perfectly capable of understanding.

In addition, perhaps she wasn't aware of the damage to the ranch caused by her "charitable" activities: the reduction in cows and calves, the daily consumption of milk, the slow depletion of wells and watering holes, and, of course, the unrestricted amount of human excrement that Cabora endured daily because of the presence of that horde of fanatics, but she should take all that into consideration and realize that it wasn't fair to the rest of the family. Also, it was obvious that the whole matter was degenerating into a fair: the booths, roving vendors, tents, dancers, bonfires, and prayers were embarrassing to decent people. He didn't doubt a bit his daughter's kindness or her desire to do good; on the contrary, he was appealing to those qualities in her so she would understand his position and agree to remedy the situation as soon as possible, starting tomorrow.

Of course, once the fanaticism and fervor had died down, if she wanted to continue making Huila's rounds, he wouldn't prohibit that, as long as it was just among the people who belonged to the settlement, but in no way was it appropriate for her to continue with the so-called miracles, with this hogwash about being a saint, and with his whole property converted into a pilgrimage site.

As Tomás spoke, he remembered the insults he had suffered in Alamos and the defiance of his own daughter, and his voice increased in volume, his gestures became more extreme. Teresa stopped listening to the words and began to observe the person. She lacked logical arguments with which to refute the cold reasoning of her adversary, but that "cold reasoning," if one didn't pay attention to the words, was wrapped in so much theatricality, so many emotions, suppositions, and defenses that it got lost. She thought of Huila again, about how she told her that language fragmented reality to such a degree that you ended up not understanding anything. She smiled. For the first time she saw her father trapped by pride into denying what he perceived with his five senses and affirming the self-serving abstractions of his intellect. The miracles were "hogwash" even though they were palpable; the people were "beggars" even if their need could be felt from afar; the ability to cure was "an obstacle to the dignified life of the family" that consisted of three people, or five, or ten, against the multitude of people seeking help. Her activity was subject to the "rules of society" constituted—of course!—by the elite from Alamos and not by the hundreds of thousands of inhabitants of the Yaqui valley. She boiled inside with a new sense of justice that was charging her with an energy contrary to the one that was produced when she was just about to perform a miracle. Her look hardened and her mouth lost its smile. She observed her father as he continued to rant and rave, and she was surprised to notice the weakness visible in his mouth, only half hidden under his huge mustache, the fear crouching in his eyes, the trembling dissimulated by his gesturing hands.

". . . so it's all decided," announced Don Tomás, interpreting her silence as agreement. "Tomorrow—not a day later—you tell those people that you aren't going to heal anymore, make up any excuse, tell them God ordered you not to, who cares what you say. . . . You're good at that. Miguel and his men can run them all off the property. You go inside the house, and if someone shows up, we'll tell them you're sick or you went on a trip. That's it, a blessed remedy, and we go back to a normal life"—he kept looking at her and his voice changed from the authoritarian tone to a more tranquil one—"like we had before when we sang at night and you and I talked about the important things in life, remember?" He reached out his hand to touch Teresa's shoulder and she stepped back; the man's hand was left suspended in air, making an absurd gesture. Don Tomás frowned, and their eyes met in the hard space that separated them. The father's voice became a growl.

"I've had enough of your haughtiness, young lady. I've just given you an order: I expect you to carry it out, and there'll be no more discussion of the matter."

Teresa stood there in silence for a moment, sizing up her enemy. Then she turned to go, but stopped when she reached the door, her hand on the knob. She looked at her father again.

"It will not be done as you have ordered. It can't be, but I'll offer you an alternative: have the blacksmith's workshop fixed up, on the other side of the esplanade, so I can attend to my patients there and leave the Big House with more privacy." She quickly walked out, closing the door behind her. When she heard the shattering of a bottle against the wall, she paused and then hurried to her room.

The man's face dissolved in the heat of his ire until there was only skin hanging on the bones, with an astonished expression burnt into it. From surprise he leapt to incredulity. The alcohol simmered in his veins like a witch's brew; reason and logic were transformed into blind rage, patience into desperation, self-assurance into entrapment, and authority into an unpostponable act of violence. After the bottle smashed against the wall, two books followed, then the kerosene lamp, a jug of water, and the cushion from the chair, whose muffled impact brought his tantrum to a halt. The silence was like a slap in the face. He ran to the cupboard, took out another bottle, and guzzled a drink that no longer even tingled as it gushed down his throat. He took his pistol from the drawer and put it in his belt. He sunk down into the armchair to order his thoughts with the alcohol's help, but his thoughts stumbled over each other, creating illogical images and phrases; Loreto and Teresa became confused in a contradictory torrent that threatened to drown him: magic and absurdity, the ridiculous and the sublime, order and insanity, reason and faith, misery and wealth, need and mockery; ideas converted into bullets one after the other until he felt that he was going mad, that Cabora was turning into a nightmare, torn asunder by a savage beast that would have to be eliminated. In his imagination he felt himself driving a dagger into the enemy's flesh, weeping with rage and pain, shooting her with his pistol, sundering his own existence, pummeling the life out of her with his fists, asking for her forgiveness from the depths of an irreparable guilt, until in his dreams he left her inert and he fell asleep in the armchair.

Teresa closed the door to her room and got into bed. From there she could hear Don Tomás's violent eruption. She was shaking all over, but the decisive step had been taken. She had no choice: she had seen reality, had lived the miracle, had touched a destiny beyond all imagination. She was committed: there was no turning back. She thought again of Saturnina-Cayetana, with tenderness this time. If not for anything else, she ought to fight this battle for them, to its ultimate consequences. When the house finally fell silent, she let sleep creep over her, shrouding her with a thin, dark blanket of numbness.

Walking down the empty corridors of a restless dream-sleep, Teresa encounters Don Tomás, who walks through the corridors of a an untimely nightmare. Teresa envisions an uncertain and cloudy future in which the enemy is still unknown; Don Tomás conjures up the past when his will was law and an order from him fixed everything. Don Tomás opens his mouth and seems to say: "Tomorrow you pack your things and go; you take your saintly hogwash with you and leave me the clean name of Urrea; you leave me my peace and solitude; you take those miserable people with you; the party is over." In the dream his words taste like salt and they dissolve like shadows before Teresa's eyes. Teresa opens her mouth and speaks with tenuous threads of light, small sparks that illuminate the oneiric corridor: No, Don Tomás, I will not go away tomorrow or the next day or the next, not for a long time, and when I do go, you will go with me. We will go far away, seeking death and leaving Cabora behind for oblivion to rule. I'm very sorry. Here the only authority is destiny." The corridors of the dream fold in upon themselves and the sleepers awake, each in his or her place.

Teresa opened her eyes in the dark and observed the silence. Don Tomás opened his eyes in the dark and, drawing his pistol, staggered out of the library. Teresa listened to the faltering steps and fixed her gaze on the door. Tomás stopped before the door of her room. Teresa heard the hammer click; the door banged open. Don Tomás raised his weapon and pointed at the luminous eyes of his daughter. She looked down the dark tunnel of the gun's barrel and didn't find her death there. The silence grew; each one recognized the other and knew that they were instruments of something inexorable. Suddenly, the stillness was broken; Don Tomás shut his eyes, lowered the pistol, and broke into a heartrending vomit of sobs that seemed to tear his insides to pieces. Teresa understood why men sometimes would rather die. She looked away so her father could leave with what remained of his dignity.

The next day the rebuilding of the blacksmith's workshop began. From then on it would be known as "Teresita's House."

✸ VII

On the day of her second death Teresa would remember with a certain sadness the calm after the storm that ended in her father's defeat. She didn't sleep anymore that night, fearful of the consequences of her triumph. When she got up, she checked to be sure

Don Tomás was still shut up in the library, in a silence that was only broken from time to time by the splash of cognac in a glass. Then she looked for Miguel.

The foreman didn't raise an eyebrow when he heard the orders to remodel the smithy; he had seen the two adversaries before the battle and had his bet well placed.

"I reckon the boss won't get out of this one alive," he told his wife that night.

She had just finished giving instructions to Miguel when Gabriela appeared on the esplanade. She was worried about Don Tomás, who hadn't even greeted her upon his return and was still locked up in the library.

"I don't know what I've done to make him treat me like this," she said, crying.

Teresa consoled her without revealing the real motive for her father's isolation, which she attributed to a bad encounter with the family in Alamos, and she advised Gabriela to leave him alone for a few days. Gabriela accepted the explanation without further questioning and during the rest of the day helped Teresa mobilize the people and the encampment and move them to the space behind the workshop, far out of sight from the library. The move took most of the day. When they returned to the Big House, Don Tomás was still locked in.

All the rest of that week the door to the library remained closed as a silent reminder of the profound wound suffered by its lone occupant. Now and then they would hear a bottle smash against the wall. Teresa began to worry: his behavior was beginning to seem like a slow suicide, for which she was not exempt of guilt. Finally she decided to send a note to Lauro Aguirre, asking him to visit his friend.

When Don Lauro arrived, Teresa was already installed in her new quarters. Although she would continue to live in the Big House, her newly inaugurated quarters would be the center of all her activities from then on. Lauro sought her out and for a long time observed her healing, taking notes in a small notebook and asking Gabriela when he didn't understand the form of treatment employed.

"What is the red earth she uses for rubbing?" he asked in a low voice.

"Rock dust. It comes from the cave up there," replied Gabriela, pointing toward the strange hill. "Teresa says that it has curative properties, but she doesn't know why."

Lauro made a notation in his book. "Power of suggestion beyond normal; possible innate ability to hypnotize. Indisputable charisma in the management of crowds."

When Teresa had finished taking care of the sick people, she went into the little house with Lauro and told him the truth about what had happened. Lauro listened without commenting until the young lady concluded: "I'm convinced that he's trying to kill himself."

"I'll speak to him. If I can make him understand exactly what it is that you're doing and how important it could be, I think he will accept it."

The two friends were secluded for a day and a half, speaking in voices so low that only a murmur could be heard from the other side of the door. At two o'clock on the second day Teresa and Gabriela were relieved to see them walk out with their arms around each other and sit down at the table to eat together. Don Tomás was pale and gaunt, but he held his head high and ate with real appetite, although in silence.

Slowly everything returned to normal. It was a few days before Don Tomás spoke to Teresa again, but when he did it was as if nothing had happened between them; neither of them ever mentioned the confrontation, and Teresa was careful not to talk about her "cures," which now at least were taking place at a conciliatory distance from the Big House.

Teresa did what she could to smooth over the situation. She docilely carried out any paternal request and avoided disobeying him even in petty things like riding bareback or taking her shoes off under the table. She took greater interest in the problems of the ranch and helped organize the visitors in such a way that their presence was felt less by her father and took less of a toll on the property. Finally, she revealed to Don Tomás the location of a new well that solved the water problem during the whole year-long drought, when the cattle in the rest of the region were dying in droves.

For his part, Don Tomás established an absolute protectorate around his daughter, so that from then on nobody in Cabora dared to criticize her. Miguel was somewhat surprised to receive from Don Tomás the order to keep the cows with newborn calves far away from Teresita's followers so they wouldn't steal the milk, to regulate the number of animals sacrificed to feed the multitude, to repair the fences as many times as necessary, and to assign two cowhands to channel the large pilgrimages along the roads in order to avoid greater destruction to the pasture land. Grumbling about his boss's foolishness and the abuses of the crowds, the foreman entrusted his wife with lighting candles to as many saints as she knew so the cows would deliver twice as many calves. The woman lit a candle to Saint Teresa of Cabora, and that year they had a prodigious number of calves.

Little by little they went back to the evenings of singing and poetry; father and daughter rediscovered the mutual pleasure of chatting until the early hours of the morning; and their love and reciprocal admiration grew beyond what they had had before the rupture. It seemed that the happy times in Cabora were returning. In April, Gabriela realized she was pregnant and immediately shared her secret with everybody: She asked Teresa for advice.

"It's going to be a boy and it will be born strong and healthy," she answered, "but it would be better for you to start taking care of yourself. It's not good for you to be standing here all day, helping me."

"But you can't do it alone . . ."

"Don't worry, I won't be alone. I'm expecting somebody. . . ." She didn't finish her sentence but raised her eyes as if she were straining to see something beyond the horizon. "She'll be here by eleven o'clock at the latest." And she hugged Gabriela and sent her back to the house.

Gabriela accepted being replaced with good humor; she was itching to start knitting baby sweaters. She asked Tomás to send to Alamos for blue yarn and everything necessary to adorn the basket that would serve as the baby's first cradle.

At eleven o'clock sharp Mariana Avendaño arrived with her mother. They came from Navojoa and were just getting settled at the edge of the crowd when a girl approached them.

"Saint Teresa says you should come forward. She's expecting you."

Mariana was not surprised by the unusual message; she didn't believe in sainthood but she didn't deny the existence of miracles. She took her aged mother by the arm and followed the girl until they reached the front of Teresita's House. The young woman was watching them from the entrance and, smiling, gestured to them to come in. Inside, the small living room was comfortable but simple; it had a fireplace, several chairs, a sofa, and a table. Teresa sat down and invited Mariana to sit next to her. Mariana had the impression that they had already met, but she didn't know when, how, or where.

"Let's see," said the young woman, "first, your mother's hand."

The old woman extended her arm with the gnarled hand; Teresa took it in hers and, turning it over, deposited an enormous glob of spittle on her palm. The old lady laughed, confused, and as a reflex shut her fingers around the saliva; then, with disgust, she opened her hand and began to shake off the spittle that covered it. Teresa and Mariana were doubled over with laughter to see the incredible flexibility of those fingers that a minute earlier had been so stiff; her daughter passed her a handkerchief and turned to Teresita.

"How did you know we were coming?"

"I've been waiting for you for some time. Come, leave your mother here awhile and accompany me," she said, taking Mariana's arm and leading her outside. There was, as every day, a long line of patients waiting to be seen. All eyes turned toward Teresita, and she made a sign that they should wait a little while longer. "Look," she said, with a gesture that encompassed the throng. Mariana looked; she contemplated one by one the raised faces, saw the small groups formed way back around the bonfires or under shaky shelters, gazed at the booths on both sides of the road, and observed a little group of children playing in the dirt. Then she turned toward Teresa.

"You need someone to help you, right?" Teresa smiled. "And I need company, a family, because my mother will be gone soon."

"Perhaps by tomorrow," Teresa said, putting her arm around her shoulder, "but don't get upset; you can stay here with me if you wish, and in exchange I promise to give you the children that you've never been able to conceive."

A few days later they buried the old woman. Mariana settled into Huila's old rooms and with no further ado began to work with Teresita. She was thirty-five years old, and she had a husband who disappeared from her life without leaving children or any sign of his passing; she didn't mind the husband's inconsistency, but she had an irrepressible yearning for offspring. With Teresa's promise she felt the first relief she had experienced since she learned she was barren. There was no doubt in her mind that Teresa would keep her promise, though she didn't have any idea how. She wasn't used to asking questions or nurturing anguish; she had a clean and healthy belief in the goodness of life. From then on she never showed any amazement at Teresita's cures, nor was she inclined to making them into a matter of faith: they were just as natural a phenomenon as any other. To exist was, in and of itself, a great miracle: why should she be surprised that there were also partial miracles?

Mariana was already integrated into the family at the beginning of that unforgettable summer of 1890, when the worst drought in ten years began to dry out the northwest. The air itself seemed to generate unbearable heat as it wafted over the land from sea to shore and from the shore through the Yaqui valley and along the dried-up Mayo River without leaving behind even a hint of humidity; it crossed the ranch of Cabora with its breath of fire and went up over the crest of the Sierra Madre Occidental until reaching the previously cool city of Alamos where, in the afternoons, Loreto fanned her rancor while she waited for the consoling visit of the bishop, who had replaced Father López y Sábana as her confessor. All of Sonora was panting with thirst. The drought was so bad that the Yaquis stopped attacking the ranches for fear that their horses would die of dehydration during the retreat; the soldiers abandoned their persecution of rebels for fear of sunstroke; the ranchhands gave up herding cattle because there was nothing to herd, and even the buzzards were shriveling up as they stood before cadavers so withered they couldn't be eaten. The drought paralyzed life, and life hid under a stone, in the shade, in the patio, behind a bush, in the cave, in the barracks, in the settlements. Only in Cabora was there any movement: Cabora was the miracle.

It was the miracle of the inexhaustible well where people drank and the cattle were watered; the miracle of the fat cows that managed to feed everyone; the miracle of the fair and the music that started up again with every sunset; the miracle of Teresita; the miracle of health and abundance. There were days with five hundred pilgrims, others with a thousand, sometimes even five thousand or more; nobody bothered to count them: they arrived, settled in, left, and others arrived. They were a formless mass, mobile and bustling, in which the individuals were distinguished only by their ailments: vomiting, diarrhea, injuries, blindness, deafness, stuttering, a numb hand, paralysis, headache, the evil eye, sterility, depression, rheumatism, pimples, fever, a buzzing in the forehead, dental problems, gangrene, gunshot wounds, body odor, typhus, coughing, loss of appetite, tumors, limping, idiocy, pregnancy, cancer, goiter, alcoholism, neurasthenia, and curiosity.

Teresa worked from dawn until the midday meal, and from five in the afternoon until sunset, day after day. Her existence became an interminable line of people waiting to be healed; endless, repetitive expressions of gratitude; a constant clamor of the multitude; a series of rituals, homages, praise, eulogies, and odes to her kindness, rectitude, tenderness, wisdom, virtue, supernatural powers, dedication, generosity, and saintliness. Miracles became the routine and she was filled with belief in herself. The early self-doubt was transformed into a certain lack of modesty in regard to the simple beliefs of the humble people who swore that on her lips they found only truth, from her hands they received only miracles and good works, in her eyes they saw only sweetness and tranquility, in her actions they felt only compassion and justice, and in her they found only perfection. Conceit began to burrow into her bones, and every day she listened more eagerly to what the people said. Veneration and the supernatural became her daily bread.

Don Lauro's visits increased in frequency during those hot months, and in contrast to Don Tomás, who never approached his daughter's work zone, the friend posted himself there hour after hour, observing, taking notes, and chatting when the young woman was not busy. He was the one who brought her the news that the priests were condemning her from the pulpit, saying she was an instrument of the devil. When she expressed surprise, Lauro responded with a philippic: he called the priests "serpents' tongues" and "antichrists," accused them of being corrupt, and predicted the fall of the church. His eyes flashed as he spoke; he was furious: how could those vermin dare criticize her, put on holy airs, tell such horrendous lies, when she spoke the truth? They predicted death, she gave health; they lived off others like drones, she never accepted remuneration for her services; they slumbered in opulence, she lived a simple life. How dare they, when so many hundreds of thousands recognized her and only her as the salvation of the poor, protector of the humble, hope of the sick and of those who loved justice? They had some nerve!

Teresa listened to it all and felt a justifiable indignation growing inside her. There was no doubt that she had enemies, but these were, as Lauro said, creatures with little heart and less soul, liars, or at best, dimwits. Truth was there, with her. Cabora was the center of the world, the point of confluence of the times. But the sting of public criticism nestled into her memory like a larva, and she found herself going back over her friend's words time and again, cultivating a secret rage and an even more secret desire for vengeance. One day she spoke of this with Mariana, who listened and then shrugged her shoulders.

"What do you expect, Teresita? I bet that if Christ himself returned, they would crucify him again."

Thus, during the candescent months of May, June, July, and August, while the heat and drought disheartened spirits and inflamed minds, while 178,000 of the region's cattle died of thirst and 23,547 diverse ailments were cured or accepted as inevitable in Cabora; while the country's newspapers lost interest in the phenomenon of the new saint and filled their spaces with news of greater profundity like the imminent total pacification of the Indians in Sonora or the signing of a contract with the Richardson Company to open irrigation canals on the banks of the Mayo, Yaqui, and Fuerte Rivers or the contract for the purchase and colonization of the fertile lands bordering the rivers; while the ship *The Democrat* of the Mexican navy sailed from Guaymas, carrying fifty infantrymen to combat the rebellious Seris on the Island of Tiburón; while some inhabitants of the region were wondering if it was true that four comets would be seen that year and others were debating the most recent opinion of the Psychic Research Center of London on the dreams of the dead; while the Wandering Jew roamed around Chihuahua, causing fear among the citizens, while the government of Sonora refused to pay the stipulated twenty-five hundred dollars to Mr. Morley for producing rain because only five drops of water had fallen on Hermosillo; while in the district of Ures all the cereal crops were lost; while the Chinese continued to arrive in Guaymas in order to impose on the population the custom of eating chop suey; while Francisco I. Madero was finishing his studies in preparatory school; while Catarino Garza was up to his usual shenanigans on the border to the great despair of Porfirio Díaz and his henchmen; while in Mexico City they were finishing construction of the most modern penitentiary in the world; while the engineer Lauro Aguirre finished up the contract marking the boundaries between Hermosillo and Ures and took the opportunity to listen to the latest political gossip; while all this and even more was happening in every corner not only of Sonora but of the whole country, Teresita's reputation was spreading from mouth to mouth, from ear to ear, from town to town, in spite of or perhaps because of drought, hunger, repression, and injustice.

The pilgrims crossed miles of desert under the lacerating rays of the sun, with thirst piercing their throats and hunger burrowing like a tapeworm into their stomachs, with pain seeping out through a leg, an eye, a mouth, or their private parts, with disease or despair gnawing at their words, their sighs, their tears, but with hope coveted in a secret part of their heart or their mind. They converged in groups of two or four, ten or twenty, and found others on the road in a long line that extended from the horizon to Cabora and another that moved in the opposite direction as far as the eye could see, spreading the news, speaking of the limp that disappeared, the miraculous fainting spell that cured 110 cases of influenza, the gentleness of the voice that reached all the corners of the ranch and the ears of the most distant visitor, the miraculous multiplication of the cows, and the water that flowed endlessly; they told of how the saint knew that Doña Lupe's paralysis was caused by the sin of incest and condemned her to ten more years of being crippled; how Teresa was in a trance and a disbeliever pierced her leg with a hatpin without her feeling anything or bleeding a drop; how a rich man arrived to have his mute son cured, and how he was scolded by Teresa because he wanted to pay her when he could do much better being generous with his workers; how, when she bid farewell at the end of each day, Teresa would raise one of her miraculous hands and there would be such a complete silence that even the babies stopped crying and seemed to listen to the saint's words of love, justice, and hope; how she made the milk flow for the new mother; how she cured with saliva Don Crisógono's wound after it had been festering for three years; how Teresa knew who believed in her and who didn't, and how she wouldn't heal those who didn't but just send them home; they talked about the miraculous cures with the blessed water from Teresita's evening bath, the perfume that emanated from her body, but above all they spoke of her infinite kindness, her celestial love for everyone, her patience with children and the aged, with women whose husbands beat them, with abandoned mothers, with men tired of living, with those defeated by poverty. Nobody left Cabora with empty hands. Some went with new health, others with resignation, others with hope, others with the memory of a smile, others with the shine of Teresita's eyes, which would keep them company in their solitude.

And thus the image increased in size and grandeur until it shone throughout all corners of Sonora and traveled with the breeze that came down from the Sierra del Bacatete and nestled into the hot valley of the Mayo and wound through the towns and villages of Sonoíta and Agua Prieta, through Magdalena, Trincheras, Aconchi, Carbó, Babiácora, Huasabas, Cócorit, Bacanora, Arizpe, and arrived at Ures, Sahuaripa, Tubutama, Cucurpe, the ranches of Bacamaya, Mayobampo and Bacamocha, Jambiolobampo, Baborácahui, Chinobampo, and Echomocha and returned, coming and going, entering and leaving the depressed minds, the desperate hearts, the hungry bellies, leaving behind believers in the living saint, the Caboric Teresa, final justice, the retribution of the exploited, the future, the wait-just-a-little-more, the it-will-happen. And gradually a belief began to form, a religion with its rituals and prayers recited in silence, at night, with sonorous phrases in which the name Teresita magically appeared. They sang supplications, lit candles, gave special nicknames to the saint, requested strength, health, vengeance, retribution; they commended a child to her so it would grow strong, a lover so he would be faithful, a husband so he would return soon, a rebel so he would triumph over the *yoris,* the dispossessed so their land would be returned to them, a woman so she would stop drinking; they were grateful for the favors she granted, and they endured with resignation the ones she saw fit not to grant, because she was wise and she judged only from the truth.

Thus, when August had run its course and the first week of September arrived with no sign of rain beside the five drops that the thieving gringo had tried to charge for in Hermosillo, and when people were convinced that celestial injustice was uniting with so many human injustices, there began to converge on Cabora those who were not searching for physical health but social well-being; they didn't want to be healed, they wanted justice; they clamored for the land that the government had taken from them as well as rain for what little land they had left, which, it seemed, God was wrenching from them through drought, taking sides with the sellout, brown-nose clergy. So it was that the representatives of all the indigenous tribes of the region began to arrive to request Teresita's celestial intervention: they wanted rain.

Teresa was frightened. The people from the tribes were determined not to leave until she made it rain. She consulted Miguel, but he looked up at the sky, shrugged, and continued mending the fence. She went to apologize to the people. She told them the truth: she couldn't make it rain. She could cure their maladies or alleviate their colds, even overcome their fear of death, but rain was something else. She explained to them that she wasn't capable of entering into a trance at will, it was forbidden for her to demand an answer to concrete questions, and she only knew what came to her spontaneously and there was no hint of rain. They didn't believe her. They asked, by means of a spokesperson, if the drought was due to their sins. Then she spoke about the lies of the clergy, their representation of God as a vengeful being, and how they manipulated through deceit in order to exploit the people. But the rain and drought did not depend on God, but on the climate. She told them to go back to their homes and wait; sooner or later it would rain. But they didn't go.

"They're still waiting," Mariana told her. "They say they're not leaving until you give them an answer they can understand. They don't believe you can't make it rain."

Their unshakable faith bordering on mulish stubbornness drove her to despair. From then on she limited herself to speaking in the least spiritual or magical way she knew. She spoke of the phenomenon of rain and its excesses or absences. She spoke of the winds and the ocean currents, hot and temperate fronts, relative humidity, spontaneous condensation, and gradual evaporation, until she ran out of knowledge. But the people wouldn't leave. Either they didn't understand or they didn't want to understand that she couldn't convoke the powers of heaven to produce the rain they needed so much. Then she got angry and told them with a firm voice that they should wait a little while, soon abundant water would fall; within a week or two, she promised them, it would rain more than they needed. To her surprise, they were convinced, they thanked her for granting them the miracle, and with her "promise" they went peacefully back to their homes to wait for the water the saint would send them.

As soon as they left, Teresa felt relieved and returned to her routine. She forgot about the whole issue until September 8 when the sky took its vengeance and night rushed in at midday. Great gusts of wind swept the region, and the rain arrived with unprecedented force. The rivers overflowed their banks, ravaged the tender crops, carried off the precarious roofs of the huts, and filled with joy all the believing hearts that had waited so patiently to see Teresita's prediction fulfilled.

The phenomenal rains continued day after day until they became national news. In the capital they reported a "deluge" in the state of Sonora that had caused serious damage to the agriculture and cattle industries and destroyed bridges over the rivers and sewers in the towns; the impetuous currents had carried away entire sections of the railroad tracks and partially suspended traffic between Guaymas and Nogales. They spoke of inundations and of waterways leaving their beds, destroying fences and carrying off cows, buildings, and even the most recent boundary markers.

So much water poured over the state that at first nobody noticed the disappearance of the Mayo workers. But that meteorological phenomenon had no sooner degenerated into a stubborn drizzle when the hacienda owners observed that the docile and submissive Mayos had abandoned their jobs, left the ranches and towns where they had lived, procreated, and died, to gather—this was discovered later—at the settlement of Jambiolobampo, within their sacred territory. The haciendas were without workers, the fields abandoned, and the cattle left to stray. The general alarm reached the ears of Colonel Antonio Rincón, military chief of the Mayo Territory, whose responsibility it was to keep the peace and enforce the hard work and total submission of any Indian who raised his head in protest. The unusual happenings gave him a bad feeling so, without even waiting for the weather to clear up completely, he set out to take action.

✸ VIII

Colonel Antonio Rincón was a man of arms, ready to fight at the slightest provocation. Along with a squadron of his best soldiers he went from ranch to ranch to confirm that there was not a single Mayo remaining except for those too young or too old to walk and the women that cared for them. The only place immune to the strange phenomenon was Cabora, where the colonel arrived on September 21, at dusk.

In Cabora, what the inclement sun and the long months of drought had not managed to do, the torrential rains had accomplished. For the first time that year Teresa was free of patients. The endless line of suffering beings had disappeared, and the two or three stragglers that withstood the first days of the deluge had finally given up, fearing that the cure of the wart or the evil eye would cost them a pneumonia that all the celestial arts of the saint would not be able to cure. Therefore, on the day Colonel Rincón arrived, soaked to the bone, he didn't find anything out of the ordinary, and certainly not the huge crowds that had been reported to him. On the contrary: he was presented with a family scene of daughter, father, mistress, and someone who resembled a maiden aunt gathered around a large table. Nobody knew anything of the flight of the Mayo Indians, and it was obvious that at Don Tomás's ranch it hadn't occurred. Colonel Rincón rejected the invitation to stay the night and galloped off to Jambiolobampo to surprise the insurgents and return the lazy, good-for-nothing Indians to their respective owners for a swift punishment of forced labor.

The unexpected exodus of scrawny, ragged, tired, and submissive Mayos was not due to the motives that the colonel suspected but to something totally different. When he arrived at Jambiolobampo with his squadron of soldiers armed to the teeth, he saw a young Mayo about twelve years old standing on a great rock, surrounded by more than a thousand followers. Men, women, and children listened while Damián Quijano, the boy prophet, announced a new deluge from which the Mayos should take refuge in the highlands.

Colonel Rincón stopped to listen from a distance. The flood would be the second for the Mayo people, the first being the one of their creation. Besides, it would come "to baptize our land with the water of new life" and to liberate all Indians from the oppressive yoke of the treacherous, thieving white man and the brown-nose mestizo. "So then the *yoris* will die, the white man will swallow his own dirt, those who have offended our gods will be washed away by the waters, and the Mayos of true heart will reign again over the valleys and mountains that have always belonged to them." Damián Quijano swore that it was not only he who had received that prophecy, but also Saint Isabel of Macochi, Saint Camila of Ilibaqui, Saint Agustina in Baburo, and Saint Irineo at the ranch of Sapochopo. In Tenanchopo, Saint Luis knew of it, in the town of Cohirimpo, Saint Juan and the blessed child called "The Light" preached it, and beyond the high mountains it was predicted by Saint Barbarita, whose sacred powers had been confirmed by the elders of Chopeque; but above all, there was a saint whose truth nobody could doubt, Saint Teresa of Cabora, who in a dream had seen the future when the Mayos would once more be the owners of their land. Teresita had foreseen the arrival of rain and the unusual force with which it would arrive, so great that it could be interpreted as the second deluge.

It seemed to Colonel Rincón that the deluge was actually a deluge of saints with a frankly subversive desire to see all civilized people die and the region return to its original barbaric state. He had a hunch that this could turn into an epidemic of the worst kind: an epidemic of insubordination, seditious mystics dedicated to disturbing the peace, upsetting law and order, and destroying progress. Even though there were no signs of revolt at that moment, one couldn't ignore the twisted intentions of those gathered there to summon a flood that was supposed to wipe from the face of the earth the heroic Mexican army, of which he was an outstanding officer for his pacification of the Mayo Territory, a feat that was being challenged at that very instant and before his very eyes by a twelve-year-old child! And all this when he had just sent, scarcely two days earlier, a telegram to President Díaz announcing that the Mayo people were completely subdued and would give no more problems in the future. Not only did all this promise to be dangerous, but it could also make him seem like a fool in the eyes of the supreme leader of the army. It appeared to be a sinister plot against him and against the true government; those recently discovered saints were actually an army of subtle enemies that could destroy his future.

"Water they want," he murmured to himself as he planned his strategy, "and water they'll get." He ordered his soldiers to round up all those present.

The capture of the sixty people gathered there who didn't manage to escape—including seven old people, three lame men, twenty pregnant women, a blind man, and twelve youngsters under fifteen years of age—and of the boy prophet was carried out immediately. This first arrest was followed by others to detain Saint Isabel and her followers, Saint Agustina, Saint Irineo, Saint Juan, the one called "The Light," and a few others they found along the way and arrested just in case. They resisted the temptation to go after Saint Barbarita and the elders of Chopeque because they would have to invade the neighboring state. They couldn't find Saint Camila in the forests of Ilibaqui because, according to rumors, she had gone to Cabora, and they didn't even mention Teresa because her last name was Urrea.

Once his mission was fulfilled, Colonel Rincón put the two hundred prisoners at the disposition of military justice for the appropriate investigation of the case. A few weeks later he informed his superiors that no proof of any subversive intent had been found beyond the express wish for the death of all Mexicans by drowning. It seemed like a resurgence of mystical deviations provoked by ancient beliefs and a profound rejection of the church. "Nevertheless," the report concluded, "since these meetings always have been a source of upheaval with serious consequences for peace, order, and progress and since they also distract honest, hardworking men from their occupations, this General Headquarters, in agreement with the Government of the State, decided to send the prisoners to work at the mine of Santa Rosalía, where they were accompanied by their respective families. I have given instructions that they be paid one peso and twenty-five cents a day, which I consider to be a just retribution, given their condition of convicts."

The first news Teresa had of the events was some time later when Lauro Aguirre recounted them to Don Tomás. They were in the library and Aguirre was shaking a newspaper in front of his friend's face. Therein appeared, duly outlined with thick, black lines, the letter of condolence that Porfirio Díaz had sent to the relatives of Colonel Antonio Rincón upon his death from fulminant pneumonia caused by bathing in cold water.

"Divine justice, in the deepest sense!" exclaimed Aguirre. Teresa remembered the visit by the Colonel, who at that moment had seemed like a good man; courteous and elegant, he had given the impression that he didn't want to bother anybody. She hadn't imagined then that a few hours after leaving Cabora he would carry out—against defenseless Mayos—the cruel and absurd military actions that Aguirre had just described. She remembered having seen a young boy about Damián Quijano's age among the solicitors of rain that had given her such a headache. The whole affair made her uncomfortable; she felt a premonitory trembling. Don Tomás looked worried; Aguirre, getting more and more excited, continued to rant and rave.

"But, wait, you haven't heard the worst, the grand finale that has no name. Two hundred altogether, men, women and children! Do you realize? The innocence, the hopes of those creatures, believing that by working in the mines in Baja California they would pay for their alleged crimes: the crime of faith, the crime of confidence, the crime of wanting to regain what is legitimately theirs, and they could return one day to their lands, their people, their homes. Oh, into whose clutches has this poor country fallen? Teresa, you've seen them, you've helped them, tell me: what harm do they do? What threat do they pose to the monster of tyranny who governs from the capital with an iron hand? They invoked your name to ask only for justice! They wanted water, a deluge, a flood that would liberate them from the eternal abuse of the powerful. But Rincón had to have his sacrificial lambs to satisfy the thirst of Herod-Pilate. They all embarked on a ship, even the smallest and the child saints, victims of spontaneous somnambulism produced, of course, by hunger. They all embarked, to the great delight of the bloodthirsty colonel, on a warship ironically named *The Democrat*, which was to take them to the peninsula. But they didn't even make it to Guaymas: they were thrown into the sea and drowned. That was the water, that was the deluge, that was the flooding, the flooding of the lungs of women and children! And all because the tyrant, the monster, the modern Herod can't live with the truths proclaimed by a child saint!" With a dull thud Teresa fell to the floor. Her face was white, her eyes rolled back, and she shook all over. Don Tomás

ran to her side, took her pulse, tried to calm her. Suddenly she
became stiff.

"My God! She's in a trance again. I thought that was all over.
She was overwhelmed by the story you told." He picked Teresa
up in his arms and was surprised to find that she didn't weigh
anything. He carried her to her room.

"That story would overwhelm anybody," murmured Aguirre,
pouring himself a glass of cognac.

When Mariana arrived to take care of her, Teresa had already
come out of her trance and was sitting on the edge of her bed,
staring at the wall. She was pale and her hands were cold, but she
didn't want to lie down again.

"It was just a fainting spell; I'm all right now. Leave me; go
take care of things out there. I want to be alone a while; I need to
think," she said. Mariana noticed that her voice was strangely
hoarse, as if it came from some deep well inside her, and Teresa,
as she spoke, did not look at her; instead, she stared straight
ahead at the wall. She quietly withdrew, but she was worried:
there was no doubt that Aguirre's account had profoundly affected the young woman.

When she was alone again, Teresa shut her eyes. In spite of
the silence, she couldn't organize her thoughts. The images of the
crime flashed through her mind in a confused jumble. She could
still hear the howl that preceded her fainting spell. It was the cry
of Damián Quijano; she saw his frightened face beneath the gulf
waters, his black eyes full of confusion, his mouth full of suffoca-
tion. Damián didn't understand. If the water was to carry away the
evil ones, to drown the *yoris* and liberate the Mayos, why had it
swallowed so many innocent people? This is what Damián's look
had shouted, and then his eyes had clouded over with the sadness
of death. One after another in the turbulent wake of the ship
called *The Democrat,* they had been thrown overboard; one by one
they were torn into shreds of fear and anguish, enveloped in the
liquid nightmare. Then silence, nothing . . . , and then Teresa
heard what she didn't want to hear: the last words of Damián,

echoing in her mind over and over again: "You promised us water, Teresa, you promised us, you promised us, you promised us . . ." like a funeral chant that gradually materialized into something terrible, confusing, dark, sinister.

She looked at her hands and touched her mouth as if they were foreign objects independent of her will. How was it possible that she had pronounced a death sentence without realizing it? What forces operated within her on the margins of her consciousness? The deaths of those poor people had been sealed with her promise of water. They weren't good deaths, they didn't belong to those who died; they were truncated existences, unfulfilled destinies, eternal mistakes, assassinations that broke the ebb and flow of life, that interrupted the cycle, the natural transformation of all things into other things; it was as if the night had rebelled against the day to impose darkness; as if the sea had risen in a gigantic wave to swallow the solid earth. They were arbitrary deaths, dark and dreadful. They hung chaotically over innocent lives that were lost in the solitude of nothingness. Those deaths belonged to her; she was guilty.

Once again she felt fear of herself, of the powers that she didn't understand and that were capable of taking on a cruel independence without her being able to foresee the results. What would Huila have said if she were alive? Would she scold her for having pronounced words so lightly, for having made a vacuous promise just to get rid of a bothersome problem? How could she have faith in herself if she didn't even understand the meaning of her own predictions?

"No," Aguirre told her when she confessed her anguish to him, "you aren't responsible for those deaths, but you have a very powerful enemy who is capable of transforming good into evil in midstream, of twisting the paths of destiny to suit his own ends, of converting you into an accomplice of his schemes. You should get to know him and understand him thoroughly so that he can't defeat you. The tyrant, Herod-Pilate, that is the enemy personified: his name is Porfirio Díaz.

Teresa started under the impact of that well-known name; she remembered reading Doña Rosaura's newspapers. Suddenly everything she had read took on an ominous new meaning. She saw the threatening image of a short man with an enormous mustache in the diffuse photograph of the paper and remembered the insidious way in which they spoke of him and his desire for power. She felt another pang of fear. How had he been able to deceive her and involve her in the murder? What frightful irony! She had prophesied the end without realizing it. Was it possible to mistake the omens or to not even see them and thus precipitate an unjust and irrevocable outcome? Could good change into evil in midstream, as Aguirre said, without her being able to avoid it? Could the enemy be so powerful as to succeed in making her an accomplice of his schemes?

That night she couldn't sleep. She tossed and turned in a dreamlike state, searching among the images that tortured her for the face of Damián and shouting at him: Why did they kill you, Damián? What evil were you doing? Explain it to me, Damián! Finally the youth appeared to her amid the turmoil and smiled, saying: "They killed me because they were afraid of me," and disappeared again.

IX

When Porfirio Díaz, in turn, found out about the existence of Teresita by reading Colonel Antonio Rincón's report, he said the same thing as Don Tomás: "Hogwash!" He had no time for false saints.

Those had been the years of the war for peace, and he had emerged triumphant. He had waged war on the rebellious political bosses and the restless opposition, the disobedient Indians and the bandits that plagued the roads, the Apaches and Cajeme's family, kidnappers and thieves; he had shot the convicts and beaten down the troublemakers; he had declared war on the

international debt and inflation, the economic crisis, and the low
production of petroleum; he had battled the national deficit by
increasing tariffs on nonexistent services, and the colonialist
ambition of the neighbor to the north by inviting foreign invest-
ment in everything, from mines to railroads, from edible products
to whore houses; he had waged war on cultural backwardness by
Frenchifying indigenous customs. He fought against the earth-
quakes that shook up his constituents and the epizootic of the
chickens, and against the defects of the race by importing tall,
handsome Italians, hard-working Mormons, musical Cubans, and
hundreds of Chinese to teach the Mexicans to eat vegetables. A
couple of times he had ordered the noisy volcano of Colima to be
silenced, and he had combated unceasingly the subversive whims
of nature: hail and floods, freezing temperatures and storms, a
scourge of locusts, drought, and hurricanes. He had managed to
submit the pride of forests to the servility of railroad ties, the
haughtiness of silence and distance to the tap-tap of the tele-
graph, and the docile entrails of the earth to the extraction of its
riches. He had waged war on the epidemics of yellow fever in the
northeast, cholera in the southeast, influenza in the northwest,
typhus in the southwest, and hiccups on the central plateau. He
had fought against boredom with an overproduction of cane alcohol, and against enteritis, weight loss, whooping cough, malaria,
itching, and pneumonia with neglect. He had detained the exodus of his countrymen at the northern border and prohibited the
incursions of the Wandering Jew in Chihuahua. He had made war
on the lack of honorable national ambitions and the surplus of
dishonorable political ambitions, on bullfights and cockfights, on
alcoholic merrymaking and on unpatriotic illiteracy with hundreds of official schools, and on anything else that was opposed
to progress.

But it hadn't all been war. He had suspended the attacks on
fairs and circuses, covertly made peace with the clergy, encouraged dancing, maintained a peaceful coalition with the rich, and
brazenly abandoned the war on poverty. They acclaimed him

"Hero of National Integration," "Defender of International Harmony," "General Pacifier," and they decorated him with the extraofficial titles of "The Indispensable One" and "The Necessary One," until God should decide to call him. All that and more he had achieved with his own bare hands, with perseverance, without straying an inch from his task, and he wasn't willing to allow the sudden increase of saints and similar hogwash to ruin his success. He immediately sent a terse telegram: "Watch alleged saint. Keep me informed. PD."

After what happened to Damián Quijano and his followers, Teresa became more quiet, almost taciturn. She continued attending to the sick, but no longer with the same joy. Sometimes she looked at them out of the corner of her eye, with mistrust, as if she were looking for something besides the simple ailment described to her. During the week after her fainting spell she had long conversations with Lauro, becoming informed about the procedures of the enemy, the organized espionage to keep even his supposed friends in line, the traps and lies, the murders, the distribution of political positions to his staunch supporters, the obligatory exile for anyone who protested. Lauro had alerted her to the possibility of spies among the pilgrims to Cabora.

"Evil never sleeps!" he told her before leaving. "For him, virtue and kindness are his greatest enemies. Be ready to fight."

Nonetheless, the rest of the year passed without further frights. On her birthday more than five thousand people sang the traditional song, *Las mañanitas,* for her. There was no party, just an extremely long line of visitors who waited to kiss her hand, wish her happiness, give her a little homemade gift: a leather pouch, a ribbon embroidered with colorful threads, a bunch of oregano, a flower. Gabriela made her a cake; Don Tomás gave her a hug but refrained from inviting guests. Since Cabora had been transformed into a sanctuary, he preferred solitude to possible ridicule and avoided all contact with society.

On Christmas Eve more than ten thousand visitors gathered to receive the Baby Jesus in the company of Teresita. They sang hymns and litanies in their indigenous language, roasted cows and lambs, and waited for the saint to pass by to greet each group. She walked around the encampment until dawn, exchanging comments or greetings with everybody. She had never seen so many people. She felt secure, strong, protected. She thought again of the Enemy. Had he ever gathered so many kindred souls around himself? Aguirre said no, all he had were potential traitors, who would turn against him as soon as the revolution broke out. Teresa didn't ask any more questions. Every time Lauro spoke of a possible revolution, she felt a chill.

Aguirre made it his duty to keep the Urreas informed and to advise them to be careful. Don Tomás lent little credence to the news.

"Your head is full of imaginary revolutions, Lauro," he said, "but Díaz has much more serious problems elsewhere. How could he pay any attention to Teresita's cures when he is facing a colossal economic crisis, the second year of a hellish drought, and the presidential elections of '92?"

"If you want to play blind, that's your problem. But there is something you shouldn't ignore: espionage! Teresa's name has already reached Díaz's ears because of that business with the "child saints," and I have no doubt that he is infiltrating the crowd out there with spies who keep him informed of everything."

Later Teresa listened as Lauro painted her a panorama of possible threats and dangers in his usual bombastic language. "The enemy is stalking you," he said; "he has a thousand ears, and eyes everywhere. He's like a crouching animal, ready to pounce on his quarry. Everything you say, he hears; everything you do, he sees. You ought to take care, never say what you really think, never do anything that could seem subversive."

"Nonsense!" Teresa said to Mariana that night. "What could I do that would seem subversive or threatening to such a powerful man?"

Nevertheless, she became more alert and began to observe that there actually were strange people mixing with the multitude, people that stood out precisely because of their obvious attempt to blend in: they never approached her, they observed from a distance, spoke with visitors, asked questions, and then disappeared and others arrived. She instructed Mariana to be vigilant.

One afternoon in mid-July Mariana came running to her. She waited until Teresita had finished with the patient whose turn it was, and then signaled to her to enter the house. She shut the door with an air of mystery.

"Outside there are three tall, bearded men, with rifles. They have been just watching all day; they don't come forward, and they don't leave. They don't seem to be from around here."

Teresa opened the door a crack and peeked out. She saw them immediately. They were standing together with serious faces, not speaking to each other, with the brims of their hats pulled down over their foreheads. One was a little in front of the others: he had black hair, a mustache and a beard, and light skin. Teresa felt strange palpitations that she couldn't explain and closed the door.

"Let's wait. Find out what you can from the crowd."

That day Teresa continued to cure, but she was uneasy. Now and then she looked at the immobile trio; they never took their eyes off her. They were like statues, full of stony patience. Later Mariana returned; she hadn't been able to find out anything. The three men hadn't spoken with anybody; they had arrived at dawn and posted themselves there, and since they were armed nobody approached them or asked any questions. Somebody thought they were probably from the mountains.

"We'll see tomorrow."

The next day they had moved a little closer, as if to get a better view, but without changing positions. On the third day, the same thing happened. Teresa decided to take matters into her own hands.

"Mariana, go talk to the tallest one, the one with black hair, and tell him that I want to see him and that we don't permit weapons here."

Mariana approached the group and delivered the message. Immediately the rough men took off their hats, lowered their rifles, and laid them on the ground. Teresa entered the house and waited next to the small fireplace. Mariana arrived, followed by the tall man, who held his hat in his hand. He stopped and looked directly into Teresa's eyes without lowering his own, in contrast to the majority of people who visited her. Seeing that look, Teresa felt the inexplicable shiver again.

"Leave us, Mariana, and take care of those who need medicine."

Left alone, they contemplated each other. Teresa recognized at once the feverish luminosity in the other's eyes and felt a little startled because they were so much like her own after she had performed a miracle.

"You have been here for three days, brother, and you don't come forward. Why are you here?"

"To see the powers of our saint." Teresa raised her eyebrows. "And?"

"What we have seen has convinced us. We want to take you with us, to Tomóchic."

He spoke firmly, without looking away or raising his voice.

"All those people outside need me, brother; how can you ask me to leave them? How many are there in your village?"

"About 250."

"Outside there are ten times that number. Think about it. Let's try to do what's just."

Teresa was not afraid, but the presence of that man, his strange look, made her uneasy. She was filled with curiosity and a peculiar excitement. She motioned to him to sit down and then sat facing him.

"What's your name?"

"Cruz Chávez."

"Tell me your story, Cruz."

Then he spoke to her of Tomóchic, the isolation of the village in the mountains of Chihuahua, the beautiful, extensive forests, the peaceful, hardworking inhabitants, how he had become their

leader, the young people obligated to work in the mines belonging to the region's political boss, the threat of the draft, the
religion that had died because the priest visited so rarely, and the
new religion that he had established and for which she was their
living saint.

Teresa listened without taking her eyes from his, which were
sparked by some internal flame and a certain magnetism that
attracted her; his voice had a rough sweetness, his words were
simple and direct, without a hint of deceit. His hands were large
and strong, like hers.

Cruz continued speaking as if he didn't realize that she was
observing him. He spoke of the love the Tomochitecs had for
their village, how they had defended it from the Apaches, how
they worked the earth, how proud they were. Then he spoke of
the painting that the secretary of the governor had tried to steal
and how they hadn't let him, and the visit of Father Gastélum,
who had denounced Teresita for heresy and demanded that the
Tomochitecs renounce the devil and the mistaken cult.

Cruz stopped; his eyes full of passion, burning with desire for
justice. His indignation at the priest's words was contagious, and
she felt it.

"And did you pay attention to him?"

"You'll see what attention we paid to him. During the sermon
nobody said a word, but we looked at each other and it was as if
we had all reached an understanding. Before he could finish his
harangue, I got up and, after me, the whole village rose as one;
we left Gastélum talking to himself."

Teresa was quiet for a moment. She felt that she was under
the influence of a great exaltation. Cruz had defended her the way
she wished that her father would. She laughed and answered his
inquisitive look by saying:

"How I would have liked to see that! To see his face when
you all turned your backs on him! What satisfaction it would
have given me to lead that march! It would have been like spitting in the faces of all those priests who have spoken against me!

You did it for me, Cruz, and I'm very grateful. Now we are brother and sister!"

Cruz's eyes did not waver from hers, and she felt uneasy; something unknown was trembling inside her. She had the inexplicable desire to touch the man, not as she touched her patients but as a friend, as a brother, as . . . She extended her hand and Cruz took it in his and kissed it very gently, scarcely brushing it with his lips. Teresa gasped; tears welled up in her eyes. She lowered her face so the man wouldn't see them. Cruz let go of her hand and remained quiet, gazing at her.

"Do you think there will be problems in Tomóchic?" she said in an almost inaudible voice.

"I'm afraid so. The elders of Chopeque told me that torrents of blood and fire would descend on my people. That's why we came, to ask you to protect us."

Teresa felt frightened. Once again she felt the enemy's threat, and she was afraid her words would be betrayed, as they had been when she spoke to Damián Quijano and the Mayo Indians. She tried to explain that to Cruz but he made her feel strangely timid.

"How could I protect you? No, Cruz, that's not possible; I couldn't . . . Surely, the elders of Chopeque are mistaken. But if they're not, you shouldn't make war, you should arrange things peacefully; you shouldn't allow any deaths, no blood should flow. . . ."

"Why are you afraid, Teresita? Isn't it true that you do the impossible? We've seen you, and we've been told. We believe in you and faith works miracles, doesn't it? If you believe with all your heart in something and fight for it to happen, it can happen, isn't that true? Don't you know that, too, Teresa?" He took her hand again.

"Yes, sometimes . . ." She wanted to talk to him about the enemy, but the man's fiery eyes stopped her; his exaltation affected her and made her afraid, afraid of herself, of the tumult of feelings that were pounding in her chest. She had the impression that something terrible was going to happen but she didn't know what. She didn't remember ever feeling so intimidated. "But it doesn't always happen that way. Maybe . . ."

"Then, that's all I ask. Let us believe in you, accompany us in spirit and accept being our saint. From time to time send us your thoughts and your words; I'll know how to interpret them for the good of my people. I don't ask for anything more."

"I will always think of you, all of you," murmured Teresa. "I will ask with all of my being that the elders of Chopeque be mistaken, brother Cruz, but promise me that you will not shoot, that you will not initiate the violence." Teresa stood up and the man followed suit.

"I promise you."

They gave each other a long, intense look. She extended her two hands; she wanted to touch him again. Abruptly, Cruz kneeled down and lowered his head.

"Give me your blessing."

Teresa felt confused, suddenly alone and empty. She gave him her blessing. Without saying another word, Cruz left the house, joined his men, and rode off toward the mountains.

Chávez's visit disturbed her. All afternoon she couldn't get his image out of her head. Mariana noticed she was distracted or, rather, engrossed, and fearing another attack, she advised her to lie down. Teresa obeyed. She couldn't concentrate on anything; she had a new voice inside her and that voice said "Cruz!" It was like a unique and powerful murmur that wanted to come out and couldn't. She slept, and in her dreams she ran after him in the mountains, but he didn't hear her or look back. She couldn't catch up to him, she lost sight of him, and then suddenly out of nowhere a wall of fire that wouldn't allow her to pass arose between them. From the other side she heard cries and human howls, and dogs barking piteously, but the fire made her retreat. She woke up trembling with cold.

A week later Lauro came to visit and she took the opportunity to tell him about the Tomochitecs. She hadn't stopped thinking about Cruz. She feared for him, for what might happen to him, but she didn't speak of that. Instead, she told him of the problems with the secretary and with Father Gastélum. Did he think the Tomochitecs were in danger?

Lauro noticed that she was strangely excited and tried to calm her. It wasn't likely that Herod-Pilate would take troops from areas where he had real problems—which was throughout the whole country—and send them to combat two hundred mountain people who had refused to be robbed of a painting. No. He thought there was absolutely no danger. Surely what was happening was that the isolation of those poor men made them exaggerate any contact they had with the outside world and think that the rest of the country was noticing them. Teresa felt a little more calm, but the memory of Cruz continued to haunt her.

It was Lauro who was left worrying. He refrained from telling Teresa what he had heard recently about the political problems in Chihuahua, the power struggles between the followers of Terrazas and Don Porfirio's supporters, and, worse yet, the logging potential that the forests of Guerrero had, many of which traditionally belonged to the Tomochitecs. Railroads! The monster's passion to connect the whole country with railroads and thus be better able to dominate and become rich with the work of others. For the railroads, a lot of wood was needed. Later, without revealing what Teresa had told him, he commented to Don Tomás that he feared there would be problems in Chihuahua in the not too distant future. Urrea was surprised, but he didn't say anything. Better for him: his friend was always announcing an Indian uprising in Sonora. Better they did it in Chihuahua, where there would be no repercussions for Cabora.

From then on Teresa could think of nothing else. Her head was full of Cruz, she saw his face as if it were still in front of her, she heard his name repeated a thousand times in her ears, she felt a desperate hunger to touch him, and every so often she stopped attending to patients so she could shut her eyes and converse with him in her mind. She called him "brother Cruz" with a familiarity that would have surprised even Mariana, and when she did so, her heart beat in a strange fashion, as if it wanted to leave her chest and go looking for the man whose visit had left her with a profound restlessness; her only consolation was the hope of seeing him again sometime.

As the days passed, Teresa became more and more confused: she didn't understand why the strange visit had made her feel like the most lonely and unhappy woman she had ever known. Sometimes she was irritable: the mute adoration of the people annoyed her; frequently she found herself responding brusquely when they tried to kiss her hand and refusing to give the customary blessing or throwing out the water in her washbasin so that Mariana couldn't give it away. Three times she publicly denied being a saint and asked that they not address her as such; she was just as human as everybody else. Later she controlled herself, thought of Cruz, and tried to be sweet again; she asked everyone's forgiveness, explaining that she was very worried about a soul brother in Chihuahua who was in grave danger.

Mariana said nothing about all her strange behavior. She attributed it to fatigue, menstruation, or the heat and tried to lighten her load. But Teresa insisted on working from morning until nightfall, devoting herself compulsively to the tasks of the day so as not to think about the mountain man. With time she stopped hoping for another visit and was able to calm down the exalted feelings that were torturing her. Slowly the image of Cruz faded and things went back to normal. Teresa believed she was cured; she was so relieved that she promised herself never to feel that way again.

In August the rains arrived and the number of patients dwindled. Don Lauro came to visit, and the nights were full of guitar music and long conversations on politics, the restlessness in the country, and the multiple uprisings that the tyrant repressed with a murderous fist. A little while after the visit from the Tomochitecs, Gabriela had given birth to a robust baby boy and spent most of her time taking care of him. She almost never appeared in the chapel any more: for the first time in her life, the woman was completely satisfied. In October Teresita had her eighteenth birthday, and once again *Las mañanitas* were sung. In November the temperature plummeted and there were deep freezes. A hard winter was predicted.

It wasn't until the second week in December that the news arrived at Cabora and Teresita found out: Tomóchic had taken up arms against the government of Don Porfirio. Tomóchic . . . the nightmare.

 X

"I'm telling you they're coming toward Cabora."

"That's all we need: rebels from the mountains! I don't like it, Lauro; I don't like it at all."

"I was right . . . Chihuahua could be the fuse. There's a reason . . ."

"Reason? Reason is what we need around here! If I didn't know you better I'd think you'd lost your ability to reason, like that crazy young woman who allows herself to be made into a "saint" by any beggar with fleas. Or perhaps you believe that a handful of rebellious mountain men can take on the forces of Díaz?"

"Force will not always conquer truth, the will of the masses, hunger, misery . . ."

"Hogwash!"

"Hogwash yourself! The day it happens nobody will be left untouched. We should prepare ourselves, but you act as if Cabora were a magic island, untouchable; under whose protection? Do you think that when the troops arrive your daughter's powers will shelter you?" Aguirre paced back and forth, his face flushed, his voice hard.

"Calm down. . . ."

"This is no time for calm! It's time to act! We've been waiting for fourteen years for Díaz to leave under his own steam and he's just dug in his heels and clung to power! The tyrant must be overthrown and for that we need weapons! You, Tomás, have the best weapon right here under your roof, a weapon that just by her presence can wake up the dormant masses. . . ."

Tomás lost control of himself. He grabbed Aguirre by the lapels of his coat and dragged him over to the window.

"You're crazy! Do you believe that innocent creature is going to lead the troops of your fantasy? Look at her! There's your Joan of Arc! Surrounded by children, women, old people! With that you're going to make your revolution? With those destitute cripples you're going to confront Díaz's troops? Don't make me laugh! You're the one living outside of reality!"

Lauro rescued his lapels from his friend's fists and looked at him, offended. Then he threw back his shoulders and picked up his hat from the chair.

"I'm off. You'd better think about what you're going to do when the mountain men get here, because they're being chased by the federal troops from Chihuahua. Oh, I forgot to tell you: Torres has already sent troops to ambush them here in Cabora. You decide . . ."

Tomás didn't say anything. He stared out the window at Teresita, lost in conflicting thoughts. She seemed so innocent, so ingenuous, so pure . . . and nevertheless, there was something hard and firm, something fiery and strong that bent the will of others. How had she gotten into this new predicament? And what if Aguirre was right? What if the Tomochitecs were headed here, with troops after them? What would happen to his beloved Cabora? Violence and destruction. Soldiers tromping on his land, violating his property, staining his tranquility with blood. No! He was not going to permit troops to enter Cabora. The best thing to do was to send Teresa away and have someone go and meet the mountain men and tell them that the "saint" wasn't there and wouldn't be back for many days. He decided that was the best he could do, but nonetheless he didn't move. He remained leaning against the window frame, observing his daughter and looking perplexed. Suddenly he saw her stagger as if about to fall; she scarcely managed to catch herself on the porch railing. Mariana ran out and helped her into the house. Don Tomás kept looking at the place where she had been and felt afraid: he realized that unconsciously he had wished for her death.

That day Teresa had woken up with a strange fright that pulled her brusquely from her sleep. Her first thought was of Cruz Chávez, and then a wave of anguish spread over her. It was not a good sign. She tried to remember if she had dreamed of him, but she could find no trace. She had the sensation that she had slept very profoundly, but the anguish persisted. When she faced the visitors that were waiting for her, she found Chávez's face repeated five hundred or more times. She had to shut and open her eyes several times to clear away the mirage. When she looked again she saw only strangers, women with their children, little ones wrapped in shawls, older ones holding their mother's hand, cripples on improvised cots, lame people leaning on simple canes . . . children, not Cruz. But Cruz's image stayed in her eyes and was superimposed on the faces she had in front of her, time and again, until she despaired. She had wanted to forget him: she had forgotten him! Why was he tormenting her again? She tried to lose herself in her work, but every child looked at her with the eyes of the mountain man, causing a new fright. She began to suffer from strange palpitations as if her heart were warning her of something, and she constantly had to look up to be sure that Cruz wasn't there, in front of her, quietly waiting.

Near midday she felt a little faint; the faces around her began to float. She lost her balance and had to grab onto the railing to catch herself. She called and Mariana came running to help her into the house. She made her lie down and took her pulse.

"Teresa, rest, your pulse is like a frog that wants to jump out of its skin." She began to caress her forehead and hair. "What's bothering you? Is there something I don't know about?"

Teresa didn't reply; she felt extremely weak. She closed her eyes and concentrated on trying to still the internal agitation; her head was spinning. She made an enormous effort to calm her pounding heart and relax, and suddenly she heard it: the voice was clear and strong: "Cruz is coming, Cruz is coming, Cruz is coming." She bolted upright.

"That's why I've been seeing him all morning long; he's on the way."

"Who?"

"Cruz Chávez. I know something terrible has happened; otherwise, he wouldn't come."

"Are you sure?"

"Yes," she said, and raised her head, but she didn't see Mariana, just Don Tomás, who had entered quietly and stood watching her from the foot of the bed.

"What are you doing here?"

"I saw you almost fall out there and I thought you were sick."

"It wasn't anything, just a slight dizziness," she said, signaling to Mariana to leave them alone. "I feel better, but since you're here, there's something we need to discuss. I had a premonition: I think a group of highlanders from Tomóchic are coming here, and I have a feeling there'll be trouble."

"That's what Lauro told me. It seems there are rumors that the insurgents . . ."

"Insurgents? So it's true!"

"Yes. Forty armed men from the village of Tomóchic have rebelled against Díaz's government; they refuse to recognize any authority besides the great power of God and . . ."

"And?"

"And the Saint of Cabora. There were skirmishes: the federal troops attacked the village. Apparently a certain Cruz Chávez shot first and started the fracas. There were some casualties, and the armed men fled to the mountains, followed by the army. It seems they're headed here to ask for your advice or your blessing or God knows what! How should I know what you've gotten into this time?"

"I didn't get myself into this! What can I do if people have faith? What can I tell them if they just look and believe? Can't you understand?" Teresa was staring directly into her father's eyes, but she didn't see him, only Cruz, who was on the way. She tried to calm down but it was too late: Don Tomás let out his pent-up rage.

"Understand? I understand! I understand that some mountain men driven crazy by the idea of your sainthood are coming to Cabora, fleeing from the federal troops, and Torres has already sent men to wait in ambush for them here! Now it's time for *you* to understand! I'm not going to allow a bunch of rowdy soldiers to invade my property! I'm not going to permit a group of upstart mountain men to implicate my family and the good name of Urrea in matters of fanaticism! I'm not going to allow a senseless massacre to occur on this beloved land! I forbid you to continue with this nonsense! I forbid you to have contact with highlanders! I . . . I . . . forbid you to move from here!" Don Tomás shook his fist at her as if he wanted to hit her, but then he dropped his hand and looked away. "What the hell! What the hell are we going to do now?" he muttered.

"The long arm of the enemy . . . ," said Teresa, with such a strange voice that her father turned to look at her. "It's true: he's stalking me. . . ."

"Enemy? What enemy? We don't have any enemies; we live in peace, we're not into politics. We only want them to leave us alone."

"That's all Cruz Chávez and his people wanted, but no, it wasn't possible. I think I understand. The enemy can't leave anything good alone: he has to kill it, suffocate it, bleed it to death. The enemy . . ."

"Who told you all that? Aguirre? That nincompoop has a sweet potato instead of brains! I forbid you to speak like he does! That's all we need! Enemies! What do I need enemies for, when I've got you? You destroy my ranch, bleed my family patrimony dry, make me the laughing stock of society, and now you're bringing highlander rebellions to Cabora! I curse the day I sent for you! I curse the day I concei . . . God damn it!" He realized Teresa wasn't listening to him; she had gone into a trance, her eyes lost in the distance. He left the room and in a harsh voice ordered Mariana to take care of her. "Let me know when she comes back. I want to talk to her."

Mariana entered, observed the absence, and sat down to wait; she was used to this. Teresa hadn't changed her position: she was sitting stiffly on the edge of the bed, her back straight, hands in her lap, her gaze lost in a space unknown to others, without blinking, without a single sound or movement; she was gone.

Teresa searches for Cruz; she imagines his gaze until she can see it illuminated inside her; she imagines his mouth full of simple words; she imagines his arms and discovers they are strong and tender. She wants to touch him and she reaches for his hand. She's surprised that it's cold, it doesn't respond to her contact . . . the hand is full of anger, full of rage. She looks into his eyes again and sees pain and fever. She wants to embrace him but his body is stiff; a rifle stands between them. She loses the image.

"Cruz, where are you? Why are you coming to me, making me an instrument of your death? I see a road, I see you coming on that road, climbing through the mountains, your face looking up, you are cold, and, yes, you're trembling with fear. Is there no other way? Can't you take a different road? Why did you get carried away by your rebelliousness? Is it true you shot first? I don't believe it; you promised me . . . or did I imagine that? Did I imagine that you took my words the way I intended them, when you were only listening to what you wanted to hear? Oh, Cruz! I was so naïve to think that perhaps some day . . . but you didn't see anything when you were here, just what you needed: a saint. No! I don't want that. Stop where you are, Cruz; don't take another step, don't come here; don't do me more harm; go back."

"I can't, Teresita, they're after me. Their horses are breathing down my back; I hear their hooves behind me and I must keep on going; they arrive at the towns after I pass through, and they find out I'm headed toward Cabora. I can't slow down, not even because my men are hungry and thirsty and cold. I'm coming, Teresa; wait for me. I need you. There's no turning back, there's no other road. There were no alternatives; they didn't want to leave us alone. Don't believe what they

tell you: it's all lies. I didn't shoot first; they came with fixed bayonets to surround the church where we were praying, and as soon as we came out they started shooting; we had no choice, we shot back. I'm sorry, Teresita, but you don't understand, you are good, innocent. . . . Their bullets didn't hurt us: you were protecting us like I knew you would. They lost two men before they retreated. Perhaps we would have killed them all, but your words were still with us and we didn't want any more bloodshed. You called out to us to lay down our weapons, that's why we retreated, that's why we ran away. We would have won, Teresita, we would have won for sure."

"This time, Cruz, but they will keep coming; they're not going to give up. Oh, how sad it is to die like that! The enemy is so evil! No! I'm not going to wait for you here, Cruz, where you will be ambushed. There's no turning back; you're ready for battle and you're going to have to fight to victory or death. I'm not going to wait for you here and watch them sacrifice you. Cruz, my brother . . ."

"Teresita! Teresita! Wake up. By God, you can't stay in a trance right now. Teresita!" Mariana was shaking her by the shoulders, shouting at her. Teresa snapped awake and looked at her friend with astonishment.

"What's going on?"

"Soldiers. They're outside. Don Tomás is speaking with the officer."

Teresa ran to the window. It was true. Mounted on the chestnut stallion, Don Tomás was arguing with a captain on horseback. Behind him forty dragoons were waiting. The rays of the setting sun reflected off the barrels of their rifles, the animals fidgeted impatiently under their riders. Evidently the captain and Don Tomás could not agree. Fearful of the troops, the multitude had retreated a little.

"My God, Mariana, I have to do something! Go tell those people waiting out there not to move away, to get closer to the house because I need them. Tell them I won't let anything happen to them. Run, it's our only hope." Teresa went out quickly and walked toward her father.

The two men dismounted as soon as she appeared. Don Tomás introduced them. Captain Enríquez greeted her ceremoniously. He was young and handsome, with light-colored hair, transparent green eyes, a trimmed mustache. She thought of Cruz's rough, strong face, his blue-black beard, his penetrating look. Compared to the mountain man, Enríquez seemed an inexperienced boy. He was contemplating her with a bit of surprise; he ventured a smile that Teresa didn't return.

"Pleased to meet you, miss. So you are the famous Teresa Urrea, the one called the Saint of Cabora? I didn't expect you to be . . . well, I didn't know what to expect. . . ."

"You have nothing to expect and nothing to do on my ranch," Don Tomás interrupted with a hard, dry voice. "I've already told you that there are only poor, sick people here who come to see Teresa to be cured. There are no rebels, we know nothing of highlanders or Tomochitecs. Your informants must be mistaken: armed men have no reason to arrive at Cabora, much less to see my daughter."

"That is the information I have, and my instructions are to wait for them and take them prisoner when they arrive. I'm sorry, Mr. Urrea, but those are my orders."

"Captain Enríquez is right," said Teresa suddenly, to her father's amazement, "the Tomochitecs are on the way, I saw them."

"How's that?" asked Enríquez.

"The same way I saw you leave Navojoa and head here," Teresa lied. "Don't laugh. Why do you think they call me a saint? Because when I'm in a trance, I can see the future; that's how my father knew you were coming, and I can confirm that the Tomochitecs are headed here."

"Do you know the mountain men, miss?"

"I've never had the pleasure, but I saw them crossing the mountain on foot, forty men armed with Winchesters, led by a tall man with a black beard and fire in his eyes. His name is Cruz Chávez, if I'm not mistaken."

"You're not mistaken. You see, Don Tomás, your daughter says I'm right. Now I hope that you will do your duty and get your family out of Cabora until we have finished with this matter. I wouldn't want to be responsible for unfortunate accidents. The highlanders are armed and very dangerous; they won't allow themselves to be taken without a fight. . . ."

"I forbid you to do battle on my ranch! Cabora is a place of peace, not a place for fighting rebels. Neither I nor my daughter will leave here until you take your soldiers elsewhere!"

"Wait, Don Tomás." Teresa placed her hand on his arm. "Captain Enríquez is only following orders, isn't that true, Captain?"

"Yes, miss. I have precise orders to wage the battle here when the rebels arrive."

"Of course. And you want my father and me to leave, so innocent people won't die during the battle."

"Those are my orders: to avoid at all cost any harm to the civilian population."

"Captain Enríquez, forgive my impertinence, but may I suggest that your superiors, when they gave you those orders, were not informed of the present situation here in Cabora. For example, they didn't know that you would find a multitude of old people, women, and innocent children surrounding the house from which you saw me come out a moment ago and toward which Cruz Chávez will head with his men as soon as they arrive. . . ."

"Don't you worry about that. By the time the rebels get here we will have the situation under control; we'll drive away the sick people and stand guard until the rebels arrive."

"That's impossible," intervened Don Tomás. Teresa looked at him out of the corner of her eye and realized that he had understood. "With more than fifty armed cowhands on horseback we haven't been able to drive them away or to prevent others from showing up."

"And while your soldiers are busy with the noble task of scaring away innocent civilians, many of whom can't walk and will have to be carried out, isn't it possible that the highlanders might

arrive and the one surprised and taken prisoner might be you?"
added Teresa.

"I can't go against my orders. My orders are . . ."

"Captain, I understand your orders very well, but you have
just said that they include not shedding innocent blood. I think
you have a dilemma: if you follow one order, you run the risk of
disobeying the other. If you allow me, perhaps I can help you to
comply with both orders. Let's suppose that, as I said before, your
superiors were ignorant of several things when they gave you
those orders, among them," and she looked at the Captain pierc-
ingly, "the exact route the enemy was taking, which I have seen
quite clearly . . ."

"Miss, it's not that I don't believe you. . . ."

" . . . because if they knew that, your superiors would never
have told you to put yourself in such a difficult situation in which
you would have to fight in an open field, when there was such an
appropriate place for a rapid and successful ambush."

"My daughter is right, Enríquez. Even supposing the highlanders were so foolhardy as to arrive here, where would you post
your troops to combat them? On the other hand, two or three
leagues up into the mountains, on the Ranch of the Alamo, there
is a deep gorge through which they will have to pass. . . ."

"That's precisely the route they are taking," said Teresa, looking at her father with admiration. "You will just have enough time
to get there, Captain, and mount a surprise attack before they
enter the ravine. Remember that they are fleeing from the troops
of Chihuahua, but they don't suspect that you will be there waiting for them. You will be a hero when you fulfill your mission
without losing one of your soldiers, but you must hurry."

Enríquez seemed doubtful. He glanced at his men to see if
they had heard the strange communication and what, at the end,
was almost an order. They were too far away; they couldn't have
heard anything. He turned back to the young woman; she hadn't
taken her eyes off him.

"You are wasting crucial minutes, Captain."

"I'll accompany you to the gate to show you the way," said Don Tomás, jumping on his stallion. Captain Enríquez thanked Teresa, bade farewell with a military salute and, mounting his horse, turned to his men and gave the order to ride out. Teresa didn't move or take her eyes off Enríquez's young figure until he had disappeared behind a hill. "The rest is up to you, brother Cruz," she murmured. Then she returned very slowly to the house, where Mariana was waiting. She looked so exhausted that the older woman put her arms around her.

"Oh, Mariana! I've done something terrible to avoid something even worse."

When Don Tomás returned, Teresa was waiting for him in the library. Father and daughter embraced.

"Well, Teresita, now we won't have to leave Cabora."

"On the contrary, Don Tomás, we should leave immediately and go ask Colonel Torres of Cócorit for protection for a few days until it's all over."

XI

Colonel Torres had no choice but to give them shelter in Cócorit since he didn't know of Captain Enríquez's change of plans and still thought that the battle was going to be at Cabora. Judging by the commotion and the troops' leaving of the headquarters the next day, Teresa supposed that the colonel had been informed of his subordinate's disobedience and was going to cover his tracks, but she couldn't find out any details. The lack of news, doubts, an incipient feeling of guilt, and the hostile environment of the headquarters submerged her in a depression that got worse as the days passed. A week later Torres returned and, without explanation, told them that it was all over and they could go back to their ranch. A military escort accompanied them to Cabora; father and daughter traveled in silence and with apprehension. Miguel was waiting to inform them about what had happened. They sat down in the library; Tomás offered the foreman a cognac and served himself. To his surprise, his daughter asked for one, too:

"I'm afraid I'm going to need it," she murmured to herself.

"Well, just as you suspected, boss, the mountain men showed up here, about forty of them, on foot, with rifles in their hands," began Miguel, savoring the cognac and the suspense he was creating. "As soon as they were two hundred yards from Teresita's house, they put down their weapons, took off their hats, and the whole group knelt down. If Enríquez had waited for them here, he would have killed them all like sheep and not one would have made a peep. They set the table for him, I reckon; they didn't even send a scout ahead to check out the premises. Like sheep, I tell you, they came like sheep. And I was watching them from a distance to see if they had twisted intentions, but no, there they were, quiet and waiting. Well, so as not to make a long story, I went up and looked for . . . what's his name?"

"Chávez," said Teresa, "Cruz Chávez."

"Yes, that's the guy, and I sidle up to him and say, 'The saint—begging your pardon, boss, but you have to speak to them the way they understand—the saint, I say, isn't here and who knows when she'll be back,' and that Cruz fellow makes a long face and turns to his men and says, 'Brothers, Teresita didn't wait for us; she probably has her reasons, but you saw how she protected us when we were crossing the mountain and how she gave us victory over our enemy,' and then I ask him what victory and he tells me about the battle." Don Tomás got up to fill the glasses; Teresa accepted another cognac, which she drank in one gulp. "Well, boss, these guys were crossing the mountain, and that Cruz fellow sees the ravine and gets a feeling there's foul play about to happen. So he orders his men to hide up high, and in a little while, just like that, just after they had crouched down, Enríquez and his men arrive—ha! that Enríquez must have been still wet behind the ears!—and they enter the hollow to get to the other side and mount a surprise attack. . . . Surprise is what the Tomochitecs gave them! The first bullet was for the young captain; he fell flat on his back!" Nobody noticed the pain that flashed across Teresa's face. "After that, soldiers ran every which way, they didn't even wait to see how many died, they just ran as fast as they could, the sons of bitches. . . . Pardon me, miss. Well, as I was saying, that Cruz fellow was real sad; they came for Teresa's blessing, but when they didn't find her here, they decided to go back to Chihuahua, making a big circle to the north so they wouldn't run into the troops that were following them." The foreman stopped talking, sipped his cognac, and looked at Don Tomás; he seemed a little hesitant.

"Is that all?"

"There's something . . . I mean . . . ," he looked in Teresita's direction as if asking permission to speak in her presence.

Don Tomás raised his eyebrows.

"If my daughter's activities are causing so much upheaval, it's better she learn the consequences once and for all," he gave Teresa a hard look, "and I forbid you to go into a trance or faint or make yourself absent in any way. Okay, now tell us."

Thus Teresa found out about the death of Jesús Chávez, Cruz's younger brother. Jesús had been wounded in the leg during the ambush of Enríquez's men. It wasn't serious, but he couldn't walk. They carried him to Cabora, but when they were going to leave, Jesús refused to accompany them.

" 'I'd just hold you up,' he said; 'leave me here. I'll wait for Teresita so she can cure me and then I'll catch up.' 'But the troops might get here first,' said his brother. 'Well, Cruz, you pray hard to your saint so they don't; and if they do, I'll hide,' he replied.

"And he was hiding here in the miss's house when Torres arrived the next day. I tried to keep him hidden, but the colonel insisted on searching everywhere, and they found him there hunched up under the table Teresita uses to heal. They dragged him out and threw him on the ground in front of me.

" 'You lied to me!' Torres shouted and I said, 'No, sir, I didn't know; he must have snuck in at night when I wasn't looking.' And the poor devil was just moaning, I don't know if it was because he was scared or because of the pain in his leg. And then the colonel gives the order to tie him to a horse and I couldn't stand it.

" 'Leave him here, general,' I begged, 'look how bad off he is; as soon as Teresa gets here and heals him, I swear to God I'll personally turn him over to you at headquarters.' But the bastard refused, said he was going to take him to justice, that he had to stand trial for rebellion against the government. Ha! The trial was as short as from here to over there!" and he pointed outside, "because as soon as they got to the edge of Cabora I heard the shot. By the time I found the body behind some bushes the boy was real dead. Torres did 'justice' to him with a bullet in his temple and left him there for the vultures."

From that moment on Teresa lived in constant tension, waiting for bad news to arrive, or the outbreak of some disaster. Mariana noticed that she was hushed and crestfallen. She suspected the reason and decided to watch her at all times in case she "left" again. But now Teresa didn't need to enter into a trance or have visions or hear voices: it was reality itself that assaulted her, her existence was in crisis: she was racked by doubt and guilt. She was tormented by the face of the young, handsome Captain Enríquez, who so willingly believed her lies, and with the illusion of becoming a hero had marched off to his death. She was haunted by the unknown face of Jesús Chávez, who had trusted in her power to keep death from finding him. Over and over again she came back to the almost infantile face of Damián Quijano, who had asked her to fulfill her promise of water without knowing that it would bring his death. She remembered what Gabriela had told her about the fetuses that didn't survive during her own deathly trance. Death, death, death, and more death, coming from her. Doubt, fear, and guilt. She struggled between fury at the thought that the enemy was twisting things and fear that she herself was the Evil One without realizing it. She reviewed the events, trying to guess what would have happened if she hadn't intervened: would the "saints" have gathered anyway, even if she hadn't irresponsibly predicted rain? Would Cruz's men have killed Captain Enríquez even if she hadn't sent him to the place of ambush? Would Colonel Torres have gone to Cabora and found Jesús Chávez even if she and her father hadn't gone to Cócorit? If she had died in that first trance, would all of the babies have been saved then? If she hadn't announced Huila's death, would the old woman still be alive? And was Cruz going to die sooner or later because of the faith he had in her? Would he die even if he didn't have that faith? What was her role in this whole tangle of life and death? What good were her alleged powers if she didn't even know who she was, what she was doing, and what consequences her actions would have?

By mid-March the cold began to diminish and once again Cabora was filled with life. The credulous, the incredulous, the curiosity seekers, and the snoops came and went. A string of booths sprang up again, selling fried foods or images of the saint, alcoholic beverages or printed prayers. The believers continued proclaiming the unexpected cures as miracles, taking the saint's advice as if it were divine and being grateful for spiritual relief when the body didn't respond. But Teresa was not the same. Something had snapped inside her: she had lost her innocence and that ingenuousness with which she previously had confronted life. Most of the time she was introspective, working without the joy of earlier days; she no longer showed pleasure at the blind people who could suddenly see or the dumb who spoke or the deaf who heard. It seemed as if nothing mattered to her. Regardless of how hard she tried to distract herself with the routine, that handful of truncated lives kept tormenting her.

At night she spent the hours in a restless state of semiwakefulness, semisleep, haunted by confusing images and fragmented memories of her life. Anastasio galloped across the plain, pursued by Don Tomás with a rifle in his hand; Cayetana lay dying in the middle of the desert, but Huila arrived to bring her back to life, except that it wasn't Huila, it was an enormous vulture, a bad omen that announced the death of Cruz Chávez. And then she herself was running after the mountain man, but she couldn't find him, she found Porfirio Díaz instead; he stared at her in silence with burning eyes. The figure of the enemy was suddenly replaced by Lauro Aguirre shouting at her with Aunt Tula's voice that it was time to wash her dirty clothes. She asked him to be quiet, not to shout so much, because he would wake the dead, but it was too late because Enríquez was already approaching, stained with the blood from a well-aimed Tomochitec shot, and Damián swollen with so much water and Jesús Chávez with his wounded leg and a small dark stain on his temple and Huila all withered up in her coffin, which had been too small for her, and all the little angels that had died while she, Teresa, was in a trance and an unknown woman who came running down the hill of the cave and stumbled on a rock, shouting, "You stole my life," and Doña Rosaura suffering the loss of her shadow and Uncle Manuel all yellow, dead from cirrhosis of the liver, and they all started shouting at her until she covered her ears and the movement pulled her out of her dream state.

Mariana observed her, worried about the suffering she could see. She noticed that Teresa hardly ate, the circles under her eyes were growing deeper by the day, she was getting gaunt, and, without being in a trance, she didn't seem to be present. The day Teresa didn't even appear at mealtime, she decided to do something about it and went to find her. Teresa was lying in her room, rolled into a ball under the sheets. Mariana sat next to her on the bed and began to caress her hair.

"What's wrong with you? Since the Tomochitecs came you changed very much. You cure without conviction, without joy, as if you weren't really seeing the patients."

Teresa shook all over. It was true: she didn't see the sick people anymore, she only saw the faces of those who had disappeared. She cured with the fear of distributing undeserved deaths without knowing, of stealing lives, of saying truths that could be transformed into lies, of living a myth created by others.

At some time she had lost control of her own existence, her acts no longer belonged to her, they just entered into a confusing and perverse pattern that she didn't understand. She tried to say that, to see if Mariana could help her find the thread, but she couldn't speak; the words stuck in her throat and began to seep out converted into huge tears that noiselessly ran down her cheeks one after the other. Mariana had never seen her cry before and, surprised, hugged her as if she were a small child, rocking her back and forth and saying, "There, there, cry my little girl; it's good to cry, there, there," and pressed the head of that child of hers, that little daughter, against her breast.

Then Teresa really cried, she cried in torrents, with sobs that seemed to come from her stomach, ripping through her whole body and tearing at her tissues. Mariana felt the tears and the mucus and the saliva fall on her hand and said, "There, there, my child, my good little child, cry, my baby," until that flood of tears gradually began to wane, changing from sobs to hiccups, from hiccups to little moans, from moans to sighs, and from sighs to an exhausted silence. For a long time the two women stayed like that, one embracing the other without saying anything. Then Mariana cleaned the other's face with her handkerchief and looked at her.

"I have good news for you. Don Lauro is here and he says Tomóchic is peaceful. Cruz and his men returned at the end of last month without ever running into army troops; since then nobody has bothered them. They even started planting so they can have a harvest by the end of the year."

"Oh, Mariana! Why didn't you tell me that before?"

"Because you needed to cry first; but now it's out. Look, I have it all here in my handkerchief, all those doubts that have been tormenting you. And you know what? We're going to burn this rag so they don't come back, so those memories leave you in peace and you can be your old self again."

Teresa laughed and took the soppy handkerchief. She looked at it for a long time and laughed again.

"And who taught you to do such miracles? Let's go! What are we doing here? If for the first time in his life Lauro has good news, let's not keep him waiting."

Aguirre confirmed what Mariana had said. Tomóchic was tranquil, and for the moment it seemed that the federal troops had retreated. After a month of hiding in the mountains the Tomochitecs had returned home with no serious problems.

"I knew those soldiers couldn't beat Cruz!" exclaimed Teresa. The familiarity with which she said the mountaineer's name surprised Don Tomás, as had the audacity and cunning with which she had deceived Enríquez: they were aspects of his daughter's character that he hadn't noticed previously.

"With elections pending in Chihuahua nobody wants to move, but just wait until they're over; Herod-Pilate doesn't forget," replied Lauro. But Teresa scarcely listened to him; she was quite content. The evil she regretted having done appeared minuscule when compared to the well-being of a whole village. She, she and Cruz together, had conquered the enemy.

"By the time the elections are over, they'll have more important things to do. Besides, if there's no rebellion in Tomóchic, what need is there to send troops?"

"I hope you're right."

The next day she smiled again and healed with joy. The storm had passed. She was almost the same, but inside there were certain scars and the memory, forever sad, of her beloved Cruz. She hid away in a secret place the image of his face, his fiery gaze, the hoarse determination in his voice. She had the premonition that she would never see him again. By saving him she had lost him.

❀ XII

Lauro Aguirre didn't share Teresa's optimism. He smelled a revolution. Rumors were spreading about imminent uprisings, and the social restlessness seemed to be reflected in the slight tremblings of the earth that during the spring of 1892 were occurring one after the other throughout the northwest of the Republic, depositing their subversive messages in the receptive ears of the engineer.

Without the Urreas' knowledge, Aguirre was weaving his conspiracy. He had created a network of information that allowed him to keep up with the events. He maintained a secret correspondence with Catarino Garza; he exchanged coded messages with antireelectionists who were exiled in the neighboring country. After the Tomóchic incident he established contact within the rebel village with a certain Benigno Arvizu, whose duty it was to keep him informed of any signs of violence. He accepted various official positions in order to be near centers of information and find out about the enemy's movements. His blood was burning with the desire to see fulfilled his daily predictions of an armed uprising that would overthrow the dictator, that murderer of women and children. But, in spite of all the signs that followed close upon each other, there was something missing: a unifying element that would coordinate all the outbreaks and give direction to the movement. Lauro decided to create one.

In great secrecy he began to print a newsletter of about two hundred copies, which were distributed clandestinely in Sonora, Sinaloa, Chihuahua, and beyond the border. The publication bore no signature or address; it was openly anti-Porfirian and dealt obsessively with the contrast between the malicious and outrageous acts of the government and the kindness and virtues of Miss Teresa Urrea, the Saint of Cabora.

> It is not surprising [declared the pamphlet] that in these times when Evil has raised a head as monstrous as the one we see leading the present misgovernment, nature is sensible enough to create its opposite: a figure of such kindness and innocence that her very presence serves to reestablish faith in Good and Justice. Yes, beloved readers, you need not despair. Our moment is yet to come, but already Miss Teresa Urrea is working miracles of health, not only on sick bodies, but also on the spirits of the just.

> *Her followers call her "The Saint of Cabora"; nevertheless—in contrast to the monster who inhabits the Capital—she is very humble and rejects any title. But the day will come when she must recognize her most elevated mission: to inspire in men the courage and strength necessary to combat the Evil that is devouring the country. For now, she is dedicated to tenderly loving the needy, the poor, the old people, the sick, and especially the children, healing all imaginable ailments with only her blessed hands.*
>
> *But she is already preparing herself for her role in the coming revolution. On her innocent lips she perceives the acrid taste of injustice; before her sweet eyes file images of crimes and assassinations too horrible to recount. Her spirit is fortifying itself, and the day will come when she will rise up to ignite the souls of the repressed and the weak and turn them into heroes.*

In another article, Aguirre expounded upon the out-of-body trips during which Teresa observed the crimes the tyrant committed against defenseless citizens; her universal ear capable of listening to even the perverse thoughts of the enemy; her transcendental vision that penetrated the souls of sick people in order to discover secret ills of the spirit; her pure sensitivity that trembled before human pain wherever it was found. Then he tried to infuse hope in the desperate, optimism in the pessimists, and faith in those who didn't believe in spiritism; he promised that the day of retribution was near: "Be prepared," he said, "to join the just and avenge the crimes committed by the masters of the present exploitation."

Benigno Arvizu served as mailman in Chihuahua, delivering copies of the newsletter for distribution among the towns and villages. In Tomóchic he gave them to Cruz, who read the articles as a sermon during the two daily masses celebrated in the name of the great power of God and of Saint Teresita, whose protection had saved them from the enemy's bullets. Ricardo Rojas crossed the border with the manifesto hidden under his clothing in order to deliver it to the political exiles, who took heart remembering that another virgin had inspired the great uprising of the War of Independence. Francisco Mojarro and Pedro Cisnea were in charge of taking copies to the inhabitants of Sonora and Sinaloa, who immediately organized pilgrimages to Cabora to see the miracle with their own eyes. Thus, the newspaper circulated from hand to hand, was read and passed on to others, spreading the good word of Teresita among hundreds and then thousands of eyes and ears hanging on every word about Cabora, some with faith, others incredulous; some attracted, others indifferent; some hopeful, others pessimistic; and one or two who reported immediately to their superiors to see what could be done about this new burgeoning of anonymous and subversive treason.

In Cabora nobody was informed of the journalistic conspiracies of Don Lauro. Calm had returned to the ranch; cures and miracles were daily occurrences and tranquility became the routine. Once again they were predicting a summer of intense drought, after the inclement cold of the winter. Don Tomás took measures to maintain the levels in the wells by posting guards at each one and rationing water to the visitors; he didn't say anything to Teresa anymore. He preferred to see her like that, busy with cures, with concrete human ailments or spiritual needs, and not involved in uprisings. Cabora was safe, Gabriela's son was growing up strong and healthy, and Don Tomás again felt the plenitude of previous times.

The peace of Cabora seemed to have spread throughout the whole state. The Mayo laborers had settled down to work again; the bands of Yaqui rebels, realizing that another difficult year was approaching, had ceased their attacks and looting to ensure at least one harvest. Chicho Huicha, the most recent leader of the rebels, had been captured and duly silenced.

The government of the state took advantage of the sudden lull in hostilities to promote the progressive development of the Mayo valley, offering the fertile expanses of land on both sides of the river to white colonists and assuring everyone that the indigenous people were totally subdued. Thus families of immigrants began to take over the fertile land between the two rivers, and the flow of discontent Mayos greatly increased, arriving at Cabora to request retribution, advice, or mere consolation. Teresa, with the events of Tomóchic still fresh in her mind, spoke to them of kindness and justice, recommended that they have faith and patience, and advised them to avoid bloodshed, futile rebellions, and other actions that would only produce death and more misery. When Don Tomás found out about this recent seizure of lands and the resulting complaints of the Mayos, he just shrugged and shook his head.

"No more politics, Teresa. There's nothing you or I can do. It's inevitable: civilization, progress . . . it has to be. Send them all back to their homes and don't speak to them of injustice. Don't stir up trouble; we don't need any more trouble."

But trouble arrived on its own at the end of April. A messenger from the state government personally delivered a document addressed to Don Tomás. They were eating when the envelope was handed to him. Everyone fell silent. He opened the letter, and Teresa observed that first he paled and then he flushed. As he read, the peace and tranquility that he so desired crumbled into pieces and were transformed into a new fit of anger.

"They demand . . . they demand that, as the owner of Cabora, I keep a register of the workers who come and go on my property and that I make it available to . . . to the army! Well, they won't receive a single report from Cabora, and they better not come for one either."

He threw the document on the table, grumbling about the foolishness of the government.

"Where, precisely, do they expect us to carry out these inquiries? In the mountains? 'Hey, you, what's your name?' 'Juan Zalamea.' 'And where are you from, Juan Zalamea?' 'From over yonder.' 'And tell me, Juan-Zalamea-from-over-yonder, are you tranquil, peaceful, the kind who won't go making revolutions?' 'Whatever you say, boss.' Ah, but if this Juan or Pedro turns out to be suspicious, if it's not perfectly clear that he comes from another farm or town where he has lived in peace, the proud, dutiful owner-commissioner-spy-interrogator-accountant-bureaucrat-citizen must apprehend him and turn him over to the nearest authority so the unfortunate man can be delivered to the leader of the nearest troops so they can carry out the appropriate investigation. Ha!"

"You're talking like Lauro," Teresa said with a laugh, but she felt that the enemy was threatening them again. "By the way, what happened to him?"

"He must be off somewhere, dreaming up revolutions. How should I know? The last time he came he was talking about enemies, people who want to harm us, spies; you figure it out!"

Spies . . . Teresa had observed again the presence of certain men who appeared one day, nosed around among the people, and then left the next. Perhaps Lauro was right: she should be more careful. . . .

May brought a heat wave that disheartened the spirits and doubled the work on the ranches since continuous movements of cattle were required to provide them with minimal food and water. Visitors to Cabora decreased, and on the first Sunday of the month there were scarcely ten people waiting outside. A moribund man only asked for Teresa's blessing so he could die in peace; Teresa spoke to him in a hushed voice for a while until she saw him smile tranquilly and slowly surrender to death. Three children were suffering from diarrhea, and she gave them the appropriate tea; a hearty young man had a tic that scrunched up the whole right side of his face; she rubbed him with saliva until the rebellious muscle relaxed and became smooth and docile. Lastly, there approached a young woman who was spitting blood when she coughed; Teresa could see the first shadows of death in her eyes.

She said her name was Anastasia, she was nineteen years old and married without children because the cough had started as soon as she moved to her husband's house and he hadn't wanted to get near her. Now he was seeing another woman and she was afraid of being abandoned. As soon as she confessed this, she began to cry: Teresa was her last hope; she needed to get well so she could have a child and hold on to her husband.

Teresa asked her why she had waited so long to come, and she shook her head. No, she hadn't waited, she had gone else-where first. She had started by consulting the doctor of the town where she lived, and he had given her some powder that didn't help at all; the same thing happened with the faith healer from Cócorit and the doctor from Hermosillo, who had charged her so much just for syrups that seemed to make her better for a while but didn't really cure her. The day she started spitting blood she decided to come to Cabora.

Teresa realized that it was already too late and knew she should tell her so, but she looked at the young woman, a bag full of bones, so alone and so convinced she wouldn't die, and she felt such pity that she forgot one of Huila's first lessons, hugged her, and took her inside the house.

"I'm going to do what I can, but I need you to help me. You must ask for a miracle and believe that you are worthy of receiving one. I know that you are, because you are young and you love deeply, because you wish to give the greatest of gifts to your husband. But you have to believe in the miracle; only that way can I help you," she said, knowing she was lying but feeling incapable of disillusioning the moribund woman.

Tenderly she helped her get undressed; then, very slowly, making each touch a caress, she rubbed earth and saliva all over her back and chest. When she finished she took her by the shoulders and looked directly into her eyes, which shone with tears of gratitude. Teresa was shaken by a chill that ran down her body.

"Leave the caked earth on until it falls off by itself and don't think about it. Think that a new strength is growing inside you, feel that strength, and guide it to the source of your ailment," and she softly touched her chest. "You should do this at least three times a day, for an hour each time, and be completely alone so that nothing distracts your concentration. You need to close your eyes and make the trip inside yourself until you find the illness and then concentrate on your faith in the miracle." She hugged her again, helped her get dressed, and, as a blessing, she gave her a light kiss on the forehead.

"Close the door as you go out," she told her; she didn't want to see her leave, struggling, alone, full of hope.

In spite of her low workload and although it was only eleven in the morning, Teresa felt tired. Anastasia's case had exhausted her, leaving her with a confused sensation of sadness and anger. If she had ever wanted to perform a miracle, it was now. Something in that young girl had pierced her heart, to a secret place where she harbored the pain over the indifference that death showed its victims. She was just about to go to the Big House when Mariana informed her that they had run out of red earth and needed to get more.

"Do you want me to send Miguel?" she asked.

"No, I'll go. I need the distraction."

During her trek up the hill she thought of Anastasia. The name reminded her of Anastasio, lost in the distance of time, part of another life, another moment, another space, all unreachable now except through nostalgia, which didn't reach anything but only produced a sad yearning. When she got to the cave, she sat in the shade, hugging her knees and contemplating for the hundredth time the smooth, beautiful expanses of Cabora.

In spite of everything, Cabora was still the same. It was, perhaps, the only stable thing in her life, in everybody's life. Cabora. It was the love she shared with Don Tomás and even with Gabriela. It had shaped their destinies more than any other particular circumstance. To the left was the pointed peak of the Hill of the Mine; down below was the wide, dry bed of the Cocoraqui Wash with its secret reserve of humidity carefully guarded against the sun; on the horizon the jagged hills slumbered in an eternal siesta like fatigued beasts; to the right, the thick grove of *huamúchiles* rose in stately elegance. From up there she couldn't hear the garrulous parrots, but she could see them flying from treetop to treetop, eating the sour-sweet fruit of the *huamúchil*. Cabora hadn't changed. It was always there, patient and peaceful, like a great mother who sheltered them all.

She was the one who had changed, slowly becoming a woman. The illusions of girlhood, the confusing impulses of adolescence, the traces of childishness had all disappeared. Her character, like her body, had affirmed itself, taking a definitive shape. On one hand she felt softer, like a fruit about to ripen; but, on the other, she felt harder, firmer, less flexible than before. She thought of her days in the settlement. If she had stayed there, she certainly would have married and had children; her duties would be the difficult, monotonous ones of any cowhand's wife. Instead of that, she was Miss Urrea, the Saint of Cabora. She had escaped the anonymity of husband and children to become someone known, the Blessed Child, the Miraculous Lady. She had outdone her father and managed to bend the paternal will to her own: Cabora was ruled by her desires and needs. As a healer, she was much more powerful than Huila had ever been and also more admired, more beloved. She wasn't lacking anything: everything she had ever wanted in life she had achieved. But deep down she felt alone, as alone perhaps as poor Anastasia with her rotting lungs and her false hope. She no longer saw the future clearly; had she lost her way? Or was it just that the goal had been reached and from then on the days would repeat themselves over and over, monotonously?

She took out the jar and began to fill it, remembering the first time in the cave when she had eaten the reddish earth as a form of ritual; that was only three years ago, but how different her life was now! She no longer suffered from the insecurity and uncertainty of those days; she was in charge of herself: she had a destiny that was a bit lonely, but it elevated her above normal beings. The power was hers, the greatness was hers; she just had to wait for destiny to challenge her again. She smiled and ate some more of the red earth—"so Anastasia will be cured," she said—she rubbed it on her chest and arms again, laughing now at that infantile act—"so the enemy will yield to the great power of God and Saint Teresa of Tomóchic!" she exclaimed. Then she dusted herself off and headed back down toward the house.

When she got there, everybody was at the table and in a good mood. She forgot her reflections in the cave and deposited a kiss on Don Tomás's cheek. Then she embraced Gabriela and caressed little Ramón. She sat down to eat with real appetite. Mariana observed her with pleasure. It had been a long time since she had seen her so content; the walk had done her good, no doubt. That day they talked about everything and about nothing. The meal lasted longer than usual. While they were drinking coffee at the table, Don Tomás spoke joyfully of the three newborn calves and the twelve cows about to deliver. Suddenly Mariana signaled to him and looked in Teresita's direction. She was stiff, sitting straight up, her gaze lost somewhere tangential to reality. She didn't move.

The trance lasted only a few minutes. Then Teresa shook her head, looked at her father, and said:

"Somebody is riding here at a gallop. I'm afraid he's bringing bad news."

Don Tomás frowned and rose brusquely from the table.

"I'll be in the library if you need me. Josefina! Take my coffee there! Gabriela, stop carrying that boy all the time; you're going to make him a sissy and I already have enough with Loreto's sissies! Don't anybody bother me!" he shouted to nobody in particular, slamming the door behind him. Josefina hurried by with the steaming cup in her hand. Then there was silence. Mariana looked at Teresa: she was frowning.

"Are you sure that it's bad news?" asked Gabriela, hugging her baby more tightly.

"No, but I felt a strong chill and that's never a good sign."

"Then I'm going to the chapel to say the rosary. Maybe that will help. Josefina," she stopped the cook on her way back, "take care of the baby for me. If he cries, let me know."

Teresa and Mariana were left alone.

"You were so happy . . . and now . . ."

"I don't like surprises," she said, thinking of the enemy.

Silence returned. Twenty minutes later the galloping hooves of a horse could be heard, then the rapid steps of the rider and the entrance bell. Don Tomás stomped out of the library, glared at Teresita, and ordered her not to move. He went to answer the door.

❁ XIII

Ricardo Rojas, as the stranger identified himself, saluted in military style and handed Tomás an envelope. The salute seemed absurd to him since the messenger didn't look at all like someone in the military. He was wearing denim pants and a dark shirt, a hat, and boots; he appeared to be just another cowhand. He glanced at the envelope: the handwriting belonged to Lauro.

"My boss," said Rojas, "ordered me to get here as fast as possible and deliver this to you personally."

"Your boss?" Tomás's irritation was growing.

"The engineer Aguirre."

"Ah. Where is he?"

"I'm not authorized to reveal that information."

The answer seemed absurd. Don Tomás stuck his hand in his pocket and pulled out a few coins, but Rojas refused to accept them.

"Everything is for the good of the cause," he said briskly and saluted again before turning to mount his horse. Don Tomás watched him ride away at a full gallop as if he were in a great hurry, and then went back into the house.

Teresa, watching him pass, perceived the tension in his hunched shoulders. She caught a glimpse of the envelope and recognized Lauro's handwriting. She felt another shiver, as if the secret contents were harmful to her. She observed the closed door and then looked outside. The sky was a sharp, discouraging blue.

The imperturbable sun seemed to deny the possibility of any cloud but, nonetheless, the cloud was there, she felt it inside the house itself, gray, ominous, threatening.

The communiqué was long, intricate, confusing, paranoid, and accusatory like everything Lauro wrote. Don Tomás read it first with irritation, then with incredulity, later with desperation, and finally with disgust: "Hogwash!"

Dear Friend:

By the time you receive this letter I will already be far from the clutches of the assassin who tried to dam up the river of truth with which I have flooded the nation. I hadn't wanted to involve you, but given the twists and turns of fate it has become imperative that you be informed. Please destroy this as soon as you finish reading it.

Back in Chihuahua I was anonymously publishing a newsletter whose only error was to tell the truth above all else. There are no deeper wounds for those who practice Evil than truth and justice. I distributed the newsletter by means of certain friends who had my complete trust, but an ambitious traitor joined our group and, taking advantage of my good faith, delivered into the hands of the Enemy my publication as well as a few incriminating messages. That was my undoing. Although an order for my arrest was issued, I fortunately found out about it in time to escape to the other side of the border, where I believe that I'll be able to gather the necessary forces to overthrow the Monster. In the meantime, I am organizing an opposition newspaper that should come out soon. Be patient, my friend, and you will see the magnificent results that we will achieve. The Enemy has already shown his weak flank by persecuting such a humble person as your brother.

Lauro's letter rambled on about possible enemies of Don Tomás and begged his friend to take the greatest care; he ended by sending his love for the whole family, "especially our beloved Teresita." Don Tomás burned the document and poured himself a snifter of cognac. He had no doubt that Lauro had put himself in danger by supporting so many supposed uprisings, but to what extent was he, Don Tomás, in the line of fire just because of their friendship, and who were the so-called enemies? He found it difficult to believe that anyone, other than his wife, Loreto, could wish him evil. He was about to serve himself another drink when his ruminations were interrupted by Miguel. A cow was having trouble giving birth.

"Call Teresita," ordered Don Tomás, as he ran to the stable. A few moments later Teresa joined him at the side of the dying animal. It wasn't the first time they had worked together to save a cow in labor and each knew exactly what to do. While Miguel and Don Tomás held the animal still, Teresa delved deep into the birth canal and extracted the dead calf. As soon as the mangled product emerged, the cow heaved a strange sigh and stopped struggling.

"She'll be all right," said Teresa as she cleaned up.

Father and daughter walked together toward the house, arm in arm. Tomás had forgotten about his foreboding and at the moment could entertain only tender feelings for his daughter. He realized that no matter what happened, he wanted Teresa to be the owner of Cabora. He decided to arrange the necessary papers as soon as possible.

"Teresa, I want you to know that if anything happens to me, Cabora will be yours."

The young woman embraced him.

"Nothing's going to happen, Don Tomás, don't even think like that."

Yet Teresa was left with worrisome premonitions, and that night her slumber was filled with confusing figures and voices, with fragmented dreams that no sooner had begun than they were transformed into another and another. She rolled back and forth in bed, trying to capture the furtive images that made her leap from nightmare to nightmare. Suddenly, everything stopped. She was facing the image of Anastasia, who held out to her a big, gift-wrapped box with an enormous red bow. "This is for you," and even though she rarely accepted gifts, in her dream she didn't hesitate. She untied the bow and took off the wrapping: inside were the bloody, cavernous lungs of Anastasia.

"They're yours," the other woman murmured. "I have new ones."

Teresa was horrified; she dropped the box and the sickly lungs began to slither across the floor as if pursuing her. Anastasia was smiling. Abruptly she disappeared, and Teresa entered a new dream. She was alone in a strange room, lying on a bed. On the wall in front of her was a mirror, in which she could see herself dreaming. And she dreamed that in the mirror she was dying for the second time or that she was dreaming that she was dreaming that she was dying. And as she awaited death in the dream, she dreamed that she was dreaming about everything she had lived through until then, including the dream in which she dreamed she was dying. Dreaming that she was dreaming, she once more felt nostalgia for life and tears ran down her cheeks, but she didn't know if she was crying in the dream that night in Cabora or in the dream of her own death. And thus she continued, dreaming that she was dreaming in an endless oneiric labyrinth that came and went from the past to the future, confusing and blending both into one.

❀ XIV

Don Tomás was closing the payroll book when Miguel arrived with the news. He had been hearing rumors all day and a while ago they had been confirmed. That very morning a horde of two hundred Mayos had descended upon the town of Navojoa in a surprise attack. They killed the mayor and two citizens; then they looted the town. The federal troops had moved to the north the previous day and hadn't been able to return in time to fight off the attackers. The inhabitants defended themselves as best they could, managing to kill seven before the rest fled to the mountains. When the troops arrived, there was nothing left to do except bury the dead.

"How strange," said Tomás, perplexed, "the Mayos have been peaceful for more than three years. What do you think, Miguel?"

"I'm afraid there's more, boss. According to some informants, the Mayos entered the town, shouting, 'Long live the Saint of Cabora! Down with bad government!' and now it seems they're headed here."

"God damn it! Weren't the mountain men from Chihuahua enough? Aren't we ever going to have peace in this house?" Tomás was pale; all at once he felt that he was fighting the inevitable and an overwhelming fatigue spread throughout his body. He turned his back on Miguel. "Go to Navojoa and find out what you can. Stay alert on the road, and any troublemaker who's headed this way, you stop him, even if you have to use bullets. Come back as soon as possible. On the way out, tell Teresa that I want to see her immediately, say it like that. Get going, and as soon as you get back, report to me, no matter what time it is."

Something in Miguel's tone of voice made Teresa leave everything and run to the library. She found Don Tomás exactly as the foreman had left him, with his back to the door, immobile, pensive. Without looking at her, he recounted the news just as Miguel had given it to him. Then he turned brusquely.

"What do you know about this?"

Teresa shook her head.

"Nothing. The Mayos who come to see me are peaceful. They only speak of their needs and ailments, never of rebellion, not even now with the massive redistribution of their lands to colonizers. What do you think it means?"

"I don't know, but something's going on. You must have said something to encourage them to revolt, something that made them believe . . ."

Teresa reviewed her words of the past few months, searching for some phrase that could have been twisted, then shook her head again.

"No, I don't think I've said anything that could . . ."

"This is the second time in less than a year that a rebel group has used your name as a battle cry and then headed toward Cabora to see you. It will be hard for Torres to keep believing in our innocence." He thought for a moment. Bandala was the new chief of the military zone; he had been named not long ago, after the death of General Carrillo. Perhaps he hadn't had time to find out about the previous events, the crowds in Cabora, and Teresita's activities. On the other hand, maybe he would manage to capture all the rebels before . . .

"Let's hope so," he said, almost to himself.

"What?"

"That they're all captured before they get to Cabora, captured or killed or hung one by one from the highest tree, just so they don't get here. Let's hope that new General Bandala gets them."

"And if he comes here first?"

Don Tomás let out a lengthy sigh; he felt terribly tired again.

"You have to convince the people out there to leave. Bandala shouldn't find crowds here, especially Indians. He's capable of arresting them just so he doesn't have to return empty-handed. Besides, if the rebels come here, we don't want them to mix with the others; that would be difficult to explain. Meanwhile, I'm going to give Cosimiro orders, in Miguel's absence, to gather all the workers and arm them as guards; any stranger will be detained immediately." Teresa made a gesture of protest, but Don Tomás silenced her: "This time we have no choice. The rebels have directly involved you in an uprising against Díaz's government and in the assassination of civilians, and those are serious charges."

At the mention of the enemy, Teresa trembled. Nevertheless, she realized that her father was right: it was necessary to disperse the people to avoid greater tragedies.

"Let's get to work," she responded. "If Bandala comes, he will find nothing but an innocent family. We will simply tell him the truth."

Tomás didn't reply. By this time he had his doubts about "the truth."

Teresa managed to disperse the majority of those who had congregated around her house by telling them that the troops were coming to Cabora and their lives could be in danger. She asked them to leave and to stop anybody they met on the road. Cosimiro, with a group of armed cowhands, was posted at the entrance to ensure that nobody came back and no new visitors got through. Teresa returned to the Big House to wait for news.

They were together in the library when Miguel arrived at midnight. He came directly in and found them sitting, silently waiting. For hours they had been going over and over the situation without finding any explanation.

The foreman confirmed everything he had said before, adding details that hardly changed their predicament except for the worse. The attackers had killed the mayor, Don Cipriano Rábago, who was a great friend of Bandala; in addition, the commissioner of Cuirimpo and his brother had died; there were two wounded. Different versions estimated the Indian fatalities between seven and fourteen. Nobody could find a logical reason for the unexpected uprising, although some, remembering the incident of the "saints" two years earlier, attributed it to exacerbated fanaticism and pointed their accusatory fingers at Don Tomás and Teresa.

What appeared suspicious was that, one day before the attack, General Otero, for no apparent reason, had withdrawn all the troops from the most important town in the region, leaving it defenseless. This detail made Don Tomás apprehensive; he remembered Lauro's message.

"Captain Enríquez was under Otero's command; so was Rincón, who rounded up the 'saints' that received such rapid 'justice.' . . . I don't like this at all. I'm afraid the motive might be revenge."

"Could he know that I was the one who . . ." She was going to say, ". . . sent Enríquez astray," but Don Tomás hushed her with a sign. She looked at Miguel. Did they have to distrust even those closest to them? She felt afraid. It was as if a subtle web were being spun around her and she was incapable of defending herself. Damián Quijano, Cruz Chávez, and now someone called Manuel Jocoricoqui were emerging as innocent pawns mobilized against her. She felt a wave of anger and struck the edge of the table with her fist. Don Tomás, thinking she was going into a trance, grabbed her by the arms and shook her.

"No more fainting! Innocent or not, you got us into this. If you hadn't been so stubborn, if you had paid attention to me two years ago and stopped this nonsense . . ." He paused, felt the enormous wave of fatigue again, and muttered: "What's the use? I don't think there's anything we can do except wait and see what happens in the next few days. I've put Cosimiro in charge of the workers; Miguel, you stay informed of the latest happenings and keep us up-to-date."

"Yes, boss."

Father and daughter stayed up the rest of the night, searching past and present events for some pattern that would reveal what the enemy's next move might be. Teresa grew increasingly upset; she didn't understand why she had such foresight for other people's problems but her prophetic powers totally failed her in matters concerning herself. She concentrated to see if some voice or sign would appear, but there was nothing—silence. That made her angry; it didn't seem fair. Don Tomás was going over various military options to decide which would be the most logical. He arrived at the conclusion that there would be something similar to what happened with the Tomochitecs or the "saints": persecution, roundup, dispersion. Then he felt more at ease. At the break of dawn he retired, leaving Teresa sitting by the window, solitary and pensive.

On the sixteenth, the early morning sky was clear. Nothing moved in Cabora, not even the workers that Cosimiro had posted in groups to stop any intruder. Most of the ailing people had gone. The unusual stillness was ominous. Teresa stayed in the Big House, which was not her custom, and only sent Mariana to be on the alert for any patients that arrived so she could send them back the way they came. At midday Mariana returned. She hadn't been able to convince a small group of people to leave without seeing her; apparently they had come from very far away, and even though she told them the saint would not attend to anyone that day or any other day for some time, they had camped in front of the house to wait. They included two cripples, a one-eyed man, and an old, toothless woman.

"I've never seen such misery! Should I tell Cosimiro to throw them out by force?"

"No, let them be. They'll get tired of waiting. I'm not going out today. We'll see what happens tomorrow."

At dusk Miguel arrived with news. Bandala was making a forced march toward Navojoa with his troops and cavalry; Otero still had not taken any action but people said he'd been informed. Evidently the news had reached the state government and possibly even the president of the Republic.

The seventeenth seemed like a copy of the previous day. The waiting stretched out before them, and no federal troops or rebellious Mayos appeared anywhere. Mariana reported that more indigents had joined the first group. Miguel informed them that Otero was marching with his troops to join Bandala in a pincers formation. Apparently there were orders from above to snuff out the rebellion as soon as possible. There was talk of some executions, but they hadn't been confirmed. The rebels were dispersing to avoid capture, and the military was arresting any stray Mayo they encountered.

"Poor devils!" murmured Gabriela, who was just finding out about the problem.

"If they execute enough of them, the bloodthirsty bastards will be satisfied and leave us in peace."

"Tomás! That's horrible. It's all right for them to bring the assassins to justice but not to persecute innocent people."

"I didn't create the present situation. I can't be responsible for the actions of a twisted, corrupt government. I just want them to leave us alone and stay far away from Cabora. Gabriela, why don't you go visit your father for a few days and take the boy? I don't think this kind of fright is good for the youngster. If the troops arrive, we'll arrange things peacefully and when they're gone I'll send for you."

Gabriela left that same night for the neighboring ranch, taking little Ramón with her. The house seemed even more strange and silent without the boy's presence. The next day Miguel returned with more news.

"It seems they've captured the leaders and a good number of the rebels near the Torobena plateau. They say General Otero didn't leave a single one alive, not even those who were traveling with their families. There are reports that the region is now completely pacified and there's no more problem. Otero is going back to Torin today with most of his troops."

"So much the better," said Don Tomás. "Tell Cosimiro that the cowhands can go back to work. Tomorrow I plan to send Teresa to take a vacation on the hacienda of a friend. By the time she comes back we'll have gotten rid of the beggars. If everything stays calm, you can go and pick up Gabriela the day after tomorrow."

The next morning Teresa awoke exhausted by the three days of tense waiting, feeling like a hounded animal and wondering where the enemy would strike next. At least nothing had happened in Cabora, but once again there was a massacre of innocent women and children and she was indirectly responsible. Despair had settled into her heart with the same stubbornness with which increasing numbers of sick people had posted themselves outside her door in spite of the threats and danger. She didn't even have the heart to attend to them. There was something she couldn't understand: what drove men to fight for lost causes with nothing but her name on their banner? It was a power that transcended her and was totally out of her control, a power that, far from curing, produced death over and over again, filling her with desperation and guilt.

At breakfast Don Tomás announced that he was sending her away for a few days and, if necessary, he would bind her hand and foot and take her personally. To his surprise, instead of resisting Teresa was pleased. Mariana would accompany her and they would be near the sea. Suddenly she was filled with childlike illusions. As soon as she finished eating, she began making plans with Mariana and packing while Cosimiro prepared the wagon. She spoke so animatedly of the upcoming holidays that Mariana soon was laughing with her as they picked out clothes to walk on the beach or ride horses or just sit on the terrace at the hacienda of Santa Rosa, chatting with the family. They challenged each other as to who would get into the water first and who would venture the deepest and promised themselves they would bring back many beautiful shells so Gabriela could make them necklaces.

"Did you know I haven't seen the sea since that trip from Santa Ana when I was just seven years old? You'll see how wonderful it is and so enormous it doesn't seem to end."

Don Tomás was waiting next to the wagon to say goodbye to Teresita when a worker came running up to him. Miguel had sent him to look for a lost calf, and while he was searching near the road he heard the sound of many horses approaching.

"There are about three hundred of them, boss, or more! They're coming in a forced march and in attack formation, with the cavalry in the lead. I came to tell you right away, and now I'm going to run and hide my wife and kids. Then I'll be back, boss, if everything's all right."

"The hell you will! You run and order Cosimiro to conceal the wagon. You, Nicolás, tell Teresa not to come out and to hide her suitcase! If they see us making preparations for a trip, they may think . . . Antonio, look for Miguel and tell him to come immediately! I'll be in the library."

When he entered the house, he met his daughter in the hallway.

"Go to your room and don't come out unless I call you. Where's Mariana?"

"She went to fetch some things from my house."

"Josefina! Send a girl to tell Mariana to close Teresa's house and come back here at once."

He had just given the order when Mariana came running up. "Here they come! Here they come!"

"Go stay with my daughter and don't let her come out," he ordered. Through the door he saw them coming; he squinted, trying to make out the face of the one in front. "At least it's Bandala," he murmured to himself. "I was afraid it was Otero."

Mariana found Teresa tense and pale, sitting on her bed. She sat down beside her and the two women embraced each other.

"Why are they coming if it's all over? I don't understand. I wish we had left early this morning! I have the feeling something terrible is going to happen, they're going to kill the poor people who are waiting out there, they're going to loot Cabora, or . . ."

"Don't say that, Teresita; be patient. Maybe it's nothing, just a routine search. They're not going to find what they're looking for here," she said to calm her, but Mariana was afraid, too.

Don Tomás stood at the doorway to receive General Bandala and escort him to the library.

XV

It was only a month ago that General Abraham Bandala had been transferred from the south of the country to the north to occupy the post of chief of the military zone of the Mayo River. He was about forty years old, dark-skinned, with thick, unruly, black hair, small eyes, a wide nose, thick lips, and an insatiable ambition, distilled in the bitter fermentations of an inferiority complex that he covered up with shows of machismo, bravery, and an unflinching fulfillment of duty. A week before the surprise attack on Navojoa, General Otero, his second-in-command, had informed him of the problems in the region, including the irregular and potentially subversive practices of the so-called saint.

"We have to keep an eye on her," he had said, "she's stirring up the Indians, and that could cause some problems."

Bandala didn't trust Otero, who was just as ambitious as he was, so he had been careful to confirm the report with other sources. What he found out worried him. Although the idea of a half-crazed young woman whose words were inflaming the downtrodden Indians to the point of rebellion was not at all pleasing to him, what he heard of the attitude of Don Tomás was even more objectionable: the thought of a hacendado, a recognized member of a wealthy family, permitting such unruliness on his property and provoking so much talk seemed so vile that it was incomprehensible. When they told him that this Urrea fellow also took advantage of the situation to extract money from the needy, he was overwhelmed with indignation and disgust and promised to do something about the situation as soon as he had an opportunity. This was provided to him by the attack on Navojoa.

Once the roundup of the rebels was completed, he decided to go directly to Cabora and carry out the order he had just received from Díaz. Upon arriving at the entrance to the ranch he ordered a halt and immediately saw the deplorable spectacle of indigents camping in front of Teresa's little house: cripples, old men, children, women, all in rags, protecting themselves from the sun under makeshift shelters, with garbage scattered about them. It was a scene of promiscuity, ignorance, and misery. He advanced to the front door. There he ordered a squadron of soldiers to surround the house and not let anyone leave. Don Tomás appeared just in time to hear the order. He strode forward with a determined gait.

"That won't be necessary, General. Nobody has any intention of leaving. They informed me of your arrival and I was waiting to welcome you."

"Mr. Tomás Urrea, I presume."

"You presume correctly, General Bandala."

"Then, with your permission, my soldiers will proceed to surround your house."

"I have no objection, but you are wasting your time; we have nothing to hide here."

In a few minutes the house was surrounded, and Bandala agreed to dismount and accompany the hacendado to his library.

"What can I offer you, General?" asked Tomás. "Please, sit down. I am sure that whatever the problem is, we can resolve it like gentlemen."

Bandala ignored the invitation.

"The purpose of my visit is not pleasant, neither for me nor for you. I wish to carry out my orders as soon as possible. Is Miss Teresa Urrea at home?"

"Yes, but . . ."

"Please, be so kind as to send for her."

Tomás felt rage churning inside him. The "please" didn't diminish the commanding tone that Bandala had assumed. He returned the bottle of cognac to its place without serving himself a drink and directly faced the general, who was about four inches taller than he was.

"I think that this is between us men," he said, controlling himself; "we don't need a woman's sentimentality to find a solution. I've been informed of the unfortunate events in Navojoa, which I suppose are the reason for your visit. You can be sure that I am the first to condemn them; as soon as I found out, I gave the command to detain any stranger who tried to enter this property, in order to turn him over to the authorities for interrogation. Fortunately . . ."

"Mr. Urrea, your daughter's name . . ."

"I know, and you can imagine the surprise . . . or, rather, the indignation that I felt when I heard they had invoked Teresita's name to commit atrocities against innocent citizens. This is inconceivable and it is your duty to stop it! We cannot permit a few barbarians to dishonor the names of civilized, progressive people in this state. Of course, my daughter doesn't comprehend these things, you understand, she's very young and naïve; she believes that by doing good . . ."

"Mr. Urrea . . ."

"Allow me, General. I was saying, she doesn't realize the evil that could result from her innocent cures, but you and I know, especially now, the consequences they may have. Even before you arrived, I had decided to call an immediate halt to her nonsense; thus I am pleased you are here so we can coordinate our efforts and avoid any further uprisings due to ignorant fanaticism, because I can assure you that my daughter had nothing to do with what happened. As you can see, I am at your disposition. If you approve, I will take charge of sending my daughter away and dispersing the sick people who have come uninvited to our ranch, and you . . ."

"Mr. Urrea, I have a peremptory order of arrest against you and your daughter, but I require her presence in order to formally read it and carry it out. If you would do me the favor of sending for her, we could finish with this unpleasant business."

Tomás's throat went dry. He had expected an occupation of the ranch by the troops, a search of the property, the detainment of the visitors, anything but an order of arrest against him and Teresa!

"There must be some mistake. . . ."

"There's no mistake. The order is signed by the governor himself and has been approved by General Díaz. Now, either you call your daughter or I will send a soldier for her."

Just then the door opened and Teresa entered.

"That won't be necessary; I'm here of my own will. I heard what you were saying, General, and decided to put an end to this farce," she said, turning to the surprised officer. She was dressed all in white; her shiny, reddish hair discreetly pulled up on her head made her seem taller than she was; her amber eyes shone with both coquetry and determination as she turned to look at him. Now it was Bandala who fell silent.

"As you can see, General Bandala," she continued, "I could not be the one inciting the Indians: there is nothing further from my character than violence. I suggest you look for the cause in the injustices that certain authorities have committed against the villages or in some element of society that wishes us evil. Here only love, kindness, and patience are preached. Here we just help the poor and the sick; we alleviate as much as possible their suffering. Never has a word been spoken that could lead to violence, nor will one be spoken." Bandala felt as if he were being enveloped in that hoarse, seductive voice; he wanted to touch the apparition before him. He thought there must have been some mistake, that young lady could not be the one called the Saint of Cabora, whom he had imagined as a crazy woman, unwashed and foul-smelling. "I am in complete agreement with my father about my leaving for some time until the region calms down. I assure you that I have nothing to do with these absurd uprisings."

With the word "uprisings" Bandala recovered his presence of mind, saluted formally, took a folded piece of paper from his pocket, opened it, and began to read:

> On May 19, 1892, in the City of Hermosillo, State of Sonora, I hereby issue the following order of arrest against Mr. Tomás Urrea, owner of the ranch of Cabora, in the district of Quiriego, and against his daughter, Teresa Urrea, on the grounds that these people were the direct cause of disturbances of the public peace. Once this order is carried out, the prisoners shall be taken to Cócorit and from there to Guaymas, where they will be detained until further orders are issued as to their final destination.
>
> Signed: Rafael Izábal, Governor of the State of Sonora.

When he finished reading, father and daughter stared at him with alarm.

"You can't carry out that order, General. This is unjust. My father and I haven't committed any crime, we haven't . . ."

"Miss, my obligation is to carry out orders, not judge them. In Guaymas you will have a chance to defend yourselves and have your case reconsidered. For now I suggest that you prepare your things; you, too, Mr. Urrea. We will leave in thirty minutes; I'll wait for you outside." He saluted again and turned to leave, but before abandoning the room he stopped and looked at Teresa. "I request that you dress discreetly for the trip and cover your face with a veil. I've heard that your followers are capable of doing just about anything for you; we wouldn't want any misfortunes on the way, would we?" he said in a cynical tone of voice and then left. Stupefied, Teresa watched him disappear through the door.

"This is an insult! A humiliation!" she shouted. "Leaving clandestinely so nobody realizes the injustice that is being committed!" She looked at her father but he had turned his back, his face hidden in his hands. The idea of having to leave Cabora as a prisoner had overwhelmed him. He dropped his arms to his sides, raised his face to the wall full of books, and without turning around, said:

"Prepare your things."

Teresa perceived their defeat and felt confused, riddled with currents of rage and desperation. She wasn't accustomed to receiving orders and didn't know how to handle her feeling of impotence. Bandala's tone had convinced her that she wouldn't get anywhere with him. They would have to leave, be humiliated for the moment, but they wouldn't give up; they had to fight in Cócorit or in Guaymas and, if necessary, reach the governor himself. . . .

"Go, now," insisted Don Tomás in the same lifeless tone of voice. Teresa left him there and went to get her things.

Before leaving, Don Tomás issued his last orders: Miguel was to inform Gabriela; Mariana would stay awhile to disperse the visitors. Cosimiro would be in charge of the ranch until there were new orders. He didn't think it was necessary to send a message to Loreto.

As they left the house, Teresa saw the wagon waiting and, with indignation, declared that she and her father weren't a couple of weaklings to be pulled along by mules: they would ride horseback. The general replied without even looking at her:

"You, miss, will ride where I tell you. I don't want you to mix with the troops; many of them are ignorant, and I've been told that your specialty is deceiving the uneducated and leading them along twisted routes. So climb into the wagon and keep your mouth shut. I don't want to have to gag you."

A few minutes later, in the wagon that was supposed to take her that day to the ocean for a vacation, they began the trip to Cócorit and began what Teresa would later call "the journey of silence." She had changed clothes; now she was wearing a severe black outfit with a veil of the same color over her face, hiding her eyes, which were flashing fire. Don Tomás traveled with his head down as if he had suddenly grown tired of holding it upright. It was almost as if he were dozing, with his chin resting on his chest. He didn't look up, not even to say farewell to Cabora.

When they reached the top of the first hill, Teresa raised her veil and turned to look back. Cabora seemed to fold in upon itself like a distant memory, an empty cradle, a barren womb destined to be forgotten. It was the enemy's triumph. A scarcely contained rage was churning inside her. She looked around for her captor: he was riding near the wagon and contemplating her.

"Lower your veil, miss," he ordered brusquely. Teresa glared at him, but she obeyed. She was afraid for the broken figure at her side, who seemed determined not to protect her any more; she wanted to say something to him, to encourage him, but she could find no words. He seemed deaf, dumb, and blind, immobile, turned inward, scarcely breathing. Teresa felt even more humiliated and made an effort to sit erect, expressing defiance with her body since she couldn't show her face.

Cabora was soon out of sight. Ahead the road stretched between low hills and the coastal plains; the vegetation was sparse, shade nonexistent, and the waves of heat struck their faces and bodies with fury. On the right, the rugged, imposing peaks of the Bacatete Mountains shimmered in the lacerating light of midday. Two buzzards traced huge circles in the sky, gliding on a tenuous, high-altitude breeze. The thick silence was interrupted only by the sound of horses' hooves on the rocks and the muffled trampling of hundreds of army boots. As she observed the land-scape around her, Teresa vowed to return some day along that same road.

The sun radiated mercilessly above the procession. Teresa struggled against the oppressive heat and the erratic rocking of the wagon to maintain her defiant posture, keep her anger intact, feed a belligerent hatred with dignified arrogance. The desert, the heat, and the fatigue seemed to be accomplices to injustice. Nobody looked at her, no one seemed to notice her, not even Bandala, who rode his horse back and forth through the rows of soldiers, from one side to the other, in order to encourage or reor-ganize the troops; not even the cavalry lieutenants who escorted the wagon and kept their gaze fixed on the road at all times; much less the troops who were divided in two columns and were walk-ing at a prudent distance from the vehicle. She began to feel hungry and thirsty; she needed to urinate; the sun was making her sleepy; the black dress was asphyxiating her at that tempera-ture. From time to time the movement hurled her against the mute shoulder of her father. If only she could speak in a hushed voice to Don Tomás. She realized she was battling a deepening depression that waited in ambush behind her diminishing rage and the suffocating silence of her father.

After two hours on the road they stopped to rest, water the horses, and eat. Bandala approached to offer food and drink to the prisoners. Don Tomás didn't even look up. Teresa was dying for a sip of water, but instead of accepting it she fulminated the general with a hateful look and retorted that she didn't want any-thing from him. Bandala shrugged and proceeded to eat and drink in front of her. He gobbled like a pig, chewing with his mouth open and making slurping noises drinking from his can-teen, until he finally finished and gave the order to move on. Then he left them alone.

As the afternoon advanced and the sun's rays threw length-ening shadows across the desert floor, the effect of Don Tomás's silence on Teresa's spirits worsened. From dejection, it deepened into aggressiveness and protest. Why didn't he speak to her when she was just as wounded and frightened as he was? Why this accusatory rejection? Her father blamed her for what had happened and condemned her to solitude. Her anguish increased; her rage and desperation were gradually redirected toward the silent figure at her side, until she could stand it no longer.

"Are you going to give up just like that?" she said in a low, challenging voice. "You should be ashamed of yourself. Cabora needs you; I need you; Gabriela is waiting for you. . . ."

"Cabora is lost," said Don Tomás in a listless voice. "You predicted it. Or have you forgotten?"

For a moment Teresa felt confused. Then she remembered the dream the night of their confrontation and she crumbled. All of her defenses tumbled as if an earthquake had struck inside her, and amongst the ruins there were just the remains of a prophecy from a dream they had somehow shared. Was this the end of the road? No, it wasn't possible. Could one's life be destroyed so easily? Could one's fate be sealed so quickly? And was it inevitable just because she had predicted it, or had it always been inevitable, and she had just foreseen it?

"It doesn't have to be," she said, but without conviction. "We can appeal to the authorities, we can . . ." Her father wasn't listening any more. He had withdrawn behind an invisible wall, his eyes fixed on the floorboards of the wagon. Finally Teresa understood that Don Tomás could be right and they might never return to Cabora. She accepted, then, his stillness, that living death that enveloped him, and sunk into the inexorability of her own depression. Destiny had been fulfilled in spite of her and behind her back, just as she had predicted, with all the cruelty of incomprehension. She heard again the voices of the dead and of her forgotten dreams rising up to reproach her, and she, too, was soon swallowed up by the silence.

They arrived in Cócorit late that night. Teresa immediately demanded to see Colonel Torres; she harbored a minute hope that

she might still impose her will on fate. Bandala informed her curt-
ly that the colonel was on campaign and wouldn't be back all
week. She and her father were locked up in separate rooms with
guards at the doors. Outside the soldiers patrolled, fearing a surprise attack from rebel bands that might be in the area. But the
night elapsed without disturbances. Teresa, exhausted by nerves,
anger, humiliation, and insolation, fell asleep at once.

Well after midnight she was awakened by a slight noise near
her cot. She opened her eyes. General Bandala was standing
there, gazing at her. Indignant, she sat up.

"You're quite beautiful, Miss Urrea. I'm beginning to understand the hypnotic effect you must have on the poor people you
deceive. Seeing you so tranquil, I myself could . . . ," he let the
words slip away. They both looked at each other in the silence of
the night. Teresa understood that with this insinuation there was
a possible way out but rejected the thought.

"General Bandala, don't even dare to think that I might harbor some feeling for you besides intense hatred. If you don't leave
immediately, I'll cry out, and I can't wait to see the expression on
your lieutenants' faces when they find you here."

Now it was Bandala who looked at her with hatred and
turned to go, slamming the door after him. The next day he
stayed as far away from the wagon as possible; he had ordered a
subordinate to watch over the prisoners. During the rest of the
trip Teresa only saw him occasionally and at a distance.

The journey from Cócorit to Guaymas transpired without
incident other than a brief fright. Halfway there a scout came galloping back with the news that a band of twenty Indians was
moving in the opposite direction and would cross their path in
about half an hour. Bandala decided to keep advancing, but he
doubled the guard around the wagon. Teresa realized what was
happening and thought that a confrontation with the rebels
would give her and Don Tomás a chance to escape: they would
just have to catch a horse whose rider had fallen. For an instant
she imagined that the Indians were coming to rescue her. After

all, if her influence was capable of inspiring downtrodden men to rise up against the fearful forces of the government, it was just possible that they would be brave enough to attack Bandala's troops to save her. She whispered this to Don Tomás, and he looked at her as if she were crazy.

"And where, precisely, do you suggest that we hide? In the Bacatete Mountains?" And he sunk back into his resentful silence.

Half an hour later it was obvious that the Indians had taken a different route. Teresa abandoned all hope. The rest of the trip progressed with maddening monotony. That night they slept out in the open, and the next day they pushed hard to arrive in Guaymas by nightfall.

They drove down the main avenue, where whole families gathered at their windows or came out on their wooden porticos to watch the troops pass by, and then they turned left on the main street that bordered the bay; the water was on their right, its tranquil waves repeating swish-ahh like slow breathing in the darkness. On the other side the kerosene lamps in the windows of the houses produced a phantasmagoric play of lights on the street. They stopped in front of the Municipal Palace; Bandala dismounted and disappeared through the entrance. Don Tomás and Teresa remained seated in the wagon, silently waiting. The atmosphere was hot and sticky with humidity; the stagnant air simmered with insects. Along the edge of the water strolled groups of young people, who stopped to look at the military men and then walked on, laughing or talking in low voices. The soldiers followed with their eyes the young girls who wore tight clothing or had notable breasts. Once in a while they whistled under their breath. The girls tried to conceal their laughter and kept walking.

A slight breeze arose carrying the salty smell of the water; sudden gusts brought the stench of dead fish and now and then a flirtatious whiff of perfume from the strolling youths. The number of strollers increased as the moon climbed up from behind the mountains and cast its silver gaze across the bay. Nobody seemed to be in a hurry or to have a fixed destination; they sauntered along casually, even lasciviously; they paused, scrutinized the guarded wagon, made some comment among themselves, and went back to their idle rambling. Teresa could hear the voices and laughter, mixed with the sounds of the port. They made her feel even more isolated, more humiliated. Obviously nobody recognized her, perhaps they hadn't even heard of her; she felt terribly alone and the distant world of Cabora seemed like a chimera before the harsh reality of her anonymity. All of a sudden she felt the enormity of her fear—the fear of being nobody, of disappearing without leaving a trace, of being swallowed up by the universe, and forgotten.

"Papa . . . !" she said, for the first time in her life, and her voice broke. Don Tomás made no move to console her. Silence returned, caressed by the soft murmur of the waves.

❁ XVI

On the day of her second death Teresa would remember the time of her imprisonment. It was only two weeks, but each day dragged along, its hours loaded with humiliation, abandonment, and isolation. As the days passed, her image became blurred as she lost awareness of herself, forgetting the definitive characteristics of her identity and being left with an amorphous, imprecise perception of her existence. From afar, from a street she could not see, came the sounds of everyday life as a constant reminder that her presence there was totally lacking in significance for others; the world didn't know her. Sometimes she was submerged in a deep depression; other times she suffered from fits of anger that, having no outlet, resounded in the void; and then there were times when she was overwhelmed with guilt for the pettiest details of her past, like a penitent before the gates of purgatory.

The peremptory order stated that Teresa's presence in Guaymas was to be kept absolutely secret, so they had decided against the military prison in favor of the Municipal Palace, which had, way in the back, two small cells with bars on the windows and bolts on the doors. Teresa's window looked out on an interior patio that somebody, probably the caretaker and his family, had converted into a pigsty. Three scrawny hogs rooted around, like a pathetic mockery of her situation. Two infants spent day and night crying for any reason or for none at all. The little breeze that entered the dingy room brought the stench of rotten garbage, urine, and excrement. Every other day a person that Teresa never managed to see came out and threw a few buckets of dirty water across the patio; it soon filled up with fresh garbage, which rapidly decomposed under the strong rays of the sun. The walled-in space was a perfect incubator for flies and mosquitoes, which invariably found their way into the small cell and feasted on the prisoner. Her arms, legs, and face were blotched with aggressive red welts as if she had the measles; they had even stung her between her fingers and on one eyelid, which became grossly swollen.

Don Tomás was in another cell far enough away so they couldn't talk to each other. She hadn't seen him since the first night. She didn't know if he was alive or dead, if he was suffering or if his situation was better than hers. Her only contact with the world was an old, deaf-mute Yaqui woman who brought her food and water once a day and cleaned the chamberpot.

The whole first week she wore herself out with expectation. Any noise, the approach of the Indian woman, footsteps on the floor above her and she leapt to readiness, reviewed her best arguments, tried to fix her hair, and waited, almost holding her breath. Finally she had to accept that nobody would come, except that walking silence that entered and left as if Teresa didn't exist. She tried to communicate with the woman; at least if she managed to break the barrier of her isolation, she could ask for help and maybe . . . But the jailers had chosen well. After several attempts, Teresa gave up; all she managed to do was frighten the poor creature, who left the room running like a fleeing animal as soon as she made the slightest movement. She went back to passing the

time contemplating the monotonous ramblings of the pigs, listening to their grunts, envying them their little fights, until she
despaired of the filthy animals and felt like screaming. Hope fled
before the onslaught of despondence.

On the tenth day she felt completely disheartened: she had
been forgotten, they would leave her there to rot forever. Desperation swept over her. She preferred to be shot rather than be
condemned to that inhuman incarceration. She began to shout at
the top of her voice and evidently her cries were heard in another part of the building, because in a few minutes a young officer
arrived to see what she wanted. He unlocked the door, entered,
and bolted the door from the inside. It was the first human face
she had seen besides the impassive countenance of the old deaf-
mute. She stood quietly, looking at the young man, and suddenly
she saw her own reflection in the other's eyes. She hadn't bathed
in ten days, she was covered with insect bites and red, irritated
blisters, her hair was uncombed, and she probably stank. She felt
an intense shame that she had never felt before and hid her face
in her hands. Underneath her ragged fingernails were half-moons
of grime. She wished she could disappear from the sight of that
clean, uniformed young man. But she was the one who shouted
in her anguish, who had called so someone would come running
to tell her that they weren't going to forget her forever.

"Is something the matter, miss? We heard you shouting all the
way upstairs. The mayor doesn't like so much ruckus when he
has appointments. People might think something's wrong. He
sent me to see what you needed."

Teresa tried to compose herself a bit. She ran her hand
through her hair coated with grease and sweat, trying to smooth
it down. She raised her eyes and attempted a smile that came out
half twisted, half absurd.

"I was afraid I had been forgotten. I need to know what's
going on and when our case will be resolved." It had been so long
since she had spoken that her voice sounded strange, gruff, as if
it didn't come from her but from one of the pigs on the patio.

"Nobody has forgotten you, I can assure you of that. Your case is being considered, but they still haven't arrived at a decision. Apparently they are waiting for orders from above. It must be complicated. Be patient."

"But they told me I would have the opportunity to see the governor to explain my case to him. When can I see him? I have the right to talk to him, General Bandala said. . . ." She realized it was useless.

"The governor is a very busy man. He has to solve problems in the whole state; you can't expect him to devote himself to your case. I assure you that everything possible is being done to bring an end to this matter. Anything else?"

"Water. I need water to wash myself. I need a bath. You can see that I need a bath."

"I'm sorry, miss. The building is not equipped with that kind of accommodations; we don't usually keep prisoners here. And we have strict orders that you are not to go out, you shouldn't be seen. As soon as your case is resolved . . ."

"At least you could bring me a bucket with clean water and a little soap so I can wash my hands and face. If you just did that, the wait wouldn't be so unbearable. Imagine what it's like being shut up here in silence day after day. Clean water and a brief visit to assure me that I'm not forgotten would be sufficient. Please . . ." The idea that the young man might leave and never come back made her anguish return. The officer nodded.

"I'll see what I can do."

The next day the lieutenant arrived carrying a bucket brimming with fresh, clear water and a bar of soap with a sea sponge. Teresa felt tremendous relief when she saw him enter: she had finally managed to communicate with somebody. She received him almost joyfully, thanked him, and asked that he come back the following day.

When she was left alone, she began to compare the quantity of available water with the size of the wound to her vanity. It wouldn't be nearly enough. She started by washing her face, trying not to

spill a single drop of the precious liquid. When the delightful
sting that she felt on her skin convinced her that it was clean, she
proceeded to wash her hair, wetting it down the best she could,
using only a little soap and then sticking her whole head in the
bucket to rinse it off. That was delicious. She would have enjoyed
leaving her head in the bucket forever, but she still had to wash
the rest of her body. The water was soapy, but she could at least
rinse off her chest and arms. For thirty minutes she completely
forgot that she was a prisoner. The next day, except for her face,
she would reverse the process and so by the third day she would
be clean from head to toe. That tiny, insignificant bucket of water
seemed to bring her back to life.

Immediately she changed clothes. She chose a light blue
dress. She combed her hair carefully until it was silky and smooth.
Then, with an old rag the deaf-mute had left in a corner, she used
the soapy water to scrub the floor, wiping away all the dirt and
dust. With the exercise the color returned to her cheeks, and
when she had finished, she felt better. The rest of the day didn't
seem so intolerable. The strong smell of soap discouraged the flies
from visiting her cell. In the afternoon a stiff breeze began to blow
away the foul odors of the patio. That night Teresa slept soundly.

When the young man came in the next day, he found a different person. The coolness of the water had diminished the
inflammation of the insect bites, which were now lost in the
renewed color of her cheeks; her hair hung smoothly over her
shoulders. She was smiling, and the sparkle had returned to her
amber eyes. This time she didn't encourage the young man to
leave so soon. The bath could wait. She invited him to stay a
while to chat. The officer hesitated; he had strict orders not to talk
with the prisoner, but she looked so harmless.

"A few minutes, that's all. I have to return before they come
looking for me."

The brief chats and the daily sponge bath made the days
more bearable. Teresa recovered something of her sense of identity and, with that, her pride. She noticed the young man was

beginning to trust her, and each day he stayed a little longer. She began to play with the possibility that he might agree to help her escape, but fate didn't give her time to even formulate a plan.

On the fifteenth day of imprisonment, a military escort arrived at her cell; the officer in command ordered her to gather her things and accompany him. Teresa immediately snapped alert; his tone of voice seemed to convey a veiled threat. She retrieved her travel bag, straightened up, and walked out surrounded by soldiers.

Upstairs in the mayor's office she encountered her father. He had aged; his hair had whitened more, and on his unwashed face there was a distant expression. When he saw her, a look of surprise flickered across his face as if he had forgotten that she was there too, but he didn't even smile. He continued to stare straight ahead. Bandala was behind the desk, flanked by two guards. He waited for Teresa to stand next to her father and then, with a satisfied smirk, began to read the document he held in his hands:

> Guaymas, Sonora, June 3, 1892. The Honorable Governor of the State, with full authority, has pronounced the judgment that Mr. Tomás Urrea, present here, and his daughter, Miss Teresa Urrea, also present, are undesirable persons who threaten the public well-being, the peace, and the progress of the region. Therefore, the above-mentioned persons shall be escorted under strict vigilance to the border at Nogales, Sonora, and dishonorably expelled from the country.
>
> As exiled expatriates, the above-mentioned are to reside in the neighboring country of the United States of America at a sufficient distance from the border so that their presence will not cause any more disturbances in our Nation. Under no circumstances may they return to their native country for the rest of their natural lives. In full knowledge and understanding of these conditions, the persons named above shall indicate their complete acceptance of the terms of this sentence by affixing their signatures to the bottom of this page.
>
> Signed: Ramón Corral, Secretary of State.

Teresa heard in the sentence the echo of her own words, dreamed that night long ago with such certainty. She realized that she had foreseen this defeat. The enemy had won; they would never return. Cabora, their beloved Cabora, would slowly deteriorate in their absence. In this life, at least, she wouldn't fulfill her promise to return. She would never see her land again, or her hills; she would eat no more vengeful earth, wake no more with the hope of performing new miracles, ride no more on her beloved Spirit. The vibrating guitar, the song of the owl, and the howl of the coyote would continue for other ears, not hers. She looked at Bandala and recognized his triumphant gaze. She closed her eyes and sighed. Then she hugged Don Tomás.

"Come on, let's sign; it's time for us to go." Her father stepped forward, placed his signature on the paper, and handed her the pen. Then she signed: Teresa Urrea, the name that she had so eagerly inscribed in all her childhood illusions and that now was hers in dispossession and anonymity. Then she embraced Don Tomás again; he put his arm around her waist and thus they left, escorted by twenty soldiers, for the station, where they boarded the recently inaugurated train from Guaymas to Nogales.

Part Three

I

I am immensely this hour.
I have this look in my eye,
and I face the shadows.
Sight only says the words
that we have taught it, and silence
is an opaque crystal; the mystery,
a wall behind which there is nothing.

—E. TAVERNIER

They arrived in Nogales, Arizona, on June 4, after a distressing train ride during which both Teresa and her father refused to admit their fears. They made the journey in silence, swallowing their doubts about the future, not knowing what was waiting for them at their destination, or what they would do when they arrived, or how they would be received in the neighboring country. They didn't even realize they had crossed the border until the train stopped. Bandala and his two assistants stood up and, without saying a word, climbed down from the car. Through the window Teresa saw the general speak briefly with someone who probably was an American immigration official, because he looked over the documents, bade farewell to Bandala, and boarded the train. The official, who scarcely spoke two or three words of Spanish, indicated to them with gestures and an impatient, arrogant attitude that they should sign and put their fingerprints on the various documents that established, in English, the terms of their exile. When Don Tomás, with his little knowledge of the language, tried to ask about a hotel, the American just shrugged his shoulders. Teresa, who never had felt such overt scorn or the gratuitous hatred born of prejudice, silently endured her helplessness. Finally they climbed down from the train. The platform was empty except for a small group of men and women who seemed to be waiting for someone. Then they saw Lauro walking toward them at the head of the group.

When he had found out about their arrest a few days after it occurred, he had traveled from El Paso to Nogales in order to receive them. Without wasting any time, he took advantage of the situation to promote his political interests, spreading the news around the Mexican community about the imminent arrival of the saint. He delivered bulletins to the local press and advised the authorities that the Urreas were fleeing from the iron hand of Porfirio Díaz. He requested a police escort for their protection and gathered a small group of friends to welcome them.

As they approached, the group broke into hurrahs for the Saint of Cabora. There was a round of applause and then many hugs. Teresa was relieved; she had feared that the total anonymity of her imprisonment would continue. Tomás, on the other hand, did not seem interested in the gaiety: he turned inward like a moribund animal. Three public security officers escorted them to a modest hotel where Lauro had made reservations for the night. The owners of the establishment were Mexican and had prepared a little reception with lemonade and cookies. Don Tomás mumbled an unintelligible excuse and went immediately up to his room, leaving Teresa with Lauro, who continued taking advantage of the situation to pontificate against Díaz. The guests wanted to know the details of the arrest, the conditions of her incarceration, the threats of the government, and, especially, what the saint planned to do in exile. Teresa was the center of attention once more. As the chatter heated up inside the hotel, outside curious people filed past the windows, hoping to get a glimpse of the newly arrived "saint." Beggars and merchants, Yaquis from

Arizona or Sonora, well-to-do women who discreetly passed by in their carriages, cowboys on horseback, and children on foot who whispered and giggled to each other: it was like a circus.

Finally they all left. Teresa was tired, but the gathering had given her new hope and she was determined to resume her activities as soon as possible. Lauro advised discretion:

"Here the people are more interested in politics than in spirituality. You must be careful. We are still not free of the enemy's machinations."

When she went up to her room, the dispirited attitude of Don Tomás, sitting there in a chair, crestfallen and enveloped in silence, was the memory incarnate of her humiliation. To avoid seeing him, she went into the bedroom and left him alone with his pain.

Even though Bandala had made them sign a document in which they promised to remain at a certain distance from the border, Lauro convinced them that the agreement wasn't valid in the United States and Teresa's presence near the dividing line was important in order to keep her memory alive and allow them to return to Cabora some day. Don Tomás shrugged and said that it was all the same to him, it made no difference whether he waited for death in one place or another. They stayed in Nogales. The Mexican community made a small house available to them and organized a collection of used furniture to decorate it. It was not at all elegant: just a living room, bedroom, and kitchen in a wooden structure so feeble that they could hear the neighbors' voices through the walls. It was in a poor Mexican neighborhood with houses built one next to the other along a narrow dirt street. Teresa felt suffocated with so many people living practically on top of each other and no space in between, and she could scarcely hide her disillusionment so as not to hurt anyone's feelings. Lauro tried to cheer her up, saying that it was just temporary and they could soon move to a better residence.

They moved into the house the next day. The furniture was stacked up and the rooms needed a good sweeping. Don Tomás immediately appropriated an old rocking chair, sat down by the window, and returned to his stubborn immobility. Teresa gazed at the disorder and filth and interpreted it as an insult: the sordid neighborhood, the humble house, the neighbors' charity, and her father's resentment all seemed to come together to put her down. Things didn't get better as the days went by. Due to all the commotion that Lauro had generated, the curiosity seekers began to arrive. They formed small groups in the street, then someone would step forward to knock on the door, and when she opened it they would scrutinize her from head to toe, as if they were looking for something remarkable. Occasionally they brought food or household goods because they knew that the Urreas had fled from Mexico with very little. Sometimes they asked Teresa to perform instant miracles in the air, and when she explained that she couldn't because she wasn't a magician, they went away with a mocking smile to spread the word that the so-called saint wasn't a saint at all. She wasn't even extraordinary, she was just a simple, kind woman with a father who was slightly touched.

The initial flurry of attention didn't last long; gradually Nogales seemed to forget them. Only the most destitute continued to arrive: foul-smelling Yaquis and Mayos covered with dirt, in ragged clothes, exuding misery through every pore. In Cabora she had never seen such poverty, such dejection. The majority of them had arrived just as she had, fleeing from injustice, fearful of being sent to the National Valley on the Yucatan Peninsula, where they would die of hunger, malaria, and sorrow. Many of them didn't even ask for help; they just wanted to contemplate her, to carry out half-forgotten rituals of adoration with a new saint. They asked her to baptize children, marry young people, and bid farewell to their aged with ancient ceremonies because there in Arizona they missed their elders, the wise people of the village, the leaders, the shamans who had remained behind or had died. Teresa realized that the majority didn't need relief from physical ailments but from spiritual ones; they wanted the identity of a community, they wanted renewed myths, they wanted to reinvent lost traditions in order to feel that they belonged to some place, to some history. They wanted what she couldn't give them, what had been left behind in another world, in another moment of time.

The spectacle of suffering and misery in front of her door disheartened her and soon put an end to the visits of those who were "better off." The neighborhood was becoming aggressive. The atmosphere was hostile, even churlish. Other Mexican families stayed away, afraid of being identified with the motley groups of Indians. Their ambition was to conceal their mestizo traits, learn English, cover up their Latino background, and become accepted by the "whiteys," or at least by the "Hispanics" who claimed to be directly descended from Spaniards. It was a difficult struggle, almost impossible, and the arrival of the alleged saint with her following of ragged Indians complicated things. What had glorified her in Cabora, vilified her here. She became a pariah.

The distance between Teresa and the North Americans in Nogales was even greater. The cultural, religious, and linguistic barriers were of such magnitude that they excluded any contact beyond the curious looks she received when going out. She was no longer Miss Urrea of Sonoran high society, nor the kind saint who healed and performed miracles. She was just another Mexican among all the refugees who crossed the border every day, an undesirable foreigner whose customs provoked first malicious laughter and then scorn, an outcast, a cultural hybrid, an abnormality within the context of Nogales. She didn't belong there.

The reporters were the worst, arriving to photograph the scene in the street in order to fill their newspapers with descriptions of promiscuity, filth, and possible contamination with exotic diseases. They said that the Nogales merchants were deceiving themselves if they thought the so-called saint would encourage business and tourism when all she attracted was human misery. When they had no other news to print, they wrote whatever occurred to them about Teresa. One day they exalted her, describing her as the brave young woman who had stood up to the ogre of Mexico; the next day they said she was unjustly persecuted by the dictator, and on the following day they accused her of being an ignorant, illiterate woman who had never attended school, who lacked any sign of culture, and who still had the nerve to preach about good and evil and to fanaticize the ignorant Mexicans with absurd superstitions. "Dirt and Saliva in the Century of Enlightenment!" proclaimed the headline of an article. "Black Magic," warned another; "Example of Kindness and Mercy Savagely Persecuted by Unjust Government," contradicted still another. There seemed to be no middle ground. One day they even published a letter addressed to the mayor requesting that he banish the false saint from the neighborhood where she lived because she was converting the area into a noxious garbage dump.

Teresa and Tomás endured everything in silence. Once the door was closed, a heavy stillness descended on the room, loaded with tension and guilt. There was nothing to say; everything she had foreseen had come to pass. Day after day they remained in that room without even looking at each other. Underneath her anguish, Teresa felt the overwhelming effects of repressed anger. She was defeated, and her impotence made her aggressive and rude with the neighbors of that hostile place. She suffered from constant nightmares filled with the faces of Díaz, Bandala, Enríquez, and Father Gastélum (whom she didn't know), phantoms that laughed maliciously and celebrated her living death. In the mornings she woke up exhausted by the impotent rage that she turned upon herself. She wondered whether it was there, in that unbearable situation, where she and Don Tomás would die, just as she had predicted in the dream.

Lauro Aguirre had gone to El Paso to attend to "a little business matter" and didn't return until the end of June. He arrived radiating optimism. The future presented a whole gamut of possibilities. He had already managed to raise sufficient funds to initiate publication of an opposition newspaper that would be called *El Independiente*. A Mexican in El Paso who owned a small press had offered to print it for a very low price. Finally, he was going to be able to attack Díaz directly without having to fear retribution. He spoke enthusiastically about the progress of the conspiracy, the increase in the number of people loyal to the cause, the spies who constantly reported events in Mexico to him. He was so engrossed in his successes that he didn't even notice the complete indifference of his friend. Teresa stopped him and made a sign that they should continue the conversation outside.

"He's not listening to you," she said when they went out to the street. "He's been that way since we arrived: shut up in his own world. He doesn't speak, he doesn't move, he hardly eats. I don't know what to do. Strange, isn't it? For him I have no miracles."

"Oh, Teresita! Exile is the sure road to oblivion," Lauro exclaimed, "unless you fight back. Only by struggling can you turn it into an interlude between the past and the future and then it will be bearable. What has happened to both of you? You look like two ghosts waiting to die. Where are your ideals, your spirit . . . ?"

"My life is so unrecognizable now that sometimes I think I've lost my way. Every day I wake up to silence and indifference or to brazen rejection. I'm a curiosity, just grist for gossip and mockery. And Don Tomás is worse; he doesn't want to know anything. For him everything ended when we left Cabora."

"Perhaps if you sent for the family, for Gabriela, the boy. . . ."

"Not while we're in this hovel. Where would we put them? But Don Tomás doesn't want to move; I can't get him to hold up his head and get started again. It's useless. . . ."

Lauro thought for a moment. From the very beginning he had considered the Urreas' exile to be a stroke of luck for his cause, but he knew he had to get them involved little by little, without pressuring them. Tomás was temporarily out of commission, but he wasn't the kingpin: Teresa was. Teresa would be the living symbol that would inspire the movement, the pure virgin, the image that the whole country would follow, as it had followed the Virgin of Guadalupe. But he had to convince her.

"I think I can help you. I have friends, but we need a plan to change this humiliating situation. Trust me."

"What are you going to do?"

"Just trust me. For now, I'll need a photograph of you."

Teresa had reservations about Aguirre's plans. In spite of his enthusiasm, his exacerbated optimism, and a tireless energy for forging new projects, he always seemed to end up ruining them, as if he lived under a negative sign that led him to make the worst mistakes precisely when he was about to succeed. But she didn't have much choice: there was no one else to help her.

Two days later Lauro took her to see a woman called Asunción who allowed the conspirators to meet in her house in Nogales. There he explained the plan to her: they would dress her as a saint and take her picture; the photograph could be sold as a religious token in order to raise money for a new residence. Teresa protested, but Asunción was already looking for the appropriate clothing in an old trunk.

"Once you move," continued Lauro, ignoring her negative response, "we can disperse the Indians and attract wealthier people who would be willing to contribute to our cause. You're not doing those poor Yaquis any good. It's more important to make it possible for them to go back home to their land, to their villages. . . ."

"And you think you can achieve that by dressing me up as a saint and making a spectacle of me?"

"No, no, absolutely not! But we have to give you back your stature, your image, your dignity. In this country things work differently: appearances matter more than reality. It's like a great theater; in order to play your part in society you have to dress according to your character. Do you think they would respect Díaz if he went around dressed like an Indian? No. That's why he wears his general's uniform, he whitens his face, he marries a woman of high society, he surrounds himself with intellectuals, and flaunts his power right and left. If you want to be respected as a saint, you're going to have to look the part, but not a backwoods saint with your shawl covering your face and your eyes always on the ground. A worldly saint! A well-dressed saint with her head held high. Asunción, the first thing you have to do is change her hairstyle and clothes. . . ."

Teresa doubted.

"Don Tomás will never approve. . . ."

"Don Tomás is dying of sorrow and who do you think is responsible?" Lauro gave her a hard look; the dart had hit home. "He doesn't have to know. You decide. First we have to create an image for you that will attract the rich people. We must reestablish your healing practice so that this society, at least the Mexican community, will grant you importance and recognition. Or are you going to allow the enemy to defeat you and condemn you to oblivion?"

Teresa remained pensive for a moment. Lauro was right. To continue as they were was slow suicide. She had to fight. She wished she had a little red earth to eat and rub on herself, as in other decisive moments of her life; instead, she opted for taking off her shawl and tossing it into the corner.

"All right, Doña Asunción, let's declare war on the enemy!"

Doña Asunción set to work while Lauro supervised the procedure and savored his triumph.

"Ah, Teresita! You won't be sorry. We're going to make you a powerful weapon against the enemy, you'll be a heroine, a defender of justice, a . . . Just leave it to me; I know about these things. Before you know it you'll be living in a decent house, your father will have his family back, and you will acquire the stature that you deserve among these rotten gringos. Together we will . . ."

Teresa stopped listening. They were the same dreams, the same schemes that she had heard on other occasions. She preferred to concentrate on the surprising transformation that Doña Asunción was achieving so quickly. First the dress, long, black, and very tight in the bust and waist. The skirt fell smoothly to the floor, insinuating, without emphasizing, her hips. She looked taller, more slender, more of a woman. Then she draped around her neck a huge crucifix carved in wood that hung from a rosary also made with wooden beads ("people are very Catholic around here; this will be a nice touch"). Next she smoothed her hair with water, pulled it back, and tied it in a knot at the nape of her neck. Without the bangs she looked older and more serious. Using a light make-up, Asunción shaded her cheeks to emphasize her cheekbones and outlined her eyes so they looked bigger and sadder. Thus she was converted from a young girl into a woman. She was astonished.

In the photographer's studio they took her picture with her standing, one hand resting on a wooden chair, the other at her side, holding a prayer book. She was slightly turned toward her right, and there were cherubs in the background.

"Now, miss, don't smile. Don't be so serious, either! Look, think about something or somebody who moves you, somebody you want to heal."

Teresa thought of Anastasia's poor, rotten lungs, and her eyes turned luminous; on her face was an expression of tenderness, with only a trace of pity.

▓ II

Lauro was lucky and his plan succeeded. An unexpected event gave him a pretext to go to the newspapers and make a fuss. The same afternoon that the photograph was taken, the mayor of Nogales, Sonora, a fellow called Mascareñas, paid a visit to the Urreas to deliver a message from General Abraham Bandala ordering them to keep their promise and move away from the border. Mr. Mascareñas appealed to Mr. Urrea's word of honor as a gentleman in order to pressure him to comply. Don Tomás shrugged his shoulders and didn't say anything, but Teresa, who had regained her self-assurance with the prospect of entering into action again, took care of the matter brusquely.

"You can inform the general that my father will keep his promise the day Bandala keeps his and allows us an impartial trial so we can clear our name of so much defamation and return home with dignity."

When Lauro found out, he immediately took charge of the matter. In the first place, he said, Díaz was probably furious, which could lead to an attempt at extradition or even a threat against his friends' lives. He advised them to go to Tucson and initiate the process to acquire U.S. citizenship. That would void a request for extradition and make any threat to their lives an international crime. Don Tomás shrugged his shoulders once more and continued rocking silently.

"We'll go tomorrow," said Teresa, without even looking at her father.

Lauro took advantage of his friends' absence to set the stage. All of Nogales immediately found out from the local press about Mascareñas's visit to the Urreas. "An overt act," it said, "of extraterritoriality in brazen violation of American laws." Señor Mascareñas, according to the newspapers, had uttered threats against the saint's life if she didn't go farther into American territory. The article included a detailed and dramatic account of their unjust arrest, incarceration, and deportation at the hands of the criminal Bandala. "The Urreas were sufficiently frightened and convinced that the Mexican government would carry out its threats so as to immediately seek protection from the American authorities. For greater security, they have traveled to Tucson in order to apply for American citizenship."

Once the door was open, Aguirre didn't stop. Another article gave a full account of the kindness and virtue of young Teresa Urrea, "who will soon be known worldwide for her miraculous cures."

A reporter who once had interviewed Teresita took advantage of the flurry of publicity to write about his experiences. He swore he had felt an electric current when he shook her hand and immediately afterward had been permanently relieved of an annoying backache that had been bothering him for weeks. A neighbor declared that Teresita's presence a few doors from her house had caused a remarkable improvement in the health of her father, who had suffered from fatigue for many years. Suddenly all of Nogales was talking about Teresa. Those fortunate enough to have met her personally were assured of invitations to gatherings that had previously excluded them; anyone who knew something (or invented something) about her life instantly became the center of attention. Lauro was the man of the hour, and there was no journalist in Nogales who didn't obtain an "exclusive interview" with "the personal friend and confidant of the saint." The newspaper with the greatest circulation invited Aguirre to set himself up in one of their offices in order to sift through the avalanche of writings about Teresa that they received daily, and that attributed to her miracles and deceptions, cures and rebuffs, marvelous powers or common vulgarities, and to determine which were true and which were merely creations of ambitious imaginations. Lauro took advantage of the offer to set in motion the second part of his plan.

The day after he started his new job Lauro placed a full-page advertisement in the paper that offered—for fifty U.S. cents or seventy-five Mexican cents—a beautiful four-by-six-inch photograph of the saint with her blessing and a special prayer on the back that would allow the holder access to Teresita's miracles. The money should be sent to the newspaper, and the miraculous image would be mailed to the interested party at once. The orders began to arrive immediately.

When Teresa and Tomás returned two weeks later, Lauro had dispersed the poor people, painted the house white, and placed potted flowers by the doorway. Already the publicity was having an effect, and Teresa received visitors from some wealthy families and from the mayor of Nogales himself, who assured her that Mascareñas would not bother her again. Lauro insisted that Teresa take advantage of the visits to tell in a tranquil but assured voice about her miraculous cures, and this served to spread her fame even more. She continued dressing and doing her hair as in the photograph. She didn't feel that that was deceitful. She received visitors, listened to their troubles, gave advice, and infused hope; her function was the same, but she had realized that Aguirre was right: in this country appearances were more important than facts. To be believable, you had to disguise yourself. That was just as inexplicable to her as her powers, but there were tangible results: her physical transformation was winning her a place of respect among the "best" families of Nogales.

On the day of her second death, Teresa would remember that period as the end of her humiliation, although not of her exile. Lauro turned out to be an extraordinary publicity agent who took advantage of every opportunity to increase her fame. With the new atmosphere it was easy for her to recuperate her self-assurance, which redounded in greater appreciation by the people of Nogales. Soon she was invited to elegant houses and treated like a celebrity by the local authorities; she was able to arrange for the poor and indigenous people who visited her to be accommodated in an empty lot next to city hall so they wouldn't disrupt traffic in the street. She attended to them early in the morning so she could devote the rest of the day to cultivating relationships on other levels. Lauro was more than satisfied with himself. Besides the wonderful publicity, the money raised by the sale of photographs was considerable.

One day he arrived and took Teresa aside. Without a word he put a heavy pouch in her hand. The young woman looked at him with surprise.

"Eleven hundred, twenty-five dollars and seventy-five cents," he announced, smiling. "More than fifteen hundred photographs were sold all over the state. You are famous, my dear Teresa."

The trip to Tucson and the sudden activity in the house finally produced a reaction in Don Tomás. He started talking again, he took some pleasure in being a host to the visitors, and finally he agreed to discuss plans for the future with his daughter and his friend: he was thinking of starting a small business in the area, perhaps a small dairy farm. He had made some friends already and they assured him that it wouldn't be very difficult. He ought to look for an appropriate place and then send for the family; he planned to ask Gabriela to gather all the gold she had hidden and bring it to him as soon as possible so he could buy some land with a house. Teresa shared with him the secret of her small fortune, and he was so pleased that he didn't even protest the sale of the photograph. He began to look for another house and soon found one that had five bedrooms and about three acres of land. It was near Nogales in a forested area called "Bosque." Fifteen days later they moved, and after another three weeks Gabriela, Mariana, and little Ramón arrived.

The family brought news. Just as Don Tomás had suspected, "Tomasito," as he scornfully called his son, had arrived ten days after his departure to take over the ranch. Gabriela had returned only once to pick up her things and the money that belonged to them. However, she did maintain contact with Miguel, who never ceased complaining about the new "boss" and yearning for the return of Don Tomás. The son was a poor administrator, a drinker, and a beastly womanizer.

"Well, at least he didn't turn out to be a fag," said Tomás, try-ing to make his voice sound natural, but his expression was gloomy. He was thinking about Loreto: had she, in some twisted way, wreaked her revenge?

The son had immediately taken his father's place, as if he knew that he would not return: in the master bedroom, in the library, at the head of the dinner table; he even tried to take the chestnut horse that Don Tomás had given Teresita, but the animal bucked him off so many times that the furious young man final-ly ordered Miguel to shoot him.

"Miguel brought Spirit to my father's ranch to save him, but since he wouldn't let anybody ride him, they finally had to put him to work in the fields. I'm sorry, Teresa."

Teresa shrugged.

"Spirit reduced to workhorse. How ironic!"

What was happening to Cabora was disheartening, and nobody could explain it except by blaming the inexperience and negligence of the young son. The summer in Sonora had been so severe that Díaz had exempted the cattlemen from paying their taxes. All of the wells dried up except for the one Teresita had dis-covered a year ago, which would have been sufficient to keep the cattle alive but they had to be herded there every day and Tomasito was more concerned with maintaining the ostentatious lifestyle that he had enjoyed in Alamos than in saving cows. He sent Miguel on such frequent trips to the city that the cattle were left to fend for themselves, and thousands of them had died during the months of July and August. In September, with the death of Doña Justina, the situation had become even more bleak. Loreto inherited a huge quantity of money and Tomasito seemed determined to spend it as soon as possible. He bought new furniture, wagons, five horses with elegant saddles, and countless other luxuries. The young man had no limits; he could spend money in his sleep. The only thing he scrimped on was the workers' salaries. The land was drying up, the ranch was deteriorating, and the cowhands were leaving in search of better pay.

When Gabriela stopped talking, Don Tomás's face was pale, but his eyes were like molten steel. Teresa looked away so nobody would see her pain. Cabora was dying; the beloved had been raped by the legitimate son. It was like a distant vengeance for which there would be no retribution. Inside each of them, rage simmered silently, in isolation, trapped underneath the exterior calm they struggled to maintain.

Mariana had news, too. In order to avoid the new boss, she had moved into Teresa's house, where she occupied herself dispersing the visitors until they stopped coming. Then the days became long and tedious. She spent her time in the kitchen, helping prepare meals and exchanging memories with Josefina. One morning in the middle of August she was in Teresita's house when someone knocked on the door. It was Anastasia, the woman treated for consumption. She was looking for Teresa to thank her for the miracle. She was totally cured, and that wasn't all: she was pregnant.

"You should have seen her, Teresa. She was like new, her face flushed with color, her body robust, her eyes shining and happy. You wouldn't have recognized her. She brought you a very pretty, bright red laying hen as a gift. I told her to keep it to help feed the baby after it was born. She was really sad not to find you."

"So it was a hen . . . ," said Teresa, remembering the dream. "I'll never understand why I see some things so clearly and yet I haven't a clue about other things that are so important. I wonder what finally cured Anastasia."

With the family reunited, its members could establish a certain routine that began to give them a sense of belonging. Don Tomás discarded the idea of milk cows and opted to invest instead in a grocery store with a friend. This kept him busy and gave meaning to his life, besides providing an acceptable income for the family. In the morning Teresa and Mariana attended to the floating population of Yaquis and Mayos, who ignored the border and came and went as they pleased, and in the afternoon she would give private consultations or simply chat with visitors. Gabriela took charge of the house, hired a young indigenous girl as a helper, and devoted herself to refeathering the nest that had given her so much security in Cabora.

Aguirre had gone back to El Paso. With his departure, the journalistic uproar died down. Teresa forgot about political matters for the rest of that summer, but Lauro didn't forget for one moment. In July he had started receiving information that kept him in a feverish state: this is the beginning, he thought.

In August he found out that Díaz had personally ordered the mobilization of troops against the "fanatics" of Tomóchic to teach a lesson to all aspiring rebels. They rode out of Sonora under the leadership of Colonel Lorenzo Torres and out of Chihuahua under the command of General José María Rangel and were joined by a detachment of soldiers headquartered in Mineral de Pinos Altos. The news didn't surprise Aguirre; he had been right about the enemy not forgiving or forgetting, just waiting for the appropriate moment. Lauro sent word to the mountain men with Benigno Arvizu, so when Rangel, planning to take the enemy by surprise, attacked on September 2 without waiting for reinforcements, the Tomochitecs were well prepared. Soon Lauro heard of the magnificent defeat that the federal troops suffered at the hands of the highlanders. In the same message Arvizu informed him:

At the end of the battle we took a wounded man prisoner—
Lieutenant Colonel José María Ramírez—and cornered Rangel
with six of his men in one of the houses. They were surrounded, and we surely would have finished them off if something
strange hadn't happened. Cruz arrived and ordered his men to
respect the lives of the enemy: "During the battle," he said, "a
young woman dressed in blue, very similar to our saint,
appeared to me and said: 'Cruz, let them go, don't harm them,
and be grateful for the help that I have given you in defeating
your enemies.'" The mountain men, hearing their leader's
order, retreated and allowed the cornered men to go free. I'm
afraid they've committed a tactical error. Although he let them
go, Cruz couldn't resist the temptation to humiliate General
Rangel, saying to him that such a young man shouldn't get
himself into a fix like this and he should go home to his mama.
Then he stripped him of his uniform, which he gave to his
nephew Santiago to wear, sending the general back to his regiment in his underwear. They've set themselves up for a fierce
revenge. I'll keep you informed.

Benigno Arvizu.

Lauro decided not to notify the Urreas yet about the events in
Tomóchic, even though the supposed appearance of the "saint"
convinced him of the importance that Teresa's direct intervention
could have in any armed movement. However, he did alert all his
followers so they would be ready for action if the highland rebellion managed to spark a general uprising. He still didn't see the
situation clearly enough. It was better to wait. A few days later he
received another message from Arvizu: "We buried our dead,
since we had some losses, too. Everything is calm. We have
observed movements of federal troops in the nearby hills, but
they haven't attacked. We don't want to confront them yet. We
managed to intercept a letter with documents for Rangel. The
enemy, under the command of Captain Francisco Castro, has
done us the favor of revealing all of our weak points and their

plan of attack. If the troops stay there, we will attack on Monday, since tomorrow is Sunday, a day for prayers." Lauro answered immediately: "Apparently Torres has had difficulty gathering the men he needs and he is stalling. Don't be too confident; I fear the worst is yet to come. L.A."

A few days later Arvizu informed him that Cruz had suspended the attack planned for Monday. The reason given by the Tomochitec leader was a message received during Sunday's ceremony in which Teresita prohibited any military action that wasn't in self-defense. Aguirre began to worry: the myth was becoming counter productive. In his next message he took the risk of stating that he had spoken personally with Teresita, who not only ordered Cruz to attack the troops immediately, before they lost their advantage, but also encouraged him to assume the obligation of organizing the general uprising against the tyrant. He didn't know if his letter reached its destination, as he received no answer.

Torres marched on the district of Guerrero in mid-September and joined the detachment of Captain Castro. In a new roundup of "saints" he arrested the "Sacred Christ" of the mountains and an old man known as San José. Saint Barbarita, a child only twelve years old, had been wounded but managed to flee. The news was heard immediately in Tomóchic, from where Arvizu informed Aguirre, filling his letter with insults for those vicious cowards who laid hands on the most defenseless creatures. Realizing that the siege of Tomóchic was imminent, Lauro sent a coded message to Arvizu, telling him to destroy all communiqués and not to send any more without using the code or signing with the password.

The next message arrived according to his instructions: the troops were "sheep"; the officers, "herders"; battle was "encounter with another herd"; Tomóchic was "the ranch"; the mountain men, "the owners"; the enemy, "hungry wolves"; and Teresa, "the Virgin." Nonetheless, when Aguirre finished deciphering it he thought that something was wrong. The message said:

> Long live the Virgin! Death to hungry wolves! Great celebration
> on the ranch after incredible encounter with another herd. The

wolf Felipe Cruz, drunk as a skunk, marched on the ranch to annihilate the owners. Confused by alcohol and surely by the Virgin, he attacked an exuberant cornfield, shouting, "Death to the owners!" and made an ample harvest of dead cornstalks. In the same state of intoxication, he reported to his superiors the "total extermination of the enemy." Once the truth was known, he was punished for inebriation. Cruz ordered a general fiesta in the town to celebrate the triumph and give thanks for the Virgin's intervention.

Lauro demanded an explanation: "In code the terms 'cornfield' and 'cornstalks' do not exist. Please clarify." Arvizu answered him that neither of the terms was in code and those were the actual events. Lauro was ecstatic: Tomóchic was leaping from victory to victory. It was possible that the news would spread, and this would encourage the other towns to revolt. Too bad the mountainmen were so isolated from the rest of the nation! But if victory was theirs, he himself would spread the word. He anxiously awaited the next communiqué, but after a message on October 12, in which Arvizu noted the absolute calm in the region, there was a sudden silence. Lauro was surprised, because the reports from Sonora revealed that Torres's troops were still in the area. Two weeks passed with no news and he began to worry. He sent a coded message demanding information, but the messenger didn't return. There was nothing he could do but wait.

The wait ended the night of November 2. Lauro heard a knock at the door. He opened it and encountered the emaciated face of Arvizu. The man fell to his knees, embraced Aguirre's legs, and broke into wrenching sobs.

"Not one was left, not one. . . ."

III

The third number of the newspaper *El Independiente,* published in El Paso, Texas, to circulate surreptitiously among the population of the neighboring country, included the long, horrible account that Arvizu told in detail, sobbing uncontrollably, and that Lauro himself had written down without omissions or additions since for the first time in his life not even he could exaggerate on the cruel reality of the massacre. To tell the truth, the tragic finale at Tomóchic did not surprise him; he had always suspected that the isolation of the town, the fanaticism of the inhabitants, and the small number of rebels made it almost impossible for the movement to gain national momentum. A rebellious Tomóchic did not mean anything. But a martyred Tomóchic took on a heroic stature. The monster had played a very risky card. In his rage and desire for vengeance he made a tactical error. The massacre of the highlanders was the definitive proof of the dictator's bloody practices. With Tomóchic as the banner one could prepare the road to revolution, but it had to be used carefully. The fact that Arvizu had been able to escape to tell the story in all its gory details was a factor the enemy hadn't counted on: here was an eye witness who could spread the word about the incredible atrocity. With renewed optimism, Lauro began to spread the news in order to fan the waning spirits of the revolutionaries, including Teresita. A week later Doña Asunción delivered a newspaper to Teresa, with a note from Lauro:

> My dear Teresita:
>
> I'm afraid there's bad news, so please read this paper in a place where nobody will disturb you. I'm sorry I can't be with you when you read it, but the recent unfortunate events make it necessary for me to stay here with my people to raise their spirits again. You will remember that I told you the tyrant wouldn't forget and that he would combat truth and justice anywhere he found it, including the most remote corner of the nation. Yes, my beloved Teresa, it has happened. I beg of you to read the bloody story carefully so you will understand without a doubt the true nature of the monster we must conquer.
>
> Your friend who adores you, Lauro Aguirre.

Teresa's hands shook as she opened the paper and saw the eight-column headline: Tomochic! Heroic Town Wiped From The Face Of The Earth!

The story began by recounting the problems that Teresa had heard from Cruz almost a year earlier and had detailed to Aguirre; then it described the first attack by the federal troops, the triumph and march of the mountain men toward Cabora to receive the blessing of their "living saint," the ambush and death of Enríquez, and the return of the highlanders to their town to live in peace, work the fields, and devote themselves to their new religion that offered them the hope of love and justice. Then it continued:

But the Tyrant Díaz could not ignore a matter that had made his "brave" troops appear ridiculous, so he ordered a mobilization of forces against a town that for more than a year had not taken up arms or raised its voice to denounce the murderous government.

He sent orders to the three officers involved in the previous fiasco, who had sworn to avenge their initial defeat. Torres, Castro, and Rangel marched on Tomóchic.

Cruz Chávez, the leader of the mountain men, heard that they were approaching on October 15, when he was planning to celebrate the birthday of the young Teresa Urrea, recognized as the patron saint of the town. The elaborate festivities were canceled, and Cruz shut himself up in his home to ponder the difficult decision that was before him. When he came out, he walked to the corral where two prisoners from Rangel's first attack were being held. He opened the gate for them and said:

"You are free to go because today is the Saint's Day of our beloved Teresita, who always preaches forgiveness toward our enemies, and who, on this day, has asked me to pardon you. You should know that we would not have done you any harm, but federal troops are headed toward Tomóchic and there will be war. Shut up in here, you would surely die from the bullets of your own people. Therefore, in tribute to Teresita on her day, you are free."

The prisoners were so impressed with the kindness and
valor of the mountain man that they chose to stay there and
fight on his side rather than return to the cowardly troops of
the government. Thus there were seventy-two combatants in
Tomóchic: sixty men and twelve boys between the ages of ten
and fourteen. That night Cruz gathered them all together and
spoke to them again about kindness and justice, but especially
about Saint Teresita, because he was convinced that she was
announcing a new era in which all people could live together
in peace, with love for each other. Since they knew the soldiers
were coming, they could have mounted an ambush to get the
upper hand, but Cruz wanted to remain faithful to the wishes
of Teresa Urrea and wait for the enemy to initiate the attack. He
warned his men that defeat was possible since the enemy num-
bered more than two thousand.

"I don't want anyone to die who is not willing to make the
sacrifice," he told them, "so whoever does not wish to follow
me can leave."

The article continued, emphasizing how none of the men
had left and they all promised to die fighting, offering their sacrifice to the saint who had guided them since the beginning of
their struggle, how they prayed all night, and how at dawn they
realized that Torres's and Rangel's men were already in the surrounding hills.

As soon as the federal troops were in position, Torres and
Rangel ordered them to open fire on the town. The
Tomochitecs, lying on the ground, withstood the onslaught
until the enemy had advanced to within sixty yards of them.
Then they all stood up, shouting, "Long live the Saint of
Cabora!" and "Death to the evil government!" and began to
shoot. Both sides were under heavy fire.

The article included the details of that first day, which ended
with the triumph of the Tomochitecs and the demoralized retreat
of the army. When night fell, the federal troops had lost seven

hundred men, whereas the highlanders had not suffered a single fatality.

> At that time Cruz could have taken advantage of his enemy's defeat, but once again he didn't want to take the offensive, preferring to encourage his men to keep up their heroic defense of their land and families. He believed that the victory and the fact that not one of his men was wounded were signs that they were being protected by a superior power, which would not favor an offensive. The brave Tomochitecs were convinced that the enemy bullets could do them no harm because of the influence of the Saint of Cabora.

Teresa kept reading, horrified by the descriptions as if she had the image of Tomóchic before her eyes and could listen to Cruz's voice instructing his men and pronouncing her name to give them courage. During the days of October 21, 22, and 23, the Tomochitecs continued the struggle, always in an open field. Each of those days the results were the same: a handful of mountain men repelled and dispersed the masses of federal troops who tried to descend from the hills to take the town. However, the highlanders never took advantage of their superior marksmanship or their continuous triumphs to pursue and destroy the enemy; rather, they retreated each night after combat to give thanks to God and the Saint of Cabora. This allowed the enemy troops, in spite of their losses, to occupy increasingly advantageous positions on the surrounding hills. On October 24, by a strange quirk of fate all five Medrano brothers—the best Tomochitec sharpshooters—fell beneath the enemy bullets. Cruz decided not to expose his men so much, and on the following day he ordered them to continue the battle from the church and his own house, which had been converted into their general headquarters.

> It was the beginning of the end, and Cruz sensed it. Once again he insisted that whoever wanted to could flee under cover of darkness from that certain death, but nobody abandoned him. From October 25 to 28 there were continuous losses among

the Tomochitecs, and even though Cruz and his men continued to claim lives among the federal troops, each dead
Tomochitec was worth five hundred of the enemy. At dawn on
the 28th, Cruz had only twenty-five followers remaining. He
gave the order to take their last stand in the church; the
Tomochitec women and children joined them to die with their
loved ones.

Supplies were running low; many had not eaten anything
solid in the last three days. Rangel and his men had taken over
the river and water was scarce in the village. Those brave
mountain men began to waver, more from the ravages of
hunger and thirst than from the threat of the enemy. And their
poor families! The children were crying for lack of food; the
mothers' milk had dried up; there was nothing to eat or drink,
but nobody wanted to abandon the struggle and risk surren-
dering to the ruthless enemies.

Having concentrated most of his men in the church, Cruz
took a few to general headquarters so the enemy fire could be
returned from two fronts. General Rangel took advantage of
their movement to have a squad of soldiers infiltrate the town;
the squad reached the portico of the church and set the main
door on fire. Many of those inside were wounded, some dying;
their wives grabbed their rifles and heroically continued the
defense. But the fire spread to the stairs with diabolical rapidi-
ty. The defenders were being asphyxiated by the smoke. Those
who managed to get out ran desperately toward Cruz's headquarters and were mowed down by enemy bullets. Two
women, not wanting to be captured alive, threw themselves
from the tower. About forty people burned to death, including
combatants, women, and children. In a little while all that
remained of the church was rubble and ashes. The soldiers
took five prisoners, who were immediately shot.

The only position left to Cruz, the seven men, four women,
and two children still alive was headquarters, from where they
tenaciously kept up the defense. Fifty soldiers surrounded their

last holdout. At midday Cruz requested a ceasefire to allow the women and children to leave, but they refused to go.

On the morning of the 29th, with no sign of a surrender by Cruz and his men, the headquarters was vigorously attacked. Some soldiers got up on the roof and set the house on fire. The battle lasted more than an hour even though almost all the Tomochitecs were wounded.

When they realized they couldn't hold out any longer, Cruz and his men came out the door, firing on the enemy. The soldiers, surprised by that unexpected strategy, took cover in the ruins of a nearby house. But the battle was lost. The Tomochitecs soon ran out of ammunition and had to put down their weapons. Immediately they were taken prisoner. In spite of the ardent protest of Captain Castro, the only one who seemed to appreciate the valor of those mountain men, Rangel personally gave the order to shoot them. One by one they were executed; finally only their brave leader, Cruz Chávez, remained. He had seen all of his followers die, and with an expression of extreme pain he asked that they kill him too, commending himself one more time to his beloved Saint of Cabora. Rangel grabbed the rifle of a nearby soldier and pulled the trigger. The proud Tomochitec buckled and fell slowly to the ground. On his face there was a strange smile.

That night the federal troops reduced the town to ashes, retreating to the hills to watch the only reminder of the highlanders' brave feats burn to the ground. The last sounds to be heard in Tomóchic were the crackling of the flames and the pitiful howls of dogs that were trying to devour the corpses before the fire could destroy them.

Don Tomás was in the dining room when he heard the inhuman howl. He ran to Teresita's room; she was standing next to the bed, all color gone from her face, shaking uncontrollably. Her hand was crumpling the newspaper. Her wild eyes were the color of a raging fire. She emitted another unearthly howl, which seemed to come from the core of her being. And then, with a series of hoarse growls, she began to throw everything she could lay her hands on, ending up tearing her own clothes and hair, until Don Tomás managed to get his arms around her and knock her down on the bed, falling on top of her. Mariana came running to help. Between the two of them it took half an hour to calm her down. Finally, when they observed that her breathing was slowing to normal, they gradually eased up. She held still without blinking, her gaze fixed on the white ceiling.

IV

The last one to enter was Juan Lungo. Outside in the hot August night his five companions were waiting, their faces already painted. Teresa smiled, greeted him, and began to darken his face and hands with charcoal. As she worked she spoke to him of justice, of the importance of the cause, of the good they were doing. She explained the difference between stealing somebody else's property and returning things to their rightful owners, since the money they would take in the attack was illegally in the hands of the enemy, who was using it to persecute innocent people. When she finished, she gave the blackened man her blessing and embraced him.

"Take care, brother," she cautioned him, as she had each of them, "and I'll see you in a few days."

Juan Lungo stood looking at her, and in that gaze Teresa saw depths of fear that she hadn't seen previously.

"Aguirre says that you are going to give us success and that you will protect us during the battle. Isn't that so, Teresita?"

In that simple phrase she heard echoes of Cruz's faith and she trembled.

"Oh, Teresita, this is the big revolt and I'm afraid. According to Aguirre, more than five hundred Yaquis are waiting for us in Nogales. As soon as we have the money, we will march toward Hermosillo. On the way, we are promised another thousand reinforcements, and with them we'll take the capital of the state, impose the first revolutionary government, and call for a general uprising. Aguirre assures us that the discontent in the country has reached such a level that even elements of the army will join us. But he promised that you would go with us to offer spiritual guidance during the struggle. You will come, won't you? Many wouldn't want to go without you; we are all very afraid."

Teresa made an evasive gesture with her head. She embraced Juan again to hide her confusion and said:

"Don't worry. Just take care of yourself, and good luck."

She was left alone, listening to the hurried steps of the six men disappear into the darkness; then silence returned like a chill. The moment had come. For the last three years Lauro had constantly spoken of the general uprising, the "big revolt," but it always seemed so distant, so far in the future, until suddenly it was an immediate reality. The first hit would be in two days. She tried to feel Lauro's tireless optimism, but the silence of the house frightened her. All of a sudden she heard the crickets.

They were just like the crickets she had heard during those nights long ago in Bosque while the wrenching images of Tomóchic tormented her mind. She thought of Cruz, his faith, his bravery, the fury with which he believed in justice. She felt that the whole weight of the tragedy was on her shoulders. Was she responsible for what happened? Had she once again served the twisted designs of the enemy? Instrument of destruction! She hated kindness, she hated justice, she hated the patience she preached: she felt it was all a lie. The yearning that brave man had awakened in her returned in full force like a cruel, secret fire. She was overwhelmed by the reality of his death; she tormented herself with the idea that possibly, through some miracle, she could have been there to die with him or maybe to save him. But she was especially afflicted by Aguirre's insinuations. If Cruz hadn't followed her advice, or what he interpreted as her advice, would he have triumphed? Would he be alive right now and perhaps there with them, a refugee also, included in the group of conspirators?

The questions, the doubts, the recriminations were endless. That annihilation carried her name, her unmistakable stamp of the angel of death: the Saint of Cabora. What good were her cures, her kindness, the humiliation and persecution she had suffered, if in spite of all that her hands were stained with blood? Perhaps it was better to kill consciously, as the enemy did. To fight straight on, without thinking about the means, just seeing the end, as Lauro Aguirre did. Anything was better than that malevolent manipulation of her by the enemy. She tortured herself for a whole week until she made a decision: Aguirre was right. The enemy had unsuspected strength; the razing of Tomóchic had proven that. He could only be combated with his own weapons: blood and fire. The pain of the massacre became rage, and the next day she sent a terse note to Aguirre: "I want to avenge Cruz's death. I'm with you. I'm waiting for your instructions."

From then on she used her natural talents to attract people to the cause, especially wealthy ones who could supply the necessary resources for the purchase of guns and ammunition. It was extremely important to create a public image of benevolence and sweetness that would exempt her from all suspicion, so Aguirre took charge of spreading the word about all of her noteworthy activities. If during her daily occupations she encountered individuals who expressed discontent with Díaz's government, she was supposed to send them to Lauro. Teresa returned to her duties with renewed eagerness, feeling that once again they had an important and specific purpose. Life in Bosque seemed to return to normal.

At the beginning of 1893, under the command of Benigno Arvizu, 20 men rose up in arms in Las Cruces, Chihuahua, hoping to take advantage of the indignation caused by the massacre in Tomóchic. On April 9 they managed to take over the town of Temosáchic, where 40 men joined them. They headed for Santo Tomás; the group increased to 115 rebels. For three days they resisted the onslaught of 3000 federal troops, but the expected general uprising never came, and on the fourth day Arvizu's men broke through government lines, leaving many dead among the enemy, and fled toward the United States. The rebellion, even though it had failed, served to swell Lauro's ranks, and Arvizu brought weapons and money he had stolen from a mail courier.

"When the courier heard that the money was for Saint Teresita of Cabora, he handed it over without protest and even wished Benigno good luck," Lauro told her later.

The rest of the year and all of the next was spent on preparations. Those were tranquil months in which Teresa could spend a little time on herself. She got into the habit of fixing herself up, and she bought more stylish clothes. Many nights guitar playing and singing were heard once more in the house in Bosque. Gabriela was expecting another baby, and her happiness was infectious. Aguirre was devoted to the publication of his newspaper, El Independiente, in El Paso; he reprinted in installments the true story of Tomóchic. He frequently wrote long articles about the virtues of Miss Teresa Urrea and the injustices committed against her by Porfirio Díaz's government. He was gratified to see that the North American press, always avid for scandal, reproduced and even exaggerated his stories, creating among its public an increasingly adverse opinion of the Mexican dictator.

Toward the end of that year Aguirre came to see Teresa again. He wanted another photograph because he was sure that the situation was finally heating up; the political unrest in Mexico was spreading more and more, and he had to take advantage of it. This time he had thousands of lapel buttons printed with her image, and he developed a publicity campaign that involved not only newspaper articles but also pamphlets containing the history of the young woman and prayers that should be said while wearing the button to become worthy of her blessing. Teresa didn't pay much attention to the stir. She was too busy, first with Gabriela's difficult childbirth and then with caring for the new baby. She was a beautiful little girl, who had inherited her mother's dark hair and Don Tomás's green eyes. For the first time in many months Teresa was distracted from her mission. She felt an irresistible attraction to the baby, which made her sit still for hours, contemplating her.

As often as possible she picked her up, allowing herself to be caressed by those diminutive hands that searched for her breast or her cheek. Mariana watched the scene without asking questions, but the secret smile that Teresa had whenever she saw Gabrielita made her remember that promise of children long ago that had filled her with such joy. Teresa was now twenty-one years old; perhaps soon she would keep her word. One day Gabriela said to her:

"You ought to think of having your own family." Teresa looked at her absentmindedly.

"It's too soon," she replied, and a shadow passed over her eyes. She had remembered Cayetana.

The new year entered with cold and snow that lasted until the end of February. Then spring arrived in all its glory. Aguirre surprised them with a visit in early March, to Don Tomás's relief; he was tired of being shut up in the house all winter. They sat on the garden porch to enjoy the sun as they talked. Teresa pulled up a rocker to listen to the conversation; Gabrielita was sleeping in her arms. According to Aguirre, the situation in Mexico was critical. Since Limantour had managed to overcome the economic crisis of previous years, Díaz felt more secure than ever in power, and he was arranging the election sham of 1896, pushing aside the "scientists" of the Liberal Union, and creating the National Porfirian Circle to facilitate his inevitable designation as candidate. Lauro considered this a mistake that would weaken the monster's power, and he intended to capitalize on it. Don Tomás didn't agree. He thought that the country's new economic boom would calm people's spirits and that they would accept the reelection of the man who had achieved it.

"The oligarchy isn't going to cut off its own head over a question of ethics. Díaz has consolidated his power by centralizing the economy in such a way that he has absolute control over the states that might start a rebellion."

"On the contrary, it is precisely this centralization that is causing so much unrest, especially in the north. Large amounts of money are being accumulated in the capital; the provinces are bleeding to death. What goes back to the states is minimal and is concentrated in a very few hands. Terrazas and Torres have monopolized almost all assets in Chihuahua and Sonora. How long do you think the people will put up with that?"

"For centuries," answered Don Tomás.

"You're wrong. There are strikes and revolts going on all over right at this moment. They can spread, join forces, and then . . . I think 1896 is going to be our year. Díaz won't survive another electoral farce." Aguirre went on to discuss the recent attempt at secession by Chiapas and Soconusco that, even though it had failed, could happen again in the future, but Tomás wasn't listening any more. Lauro's diatribes tired him; actually, it was all the same to him. He had lost all hope of ever returning to Cabora. There the problem wasn't so much Díaz as it was Loreto and her sons, who had taken over the property. Why go back? He was distracted by the movements of his little daughter. She had woken up and was struggling against Teresa's embrace as if it were making her uncomfortable. Teresa didn't seem to notice. She was engrossed in Lauro's conversation. Don Tomás picked up the child and took her inside.

Aguirre took the opportunity to tell Teresa to get prepared. He had left the newspaper in good hands and was going to devote his time to training a revolutionary group. In spite of Don Tomás's opinion, he was convinced that the decisive moment was approaching. Teresa nodded; she had just become aware that her father had taken the baby from her. She felt a peculiar emptiness.

During the summer the tension in the area near the border increased. The newspapers frequently published reports of "Indian bands" that assaulted Mexican communities, taking money and weapons, killing people, and fleeing across the border to the United States. The Mexican authorities complained about the lack of cooperation from their North American counterpart in the persecution of the criminals, "who were not revolutionaries" since the country was at peace under the firm and secure hand of its president.

The rumors of an imminent armed uprising in Mexico took on new credibility in the North American press, and reporters saw possible conspiracies in every gathering of more than ten people. In the house in Bosque the nervousness increased with this news, which seemed to confirm Aguirre's suspicions. Father and daughter read everything that was printed about the matter and looked at each other, not daring to state an opinion. One intrepid reporter dredged up stories about the almost forgotten "Saint of Cabora," affirming that this "deranged woman" had appeared in the town of Presidio, surrounded by hundreds of fanatics. According to the version published in a Nogales newspaper, when the authorities tried to arrest the hysterical woman, a riot broke out that ended in two fatalities and several wounded. The so-called saint had mysteriously disappeared and hadn't been seen since. Don Tomás was furious.

"Isn't it enough that they kicked us out of the country? When will they leave us in peace?"

"Never," replied Teresa. Being the subject of newspaper articles again made her shiver. Throughout the summer she had received secret messages from Lauro that kept her up to date on the movement and advised her to act cautiously without ceasing to influence the Mexican population. Tomás didn't know anything about this, but Teresa's spirits had been rising. She could perceive the discontent, she lived the enthusiastic response of the people, she was inspired by Lauro's growing excitement, and hope was growing inside her once more. She also had been convinced that the impossible could actually happen. The moment was near: she had to involve her father so he wouldn't impede her participation.

Outside the window the sunset tinged the sky in shades of orange. The sad call of the mourning dove punctuated the silence. Teresa looked at Don Tomás. He had aged: he had white hair at his temples and his macho stance had mellowed; his previously straight spine was slightly curved, lending a certain flexibility to his body that was almost tender. His new posture made him more accessible, inviting intimacy. It was as if giving up the struggle had ennobled him. For a moment she doubted: she questioned her right to disturb that premature old age, to stir up the anguish and rage, to create the challenge that would shake his new tranquility. Then she remembered Cruz and Tomóchic; the image of Damián Quijano returned to her, and she relived her humiliation at the hands of Bandala. She began to speak, first in a hushed voice but then with a growing conviction that made her savor what she was saying. She spoke of the obligation to do something, the cowardice of sitting with crossed arms while tremendous injustices were being committed. She confessed that she had been collaborating with Lauro because somebody had to take the first step, and she didn't see any other possibility. She told him she wouldn't renege; if necessary she would leave the house, but she was going to continue the struggle. She told him of those who sought her out, not to cure their bodies or their souls, but to cure the social evil that was defeating them. She spoke of destiny and how it weighed on her life and the impossibility of eluding it and then the optimism she felt through the hope of others. She talked to him as she had never done before, feeling the urgency of her words, excited by the role that history had assigned to her, observing her father's face as it reflected first doubt, then surprise, and finally determination. When she was finished, the sun had set and the nocturnal shadows softened the silence. Don Tomás looked at her.

"I'll help in any way I can," he said; then he got up and left the room.

 V

In September, Aguirre arrived with both good and bad news. The unfortunate news was that Díaz's government suspected Teresita's complicity with the movement, and even Don Tomás was implicated. Lauro feared for their safety if they remained near the border. Fortunately, he and his associate, Manuel Flores Chapa, had already found a much safer place from which to foment the revolution: Solomonville, Arizona, a community outside the border zone and thus with no Mexican authorities in residence. He had moved there a month ago and had found someone to do the printing for him. He had taken the liberty to locate a house for his friends, much larger than the one they occupied in Bosque, and for less money.

They were not sorry to move. Teresa had developed a deep, unvoiced dislike of Nogales. The town was dirty, and the people lacked the kind of dignity that didn't have anything to do with money or social position, but with historical identity. Don Tomás had suspected that Aguirre's activities would put his family in danger, and he was glad to move them away from the border. They hurried to organize the change, while Lauro was busy leaking the news to the papers that the Urreas were leaving due to overt threats by Díaz's government. On the day of the move some of the neighboring women who had been healed by Teresa came to say farewell; one of them cried. The young woman embraced her without emotion and promised vaguely never to forget them, a promise she broke as soon as she had turned her back on the town. Moreover, she didn't even think about Nogales again until almost a year later, on the night of August 9 when she was blackening Juan Lungo's face.

The day after the Urreas moved, a note written by Aguirre appeared in the local paper lamenting the great loss that Nogales suffered with the departure of "such a beautiful and virtuous young lady whose moral character and marvelous cures have earned her the title of saint."

The mining town of Solomonville stood at the foot of the Gila Mountains. It was smaller and cleaner than Nogales. On one side rose the enormous peaks of mountains covered with thick forests, and on the other the immense plain stretched before them. Contemplating the distant horizon, Teresa felt she was recovering some of the vast expanses of Cabora. The inhabitants included the owners of the mines, the merchants who supplied them, and the workers who lived in their own neighborhood, somewhat removed from the center of town. Lauro, together with Flores Chapa and Ricardo Johnson, had rented a small house in the merchants' neighborhood in order to be near the post office and the press, but the one he had chosen for the Urreas was in the area inhabited by the owners of the mines. It was a two-story house made of wood, with six bedrooms, a living room, dining room, study, kitchen, and a porch that faced a large garden. It was situated on twelve acres of pasture land, which Don Tomás promptly populated with dairy cows.

The Urreas were immediately accepted by the local society. As soon as they moved in they began to receive visitors who offered them their homes and their help with any problem. One of the visitors was Juana Van Order, a Mexican married to a kindly, rich Norwegian who had been living in Solomonville for many years. She was tall and handsome, about thirty-six years old, and she radiated dignity and respect. Teresa liked her from the first day.

The remaining months of that year were the happiest that the Urreas had known in exile. Don Tomás was completely caught up in his dairy business; he left early in the morning and came back at dusk, burnt by the sun, smiling and singing. Gabriela, with Mariana's help, reinvented the daily routine, caring for the house and children, creating culinary works of art, weaving tablecloths, designing clothes for the children, or just sitting on the porch, saying the rosary as she waited for Don Tomás to return. Teresa was not known as a "saint" in Solomonville, and she began to enjoy a freedom that she hadn't known since her days with Chepita. In the morning she would stop by at Juana's and the two would take long walks in the country and talk incessantly. She frequently ate at her friend's house with her husband and two adolescent children, John and Harry, who listened, enthralled, to the tales of Cabora, of the exile, and even of the bloodshed in Tomóchic, which Teresa was able to verbalize for the first time. She didn't remember ever having shared such a happy, united home. As the days passed, the friendship between the two women

deepened. Teresa discovered that she could share her most intimate thoughts with Juana: the confusion and anguish her powers
caused her, her sudden infatuation with Cruz Chávez, the guilt
she suffered because of his death, and the conviction that the
enemy, time and again, managed to twist her destiny. Everything
that she had never told Mariana or anybody else came tumbling
out. Juana seemed capable of understanding and accepting everything, even the bizarre dream about Anastasia and the malevolent
way she sent Captain Enríquez to his death. In turn, her friend
spoke to her about spiritism and reassured her by saying that all
her powers had a logical explanation and her actions were
responses to a superior plan that she should always follow. When
Teresa confessed her participation in Aguirre's anti-Porfirian
movement, Juana congratulated her and promised to put her in
contact with other people in the district who would be willing to
collaborate. They started to attend Lauro's meetings together and
to help him with his plans.

During the month of December, Juana and her friends
worked secretly with Teresa, Don Tomás, Lauro, Ricardo
Johnson, and even Mariana on the primary document of the
movement: The Plan of Reform and Restoration of the
Constitution, which would be published and circulated widely
toward the beginning of the following year, before the so-called
elections. Everybody's enthusiasm was growing. The document
made official accusations against Díaz and specified the changes
that the opposition proposed for the country. It mentioned the
vile assassination of men, women, and children in the massacres
of Veracruz, Oaxaca, Jalisco, Sinaloa, and Sonora; it recalled the
slaughter at Tomóchic and Temosáchic and of the Tarahumaras.
It accused the regime of having used the Fugitive Law authorizing guards to shoot fleeing prisoners and of having suspended
human rights by imposing capital punishment on innocent citizens. It proposed the reestablishment of the vote, the return to
constitutional legality of the government, respect for private
property, the end to concessions for foreign companies, and the

right of communal holdings for indigenous peoples. It denounced the monopoly of agrarian land by the hacendados, demanded that the peasants be given adequate land to plant, and requested a limit to the acquisition of agrarian land by one individual. It also demanded the repartition of mines so that each worker could benefit directly from his labor. It denounced the violation of freedom of expression and demanded respect for thinking, writing, and teaching in any form. The military would be structured so as to defend the nation instead of protecting its tyrannical government, and, for the first time, women would be equal before the law as they were before their creator.

After eleven pages of accusatory "considerations," the document called for an armed rebellion based on the Constitution of February 5, 1857; it invalidated the functions of all present authorities, federal and local, and declared the supreme leader of the revolution to be the supreme leader of the Republic until that time when new constitutional powers would call for elections.

When they finished perfecting the document, there was general euphoria. Even Don Tomás, who was usually a skeptic, was gripped with enthusiasm as he reread what for him was the first useful piece of paper produced by his friend.

"Well, Lauro! I'm beginning to take you seriously. Where do I sign?"

Teresa laughed and hugged her father. It was the first time she had seen a spark of hope in his eyes since they had left Cabora.

"I'll sign, too," she said, "and Juana, and everybody . . ."

"I can't sign, Teresita," her friend interrupted. "I became an American citizen a few years ago. But I agree with you on everything, and when the revolution triumphs I'll become a Mexican again so I can vote in the next elections."

Don Tomás took out a bottle of cognac and served a round.

"This is for the signers, so their hands don't shake."

All toasted and drank and served themselves again.

"A toast to the year 1896; may it be the beginning of a new Mexico," exclaimed Lauro. "Here's to the death of the enemy."

Teresa frowned but immediately reconsidered. It was just Lauro's manner of speaking; they had already agreed that the tyrant would be subjected to the same fate that they had suffered, that is, expatriation, "so he can rot in solitude, far from his country," they had said. She raised her glass, too. Then Lauro called for silence and waited for everyone to be seated so he could address them.

"The document will have Tomóchic as the place of dispatch, in honor of the brave men who were its precursors, and it will be published on February 5 in commemoration of the date of our legitimate constitution."

All present agreed. But when it was time to sign, Lauro held Teresa back.

"No, you are too well known and important to be implicated at this moment. Soon you will have an opportunity to make your ideas known. Those of us who head this crusade must not be exposed ourselves: without leaders there is no movement."

Teresa felt frustrated, but she handed the pen to Tomás, who for security reasons decided to use Loreto's paternal last name, Esceverri, instead of Urrea. Then came the signatures of Isabel Figueroa, Amada Moreno, Pascuala Terrazas, and Isaura Chavira, all Juana's friends; then their husbands signed, and, lastly, Mariana took the pen and looked at Teresa with pride.

"My signature is yours, too, so don't feel bad. Don Lauro is right. You shouldn't expose yourself right now. Nobody knows us and they won't know where to look for us. With you it's different."

On February 5, 1896 the proclamation was published. Two days later Lauro received a coded message from Rafael Ramírez, who was in charge of keeping him up-to-date on governmental activities in Mexico.

> Document received and widely distributed. Work continues successfully; more than three hundred cattle have been rounded up. Herders are ready to move as soon as weather permits. Nobody is afraid of the sheep; without a doubt they will join the herd as soon as they see the quality of the grass on the other side of the

fence. A lot of rabbits running through the fields; they recognize the hand of the angel who is helping us. Take good care of it!

Lauro went straight to the Urreas' house.

"The die is cast," he said. "The proclamation has been received with great joy by our people, but the enemy has copies and, in spite of the precautions we took, the three of us are implicated. It seems they have spies in this area, probably among the American authorities. They know we're here and that the people who signed the document are our friends. It's time to jump into the ring. I'm counting on you two. I'm leaving tonight for Nogales with Manuel. We still don't have enough weapons and ammunition to be able to make a major move; we'll carry out a few minor, low-risk incursions to get what we need. I'll keep you informed; meanwhile gather all possible resources among our friends and get prepared to move to the border when the real action begins. It's essential that we all be present when the first important city is taken so we can establish the new government immediately and begin to function. Tomás, I'm leaving you in charge; I'll need Teresa with me to encourage and inspire the troops. Get ready; there's no time to lose."

Teresa and Tomás glanced at each other.

"I'm looking forward to seeing you as the supreme leader of the first revolutionary government," she said and smiled. "I'm not sure how I'll do at the front."

"You won't be in any danger," Lauro insisted; "we just need your presence in camp to get the men fired up before the battle. . . ."

Once more a shadow crossed her face. She was convinced that there was no other way, but the image of the dead and wounded implied by the word "battle" overwhelmed her.

"I'm not afraid for myself, Lauro, it's just that . . . oh, forget it. We'll be ready."

"One last thing, Tomás. If something happens to me, you two should move immediately to El Paso. You're my only hope that the movement will continue and triumph. I've already told everyone that when I'm gone, you will be the new leaders."

Don Tomás embraced his friend.

"Take care. My thoughts go with you," he said, his throat feeling a little tight.

On the night of March 7, Lauro Aguirre, Manuel Flores Chapa, and Ricardo Johnson secretly left Solomonville and headed toward Nogales. Before he left, Aguirre signed a form at the local post office authorizing his mail to be delivered directly to Mr. Urrea. Two days later Teresa and Tomás were surprised when they opened the newspaper and read:

MEXICAN EDITOR PLANS TO CROSS BORDER WITH ARMED FORCES, ATTACK DIAZ

Nogales, Arizona, March 9, 1896. A communiqué from Sam F. Webb, customs official in Solomonville, informs us that Lauro Aguirre and Manuel Flores Chapa are headed toward this town with an armed force to enter Sonora and initiate a revolution against the Mexican Government.

A week later Tomás received a message signed by Johnson. Lauro and Manuel had been arrested upon their arrival in Nogales, but Ricardo didn't believe there was cause for worry. There was no proof against them since the authorities had rushed to arrest them before they had a chance to organize any incursion or assault. He was convinced that the law of neutrality would protect them and that the arrest could even turn out to be beneficial because once the trial was won, the American authorities would be more cautious about acting on future tips from the enemy.

▦ VI

Just as they had suspected, the trial was a farce. The basis of the accusation was the February proclamation, but for neutrality to be violated, the law demanded proof of an armed movement. The North American press had a field day celebrating the absurdity of two powerful governments conspiring to punish a couple of poor editors for predicting a revolution in Mexico when in the senate of the United States help was being solicited to support a revolution in Cuba. After the trial, both were set free immediately, and Lauro, overflowing with optimism, informed his friends.

"The defense was brilliant," he said, laughing; "They showed that one of the witnesses had been bribed by the Mexican government to testify against us, and the prosecution fell apart. It was ridiculous. They even absolved us of writing the proclamation since our signatures weren't on it, and the only thing they could prove was that we published an anti-Porfirian newspaper, which is perfectly legal in this country. The judge was furious; he called our cause a 'paper revolution' and severely admonished our accusers for having wasted the time of the American authorities with such nonsense. Ha! Paper revolution!"

Teresa was infused with Lauro's optimism when she heard that news of the so-called revolution had reached Washington and that upon Porfirio Díaz's instructions Matías Romero had requested the intervention of the U.S. government. This seemed to prove that Lauro was right: the situation in Mexico was so precarious that the dictator feared any movement, no matter how small. Everything indicated that the uprising would occur just as Aguirre had predicted. She was already dreaming of returning to Cabora.

Suddenly, the thought of Cabora made her conscious of the fact that she hadn't had a single premonition for a long time. She couldn't even remember having a significant dream, as if her vision had been anchored in the present. "I've lost my objectivity," she thought. "I'm too involved and I can't see anything anymore."

The Urreas decided to move to El Paso to be ready. During the journey, Don Tomás was once more silent. Again this man, her father, was traveling away from his loved ones in order to follow her. Why was he doing it? Was it love, or was it the macho response to challenge? Or did he just want to keep his promise to Lauro? Did her father have secret ambitions? She wanted to ask him but was afraid of getting only silence in return. Upon arriving in El Paso, Lauro's irrepressible enthusiasm lifted her spirits, and she busied herself helping with the preparations.

From March to the end of July they devoted themselves to recruiting people and gathering weapons, ammunition, and money. Teresa's arrival in El Paso once more stirred up contradictory reactions as the local newspapers did their best to make much of the Mexican saint. "False Reports About The Saint Of Cabora," cried one, asserting the falsehood of Teresa's supposed participation in future revolutions. "Famous Saint Causes Stir On Both Sides Of The Border," announced another, pointing out the growing pilgrimages that crossed the invisible line to visit the acclaimed saint; another denied that Teresa's so-called powers had any political implications and called her a "deist." Lauro himself couldn't resist the temptation to take another swipe at Díaz by publishing his own version of Teresa's activities.

THE NORTH AMERICAN PRESS AND MISS TERESA URREA

Finally the North American Press has begun to favor Miss Urrea, which means that it is turning against the assassin of Veracruz and incendiary of Tomóchic it has previously praised so extravagantly. This means the day is not far when the newspapers will declare war on one of the most criminal dictators to bloody the pages of Mexican history.

Judging by these indications, the United States certainly will abandon the Mexican government soon, because in that country the press controls public opinion and both impose their will on the government in Washington.

Although she was increasingly visible in the papers, in person Teresa was very cautious and rarely left the house. All of them were convinced that there were spies everywhere, and their nervousness kept them constantly alert. Faced with the increasing anxiety around her, Teresa preferred to leave any decisions to Lauro and to simply follow his orders. She discovered that by not thinking about the ramifications of what she was doing she was better able to carry out her duties. It was an almost unprecedented relief to place her fate in someone else's hands; for the moment it allowed her to endure the growing tension that was affecting them all. The atmosphere was heavily charged as accusations and denials clashed in the newspapers and the time to act drew near.

The assault on the customs office in Nogales was scheduled for early September. But during the first days of August a gale struck the border towns, unleashing on Nogales, Sonora, a rainstorm of historic proportions, and Lauro announced that the date of the assault would be moved up to the following week.

Don Tomás protested, but his friend assured him that the downpour would keep the authorities busy, and this would practically ensure the success of the assault. The date was set for the 11th, and with the urgency to set the plan in motion none of them had time to doubt, much less Teresa, whose responsibility it was to prepare the leaders of the expedition, who were to leave for Nogales on the night of the 9th.

That evening, after blackening the faces of the six men, she was left alone with her thoughts and the memories evoked by the singing of the crickets. She was filled with doubts and fear, and Lauro wasn't there to scare the ghosts away. One by one the phantoms began to come out of their hiding places. How had she accumulated so many? Damián with his anguished face and the drowning child saints; the unknown woman dressed in such a strange fashion who stumbled over a rock, shouting, "You stole my life"; Captain Enríquez radiating youth and inexperience; an impassioned Cruz, swearing he had never taken the offensive; the Mayos of Navojoa sacrificed without a trial, scapegoats for others; and Cruz . . . Cruz . . . always Cruz. Time had not been able to wipe out his image or the memory of that first encounter. What would he say now? He would repeat her own words: that one shouldn't shoot first, never take the offensive, that violence is bad even when shedding enemy blood. Words, empty words. Now the world was upside down. Goodness was taking the offensive; kindness demanded vengeance by blood and fire and the destruction of the enemy. Good men painted their faces black and crept into the night like criminals. The "saint" gave them her blessing so their bullets would find their targets, so their hands would be skillful at theft, so their souls would be insensitive to the suffering of others, and their courage unwavering as they strove for their goal. She, Teresa, the one with miraculous hands . . .

She tried to remember all of Lauro's arguments, but her mind grew fuzzy and his abstract ideas were lost like puffs of smoke in the night. Behind the cricket's chirping, she heard the silence of the men who were secretly running toward their destination. She felt the dark shadow of her fear. Would they manage to take the customs office in Nogales, steal the money necessary for buying weapons, and initiate the march on Hermosillo? Would the enemy be defeated? Would the first freely elected government be established? When? How long would it take? How many deaths? Would she and Don Tomás see the end some day? The only response was the monotonous singsong of the crickets.

There was no one in the house. Don Tomás had gone to Solomonville to alert the family. Lauro, Manuel Flores Chapa, and Ricardo Johnson were hidden somewhere in Nogales, organizing the decisive step that would follow the successful assault on the customs office. Juan Lungo, Loreto Rivas, Miguel León, Franco Vásquez, José Salcido, and Luis Liso were on the road. There was no turning back. All Teresa could do was sit and wait in the silence that slowly filled with frights and starts.

She put out the kerosene lamp and lay down in the dark, trying to think how it would be after the revolution; but implacable images of the upcoming battle invaded her mind. In the hushed darkness hundreds of thousands of dead people filed past, rivers of blood ran by; the stench of unburied, decomposing corpses filled her nostrils; the cries of mothers deprived of their sons, women left without husbands, and children without a father reverberated in her ears. The devastating reality of civil war was revealed to her in all its chaos and confusion. She sat up without lighting the lamp. Those visions . . . were they a premonition or just the effect of her rattled nerves? How many times had she heard Lauro speak of revolution? She had dreamed of the good it would bring to the country, of being part of a new reality governed by justice. But talking of war was like talking about death: it was always projected into the future, into an amorphous time that didn't seem threatening. But now it was upon her with all its indisputable fright.

Would August 11 be the first day of vindication for the poor and oppressed? Or would the enemy triumph again? She tried to think about Díaz. She remembered seeing his photograph and being surprised by his short stature, his brown skin, his amiable, almost paternal expression; and that bushy mustache, so similar to Don Tomás's that it had made her laugh. *He* was the enemy? It wasn't possible. That little man? She had always imagined him as the monster described by Aguirre, an impressive hulk that radiated savagery and tyranny, a giant with fiery eyes and a cruel, twisted mouth that reflected the enormity of his unjust brutality. But as she looked at the photograph, she had the impression that by talking to him, by talking to the enemy, she could convince him of his error and guide him back to the path of goodness. Lauro took it upon himself to enlighten her.

"Evil is blind," he said. "It can't see itself because if it did, it would be defeated. The enemy is incorrigible; he sees assassination as justice, destruction as progress, violent repression as peace, uncontrollable thievery as administration. If Díaz appears tranquil, it's because he loves his tyranny, because he considers himself a savior, and because he has lost the ability to perceive evil. That's why the only road to change is revolution. Only goodness and justice can recognize evil and rebel against the bloodthirsty acts of the perverse dictator."

It had sounded fine then, but now doubt gnawed at her: if evil was blind to itself, what assurance did good have of being the absolute good? If goodness was not good, just self-deceived evil, how could you tell them apart? Who was to be the judge? Good men, Lauro had responded, those who love justice, defend life, and promote kindness. Good cannot be relative, he had said;

goodness recognizes itself and cannot be deceived. Díaz speaks of goodness to confuse us, but his actions reveal his lie: could killing innocent people, stealing from the oppressed, persecuting those of us who tell the truth be good? Obviously not. She had allowed herself to be convinced because back then everything was clear: those were the days when she was healing while Díaz's men were murdering, when she was giving to the poor while the dictator confiscated their lands, when she preached patience while international companies were looting the country with the tyrant's blessing. But, what about now? Tonight and the days to come?

She thought again about what Lauro had said: "The maximum good is love in its most complete expression." Love . . . another word that lacked meaning. What was love according to her friend? Had she ever loved? She had ardently desired to be a part of Cabora, but had she really loved that land the way Don Tomás loved it? She had emulated her father to the point of surpassing him, but was love her motive? Or had she merely coveted the power he had? She tolerated Gabriela, she appreciated Mariana's services, but did she love them? Cruz had made her feel an emotion so strong that it tore her apart, but was that love? When people spoke of her infinite love for the poor, had they really seen something in her or were they imagining what they wanted to see? Was it for love that she had blackened the faces of the conspirators? And the farewell hug, wasn't that more like an embrace of death? Lauro said, people said, Don Tomás said . . . Words, they were all just words and, as Huila had taught her, words serve to fragment our existence: everything becomes little pieces of reality, all relative and interchangeable.

When Tomás returned the following morning, he found Teresa in such a nervous state that he was frightened. She was standing by the window, and when she tried to explain her doubts and fears to him, she stammered and became confused. Her father took her arm and led her to the bed; then he sat next to her and silently caressed the back of her hand while looking into her eyes. Finally he spoke.

"Teresa, tonight you and I have a date with destiny. What happens today will determine whether history remembers or forgets us, but nobody can take from us the merit of having assumed our responsibility to act."

Teresa looked at her father, and it seemed to her that she was seeing him for the first time. Underneath his egotism, underneath all his weaknesses, underneath the ideal that she had constructed of him, she saw a courage that she had never perceived before, an integrity not exempt of pride, a commitment to the circumstances that revealed not only vanity but also love whose obvious object was life itself. For the first time in her twenty-three years she realized that she wasn't alone, that the future didn't depend on her, and that regardless of the results, she had made the only possible decision. She had never felt so human as in that moment, sitting there holding the hand of her father, who didn't ask her to be heroic or saintly or supernatural but just a person playing the part that life had assigned her. She would have liked to hug him, but he had turned away, assuming the conversation was over.

That night they sat together in silence, waiting for news.

▦ VII

The newspapers were filled with stories about the failure of Lauro Aguirre's "revolution," the triumph of the combined forces of the Mexican and U.S. governments, and the death of the "fanatic followers of the Saint of Cabora," among them, Juan Lungo, Loreto Rivas, Luis Liso, and José Salcido. The defeat provoked a stampede away from Aguirre, and the movement was decimated. Teresa, Don Tomás, and the family went into hiding, fearing for their lives. Not only had fourteen of the fifty assailants died without obtaining the desired booty, which the customs official had wisely hidden away in the consul's house, but the authorities had also found among the clothing of the deceased some copies of *El Independiente*, photographs of the saint, and instructions for the uprising.

Gradually the declarations of the captured assailants were published in the papers. José Morales said that he didn't know the leaders and that he only knew that they received instructions from the Saint of Cabora. Franco Vázquez declared he had been recruited by Benigno Arvizu, who told him to go to Nogales in order to get arms and ammunition and rob the customs office and then head toward the Yaqui valley; according to him, Teresa Urrea ordered the assault and provided them with the prayers and letters they were carrying. José Arsic swore he didn't know the leaders but that one of them told him that he was sent by the Saint of Cabora. Alejandro Suárez declared that the leaders assured him that the plan was for the sake of liberty. Ramón Caberos confessed that Benigno Arvizu had spoken to him about the apparition of the archangel Gabriel to the Saint of Cabora to deliver a letter from God ordering her to foment religious fanaticism for revolutionary purposes. Enrique Acevedo observed that the assailants shouted, "Long live God, the Saint of Cabora, and Lauro Aguirre!" and that they intended to take the money from the customs office and deliver it to the saint in order to provide resources to defend their rights and to demand autonomy for the Yaquis. José Morales affirmed that Aguirre was a close friend of Tomás Urrea and his daughter, and Pedro Gómez, whom the Urreas didn't know, swore that Lauro was Teresa Urrea's lover.

The declarations left Don Tomás in the grip of an almost uncontrollable rage, and the subsequent interpretations submerged him in despair. They spoke of the bravery of the authorities killed in the battle against fanaticism and ignorance; the so-called saint became a modern sorceress, the Witch of Sonora, believed to be in communication with the devil. "It would be impossible to attribute the attack to motives that guide the lives of healthy people," said one article; "the truth is that it is the work of infamous half-breeds, steeped in ignorance and encouraged by the zealotry of a crazy sorceress who prophesies the downfall of Díaz's government." "The senseless death of valuable members of the community," complained another, "is mainly a result of the twisted, muckraking journalism of one Lauro Aguirre, who has been dedicated to affirming the divinity of a poor hysterical woman called Teresita and to convincing the ignorant that she is capable of freeing them from slavery and giving them power."

A few days later Tomás received a communiqué from Lauro, whose unflinching optimism in the face of crushing realities made him seem deranged. He insisted that defeat was merely a stroke of bad luck, that the uprising was just about to occur, and that they needed to carry out the other assaults they had planned in order to recruit more men and gather more supplies. By return mail Don Tomás told him he was crazy, he should stop deluding himself and as soon as possible publish an article denying Teresa's involvement in the assaults. Lauro ignored the order. Two weeks later the attack on the customs office at Ojinaga had the same results as the earlier assault. The survivors marched on Las Palomas in Chihuahua, but the federal troops were forewarned and well prepared to thrash the rebels, and those who escaped death had to flee to the United States. The newspapers on both sides of the border named Teresa as the instigator of the attacks and Don Tomás as Aguirre's accomplice. The word was that Díaz was requesting the extradition of all three to subject them to a trial under Mexican law. According to the papers, there were possible attempts on the life of the supposed saint by government agents. The Urreas were afraid to leave their house and any knock on the door became a threat. After the attack on Las Palomas, Lauro disappeared completely, all revolutionary activities were suspended, and a strange, tense silence reigned. Nobody knew where the rebel leader was. The "revolutionaries" had dispersed. The earth—or federal bullets—had swallowed them. Tomás took advantage of the calm to return to Solomonville with Teresa to prepare the rest of the family for the worst.

By the end of the year, the landslide reelection of Díaz seemed to have influenced the ambivalent attitude of the neighboring country, and the United States government reacted to the

Mexican insistence that they resolve the problem of border attacks. In March 1897 Don Tomás received an official memo from the U.S. Immigration Service.

"Either we move even farther away from the border and abandon all subversive activity against Díaz's government or they will allow our extradition," he said with the communiqué in his hand. "I don't think it's an empty threat. Díaz's dictatorship has never been so powerful. Lauro was wrong. There wasn't even a slight shudder among the oppressed classes. The so-called revolution was stillborn. If we want to get out of this alive, we must accept the conditional protection this country is offering us."

Teresa listened to Tomás without a quiver. She didn't feel anything. She had lost all hope. She recognized in the failed assault the inevitable fate of Aguirre. He was defeated by an insane optimism that didn't allow him to see reality. The enemy had not only triumphed, he had come out even stronger. The movement was dead: there was nothing left to do but survive. She was convinced that her prediction was true: they would never return to Cabora. They had lost. She only found consolation in the last words that Don Tomás had said to her: failed or not, they were part of history; what Lauro predicted would happen sooner or later and they had taken the first step, an almost suicidal step, but it allowed them to transcend the anonymity of their individual existence. She felt tired. She was twenty-four years old. During the last five years she had been an instrument of destiny and a possible participant in history, but she didn't want any more of that. Suddenly she had an insatiable desire to live her individual life, without importance, without ostentation, lost among all the other nondescript beings who only asked that history not make waves so they could continue an everyday existence that she had never known.

They advised the U.S. government that they were moving to a small town in Arizona called Clifton. Under oath to tell the truth, they swore that they had nothing to do with the assaults on the customs offices and that they were not involved in any movement to overthrow Porfirio Díaz. They requested personal protection because they feared attempts on their lives by Mexican agents. They promised not to participate in any armed movement or conspiracy, and in late April they moved to the tiny mining town perched in the mountains, far from any possibility of revolution.

For the first time ever Teresa experienced real tranquility. In Clifton nothing ever happened except the occasional threats of floods that kept all of the inhabitants alert. For the next three years, as they awaited the new century, which, with great fanfare, was predicted to be the end of the world or the beginning of utopia, she spent her time making friends, healing the sick, helping Don Tomás with his two businesses, dairy and lumber, and spending long hours with the family. Gabriela had three children by then, two boys and the little girl, whom Teresa adored.

The residents of Clifton didn't make much fuss over her cures or spread rumors about her. Teresa was accepted as a part of daily reality, just like the inevitable overflowing of the river once a year or the visit of familiar ghosts at the end of October. She was welcome in the best homes and she felt loved. Among the Mexicans, most of them workers in the mines, the myth of her sainthood still circulated, but she had so little contact with them that it really didn't bother her much. Once in a while a wounded miner or someone suffering from the natural illnesses of his profession came to her and she would cure him, sometimes against the medical prognosis. She took that in stride now, not demanding any explanation. If she felt a nagging doubt, she would remember Don Tomás's words and imagine herself as the instrument of a blind and unknown destiny. Perhaps some day one of her patients would take part in the big uprising; he would be one more instrument, thanks to her, in the creation of a future that she didn't even dare to define as better, just different, part of the unavoidable ebb and flow of life.

In the beginning, the only person in town who criticized her healing methods because they weren't traditional was the local doctor. Beloved by all, Dr. Burke was a good man who didn't demand much of life: to live in peace, have an honorable medical practice, and go fishing on weekends. However, when he heard that his third "incurable" patient had recovered after only one consultation with Miss Urrea, his curiosity was piqued and he decided to pay her a visit to find out the reason for such amazing results.

Teresa liked him at once. He was a learned man, especially in his own field; he tried to keep up with new scientific developments without being showy about it, so he was well informed about the most recent discoveries. He was amiable, frank, and very sincere. He told her that he didn't understand how she had cured Juan Sánchez, whom he had given up for dead. She confessed that she didn't know either, and that's how the friendship started. Burke shared everything he knew about the most modern medicine without affirming that it was the only alternative. He was convinced that science only touched on a few relative truths, not absolute ones, and that they were useful in certain cases but totally ineffective in others. He didn't call Teresa's cures miracles, but he didn't deny the possibility that they resulted from something as yet unknown to scientists. Most of all, he was curious. Teresa realized that his amiable inquisitiveness was a third possibility that she hadn't considered until then. New doors opened for her. Between belief and disbelief lay human curiosity, an endless road that newborn reason was staggering along; there were no definitive answers, but that didn't negate the possibility of asking questions and, in the process, finding oneself. Suddenly curiosity appeared to her as the most astonishing of human capabilities, the urge that left nothing in peace, that had to find meaning in everything. Dr. Burke became her best friend. Together they spent entire afternoons analyzing the facts—not beliefs, not inventions, not products of blind faith—just the plain facts: that Don Jesús had been cured of chronic arthritis after only three visits; that the Arellano child didn't die of the pneumonia that was devastating her but, rather, gained weight and was completely healthy a month after Burke's fatal prognosis. And then there were the simpler cases: Peter Cummins, the owner of one of the mines, had been cured in one day of his long-term alcoholism by a single conversation with Teresita; Doña Ursula Cabañas had been cured of her wayward heart and converted into a loving wife by drinking a tea made of geranium petals that Teresita had prescribed. All this interested the doctor, without his questioning its practical application. He couldn't deny the tangible results: he could only think that the logical explanation was still unknown to him.

Her friendship with Dr. Burke helped Teresa to become fully integrated into the community, which from then on paid attention to her in a reasonable and measured way. Thus she was able to devote herself to helping others, worrying about their everyday problems, and trying to satisfy their needs in such a natural way that it didn't seem to require any miracle, or even any effort. She became part of a human community.

A new and unexpected atmosphere of normality enveloped the whole family, and nobody thought much about the future except as an extension of the present. They heard that after a while Lauro Aguirre had gone back to his usual occupation, publishing subversive newspapers and even using Teresa's name for certain revolutionary articles, but the peace and tranquility that surrounded them lent a sense of security that was so new and desirable that they didn't pay any attention to their friend's seditious activities.On October 15, 1899 Teresa had her twenty-sixth birthday and invited her friend Dr. Burke to the celebration. At the end of the evening the doctor proposed that the two of them organize the construction of a hospital for Clifton.

"The old building where we tend to the patients is not adequate. In order to take advantage of advances in medicine as well as your cures we need more modern equipment and surroundings. Perhaps we could invite scientists to come investigate your supposedly miraculous cures. You never know, before we die, we just might find an explanation," he said, winking at her.

Teresa immediately committed herself to working on the project. Even Don Tomás enthusiastically offered to help with finances as much as he could.

"The first to benefit should be the miners," he said; "I'm sure that the diseases they suffer aren't incurable, they're the result of unsanitary working conditions. A scientific analysis of the situation would be necessary to determine the cause of their ailments and to remedy the problems at the work site."

Don Tomás believed that health problems, just like social ones, should be dealt with at the grass-roots level and not with armed movements that didn't produce anything more that pretty words, "highfalutin" ideas, and chaos.

"The individual is what counts; the common man must be sufficiently convinced in order to change, thus slowly changing society itself."

Teresa felt content. The task she had before her was concrete and didn't demand that she perform miracles or lead movements. It seemed even more important than what she had been doing before. Those were extraordinarily happy and tranquil times. The plans for the hospital included almost all the inhabitants of Clifton: the town felt it had a goal and united to achieve it.

The new century arrived without any cataclysmic event.

▨ VIII

His name was Guadalupe Rodríguez. They called him Lupe. He was the foreman of the most important mine in Clifton. The workers respected him, as did the boss. He was quiet and efficient. Teresa had seen him many times from a distance. One day she ran into him at Dr. Burke's office. Her friend introduced them, and after Lupe left he commented that the foreman was an intelligent young man, but somewhat strange. Teresa didn't pay much attention. It wasn't until the first meeting to plan the future hospital that she noticed him. She saw him walk into the room and perceived in his profile an unusual beauty that she would remember later. Immediately he turned as if he had felt her gaze. They greeted each other with a smile. Afterward she would discover in the luminosity of that smile a hint of the deep, radiating pain that she would know later.

During the meeting, her eyes settled on him one or two more times. He was talking with the group of men who were elaborating the plan of services for the miners. She and the other women were dreaming up ways to raise the construction funds. She looked at him with no particular intention, in an absentminded way; then she turned her eyes to the window and contemplated the intense blue color of the sky, the golden tones of sunlight that illuminated the afternoon, and the mysterious, green shadows of the thick forest in the distance. The landscape filled her with joy, and she was distracted by an intimate desire to go outside and join the secret delirium of the languishing afternoon. She looked again in the direction of the young man and once more perceived his beauty, with no desire of possession, but rather as one would contemplate a figure in a work of art and be astonished by its perfection and its harmonious integration into the rest of the painting. A question brought her back to reality, and she realized that she had lost all notion of where she was and why.

Actually, they didn't even know each other. They had never exchanged more than a few insignificant phrases. Their lives moved in different circles. Therefore, Teresa was surprised when that very night he arrived at their home for a visit. She assumed that he wanted to continue talking with Don Tomás about the needs of the miners. She led him into the dining room, where they sat around the table, drinking coffee. For a while they spoke of plans for the hospital. Lupe had a pleasant, husky voice; he spoke slowly, as if he thought out each sentence before uttering it. Teresa watched him: she liked the way his lips formed the words, his easy smile, the intensity reflected in his gaze when he was discussing something he considered important. Don Tomás reached for the bottle of cognac to serve him a drink, and Teresa held out her glass for a refill. Mariana suggested a toast to the hospital project, and after they had all toasted she distracted Tomás with a problem that had developed with the cows in the stable, and they became engrossed in a discussion about whether or not they should enlarge the animals' quarters. Gabriela excused herself and went to put her children to bed. Teresa turned to Lupe to ask him a question, and when she met his gaze she experienced a strange, internal quivering. She realized that she had blushed. Lupe was looking at her as nobody had ever looked at her before.

From then on the miner's visits became part of the routine. He usually arrived a little after dinner and stayed late into the night, chatting with Don Tomás. Teresa realized that she spent all afternoon waiting for him, and when he didn't arrive she became so out of sorts that she went to bed immediately after dinner. She understood that for the first time in her life a man had managed to waken something in her that was more than the chimera she had experienced with Cruz.

What happened, she never knew. It was a hot summer night; Lupe stayed later than usual. Dr. Burke had arrived and was talking enthusiastically with Don Tomás about the future hospital. Mariana and Gabriela had retired for the evening. Teresa felt wrapped in a warm, exciting ambience that seemed to emanate from Lupe seated at her side. Teresa wasn't even listening to the conversation; she was caught up by an unknown emotion, something indescribable. Lupe extended his hand under the table and took hers; she felt a shiver run through her. Frightened, she glanced at her father, but he was still talking with Burke; she responded in kind to the clandestine caress. She began to speak of the hospital without even noticing what she was saying in order to cover up the secret urgencies that the contact had awakened. It occurred to her that in all her twenty-seven years nobody had touched her like that. And she was filled with desire, with infinite yearning. They kept their hands intertwined, inscribing fiery messages on each other's palms, covering up the sensual dance of their fingers with meaningless words.

The world disappeared in a tangle of secret touches. Their knees and their hands spoke the ardent language of an impulse heretofore unknown to her. Teresa felt that her being was opening wide before the unfamiliar onslaught of desire. There was no modesty in her. Her eyes offered Lupe all the caresses that she had bottled up for so many years. Only the presence of the others held her back.

Suddenly Lupe withdrew his hand and stood up to leave. It was then that she realized how gaping the wound was. She felt that she was bleeding words unsaid, possibilities not admitted, cravings denied. When he said good night and thanked them for their hospitality, she noted a peculiar ambivalence in his voice and tried to look him in the eye, but he turned away and spoke to Don Tomás. All at once she was overtaken by the pain that lay in wait behind the delirium. Lupe left without looking back.

That night she could not sleep. Internal confusion divided her between desire and fear. Alone in her room, she recreated Lupe's face, the warmth of his hand, the thousands of cryptic messages they had sent to each other, and that chaotic abyss that she had discovered in herself. In comparison, the encounter with Cruz had been mystical: it had nothing to do with her body, with that strange, inner urgency that seemed to rebel against any control. Her body had always been a docile vessel, with no requirements beyond eating and sleeping. Nevertheless, with just a few caresses, it had become a mare in heat, neighing and pawing at the ground, demanding that its desire be consummated. Teresa felt she was losing her mind. Never, not even in fantasies, had she imagined that such a thing could happen to her. Everything had been so calm! Her life had been resolving itself into a tranquil flow of days with the family, enjoying Don Tomás's tender affection, Gabriela's serenity, the children's rambunctiousness, and Mariana's friendship. What more could she ask for? But what happened took her by surprise and she was defenseless. She surrendered to a painful eagerness comparable only to the ecstasy of death.

She tried to think about her father, the hospital, Mariana, Gabriela, the beautiful little girl who filled her idle moments with joy, but she realized that nothing except Lupe mattered any more. She imagined that at one time that was what Cayetana had felt for Don Tomás, and the memory filled her with tenderness. Perhaps she finally understood her mother, whom Huila had called "an animal in heat." She went back to thinking about Lupe, with a blind passion that left no room for questions as it closed in upon itself. Her whole body ached as if there were no more room for the caresses that multiplied within her, or for love, or sadness, or patience, or dreaming; there was only room for her obsession to see Lupe, to speak with him, touch him again, feel his luminous gaze on her face. Desire immobilized her, and dawn found her curled up in bed, hugging her knees and her pain.

Much later she would understand that she had been bordering on insanity. She would remember Lupe's evasive attitude the following day, the confusion she felt when she realized that he didn't want to hear of her desires. With everything she wanted to say to him, she couldn't speak a word. She encountered his hard gaze and a voice full of farewells. Her words stuck in her gut, burning her insides. She saw him take refuge in his work: he had a lot to do, he felt awkward about these things; he turned his back on her and left her like a skewered deer, with wide, uncomprehending eyes, turning slowly over an open fire. Silently, she walked home, torn between rage, passion, and doubts. He had provoked her. Why was he rejecting her now? Was he afraid? He was younger and he belonged to a different social class. Was that it? Why then had he dared to awaken the burning urgency of her body? Hadn't he felt the same thing? She would have sworn he had: she had seen it in his eyes, felt it on his skin. So what had happened?

Delirium reigned. For days she made up any excuse to run into him: she asked for his advice about the hospital, she requested his help, and every time she saw him the desire was renewed, with ever increasing strength. It didn't take Don Tomás long to realize that there was something between them and he absolutely forbade the relationship. Teresa hardly noticed; she was only interested in breaking down Lupe's barriers. Little by little he conceded; his initial timidity opened up to small gestures of love. She was careful not to frighten him, allowing him to take the initiative. Don Tomás was as jealous as if he were her husband; he shouted at her that Lupe was unworthy of her, he belonged to a different social class, he could never be part of the family. Teresa sarcastically reminded him of her own origins, her birth in the settlement, her illegitimacy, her whoring mother. The house became a battlefield between father and daughter. Teresa had to seek out Lupe surreptitiously.

When they were together, they spoke very little, dumbfounded by the attraction that joined their hands, locked their gazes, and finally, after months, produced that first kiss so full of voluptuousness that Teresa could no longer contain herself.

"I want to go away with you," she murmured.

"We would have to get married," said Lupe, after a long pause.

She said no, Don Tomás would never accept it, the best thing would be to elope together, but he insisted.

"We have to get married. Are you willing to go anywhere with me? Wherever I say?" His voice had turned hard and had an edge of anxiety. Teresa tried to calm him.

"Wherever you say," she answered. Suddenly, Lupe turned toward her, determined.

"Tomorrow, then. Tomorrow we'll get married. I'll come by for you at noon; we'll go see the judge. Have your things ready, because I have a house about twelve miles from here where we can live. Now go, and don't say anything to your father; this should be handled man to man."

At home Teresa didn't speak to anybody, fearing that her own emotion would betray her. She understood that she was about to wound Don Tomás as she had sworn never to do again, but she defended herself by thinking of her prolonged celibacy. He had Gabriela and the children, and she had the right to make her own life. She filled her mind with thoughts of Lupe. She didn't want to foresee the future; just the immediacy of their plan.

Lupe arrived at midday, rifle in hand, face set with determination. Teresa was surprised by the firearm, but she had never seen him looking so handsome. Don Tomás stepped out on the terrace; Teresa followed him and stood paralyzed at his side.

"I'm marrying your daughter, Mr. Urrea," he said.

"By shotgun?"

"If necessary."

"You'll have to kill me first, Lupe Rodríguez. My daughter is not going with you. Go find someone of your own class and stop bothering decent people." He made a motion as if he were going to draw his pistol and the other man raised his rifle. Teresa jumped, detaining her father's hand.

"No, Don Tomás, let us be. I'm an adult and Lupe has asked for my hand. I'm going to marry him; please don't try to stop us. I'm very sorry." And she walked to Lupe's side. The last thing she remembered seeing that noon was the painful astonishment on Don Tomás's face; she hadn't seen him like that since their departure from Cabora. He looked at her with a defeated hatred that would admit no pardon. She and Lupe turned their backs on him and walked arm in arm to the horse. From her house, Teresa took only a few changes of clothing that she had already packed. They went straight to the courthouse and in a terse ceremony, with strangers for witnesses, they got married. Lupe didn't speak except to say, "I do." He had a gloomy air that disconcerted her. But when she got up behind him on the horse, the desire of the first touches was rekindled. She held onto him as tightly as she could and closed her eyes.

They galloped for an hour in silence until they arrived at Lupe's shack near the railroad track. Teresa dismounted first and entered through the open door. It was a wooden structure with just one big room, but it was clean. Against the wall was a cot covered with a faded blue blanket; in the corner, a small table; on top of that, a kerosene lamp. In the middle, a table with three chairs constituted the dining room, and in front of the only window was a wood stove; the windowpanes were opaque with grime. In some ways it reminded her of her aunt Tula's hut in the settlement. She had the sensation that time was going in circles, but she was so full of the emotion of being alone with Lupe that she couldn't worry about details. She plopped her bag on the bed, crossed to the window, opened it, and felt the gust of fresh air. A shadow made her turn toward the door. Lupe was standing there, contemplating her. With the light behind him, she couldn't see his expression. She smiled.

"I can tell you don't like it," he growled. Teresa was startled by his tone. She hesitated.

"But I love you, Lupe Rodríguez," she murmured. He mumbled something she didn't understand and entered the room. He threw his saddle into the corner, approached her, and grabbing her hair, kissed her violently. She returned his kiss and was just about to put her arms around him when he pushed her away so abruptly that she had to grab onto the stove to keep from falling. Lupe walked to the other side of the room, and with one kick, knocked over the cot; he kicked it two more times, then with a swipe of his hand sent the lamp crashing against the opposite wall. He grabbed Teresa's bag and threw it at her feet.

"Pick up your things! We're leaving now!" he shouted at her.

Teresa looked at him, incredulous. She was beside herself, her eyes aflame with anger.

"Didn't you hear me?" he shouted again. "Pick up your things and follow me!"

"Where do you want to go?"

"We're going to Mexico, right now."

"Lupe, you know I can't go there; if I cross the border they could kill me. . . ."

"I don't care. You're my wife; you married me and now you have to obey me. I'm telling you we're going to Mexico this minute. You promised you would go wherever I wanted and now you're going to keep that promise. It's not my fault you got yourself into trouble. I have to take you to Mexico now and I'm going to do that even if I have to drag you all the way there, understand?"

Teresa listened, but she didn't understand. She stood in the middle of the room, paralyzed. Her passion had been abruptly transformed into a violent wound. Lupe avoided her gaze, stomping from one side of the room to the other as if he were looking for a way out. He spit insults at her, calling her a whore, bitch in heat, shameless harlot, traitor, stupid bitch. Then he took his rifle, walked toward her, and grabbed her arm brutally. It wasn't until she raised her eyes that Teresa saw his torment. Faced with her direct gaze, Lupe began to tremble. He dropped her arm and ran out of the house, shouting like someone possessed that she should die, she should leave him in peace, she should go join her whore of a mother. Teresa ran after him: she wanted to hug him, to cure the tortured madness she had seen in his eyes, to beg his forgiveness, and to cuddle him until he fell asleep. She pursued him without thinking, trying to catch up to his fleeing figure. Lupe was running along the railroad track, but when he heard her shouts he stopped, turned around, and fired a shot that stopped her cold. She wasn't wounded, but the rifle's discharge brought her back to reality. She realized that Lupe wanted to kill her but couldn't, or that he could kill her but didn't want to; he was crazy. She watched him run away down the tracks, stumbling, shouting obscenities, and she suddenly felt the impact of the void.

After that, she completely disconnected herself from reality. Some neighbors found her walking toward Clifton, dragging her bag behind her in the dust. They took her to Don Tomás's house. He wasn't there. Mariana received her. Teresa didn't seem to be aware of anything. Once she was in her room she began to howl, without tears, as if there were something inside her that she wanted to vomit out, with great, wrenching cries that shook the walls of the house. Mariana put her to bed without resistance, but the inhuman cries continued, and her body seemed about to explode with violent shaking. She left her there, locked the door, and ran to get Dr. Burke.

The doctor administered a sedative, but nothing seemed capable of calming her. Burke advised leaving her alone to shout all she wanted until she had exhausted the demon that was tormenting her. Teresa's screaming fits continued for three days. In the afternoon of the third day there was finally silence. In a while she came out of her room: her face was emaciated, her eyes swollen, and the dark circles under them contrasted with the pallor of her face, but she had changed clothes and pulled her hair back carefully at the nape of her neck. As soon as he saw her, Don Tomás got up and left the room. She sat down at the table without saying anything and ate in silence.

All of Clifton found out about the tragic event. Lupe was arrested before he crossed the border and imprisoned in the local jail; it was obvious that he was totally deranged. At times he wept disconsolately, shouting Teresa's name and swearing that he adored her, and at others he shouted like a lunatic, declaring that he hated her, that he was an agent of Porfirio Díaz sent to eliminate the vermin that were undermining the peace of his homeland; then he would cry again.

Teresa sank into a deep depression. She didn't speak, hardly ate, and spent her days shut up in her room, staring at the wall. At night she paced back and forth incessantly. Sometimes they heard her crying for hours, and then, silence once more. Mariana tried to calm her, to make her see that Lupe was crazy from the start, that he was going to kill her, but Teresa wouldn't listen, she covered her ears and turned inward. The house took on the air of an insane asylum: Don Tomás also refused to come out of his room; Gabriela had taken her children to spend a few days with a friend to get them away from the tense atmosphere. Finally, Mariana went again to get Dr. Burke. He shut himself up in Teresa's room and asked that nobody bother them. He watched her for a while without saying anything. She didn't even look up. Suddenly he approached and gave her a hard slap across the face.

"Enough! That's enough nonsense! What do you think? That you're the only woman who has ever been in love? You made a mistake; that's human, but now it's time to repair the damage. You're destroying yourself for something that wasn't your fault."

He spoke with a harsh voice. Teresa didn't move. He changed tactics, sitting down next to her and speaking softly, "Do you think I don't understand you . . . ?" Teresa leapt up and turned to him with a wild look in her eyes.

"What can you understand? What do you know about my life? Do you know how it feels to want to do good and over and over again turn out to be an instrument of destruction? Do you know who killed Lupe Rodríguez? I did. Because Lupe is going to die because of this; he won't be able to live with it. Do you know how it feels to kill what you love most in life? No, you can't possibly know. You cure, but you don't drive people crazy, you don't make people lose touch with reality. You didn't kill Damián Quijano, or Saint Barbarita's family, or Cruz Chávez. . . . Oh, Cruz! Why did you let them kill you? I want to die, too, but I can't even allow myself that luxury. Do you know why? Because I don't have a single answer; because I haven't managed to understand anything. My life has been a lie. I don't even know if I exist or if I'm just a fabrication. No, you can't understand. I didn't even understand that first ambivalent look with which Lupe tried to warn me. That first evasive move was no more than an attempt at salvation; he was trying to save himself and to save me because he loved me, because he realized that he would love me when we looked at each other that first afternoon. But, no. I was crazy; I didn't see anything. I wanted him, I wanted him for myself, above all else. I thought that without him I would die. But he was the one with death in his eyes, and I was blinded by egotism, by passion. . . ."

"Teresa!" He shook her by the shoulders; she was sobbing uncontrollably; she didn't want to hear any consoling words. She didn't want to get better. She wanted to impose an irremissible punishment on herself for the loss that was destroying her. "Teresa! You'll end up mad, too, if you don't control yourself! What about the others? Haven't you thought about what you're doing to the rest of the family, to the children? If you can't get ahold of yourself, then you should leave. You say you don't want to be an instrument of destruction, and you're destroying your

open the door when Mariana knocked to tell him there was
news from Teresita with messages for him. He had been shut up
in his room ever since his daughter left. He had abandoned his
business; nobody, not even Gabriela, saw him. Now and then he
asked for another bottle of cognac, that was all. The food they
left him outside his door was returned half-eaten, or not even
touched. Mariana was working for Dr. Burke to help with the
expenses of the house, but there were no joyful times. She did-
n't include any of this in her letter to Teresa. She described
things as she wished they were: tranquil, everything in its place,
and life back to its normal rhythm. The doctor had advised her
to write that; he saw in Don Tomás's withdrawal the signs of a
gradual suicide.

"Why bring her back? She has suffered enough and Don
Tomás is not going to recuperate. His depression is too deep. He
only wants to die. Let her travel. Maybe she'll find a little happiness along the way."

At the end of the year everybody received Christmas cards
with news from Teresita. She was adapting to life in San
Francisco, even though she was still surprised by the people's way
of life. They were colder, with a certain forced happiness that only
came through once in a while amid the rigid customs that
demanded moderation and dignity at all times. They never
seemed to relax. She missed the guitar music and the singing, but
she was content. The Rosencranzes treated her like family. A few
weeks earlier she had agreed to perform in a public event spon-
sored by the medical company that was still very interested in her
phenomenal cures. It took place in the main theater, and the
audience surpassed their expectations: more than fifteen hundred
people! It had been difficult for her to perform cures on stage,
surrounded by colored lights and sound effects, but everything
turned out all right, and after the event the directors of the
company offered her a contract to travel throughout the United
States and Europe and demonstrate her powers. She hadn't signed
anything yet, but the idea was exciting. Seeing so many new

family. You can't keep this up. I'm telling you this as your friend:
you need to go find yourself. I'll help you."

One week later Teresa left for San Francisco with the
Rosencranz family to attend to their deaf son. Don Tomás didn't
even come out to say goodbye. He hadn't spoken a word to her
since the day she returned. His silence filled her with remorse.
She understood the absolute way in which she had destroyed
him. She thought that after Lupe there would be no pardon. She
had lost Don Tomás, the father who had been her first illusion
and her only bastion against the tides of destiny.

When she passed through Solomonville to bid farewell to
Juana Van Order, she learned of Lupe's suicide. He had hanged
himself from a beam in his cell. She didn't even cry. She was consoled by the fact that he no longer suffered. When she climbed
into the carriage, she looked back at her friend's house; Harry, the
younger son, was watching her from the window. She realized he
was crying.

▦ IX

Juana Van Order was pondering the personality changes in her
younger son, Harry, who had tended toward extensive silences and
long absences from the house ever since Teresa had left, when she
received the first letter. It was dated August 2, in San Francisco.
She sat down on the porch to read it. She was alone; the boys had
gone out and John, her husband, was at the mine. The afternoon,
freshened by a recent rain, promised to turn into one of those tranquil nights full of stars and singing crickets. The letter was written
in a precise handwriting that didn't belong to Teresa.

Dear Friend:

Finally I have found someone who will write for me, since I
have never been able to master the pen. You'll be pleased to
know that I'm in much better spirits, almost completely cured

of fright and madness, although the memory of Lupe still makes me sad. I try to understand what happened, but the answers don't come easily. I wonder if it's because I have never known love in the way that you have: tranquil and everyday. When I think of my father, I am filled with pain. Mariana is taking care of him, but I fear for his health. I wish so much that I could ask for his forgiveness, but I have no idea how to do it.

The Rosencranz boy has improved a little, and his parents are satisfied. He was born deaf and seems to be incurable; nonetheless, his deafness wasn't total until it was complicated by an infection. I prescribed some medicine for him and that cured him of the secondary affliction. He's recovered enough to go back to school. The most serious problem I have is finding the herbs that I used in Sonora for this and other cases; they just don't exist here. Fortunately, the Rosencranzes have put me in contact with a medical company whose chemist has supplied me with some commercial substitutes that are quite acceptable. Even the company experts are surprised at the level of success that their medicines achieve when I apply them. We're back to the question of faith. I wonder if human diseases reflect an unconscious desire for death. As you can tell, I'm still dealing with my doubts. Perhaps now, with this new life that is opening unexpected doors for me, I will have a chance to find some answers. The Rosencranzes have suggested that in other places, New York, New Delhi, Paris, Germany, and who knows where else, there are people who know about phenomena like mine and can give me logical explanations. How I would like to see my so-called powers reduced to an everyday practice! That day I'll get married, I promise you, and I'll devote myself to having children.

Speaking of children, how are those two marvelous sons of yours? I admit that I've envied you in spite of the enormous affection I feel for you. Your life is so full of blessings and the constant companionship and love of your family. What joy! Sometimes I ask myself if I've taken the wrong path. Give my

love to John and especially to Harry. Tell them I miss them and that I won't ever forget them. I hope I can return soor share those tranquil afternoons of conversation with you a

Until then, love always, Teresa.

P.S. I might get to travel to those places I mentio order to speak with the experts about my powers. The r company wants to publicize my cures more widely. I'll know when I'm sure.

On about the same date, Mariana received a lette

Dear Friend and Companion:

You don't know how much I miss you and how mu you sometimes. Nevertheless, my mind is more at e ing that you're taking care of Don Tomás; even s about him constantly. Please let me know how he's he been able to forget a little? Has he gone back to h Oh, Mariana! So many things were left unsaid betw were to die, I would choke on it all. Take good because I need to talk to him some day when he can forgive me and forget what happened. I wan I can give him back all the affection that I've red be my advocate and convince him to take me ba

As far as everything else goes, I'm fine. I s plans to return to Clifton; there are a lot of ne for me in this place. Every day I learn sometl must confess that English just doesn't stick in to depend on Mrs. Rosencranz, who is an ang I wouldn't have the slightest idea about around me.

Hugs and kisses for Gabriela and the ch cially for Don Tomás, who up to now, with been the greatest love of my life.

In her reply, Mariana didn't have the her father refused to read the letter. He

places and having the chance to speak with renowned scientists who could explain her powers! It was definitely a once-in-a-life-time opportunity.

Then there was a long silence. In January Don Tomás went back to his business, but his health had been undermined by his prolonged drinking. He didn't speak with anybody. He went back and forth, from the office to his home, resolving problems silently, barely giving the necessary orders, and returning to his room at sundown. Gabriela lived like a widow, but a fourth child had arrived to fill her solitude. Besides working in the doctor's office, Mariana took charge of all the duties in the house. Sadness and desolation had become the routine.

In February they received a postcard from Denver, Colorado.

Passing through the Rocky Mountains was the most marvelous experience of my life. I've signed a contract with the medical company to travel around the country, doing public demonstrations. At each place I will attend to outstanding cases and speak to different specialists about my powers. I have great hopes of finally finding some credible explanation. But the best part is that at the end of the tour they will pay me ten thousand dollars, which we can use to build the hospital in Clifton. Tell Dr. Burke. A big hug for my father. Ask him to forgive me.

Teresita.

Juana, who hadn't heard from her friend since the Christmas card, received a letter toward the end of February. This one came from Kansas City, Missouri.

Dearest Friend:

I've become a roadrunner. I am crossing this beautiful country, marveling at the landscapes, although I can't say that I'm entirely happy. I miss my family and you, my dear friend. Yes, solitude is never cured, except when you are surrounded by love. With all the attention, all the people around me, I still feel completely alone. Could that be my destiny?

The worst thing is not being able to speak the language. As I get further away from the coast and the border, it's more and more difficult to find someone to interpret for me. Last night, at a public function organized by the company that contracted me, I had to give up on helping an old lady who just could not make herself understood. I felt so useless. The company directors were obviously bothered, and they immediately started to look for somebody bilingual to accompany me on the rest of the trip. I must confess that the idea of having a stranger as a constant companion is terrifying to me. How can I ask you this favor, knowing how close you are to your children and how much you need them at home? But it occurred to me that they could benefit also from the marvelous experience of this trip. I'm daring to ask, while recognizing your absolute right to say no. Would it be possible for John or Harry to accompany me and be my interpreter for the rest of the tour? I can't stand not being able to communicate. In a few days we will be in St. Louis, Missouri, where we will stay a week. Then we go directly to New York. Don't you think it would be wonderful for a young man to see the big city? You know that I would take care of him as if he were my son. If it is possible to grant me this wish, I will be eternally grateful. John or Harry could join me in St. Louis, and we could travel to New York together.

Your eternal friend, Teresa.

Juana Van Order wasn't sure what answer to give to her friend. She had absolute confidence in her and didn't doubt that such a trip would be a good experience for either one of her boys, but she resisted their leaving the nest. Harry especially worried her; he was the most emotional and excitable; he was at a very vulnerable age and, besides, thought he was in love with Teresa. John, already eighteen and aloof like his father, was more stable and mature, not as impressionable. Perhaps it would do him good to be separated from the family for a while, to be independent and search for his own path in life. Juana spoke with her son; he accepted immediately. So there was no alternative; she had to let go of John, but just for a while. She wrote to Teresa and gave the letter to her son so he could take it to her personally. John left the next day, feeling extremely important because of his mission and excited about the opportunity to travel.

For two days Harry moped around the house. Juana waited. She imagined that sooner or later he would reproach her for her decision. She was right; on the third day he confronted her:

"I'm never going to forgive you for sending my brother. I thought you understood. I love Teresa, and when she returns I'm going to ask her to marry me; it doesn't matter to me that she's older and that some people consider her a 'saint.' I'll tell you one thing, Mama: if I don't marry Teresa, I'll never marry anybody." He turned and walked away, leaving Juana with her mouth open, frightened by the seriousness with which her young son had spoken. But it was too late. She wrote Teresa another letter, asking her to send a note to Harry because his feelings had been hurt that he wasn't the one chosen. She hoped that would remedy the situation.

The requested letter didn't take long to arrive, along with another addressed to Juana, who recognized the careful handwriting of her son on the envelope. So he was already serving as her secretary. Very good. In the letter, Teresa was deeply grateful for the "loan" and spoke of how marvelous it was to have John's company. She announced that they were leaving the next day for New York, and she would write again from there.

During lunch, Juana gave the other envelope to Harry. He looked at it angrily and tore it up without opening it.

"Didn't you say you loved her?" she asked with surprise.

"My brother wrote that! Teresa can't tell me what I want to hear as long as he's there. I can wait. When she comes back, I'm going to talk with her, just the two of us. And don't you mess with my life anymore."

A week later Harry found a job. Within a month he was living alone. He only agreed to visit his mother once in a while.

Juana felt as if she had lost her son; with the other one far away, she felt very much alone. She wrote to Teresa, but she was careful not to reveal the real reason for Harry's moving out. She asked her friend to send John back as soon as possible since it was very difficult for her to manage the house without his support. She waited for an answer. A month later, surprised that she hadn't received any, she wrote again. It was September and John had been in New York since March. Weren't six months enough for him to finish what he had to do and return home? If Teresa was going to continue her trip around the world, then John should return home right away. Under no circumstances would Juana allow him to go with her. Once again there was no answer.

The year 1901 ended with an unprecedented winter. The newspapers reported that New York had suffered blizzard after blizzard and the accumulated mountains of snow made daily movement impossible. People couldn't leave their homes. The city's businesses were closed and ordinary life was at a standstill. Juana was so worried that she sent an urgent telegram to John, begging him to at least let her know that he was all right. Ten days passed before she received an answer. He didn't say anything about his possible return. Juana read the brief message over and over again, trying to find a clue somewhere between the lines. Finally she read it to her husband.

"'Dear Mama,' it says, 'Don't worry about anything. Remember that I'm a man now and can take care of myself. The winter is very harsh and we can hardly go out, but we are comfortable and have enough firewood to heat the small house we live in. Because of the winter, Teresa's clientele has diminished, and we have to wait until spring for her company activities to be renewed. Meanwhile, in order to create some publicity, the directors have asked Teresa to enter a beauty contest, which will take place next month, and for that reason they've transformed her into a gorgeous woman. You wouldn't believe the change. I'm sure she'll win. I send you a kiss. John.'" Juana put down the letter. "What do you think?"

Her husband shrugged his shoulders and smiled.

"What do you expect me to think? A dashing young man and an attractive woman are shut up together for weeks in a cozy house. . . . I think your son is finally going to become a man. What are you worried about? It can't be anything serious; John's too sharp for that. The only thing he's interested in is making money, and fast. He won't take long to come back if I offer him a good job in the business. But first I want him to learn a little, to experience something in life. You'll see."

His answer, far from calming her, caused Juana even more apprehension. She knew that Teresa wasn't a saint in sexual matters, especially after what she had heard about the incident with Lupe Rodríguez, but as a friend she had proven her loyalty. She wouldn't be capable of . . . She wrote again, this time with a severe tone, requesting the immediate return of her son. Once again the answer was a prolonged silence.

In June, Juana received an unexpected visit from Mariana. Juana feared bad news about Don Tomás's health, but Mariana assured her that even though he wasn't as strong as he used to be, he was more or less the same. Then she looked uncomfortable, as if she had something to say and didn't know how to start. Juana asked her if she had news of Teresa. Mariana nodded and, without looking at her, took a letter out of her bag and handed it to her. Full of anguish, she began to read.

Dear Mariana:

I tremble as I write you this letter. I don't know how to begin to tell you about what has happened. You know that since March of last year John Van Order has been with me. He turned out to be an excellent companion after all the months that I've traveled alone, separated from everybody by the language and customs of this country that I have still not been able to understand. John is the first person with whom I've been able to speak sincerely since I left home. Of course, he has confided in me many of his secrets, and even though we aren't at all alike, we have begun to love each other in such a tranquil, beautiful way, so different from everything else I've ever known that . . . How can I tell you? How can I ask you to tell my friend Juana? I don't know if she'll be able to forgive me. I'm going to have a baby with John. It wasn't my intention, nor his, but when we least expected it, we found ourselves in each other's arms and he was asking me to marry him. I knew that was impossible because my situation with Lupe is still pending, but I was so grateful to him, he felt like such a part of my life that I wanted to give him something worth more than anything else. I gave him myself. Oh, Mariana! Can you understand if I tell you that I can't regret the sweetest thing that has ever happened to me?

Ever since then, we love each other. When we go back to Arizona I'm going to ask Dr. Burke for Lupe's death certificate so we can get legally married. We'll recognize the child as legitimate, and we'll live like any other married couple. All of this will be hard for Juana to understand, that's why I want you to tell her, to let her know that I will love her son as much or more than she does. Tell her that we'll be with her soon so she won't feel so alone, and then she'll experience the joy of having a little grandson or granddaughter. Will you tell her for me, Mariana? I can't write to her, even though she's written many letters to us. I need you to be there, to mediate.

I hope we'll see each other soon, very soon.

Yours, Teresita.

P.S. By the way, I won the beauty contest. How about that?

Juana was pale when she finished the letter. She didn't say anything. Her son was so young, so inexperienced; it wasn't fair for him to have the burden of a wife and child already. It made her nauseous to think that Teresa, her friend, had sexual relations with John; it seemed almost incestuous, even though there were no blood ties. Juana had trusted her, had lent her son to her, and she had betrayed her like a common slut. How could she do that?

Why, when she realized what was happening, didn't Teresa send John home? That's what she should have done; that was her responsibility as a friend. But she didn't do that, she only thought of herself, and now there was no solution: they were going to have a baby. Juana felt sick.

"They're not even married."

"They will be soon. Juana, I sincerely believe that Teresa loves your son. . . ."

"My son is a child! Teresa is more than ten years older than he is, and she was already married, whether or not the marriage was consummated. She has no shame. How could she do this? Stealing my beloved son after I trusted her enough to send him to her."

"I don't think that was her intention; she felt lonely, and they were together. . . ."

"Don't talk to me about that!"

"I have to talk to you. Teresa asked me to try to help you understand. . . ."

"What should I understand? That the one who called herself my best friend enticed my son because she was lonely? And what about me? Aren't I alone? I've lost a friend and a son, and my other son's angry because I didn't send *him*. Teresa has taken both of my sons from me, one way or the other. Is that what you want me to understand?"

"Maybe they'll be happy," suggested Mariana.

"I doubt it. John's too much like his father. He likes his freedom; he'll soon get fed up with being tied down. That's what surprises me the most. If it had been Harry, I'd understand, but John? Harry was right: John never paid much attention to Teresa. He made fun of my friendship with her, of her supposed powers; he said she was crazy. She'll pay for this. As far as I'm concerned, I hope she rots!"

Mariana returned to Clifton. At home she hadn't said anything about the matter and she decided to leave it at that until Teresa came back. A month later Juana received a telegram from her son: it was a girl and they had named her Laura. Not a word about the possibility of returning.

On September 22, 1902 Don Tomás Urrea died without finding out that he had a granddaughter. Gabriela and Mariana were with him until the end, which was brief and absolutely silent. Not even when he realized that he was dying did he mention his daughter. The next day Mariana sent the news to Teresita in a telegram. A few days later she received a letter from New York dated September 22.

Dear Mariana:

We're still here, but I'm terrified by the thought of another winter like the last one. Things aren't going very well. I don't know if I've lost my healing powers or if the indifference of these people paralyzes me. I spend a lot of time in a state of depression. The medical company doesn't want to keep its commitment to continue the trip to Europe; they say that I no longer attract much of an audience and it bothers them that I have a daughter. They think that's what took away my aura of "saint." Up to now they haven't said anything; I don't know how long we'll be in this hateful city doing presentations twice a week, but with the small attendance we've had I don't think this will last much longer. As for me, I'd like to end my contract now, but it is valid until the end of 1904, and the company lawyer says that I can't shorten it.

Juana's silence depresses me also. I received your letter in which you describe your visit. Thank you for telling me the truth: it was just what I expected. Perhaps with time we can close the wound. It seems that the lack of work and the approach of winter has affected John's temper as well. He goes out a lot, leaving me alone, and when he's home he's always in a bad mood. He's bothered by the fact that I refuse to accept money for my services, which puts us in a fairly tight economic situation. I've explained to him that I can't charge for something that was given to me freely; it would be like stealing, but he likes luxuries and the good life and says I'm very selfish, that I only think of myself and nobody else. Could that be true, Mariana?

Every day I think more about my father. Today I woke up with the premonition that I would never see him again. You tell me so little about him in your letters that I know he still hasn't forgiven me. If only I could speak to him just one more time, but I'm afraid that won't happen. The premonition is very strong.

What can I tell you about Laurita? You see I'm keeping my promise to you. She's a beautiful baby, full of life and joy. You're going to be delighted when you see her. She has blond hair like Don Tomás and black eyes like her father. I'm with her almost all day since she is the only thing that alleviates my sadness. How I wish I could go home and never leave again! I wonder, dear Mariana, if you are the only person in the world capable of not judging me, of accepting me just as I am without reinventing me as a "saint" or as a "devil." Do you remember how excited I was about this trip because I hoped to find the answers that I have always sought? That makes me laugh now. Actually, I haven't discovered anything new. There are no answers. We are defined by life itself and only in life can we see ourselves reflected. And I? I have been a little bit of everything: a little saint, a little virgin, a little married, a little in love, a little idealist, a little revolutionary, a little visionary. Who am I, after all?

I'm sorry, Mariana, I shouldn't write to you about my sadness. I'm really okay, even though I've had a bit of a cough lately. It must be because of the cold, damp weather during the winter. Write to me soon. Your letters always give me strength, and knowing that my father is still alive and well motivates me to return as soon as possible.

Mariana sighed and folded the letter. She saved it in a box with the other things, the photographs, the newspaper clippings, the prayers that Lauro Aguirre had printed, the lapel buttons with Teresa's picture, and an old pink ribbon that Teresa had given her for safekeeping. "For the day of my second death," she had said.

▦ X

On the day of her second death Teresa would remember her father, as she had almost every day of her life. Once again she saw his green eyes and the bushy mustache that hid the only external sign of his weakness: his sensual lips. She could listen to his voice and perceive the facial changes that preceded an explosion of rage or of laughter. As usual, the image produced a feeling of nostalgia and a profound sense of frustration. In spite of all the years together they never were able to dissipate the tension that made true closeness impossible. Like a gray film laid over every photograph in an album, the recollection of the uncompromising distance between them darkened all other memories. When in New York she learned of his death, she experienced conflicting emotions: profound sadness, a wrenching grief that rebounded in the void with the echo of what was never said, but also an infinite relief that finally erased the torment of guilt that she had suffered throughout so many years: she could no longer hurt him, and neither could he hurt her. She understood, because of Mariana's silence, that he had not forgiven her; he had gone to his grave determined to punish her. She was never allowed to share with him the ultimate irony: he who had never been able to accept the supernatural in his daughter was also incapable of accepting what was clearly human in her.

From then on her hunger to return to her family intensified; she longed to go back to Mariana, to Gabriela and the children, to her friend Juana, if possible. Fortunately, the medical company decided to return to San Francisco to see if Teresa could recover some of the fame she had lost in New York. Teresa accepted the proposal immediately. Her relationship with John was almost nonexistent, since he rarely set foot in the apartment before midnight. The attention that little Laura required was increasing, and she didn't have anybody to help her. In California, at least, she had friends who would lend her a hand. Besides, she urgently wanted to finish the paperwork on Lupe and legitimize the birth of her daughter. John didn't mind, either. New York didn't offer him the possibility of becoming rich, and he was beginning to long for the prosperous inheritance of his father's mines, which would allow him to live the easy life of his dreams. During the long return trip they had ample time to talk about the future and to realize that they didn't have anything in common with which to make a life together. They sat down to make plans like good friends. Their marriage wouldn't be more than a formality to protect their daughter. John committed himself to staying with her until they returned to Arizona.

They were married in a simple civil ceremony in San Francisco toward the end of 1903. Afterward, the Rosencranzes gave a little reception in their house during which John was more charming than usual. Appearances invented a brief reality, and they went back to loving each other again for a few days.

Within a week, Teresa knew she was pregnant, but she kept it a secret. John had fulfilled his duty and was ready to go home; the only problem was the medical company and the contract, which was still valid. That caused several fights between the newlyweds, because Teresa argued that the money invested in the trip obligated her to honor the contract. Finally John confessed: the company, with his help, had been charging the patients she attended money, contrary to the terms of their agreement. He was willing to testify in order to nullify the contract. Once the deception was uncovered, Teresa felt released from all commitment and cut both ties: the contract and the tenuous affection for her husband. She didn't even get angry. She was free to go home again.

The journey to Solomonville was long and tedious and resulted in Teresa's giving birth prematurely. She had no choice but to accept Juana's cold hospitality. Her friend had no intention of forgiving her, not when she learned that they were married, and not even when John told her that he was staying at home. The baby was a girl, whom she called Magdalena. She was born small and sickly, and Teresa had to wait a month for her to gain

weight and enough strength for the trip to Clifton. Teresa
endured the uncomfortable situation as best she could until they
were able to travel. John accompanied her to the station, and
they said farewell as friends. She was certain that they would
never meet again. She thought that all of her life had been a series
of goodbyes. Holding Magdalena in her arms and Laura by the
hand, she boarded the train. She refused to look out the window
so as not to see that John hadn't even waited for the locomotive
to start up before he quickly walked away to rediscover his own,
youthful freedom.

It was the month of September. Teresa had been away for
almost four years. Returning with two daughters and more than
one disillusionment, she had never been so distant from her days
in Cabora as at that moment. She even felt as if she had lost the
powers she once exerted, as if the rigid profile of daily reality were
capable of doing away not only with illusion, but also with miracles. Mariana, Gabriela, and her old friend, Dr. Burke, were
waiting for her at the station. Gabriela had aged, and she wore the
immutable black of the widow, but the years seemed to have
bypassed Mariana, who immediately took charge of the two girls
while the doctor brought Teresa up to date on the hospital project. It hadn't progressed much, due to lack of funds.

"We'll finish it now," she said, as she handed him the check
for ten thousand dollars from the medical company.

Construction was finished by the middle of 1905, and the
hospital, named for Teresa, was inaugurated with the participation of the whole town. It was the only work that Teresa felt she
had completed in her life. Everything else seemed to have been
truncated or to have failed. From then on, she and Dr. Burke
attended to the patients in the new building. It was an exceptional
year; by December not one of their patients had died. The doctor
was predicting great things for the future. The two of them made
plans to bring in a young doctor and two nurses to help with the
patients. The hospital had only six rooms, but there was a lot of
space for expansion. On the night of the 23rd, Teresa, Mariana,

and Gabriela were at home finishing Christmas decorations for the hospital when the flood struck.

It had been raining constantly for four days; the San Francisco River, which passed through the center of Clifton, was about to overflow, and the families who lived near the banks had been evacuated to higher ground. The whole community watched anxiously as the water rose. That morning it looked as if the sky was clearing; the sun came out awhile, and the inhabitants of the little town breathed more easily, but at four the afternoon grew dark and an unexpected rainstorm lashed the nearby mountain. The clouds dropped their sheets of water in a matter of minutes, and at eight o'clock that night the residents heard the unmistakable roar of the torrent. Not a herd of buffaloes, not the derailment of a whole train, not ten simultaneous explosions in the mine could have caused such a threatening rumble as that sea of mud and water rushing down the canyon. Teresa immediately understood the danger, and to Mariana's surprise she shouted that she was going to the hospital to help. She covered herself with a cape and ran outside.

Gabriela and Mariana waited all night, but Teresa didn't come back. The next day they went to look for her. Dr. Burke said that as soon as she realized that everything was fine at the hospital, she had gone out to help the others. The waters were already going down, even though it was still raining. On one of the riverbanks they had found six corpses; twelve more were found at the point where the river left the canyon; they had been caught on the bell tower of the church. The total number of fatalities reached eighteen: twelve men, four women, and two children. They didn't find Teresita's body although Mariana herself joined the rescue groups to be sure that they looked carefully. She was afraid that Teresa was dead.

"If she were alive," she told Gabriela, "she'd be helping everybody else. However, if she were dead, we would have found her body in that horrible pile of mules and dogs and people that got hung up on the bell tower. But not even a shred of the clothes she was wearing has appeared. All we can do is wait for a miracle."

They waited all that day and past midnight on a Christmas Eve that nobody would celebrate. At three in the morning they heard loud knocks on the door. It was Don Joaquín, the old messenger that worked for the mines: he had Teresa slung over the back of his mule like a sack of charcoal. She was alive.

"I was making the last delivery at about twelve o'clock when on a hill across the river I saw a light shining like a star: white, all white," the old miner told them after they had put Teresa to bed. "Well, seeing as how it was Christmas Eve and everything, I right away thought it was a sign announcing the birth of Christ, like in Bethlehem. That's what I was thinking when the light began to wink at me, as if to show me that it was real. It would disappear for a little while and then start shining again. I was curious so I crossed the bridge they put over the river for the rescue efforts and climbed up the hill. And you're not going to believe it, but there was Miss Teresa, stuck up in a tree like the star of Bethlehem. And nice and dry, as though not one drop of rain had fallen on her. Well, I don't know what you think, but I think it's a miracle. A miracle, I say."

During the next few weeks, Dr. Burke waged a stubborn battle against the fever that was determined to take her away. Mariana thought it was so serious that she sent a telegram to Cayetana, who now lived in Nogales. She arrived three days later. During the seventeen years since she had last seen her daughter she didn't seem to have changed except for some gray hairs at her temples. With the same shadowy quality as in the days when she lived with Tula, she entered the room and stood against the wall, looking at the strange woman who was breathing with such difficulty. Teresa opened her eyes and smiled when she saw her. She made a weak gesture with her hand and Cayetana approached the bed, kissed her on the forehead, and then, looking a little confused, retreated again. They didn't exchange a single word. Teresa fell back into semiconsciousness. She was not even aware that Cayetana said goodbye to her the next day.

After January 1 Teresa began to improve slightly. Her fever went down; she recovered her appetite and began to speak of all the things she had to do that year. Dr. Burke was hopeful and assured them it was possible that she would recuperate fully in no time. Every morning Mariana took the girls to see their mother and then accompanied them outside to play. She loved them more than if they had been her own, since she had waited so long to receive that promised blessing. Teresa was glad; she didn't have the energy to deal with the little ones and, deep down, she suspected that Mariana would be a much better mother than she could ever be.

Little by little, as the days passed and the cold subsided, Teresa began to leave her bed, first to sit in the sun next to the window, and later to walk around the bedroom. On January 11 she announced that she felt well enough to come down to have lunch with the family. Laura, now four years old, and two-year-old Magdalena rushed to hug her when they saw her appear at the dining-room door. It was a beautiful day, with sunshine they hadn't seen since December. The breeze was beginning to carry signs of spring, and there was a delicious warmth in the air. After the meal the girls went out to the garden with Gabriela's children. The three women remained at the table a while longer, making plans for the future.

Suddenly Teresa felt a shadow pass across her eyes, and something strange enveloped her in a translucent opacity. Even though she didn't feel sleepy, she thought it might be fatigue and decided to go lie down for a while. When she got up from the table, she felt imbued with an extreme lightness that gave her the impression of floating away from herself.

She asked Mariana to bring her some tea at five o'clock in case she fell asleep. As she climbed the stairs, she felt once more that peculiar sensation of detachment, as if she were slightly intoxicated. The walls lost their rigidity, the steps stretched before her, and her feet seemed to be walking on a liquid surface.

Warm, brilliant sunlight entered through the window of her room. Outside the children's voices could be heard and, in the distance, the tranquil passing of the river with its familiar song. Teresa lay down on the bed and covered herself with a blanket.

From the opposite wall, her image in the mirror seemed to contemplate her in an odd manner. She was a little cold. The sensation of extreme lassitude and detachment wasn't at all bothersome; it seemed to blur time and space, dissolve the walls of the room, and fill her mind with all kinds of memories: the hut in Santa Ana, the journey to Sonora, the first glimpse of her father, so handsome and young on that enormous stallion, Anastasio and his guitar, the rides around the expanses of Cabora, Aunt Tula's face when she saw her saliva, the first night in the Big House, each one of Huila's wrinkles swirling into a smile when she learned her lesson well, the birthday party and the carefree times with Chepita, Lauro's supposed revolution, the nights of singing and guitar playing with Don Tomás. The images seemed endless. She felt strangely old, as if she had lived a long time, perhaps many lives. She was barely thirty-three, but her memories could fill three times that number of years. She saw Cruz's intense face, looking at her with adoration, and felt her confusion when she deceived Captain Enríquez; she rode her chestnut colt once again and heard the voice of the mute man who spoke for the first time after seeing her. Cabora, in striking sunlight, presented itself in all its expansive glory, prosperous and tranquil. She remembered Lupe with tenderness and John with gratitude, and she saw the newborn face of Laura with the little smile that had surprised her so. She had closed her eyes to see better when she encountered the memory of Anastasia, the fragile, moribund Anastasia who came back healthy to offer her a gift in her dream, that dream in which she had dreamed the day of her second death, when in dreams she dreamed she was dreaming the dream of her whole life.

Mariana opened the door and saw Teresa propped up on the pillows, her eyes closed, a delicate smile on her face. She thought her friend was sleeping and tried to awaken her.

Epilogue

On January 12, 1987 the daily newspaper of Navojoa reported several strange incidents that had occurred in the last twenty-four hours, including a dust storm of such intensity that it darkened the sky for several hours and deposited a thick layer of grit over the whole town, a general blackout that left only the hospital generator running and could not be corrected until after midnight, an eerie howling of coyotes that seemed to come from the very streets of the city, and, lastly, the extraordinary resurrection of a young, unidentified woman who had been given up for dead. This last bit of news deserved an eight-column headline on the front page: "Unidentified Dead Woman Comes Back to Life: Claims To Have Descended from Heaven."

STRANGE OCCURRENCE IN THE GENERAL HOSPITAL

Navojoa, Sonora, January 12, 1987. There was general alarm yesterday in the local hospital when a woman presumed dead suddenly came back to life and began to talk about strange things. Since last November an unidentified woman has been hospitalized here after being found unconscious on the steps of this institution. It has not been determined how she got here, who brought her, or where she came from. She wasn't carrying any identification and nobody has shown up to claim her.

During the time she was in a coma, the doctors did everything possible to save her, without any success. Yesterday at five in the afternoon she was declared dead, but when hospital workers were just about to take her from the room to prepare her body for burial, the unknown woman sat up and looked at the astonished nurses.

Since then, she has been delirious. The patient says her name is Teresa and she has been in Heaven. According to her, she has come to bring kindness and justice to the world. The doctors diagnosed a psychosis induced by a death experience and moved her to the psychiatric ward of the hospital. Apparently, the physical strength of this poor madwoman is so great that they have to keep her sedated. They are studying the possibility of applying electric shocks to erase the traumatic experience and bring her back to normal.

At the bottom of the same page was an announcement in small print:

> Would the owner of a brown briefcase left on flight 901 from Mexico City on November 11 please come to Aeromexico's ticket counter to claim it.